TWICE-TOLD

A COLLECTION OF DOUBLES

EDITED BY C.M. Muller

CHTHONIC MATTER | St. Paul, Minnesota

FEATURING 22 UNIQUE VISIONS OF THE DOPPELGÄNGER

THE LAST SALVADOR

Tim Jeffreys

SALVADOR CEASED BEING able to distinguish between his dreaming life and his waking one the day his parents took him to the graveyard and informed him—in all seriousness—that he was the reincarnation of his dead brother, also named Salvador. As he stood there amongst the crypts and headstones which looked to him like a miniature city, a city of the dead, staring down at the headstone upon which his own name was etched, he began to suspect that he himself was a dream. Either that or he was some wild conjuring of his parents, some black magic; or perhaps he was a ghost, the ghost of the boy whose bones lay in that grave.

"You are alike in every way," his mother said. "Like two drops of water. The good Lord returned him to us. Another chance."

"Our Father saw how unjust he was in taking away our son," his father added, looking directly at Salvador with the same stern expression he always wore, "and returned him to us anew."

Following this excursion, the fantasias that filled Salvador's sleeping mind seemed no more fantastical to him than a procession of ants across the patio tiles or the faces of his family. If the grandfather clock

1

that stood in the hallway of his home had one day melted into a puddle before his very eyes he would not have been at all surprised. Indeed, some mornings he sat on the stairs, staring at the clock through the spindles of the banister, waiting, willing it to buckle and to wilt. The bottom had fallen out of what they called reality and nothing now could be trusted to be what he had until now imagined it to be.

How many times did they return to that grave? How many times did his parents tell him that he was the first Salvador given to them anew, reborn almost nine months to the day of his death?

He was alone in his sunlit playroom one day when a shadow fell on him and he felt a chill. A figure stood in the doorway, a boy of perhaps six or seven years old, a silhouette cast against a blaze of sunlight from the patio. Salvador understood at once that this was the first Salvador, come to check up on him, to see that he was living up to the standards which had been set. Marshaling his toy soldiers, Salvador trooped them across the tiles and managed to dispel the visitation. He knew, though, that his brother would return.

It was in the cold cavernous toilets at his school, where a tap dripped eternally and the plumbing clanked with doom, that Salvador saw his brother gazing back at him from the grimy mirror above the taps. As he fled along the row of sinks, he saw in the mirrors above them other Salvadors, other versions of himself. These Salvadors were awaiting their chance to be born should he—the current version—contract some ailment and die, or be killed in an accident. Hadn't he almost stepped into the path of a tram one day when out walking with his father? Too busy imagining clouds forming faces in the sky, and earning himself a clip around the head? Dying was too easy, too easy, and all these other Salvadors were just waiting for their chance to replace him.

The thought of being ousted from life by another Salvador, the way he believed he had ousted his brother, terrified him.

"I'm the last Salvador!" he yelled at the mirrors. "I'm the only one!"

Back in the classroom, he pictured an assembly line where Salvadors were made. He saw the moulds, he saw Salvadors lying across tables having their features painted on by a bored old man who from time to time consulted a photograph of his brother, the first Salvador. He saw his mother shopping for Salvadors, entering a shop stuffed with boys just like himself, all still as manikins and wrapped in plastic, filling the shelves, awaiting a breath of life. He saw his mother examining them and deliberating. He wanted to scream.

It might have been then that he resolved to be a version of himself that had not gone before and which could never be repeated. The one Salvador they would all remember. He would break the mould. He would smash it into the tiniest fragments, smash it so that they could not cast it again, so that none of these other versions, none of these other Salvadors, could ever be. And he would not die, he would not die, he would *not*.

He waited. When he discovered the line of his father's ancestry led back to Llers, a town said to have been infested with witches in the seventeenth century, he was even more convinced that some kind of curse was upon his family. Death stalked him, in the shape of his brother, throughout his childhood. In dreams he sometimes saw the first Salvador astride a skeletal horse which tried to run him down as he fled, heart in mouth, across empty, sun-scorched landscapes. In other dreams, which at first appeared innocent, objects or shapes in the landscape would suddenly coalesce to form his brother's leering face, accusing eyes, and mouth that roared from the other side of existence. *You're next!* the mouth bellowed. The voice was like a sucking wind, which dragged at Salvador's hair and clothes. *Give it up! You had your chance! Others are waiting! It's your turn to die! Your turn! Your turn! Your turn!* And, turning his face away, Salvador would see them at the mouth of a cave, these other Salvadors—no telling how many! how far the line stretched back into the darkness! There they were, lined up one after the other, waiting.

He would start from these dreams slick with sweat. His heart beat in odd, irregular patterns. Had he died in his sleep? Was he now a ghost?

There was only one way to find out. He would perform tests to make certain: repeatedly throwing himself down the stairs much to his mother's horror. The pain told him he was flesh and blood.

His next idea was to offer a sacrifice. Perhaps death could be diverted. If the void must be satisfied, perhaps something or someone else would do. One day, on a whim, he tossed the family cat—a black Bombay with mustard eyes which he had long suspected of being a spy for his dead brother—out of an upstairs window. But the blasted thing survived. He was determined to try again, and again, until he had extinguished all of the damned thing's nine lives, but from that day forward the cat would dart for the shrubbery at the end of the garden whenever it saw him coming. Another day, on the way home from church, when he and a school friend were crossing a newly constructed bridge that did not yet have a railing, Salvador saw an opportunity and pushed the friend off onto the jagged rocks fifteen feet below. For days, whilst the school friend wailed and bled in bed, Salvador ate cherries and waited for the boy to die. But again he was thwarted! Within a week, the boy was on his feet again. In frustration, Salvador stormed from the house and, coming across a dead bat crawling with ants, he picked it up and bit into it. *Death, I will eat you!* he thought as he chewed. Ants crawled across his hands and inside the cuffs of his shirt. Then he flung the rotting thing aside and screamed out, "So be it! Take me! I know there are others waiting, so let's get it over with!"

The clocks in Salvador's dreams turned to liquid. Time slipped away. Days passed. Months. Years. Out walking the streets, he would flinch at the sound of a horse's hooves, sure that this was his dead brother come to run him down at last. As a way of keeping death at bay, he spent much time engaged in furious masturbation. This often took place on the plot of waste ground behind his house, where abandoned farming machinery lay amongst scorched grass and shriveled weeds like the skeletons of long extinct beasts, where ants would crawl onto the backs of his hands and tickle his shins, and where a chorus of cicadas drowned his gasps for breath at the moment of orgasm. However, he ceased this practice after two incidents that occurred almost simultaneously. First, he dreamt one night that boys just like himself, doppelgängers—only small, green, elongated forms at first—grew like tomato plants from the waste ground dirt where he had spilled his seed. Next, he came across a book which his father had left open on the lid of the pianola in the lounge. The book was filled with explicit photographs of people suffering in the advanced stages of venereal disease. His father perhaps left it for the boy to see as some kind of warning or education, or perhaps he had left it open in a moment of carelessness. Whichever it was, after looking through the book Salvador came to associate sex with only rot and decay, and this combined with the dream of the tomato plant Salvadors convinced him that, rather than being a life-affirming affront to death as he'd imagined, to masturbate—or to indulge in sexual activity of any kind—was in fact to hail the Grim Reaper as one might hail a cab on *La Rambla*.

With each passing day he attempted to stay alert to any sign that death was coming for him. An owl hooting in the lemon tree outside his bedroom window: death! An unlit candle in the church: death! A man dressed in black seen walking along the Placa Gala: death!

In the end, it was not he who died, but his beloved mother, the sickness rapidly overtaking her so that by the time of Salvador's sixteenth birthday, there on the cusp of manhood, on the edge of victory, she was dead. After the funeral, he dreamt that his mother walked alone through some sand-colored flatland. When he was awake he saw the shape of her brow in the cliffs, whilst figures on the beach formed the outline of her nose and lips. He knew she was not gone, not entirely. She was still present somewhere, ethereal, waiting to be recalled back to the world. Silently, he willed his father to conjure his mother to life again, by the same means, whether prayer or witchcraft, that he had used to recast the first Salvador in the form of himself. But the best his father could do was to marry his deceased wife's sister who was not an exact replica. Not at all. Still, brothers replaced brothers, sisters replaced sisters. In time, Salvador accepted his aunt as the new version of his mother. They had, after all, the same eyes.

On leaving school, Salvador was encouraged to study law, the same plan he imagined his father had had for the first Salvador.

But no! Not for him his brother's outgrown clothes! He had an idea of his own.

He already knew that the world was a lunatic, and in his attempts to break the mould and stay ahead of all those other waiting Salvadors, to remain alive and never be replaced, he did the only thing he knew his older brother would never have done.

He decided to harness those scenes and images that played behind his eyes when he slept, to capture them like bottled screams, and he would use them to fill the world with even more lunacy.

He would go to art school.

And he would remain, forever, the last Salvador.

DETAILS THAT WOULD OTHERWISE BE LOST TO SHADOW

———•———

Clint Smith

A RATIONAL READER would certainly prefer I begin at some accommo-dating sequence, but I'm afraid I must start here: standing at a second-story window in a room, in a house that is not my residence, looking through the glass at my own home across the street.

What I see is my husband getting out of his sedan, a smile apparent even from this distance: the tracer of some joke as he rounds the rear of the car to help our daughter from her car seat. They pick up whatever riddle they're sharing, but I'm less interested in this interaction than I am with the woman who emerges from the passenger side, unnaturally rising out of the vehicle.

Yes: she is a stranger, but the similarities seize me—same build, proportions, same hair color and length; conversely, it's the contrasts which momentarily paralyze me. Her complexion is gray, her hair scrambled, fresh from a nap on an asylum's padded mat. She's wearing a tattered sun-dress which may have once possessed a floral pattern, though from this distance the petals' edges have smeared. She moves with a stilted gait that calls to mind a brittle assembly of bones—a ballerina in a production which mocks human movement.

And as my daughter trots up the drive, the woman—this other woman who Ben's brought home for some reason—reaches out toward Brooke in what may have been an otherwise affectionate gesture but is rather something more aggressive: that hand of hers extending, unco-ordinatedly taking a slow-motion swipe at my little girl's trailing hair—those flexed fingers appearing like a talon compromised by rigor-mortis coordination.

I still imagine that scene with a passive clarity of focus: Ben, briefly placing his hand on the small of the woman's back—so sensitive as to be obscene. The thing I am watching in helpless petrification. A dull, though familiar, ache pulsing along my right leg wakes me and I am moving, running out of this house that is not my own. In which I am a prowler.

I'll come back to this. Promise.

WE'D MOVED TO Olmstead Estates seven months earlier. This after a grueling period of attempting to negotiate alternatives. Essentially, Ben's company provided several choices, all involving relocation, and the outskirts-of-Detroit option was the most feasible and, for a number of reasons, the most appealing. Ben's income increased, but so did his daily commute.

Nine years before this Ben and I, having not been married long, were living a twenty-somethings' existence in Chicago. Back then, Ben worked downtown, and our respective lines of work had afforded us, and continues to afford us (though more so, now, on Ben's end), nu-merous comforts for which neither of us has ever apologized. If either of us were typical, we'd not have suited each other so well. We are, I suppose, conscientiously cutthroat, though having a daughter altered our lukewarm ruthlessness.

Back then, we were both profiting by catering to the affluent whims of those living in the suburbs to the north and west of the city. My routine in those days was almost shamefully selfish. I'd wake before Ben, slip into my running gear and be on the sidewalks and streets by 4 a.m., sneaking in three or four miles and making it back in time to trade places with my husband, sliding into the shower just as he was drying off.

After Ben was out the door, I'd fire up the computer and get ready for what lay ahead: most days were occupied by coordinating site visitations with clients, colleagues, or real estate agents who'd scheduled interior stagings for a shoot. Lunches were breezy things, usually conducted with a cell in one hand. Meetings and responsibilities would typically recede around early evening, when Ben and I would reconvene at the apartment, split a bottle of wine, laugh until we grew drowsy; then we'd begin the work-week routine again. Embracing our lassitude. We were frivolous with time, not with each other.

But I'm a long way from Chicago, and on some days—like the day I'm presently disclosing—I'm a long way from that ambitious interior designer with a niche startup sipping wine in a Brownstone on the fringe of Lincoln Park.

BEFORE I GET us back to that second-story window in the Motley House, let me draw your attention to our current subdivision of Olmstead Estates: a long-established residential area, totally idiosyncratic in my experiences. Built in the late-70s, and developed into the early 1980s, Olmstead Estates began as a secluded tract of land within a heavily-wooded stretch, the neighborhood proper completely invisible to nearby thoroughfares and the interstate, with a single, sinuous road acting as the subdivision's sole entrance and exit.

Any 101 urban planning class will illustrate the functions of boundaries. Essentially, boundaries lend themselves to the identity of a neighborhood: too flimsy or permeable, a neighborhood will not maintain its character; too rigid and energetic, transactions will grow limited, and so too will the personality of that particular environment. Boundaries have a certain "charge" in peoples' minds because of our recognition of zones and gateways (often tacitly so).

I do the neighborhood and its opulent homes a disservice by my description, as it is a coveted swath of real estate.

Ben and I had taken great care to acclimate and ingratiate ourselves with the neighbors along our street—not that the fall and impending winter allowed us much time for front yard small talk. Still, we've made friends. But the house across the street. That is different. I'd grown puzzled by it, the Motley House, immediately after we'd moved in.

I'd taken to calling it the "Motley House" due to the schizophrenic selections made by the designer. Part of this had to do with mere composition: caught at a particular perspective, portions of the house bore peculiar tilts, the roof—with its dissonant imbrication of shingles— appearing at a visually unappealing pitch. Still, more had to do with sheer aesthetics. As I'd mentioned, many of the homes were constructed nearly forty years ago; and while there are indeed touches which signal that period, others are sheer anomalies: take for instance the second story: a board-and-batten scheme along the facing and dormer windows, while the sides of the house are all brick and windowless. Now toggle to the lower level, where wide swaths possess Tudor-style exposed planking, while other segments are composed of cut cobblestone with thick spaces of mortar. A bay window bump-out skirted with brick, capped with discordant shingles. To describe the effect concisely, it is as though four or five capable craftsmen had lent inimitable elements, and could only compromise by installing their own portion, no matter how incongruous.

I'd only seen snatches of activity over there. Lights shone in the windows infrequently. The driveway remained unshoveled throughout the winter, not a single tire track or boot print over the course of those seemingly relentless storms. I'd only mentioned my curiosity about the place to Ben on a few occasions. Anyway, as it is my discipline and my craft, conjuring images of a floorplan, and how the interior décor was composed in such as strange schematic, became a tepid obsession.

Then, in early April—after an arduous release from winter's frigid grip—a FOR SALE sign appeared in the front yard of the Motley House.

This, I thought, would serve as a conceit to meet the occupants and, perhaps, sneak a peek at the interior. And so I assembled bits and pieces of discarded plans, consolidating them into one. I'd simply approach the house under the guise of curiosity: *"I saw the sign in your front yard and wanted to say hello before you left the neighborhood...so sad to see you go"*—something like that. I didn't need a bullet-proof scheme, just a crutch to make it to the door.

And so, there we were: a spring morning.

I'd kissed Ben goodbye just before dawn and had dropped off Brooke at school a few hours later. Truth told, it would be an ideal time to update the website, or catch-up with former colleagues, test the waters for new clientele. But the creative atrophy I'd allowed to settle in over the past nine years had become (though lingering insolence would have prohibited me using the word) debilitating.

It was still early, before 10 a.m., when I walked outside and began a pre-run stretch (never *not* a painful affair), watching the house in narrow glances as I had for the past seven months. And so I started toward the house, cutting across the street at an angle to their drive, a crumbling mess. With spring here, green stipels and unknown growth were beginning to whisker their way through uncountable cracks (I made a mental note to contact the HOA).

Adopting the gait of a friendly neighbor (which I was, I suppose), I made my way along the walk which collared the front of the house, casually inspecting the front windows which were curtained.

Three concrete risers lifted me to a glass storm door protecting a sturdy-looking and rather elaborate front door (painted a hideous tint of what may have once been hunter green). I pulled open the storm door and, after a blink-steeling pause, knocked on the front door, noting a digital real-estate lockbox secured over the doorknob.

On the final knock, I froze with my knuckles in midair. Each of my raps was repeated in a series of staggered echoes. Initially, I thought someone was toying with me, imitating the sound on the other side of the door, but when I knocked again, the sound certainly existed but was distant, as though I were knocking against a barrier which opened into something cavernous. I held my breath before giving the door three punctuated knocks, and again, from the other side, the sounds fell away in mimicked echo.

This time I pulled away, gently closing the glass storm door as I cautiously stepped off the risers, appraising the mismatched face of the house. The scale math didn't add up. Had I missed something? What sort of interior layout existed which would produce that unsettling, rib-vault reverberation?

And there was something of a challenge in this now—my clueless-ness about the inside. I felt less shy about piquing my need to under-stand, to see, and I started off toward the side of the house.

I reset, addressing the house from the ruined driveway, passing the garage on my way around back. A tall, wood-plank fence totally hid the backyard from view. I proceeded into the rear of the property not unlike the sociable neighbor I was (or was portraying). I thought about the strange contours of the Motley House itself—how it had been expertly pieced together to evoke unison. It bothered me: that discord-ant chorus of harmonious intent. The builders may have fooled some, but not me.

Though the fence was tall, I could see the tree-shrouded second-story levels of two or three adjacent homes—no doubt the backyard's condition was no secret to these folks. And it wasn't all that outra-geous, just unkempt and uncared for. Trees hung low, their barky torsos covered in verdigris-colored lichen. The dull grass was uncut and hunched, tinkling with dew in these early morning hours.

I crossed through the tall grass and made my way to a rickety patio, an old layer of paint scabby across its warped planks.

The wide, sliding-glass panels provided a reflection of myself as I crossed the elevated patio deck; reflected too was my vaguely hitching stride, something, even after all this time, I was still unaccustomed to witnessing with some objectivity. I had to avert my eyes as I moved closer to the glass.

With the awareness that someone might be eyeing this interaction, and still embracing the affectionate semblance of amiable neighbor, I approached the sliding-glass doors and called out while striking my knuckles on the surface. "Hello? Anyone home?"

Nothing budged behind the vertical blinds. No cathedral echo issued from within. Still, I gave it another try, this time pairing the knocks with, "I just wanted to introduce myself...I'm your neighbor from across the street."

Morning sounds. Birds in the trees.

Disappointed but not done, I swiveled from the sliding-glass doors, canting my head as I noticed an enormous shrub growing directly against the backside of the house, something unusual about how it hugged the brick. It reminded me of a prodigious, kelp-covered starfish cleaving to a hull that was this home.

Staring, I noticed the shrub was obscuring a shape against the house itself, a dark rectangle—I caught the dull gleam of something. A knob. Suspicion confirmed: a door. I flexed-back a few limbs, getting a clearer shot.

The door was dark, blending in with the dark nervous system of the shrub's interior. I could imagine this leading to a garage or mudroom, but the layout was wrong—I'd passed by the garage on the other side of the house. Biting my lower lip, I reached out, fully expecting any sort of test to result in a solidly locked door; so when the knob twisted and the door creaked open a few inches, I pulled a small inhale of shock.

With the shrub acting as concealment (my unkempt accomplice), only shards of sunlight punctured the dim space. Awkwardly, I hunch-pressed myself between the shrub and the side of the house.

I could see a narrow corridor, the walking space carpeted with a traffic-worn, burnt-orange pattern populated with lantern-like swirls, a style I associated with the mid-70s. Again, I gave an innocence-tinged call. "Anyone home?" Silence, even from the morning birds.

To answer your question: yes, of course it occurred to me that this was grossly illegal, and I was aware that entering a home under these circumstances amounted to simple trespassing or criminal mischief (though intent obviously dictates either criteria). But the clueless concern of a good-natured neighbor certainly wouldn't qualify for these charges, would they? And sure, I'd considered the possibility of an alarm; yet, like many of the exterior's non-contemporary features, no up-to-date blips or bleeps sounded from within. Besides, my intent was driven by two things: the bloodless need to *know* and the designer's-eye desire to assess the persona of its occupants. My career had been about telling stories not with words, but rather with things.

I stepped over the threshold, the door hanging open behind me, allowing in a wedge of sunlight.

My pacing increased as my eyes slowly adjusted to the corridor's dimness; the passage eventually terminated, opening to my left, to a kitchen.

Meager morning light filtered through the crepe-like drapes, providing a diffuse hue, fabricating the illusion that a frail mist permeated the house.

The layout, no surprise, was an amalgamation of schemes: touches of split-level step-downs, stylish load-bearing dividers separating rooms. There was a large, inglenooked fireplace in the living room composed of mini-boulders, lending a cave-like quality to the space. And though the architectural skeleton was clearly from a bygone era, the residents had done a deft job of creating a refined living space.

In my early twenties, one of the design teams at the university had researched the Japanese discipline of *Wabi, Sabi,* and *Shibumi*: the restrained principles of home and interior design. While the latter component reflects taste in its conscious reservation, the former elements concentrate on how the aesthetic elements—organic and inorganic—are gripped in time itself. Understated austerity and reduction of excessive visible distractions are chief focuses of *Wabi*. *Sabi*, which literally translates to "rust," are design elements which have been age-worn, achieving a serenity in their distinction from the new.

As I wandered the first floor (not delving into any of the nearby darkened hallways, mind you), I called up this ethos and how well (and, again, incongruently) it applied to the feel of the Motley House.

Often, these alterations are rushed—people, in other words, temporarily change habits in order to provide the guise of good taste. That said, as bizarre as some of the spatial choices had been, there was something cohesively comforting in how the disparate elements transitioned so seamlessly from room to room: a sensible respiration for how the first-floor spaces were so elegantly sutured together. There seemed to be something, here, in the ritualistic aesthetic—an enduring, holistic ethos.

Gradually, I gravitated to the front door vestibule, assessing the surrounding space, contemplating what sort of depth and impediments could have created that eerie echo. Biting my lower lip, I lifted a knuckled fist and knocked on the door—one, two, three. Silence.

Then movement, from the margin of my vision, swivel-snagged my attention.

A shadow at the top of the stairway—only catching its sudden, receding slide down the second-floor wall. The erratic rhythm of my heart—though refreshing and calling to mind many a long-distance run—flooded my aurality with static. I took the stairs two at a time, using the railing to haul myself up. Pain forked up my lower leg with each exertion.

And then I crested the landing, listening for a few seconds, trying to hook to any sound. Nothing. If this was indeed some sort of game, I would have to wait for my partner (or adversary) to make the next move.

The second floor teed to the left and right, the doors in either direction all closed, except for one, its opening framing a rectangle of inviting, morning light. Warily, I peered into the room.

A generous space, dedicated as a large den or study. Wide windows with slender muntins overlooked the neighborhood. Sleek bookshelves lined the far walls. A small sofa, a reading chair, an ottoman. A potted fishtail palm stood near the window, and I approached just as much to get a better view as to see if the thing was an imitation. I ran my thumb over one of the wide, silky leaves, confirming verdant life.

The panes provided a generous snapshot of our tree-lush subdivision with which I, and perhaps Ben too, was still growing accustomed.

Contrary to what some may assume, with windows, it's not the provision of light-wells to which people are attracted, but rather the access to meaningful views. Office workers, for instance, feel a need for refreshing vistas which open to lives, and often worlds, other than their own.

A few intruding tree limbs cross-cut the view, and it clicked then that perhaps these were the culprits of the shadow I'd seen tickling the wall—a play of the slowly ascending morning sunlight.

The view favored our spacious house across the street, and I felt a pang of guilt for some of the things I'd said to Ben about it—about the neighborhood, the tectonics of relocation in general. In truth, he really had no choice. Well, not true: it could have been so much worse. I pulled away, appraising the room.

It was a tidy, balanced space. Too often in my line of work, I'd forfeited meaning for creating a pretentious *mise-en-scène* for prospective buyers or staging for clients who were too easily seduced by artificiality. The truth is that one must strike a balanced point-of-view: equilibrium between the perception of the inhabitant and the POV of those who enter. While there are standards, too often clients are clueless about their own needs and are unaware of how much (to their detriment) they want to impress strangers (or people who will never actually witness their living space); and though I admit to practicing some of these methods, interior designers are all too willing to exploit the anxieties of clients who have no direction about the expressive process of reflecting *meaning*.

I approached the desk, aimed at an angle to the window. Just to get a feel for the space, I gently pulled the chair away, hesitated, then descended into the seat. A small stack of clean stationary was placed in the middle of the desk, the sheets curled with creamy contours. A tray containing gleaming ink pens was nearby; I picked one up, and with a smirk, imagined myself to be on the brink of some brilliant declaration. I was once assigned to a physical therapist who, aside from the merit of our daily routines, was an intrusively insufferable woman. Still, she infrequently suggested that, as a healing exercise, I write down some of my resentments—not just with my physical state, but with the fears I'd been unwilling to articulate—to place what's inside, by whatever means, on the outside. I estimated her at the time to be rather presumptuous, and my terse responses during PT clearly reflected this subscription.

With melodramatic flair, I scrawled, *My name is Tara Keltz, and I was in an accident.* There was something too ordinary in it. Directly beneath my first lines, I started again: *My name is Tara Keltz, and I was nearly killed ten years ago.* Was that too overwrought? Affected? I thought not. Though my leg was almost ruined, it could have been my spine, my neck. My brain. Now, I looked down at the words—the brief skating of the ink pen over paper felt alleviative, as though a small amount of malignant liquid had been leeched.

And though a person can admit that pain is acceptable, often it is difficult to remove oneself from how close one came to the cleft of the worst. The ink followed a path along the paper, just as I'd been following a path that morning a decade before.

It was still in our Chicago days, the years (though not too many years) before Brooke was born. I was faithful to my morning routine: on the sidewalks and streets before daylight to stretch and prep, headphones on, sneakers on concrete.

It was this consistency which I applied to my life and made me an appealing commodity for clients. It was a consistency I'd abandoned and mourned in the preceding years.

I'd been intent on some coincidental lyric in a song—one of those moments when you see something, a color perhaps, or a number on a sign, at the exact same instant a line is spoken. I remember the headlights to my right, slashing across the crosswalk. And then the black impact.

The front end of the vehicle briefly transformed my body into an acute "less-than" sign (or "greater than" sign, depending on a witness's point-of-view), the collision simultaneously causing my lower leg to get kinked between the car's right corner-panel and its wheel well, my shoulder connecting with the poorly patched street as I scraped to a stop against a parked car. I never lost consciousness (until the hospital); and though I was instantly furious, my body would not respond to the rage. It, apparently, was too focused on the pulsing volts of pain radiating from my lower leg.

The car was idling in the intersection, one headlight shattered. I was able to snag an agonized glimpse at the driver: a young man whose face was brushed with sodium-vapor glow from the streetlamp. Sometimes, that smooth face crumples with creased contrition before the driver stabs the accelerator. Still, other times my mind's-eye plainly sees the dismissive sneer of a young woman—coming home too late from a club, perhaps—as the car's tires yelp on the pavement and the taillights fade.

The major injury was to my tibia. Like most compound fractures, it was hideous to behold. It reminded me of some sort of gory imitation of a tipi: the jagged wooden poles of my bones protruding through the torn fabric of my flesh. Most vividly, at the hospital while they were working on me, I recall the sense of violation: that something which had been so intimate a part of my interior had ruptured the exterior, exposed.

Later, the same physical therapist I'd mentioned previously echoed similar sentiments from various doctors: that the fibular fracture did not cause irreparable damage to the peroneal nerve, which could have resulted in something more severe than occasional aches and an altered gait.

I stared at the stationary, at the words I'd written. *My name is Tara Keltz, and I was nearly killed ten years ago.* I was about to remove the piece of paper, when the sound of a car door being slammed compelled me to the window.

Heart racing, I glided over, out of sight. The driveway here at the Motely House was empty. Relief was brief, though, as I ticked my focus across the street, over to the scene unfolding at my own home.

And you already know this next part: where we began.

Ben was in our driveway. Sliding out from the passenger seat was the pale woman. *Was she in trouble? Had he brought her home from the office?* Ben had his flaws, but I doubted he was dimwitted enough to try to engage in some morning tryst suspecting I was out of the house. Never mind the flawed calculus of my car being in the garage.

She began moving toward the house with those somnambulatory baby steps, as if a storefront mannequin had organically sprouted gray matter.

And then there was Brooke, her little backpack a point of color. Why had he picked Brooke up from school so early in the morning? A new question: Was our daughter sick? Then the woman lunged at Brooke— an ungainly rake at her hair.

And then I was moving, too quick to avoid clumsiness. Retracing my steps, I sped down the stairs and through the house, trying to comprehend a rational narrative for what I'd just seen.

I jogged down the side entrance corridor, the open door urging exit with a glow of illumination. Stepping through the threshold, I was confronted with the barrier of the shrub; I forced my way past its rigid, inhibiting limbs.

Through the gate, across the street, back in my own driveway; I was sucking in snatches of air as I strode through the garage and into our house.

Not slowing, I passed through the mudroom and rounded the corner which fed into our kitchen; I stood there on the cusp of it, not moving, hearing my racing heart but trying to listen for anything—the sound of this other woman's voice.

What I saw instead was Brooke, perched at our dinette, hovering over some coloring project, her backpack having spilled its first-grade contents; she didn't look up as I, trying to control my panting, stepped in.

"Hi, sweetie," I said tentatively.

"Hi, Mommy."

I waited. "Where's Daddy?"

Brooke remained intent on the colored sheet in front of her. Her tiny shoulders shrugged. "I don't know."

Commotion down the hall, toward the master bedroom. I sliced through the kitchen, stanching the impulse to affectionately stroke my daughter's hair, as I'd witnessed the pale woman do only minutes before. In seconds, I pushed through the partially closed bedroom door. Ben was in the bathroom, pulling off his office attire. He said, "That you, hon?"

Barely moving, barely blinking, I sight-scoured the room for her—hiding, erect and discreet behind the bedroom door, maybe, or crouched low on the other side of the dresser, her knees drawn up to her chest like that preserved corpse from Chile, the mummy of the "tattooed lady." I rejected the urge to sink to the floor and check under the bed, salvaging a bit of dignity in doing so.

Nothing. "Yeah," I said, licking my lips.

"Go for a run?"

"I, um—yes. Just got back." And as I was about to ask why he had shown up in the middle of the morning with both Brooke and a strange woman, I saw the clock on the nightstand. 4:30. An icy sensation, like chilly tendrils spreading under my skin, thrived with my understanding that the slant of light was not at all right for the morning.

Tugging on a T-shirt, Ben came out of bathroom. "I tried calling earlier. Got out a little early, thought I'd surprise Brooke"—he began, but stopped, scowling at me—"Geez, hon, what happened to your face?"

One of my hands instinctively rose to my cheek, fingers testing the flesh. Sure enough, a soreness there. I frowned, rounding the foot of the bed in pursuit of the bathroom mirror. Ben hovered nearby as I inspected my reflection. Slender scratch abrasions were visible from my temple to the lower hinge of my jaw.

Wincing, Ben gently placed his hand on my back. "Did you fall or something?"

I blinked, my eyes joysticking—mentally backtracking and realizing: the shrub at the back of the Motley House, its witch's-broom branches. During my hasty retreat, I'd swatted through the tangle of limbs. My awe elicited a long pause; I finally licked my lips. "No. I—it was a tree branch. Hanging too low. Wasn't paying attention."

He made a light, seething sound between his teeth. "At least you didn't break the skin," he said. "You should slow down, sweetheart." Ben's finger pulled a strand of hair from my forehead and tenderly hung it over my ear. I nearly recoiled at his touch—not because of him, but because of her. I wanted to know who had emerged from the passenger seat of his car; but I realized that it wasn't just my misunderstanding of time, but that I had more than one thing wrong here, namely the woman and me.

In the mirror, I angled my eyeline from my own reflection to Ben's. He was still frowning, still waiting to see if I was all right. My lips drew into a small smile. The question on the tip of my tongue was, *Who was she?* But the words slid off, replaced with something dismissive. Something that kept the more difficult questions at bay.

THAT NIGHT IN bed, I listened to Ben's steady breathing and stared at the ceiling. To compensate for the lack of street noise, Ben and I'd taken to running a box fan.

It'd been less than an hour since tucking in Brooke (we were still in the phase where she wanted one of us to lie with her before she fell asleep). Ben was out when I slipped back in and turned off the reading lamp. As my eyes adjusted, my mind—finally freed from the mundane, evening's-end obligations—recounted what had happened.

Bothering me the most, of course, was glimpsing the strange woman and the perplexing passage of time.

Taking a deep breath, I attempted to soberly consider, with scalpel precision, what I'd seen through the second-story window, trying to dissect anything I'd missed. The scene remained the same: the pale woman's ungraceful progression into our house...her long fingers at the end of her long arm taking a swipe at my little girl...

What have you missed?

And then something else came. Unintentionally, I gasped and sat up. My mind rewinding a few more paces—to the desk...to the stationary: *My name is Tara Keltz...*

Whatever else had happened—my confusion with the woman, my confusion with how the previous day's hours had passed from morning to late afternoon—seemed like absurd figments, their fabrication less important than my neglect of concrete evidence. The mitotic complication which would arise from such invasiveness stimulated a heart-pulsing nausea.

Resting on my elbow, I considered the embarrassing and convoluted excuses I'd have to submit if someone—not the least of which the homeowner—read the lines on that sheet. I might as well have written, *My name is Tara Keltz, hapless trespasser.*

After a few calculations, I slipped out of bed. A few minutes later I was dressed and silently moving through the house. In the kitchen I retrieved a flashlight, clicking it on and off to confirm life. At the front door, I disarmed the alarm and quietly made my way into the night-chilled air. On the front walkway, I only accumulated a few paces before shuffling to a sneaker-skidding stop.

Across the street: in the second-story window of the Motley House—the window of the study, to be precise—a light was on. My eye-line was then drawn to the driveway over there, to the parked car, a rib-bone of moonlight catching its bumper.

My plan to extricate myself from a foolish intrusion dissipated. Then, up in the second-story window, a shape coalesced, a figure emerged. Tall, slender, the faint, sagging-fern shape of a deranged mane. Absent of details, it was nothing more than a lithe silhouette; but it was intent on me—the rigidity of its presence.

Slowly, I backed away, retreating into the shadows which my own house had created, reticent to pull my eyes away from that figure in the window.

I slipped back into my home, re-cued the alarm, and returned to bed.

Uneasy sleep overtook me, at some point.

I'D SPILL MY guts. With sophistication. Contrition.

I'd just drop by (again) and attempt to introduce myself (again).

As I prepared Brooke for school, I intermittently peered through the blinds, checking on the car in the driveway at the Motley House. Now in the light of day, I could see that it was a dark blue Mercedes, 70s-era, like the house itself.

Ben said, "You expecting company?"

I withdrew my fingers from the blinds and sheepishly returned his smile (Ben continues to be disarming). For the sake of simplicity, I thought about being dishonest; but I had no reason to be. Ben had never given me a reason to be. "Just. I saw a car parked over at the Motely House."

He finished filling his travel mug with coffee, coils of steam curling from the top. "Yeah, I noticed that."

I brightened a bit. Not that I was fully convinced I was imagining its presence, but to have someone acknowledge something tangible added another layer of affection for him. "You think it's an agent?" he said.

I shrugged, putting the finishing touches on getting Brooke ready for school. "Who knows." As he was saying goodbye to Brooke, I re-entered the kitchen, wrapped my arms around him and kissed him. Just like the old days.

I WAITED AN hour or so before changing, occasionally slitting the blinds, checking for activity.

And so, mimicking the friendly momentum I'd adopted the day before, I crossed the street to the Motely House; and like the day before, I pulled open the glass storm door and gave three tight knocks. This time, though, there was no succession of echoes, no taunting reverberation into penetralia. Instead, there came a curtain-twitch at the window. Considerate of boundaries (at least wanting to imply as much), I took a step back, allowing the door to close on its own.

The unrushed sound of locks being unfastened sounded before the knob twisted and the door drew open several cautious inches, just wide enough to reveal a small, paunchy old man. I smiled and gave a care-free, sternum-high wave.

Friendly-looking, he widened the aperture of the front door and creaked open the storm door. "Yes?" he said, eyes glittering.

"Good morning, I'm Tara Keltz."—I gestured back over my shoulder—"Your neighbor." I extended my hand with blithe flair.

His mouth was a small "o" as he nodded. "Oh, yes—the three of you. Moved in last autumn." His diminutive hand pumped mine several times before letting go.

With that cordial, physical contact, a wash of normality spread over me. I laughed. "Yes—that's right. We've been meaning to introduce ourselves to everyone, but the weather turned nasty so abruptly last fall and didn't let up." Still smiling, he stared at me as though the winter recap were just delivered to him. He had a full head of white, wiry hair, scrambled as if I'd woken him. According to the wrinkles lining his exterior, I gauged him in his mid-eighties. Growing self-conscious of the inordinate seconds of silence which passed, I said, "Well, we just love it here. Such a one-of-a-kind neighborhood." His grin widened—his glittering eyes now companioned by glittering, nub-yellow teeth. "Have you lived here long?"

The waxy wrinkles wrenched, his friendly features contorting under confusion. "Oh"—he cast a brief glance behind him, at the darkened, shadow-shaded interior—"we've lived here for ages. Since the beginning." I now noticed something oddly neutral about the timbre of his voice, an asexual quality that was simultaneously sonorous and shrill.

My expression implied wonder. "Wow. That's amazing." Risky, but I pushed: "You say 'we'—so you're not alone?"

His hand still holding open the glass storm door, his face whorled with what was clearly a growing bewilderment. "We...my family," he said, "all have our own rooms." His stricken expression hung on me a few ticks too long. Something about his features was no longer charming, his shriveled aspect suddenly appearing to me like some sentient, overripe root vegetable. I took a step back.

"I'm sorry," I said, as kind as I could, "what did you say your name was?"

His expression was abruptly cheerful, and he regarded me as if I were an old friend. "*My name is Tara Keltz,*" he said, his voice lilting with a mocking, patty-cake pitch, "*and I was nearly killed ten years ago.*" The old man continued grinning as I took another step backwards off the risers.

And then, from behind and above him—from the backdrop of light-lessness—emerged a gray hand. It came out of the darkness slowly, the pale forearm hooked around the side of the door, concealing its owner.

The lissome appendages of the splayed hand searched for a moment with cave-creature blindness, finally came down on top of the old man's head, where the fingers spasmed, snagging his hair; his teeth clenched and his neck strained in response, jiggling the waddle of his throat. And then the arm was retracting, slowly pulling the old man back into the darkness of the house by his hair, his hand slipping from the storm door. Then, devoid of any violent crescendo, the front door simply, and soundlessly, eased shut.

I pivoted. I pivoted and ran.

THAT NIGHT I lay in bed and waited for Ben to fall asleep.

The evening had unfolded predictably. At some point between Brooke finishing her homework and the commencement of dinner, the Mercedes disappeared from the driveway across the street. I'd then spent the meal mentally committing to returning to the house.

And so here I was once more: stealthily slipping into dark clothes and retrieving the flashlight, disarming the alarm, creeping outside. (Over the course of these past two days, I'd undergone a remarkable makeover as pseudo intruder.)

The sky was cloudless and clear. Stars shone like quivering mercury, but the moon and its crisp circumference held suspended supremacy. My shadow trailed behind me like a distorted compass needle as I unlatched the back gate and crossed the patio deck.

The large shrub cloaking the door looked darker under the moon-light. I clicked on the flashlight, using my fingers to dull the glow. I pressed myself between the brick and the limbs and clasped hold of the knob. The door gaped open, widening with what sounded like an agonal gasp. I slipped through, sweeping the door shut behind me. As with my initial entrance, the corridor's burnt-orange carpet led me into the interior.

Shadows leaped and receded as I entered the kitchen. Beyond, over in the inviting convolution that was the home's interior, my flashlight compelled dark projections to spring open and fall flat, as though I were walking through a pop-up book, its black pages guided by an incoherent hand.

Again: despite my multiform, self-inflicted failures, my innate impulse remained—visual dissection, interpretation. I didn't need to ask too many questions about these occupants, as the answer to most people's stories lay exposed before us. And so it took some self-control to maintain pace and stay on task.

I arrived at the vestibule adjacent to the staircase. The spindles of the banister cast jail-cell shadows, dozens of bars creating a sort of gyroscope.

Fingers, wrapped around one of the spindles, withdrew as I approached; a figure, barely discernible through the vertical shadow-bars of the banister, scuttle-scaled the stairs. "Wait!" I called, gripping the banister and racing up the risers. Panting, cresting the landing, I angled the beam down the empty hallway and, trembling, clicked off the light and tried to calm myself, waiting for my breathing to steady. The house was silent.

In the study, generous moonlight streamed through the wide windows, the powder-blue glow through the muntins created tiles of light on the carpet. The tree limb outside cut a crooked silhouette.

The once-lush palm next to the window was dead. Anemic leaves were scattered beneath it, skirt-like. Verdant two days before, it stood now like some enormous, withery neuron, its dehydrated dendrites bare and vulnerable. I was conscious of the under-current-thrum of my pulse.

Despite my awareness of the wrongness of this whole thing—the palpability that I'd stumbled into something I didn't comprehend—I simply couldn't expedite the imperative: grab the stationary off the desk and get the hell out of the house. I side-stepped the ottoman on my way to the desk. Though I recognized that using the flashlight here near the second-story window to be reckless—though no more negligent than the intrusions I'd already committed—I could not resist but clicking on the light, using my palm to deaden the beam.

The paper was where I'd left it; but my midsection crimped when the dull light touched the surface. The opening line was there—*My name is Tara Keltz*—but added to it was either a child-like or deranged endeavor in ink: black latticework of lines and scribbles, an ivy of invective forming obscenities in precious cursive. The looping script of BITCHROT has lingered with me.

Pursing my lips and clicking off the flashlight, I slid the paper from the desk, folded it, and slipped it in the pocket of my pullover. I made it merely two steps and halted, my entire awareness arrested by the tall, pale woman standing in the doorway.

Though her ghastly pallor had a contrasting effect with the darkness, the shafts of moonlight illuminated her, flesh seeming to radiate a gray-blue hue. She stared at me, her lips bent in a tired simper. Her dark hair hung over her shoulders in ratty panels; she was wearing that forsaken sundress which exposed her shoulders, arms, shins. I recognized it now, a garment I'd given to Goodwill over a decade before. I could describe her to exhaustion, but—notwithstanding the rot-mottled condition of her flesh—the enterprise would be as mundane as imparting what I'd seen in the mirror each day most of my adult life.

I managed a step toward her and she responded by doing precisely the same (albeit with a hitching stagger); and as I summoned another step, so too did she, until we were standing only several feet from each other within the window-tiled moonlight.

We lined up symmetrically, in height, in the set of our bodies. I ignored the requisite repulsion in encountering such a cadaverous essence. Her purple lips still bore a small smile and I realized that I (though I had no idea why) was smiling, too—a distant recollection asserted itself.

A long time ago, there was a television station that played old movies in the middle of the night. This was before Ben and the night-time—used for studying, mostly, for getting a "leg up" on my academic competition—suited me. Flipping stations, procrastinating between chapters, I'd stumbled on a Marx Brothers movie—that mirror scene in one of those black-and-whites where Groucho and one of his brothers amusingly duplicate each other's movements.

Tentatively, I lifted my hand, palm-out, in a gesture which was intended to reflect a greeting, or a sort of truce.

Her forearm—as violent as a suddenly unencumbered coil—sprang out, her frigid palm and long fingers cinched my throat.

A wash of acidic sobriety sluiced through me, my momentary reverence and awe disappearing in a synaptic shiver. Her expression had not changed; her cracked lips still bore that simper, her eyes were wide, unblinking—the moonlight reflecting slender sickles in her slick sclera.

Shock-stalled, I was now aware I couldn't breathe. This reshaped the inflectional state of my perception and brought an objective immediacy to what I saw before me—to what I see happening to Tara Keltz.

Tara's eyelids flutter as shadows in the room double and coalesce, overlay and assimilate. As the decayed figure tightens its grip around her throat, Tara staggers, catching herself on the corner of the ottoman. The moonlight is fading; she feels the weight of the flashlight in her hand. Tara lashes out, punches wildly. One of the clenched strikes connects with the woman's chin. Tara summons another more accurate blow, this one eliciting an audible crunch as it lands squarely against her nose. The icy smile is still there. Even with the rills of blood freely streaming over her philtrum, the smile is still there.

The woman's grip compresses with renewed intent, and Tara understands that she is supposed to close her own eyes now. Through her narrowing awareness, she thinks of Ben and Brooke. She thinks of pain—how it is inflicted in forms of casual cruelty, in manifest forms of wonton physicality. She thinks of the excuses she's made to conceal her own pain in an effort to present herself as superior. Tara Keltz thinks of the aberration of exposed bone—that obscene tibia-tipi draped with the gore of torn flesh.

My leg, thinks Tara. *My shin.*

Tara claws at the last threads of consciousness, shifts her weight, and spears her foot out and down in a vicious kick, her sneaker connecting with the other woman's lower leg.

The howl does not ascend in volume as much as it is just instantly *here*—funneling out from the rotting woman's midsection, echoing down the hall. The house's atmosphere itself, agonized.

The decay-corrupted woman releases her hand and collapses; and though Tara feels like doing the same, she braces herself against the bookcase, wincing as much from the pain as from the sustained keening. The other woman is on the floor, cradling her lower leg, the moonlight catching the glint of blood-streaked bone.

Then Tara is limp-hauling herself across the room; the pale woman removes one hand from her strangely angled shin and takes a swipe at Tara; but she sidesteps it on the way to the hallway.

Tara does not look back as she clicks on the flashlight—the shadows of the staircase risers rush toward her, as though she's running down the wrong way on a malignant escalator. Then she's in the kitchen and when she sweeps the light over the space she falters. None of the shadows move here, but hang static behind each corner, each shape, disorienting Tara for a moment. The sound of something thumping its way in pursuit gets her going again.

Tara turns the corner to the side-hall corridor. Licking her lips, she runs the length, yanks open the door and propels herself through the threshold. The screaming ceases and she draws in achy gulps of night-cool air. With the large shrub netting itself around her, the light playing along the limbs creates a veiny, incessantly reweaving animation.

Tara leans against the side of the house, begins to slide away but is roughly seized. She whips the flashlight beam down to her ankle, to the shackle of a decay-riddled hand protruding from between the door and the jamb; but the grip is weak, fever-meak. Breath coming in ragged gasps, Tara slowly reaches down and tenderly unfastens those stiff, gray fingers from her ankle. She does not glance within as she gently hinges the cold forearm back through the black breach and solemnly pulls the door closed.

THAT WAS A long time ago.

And the greatest challenge in those following days was concealing the clamp-shaped bruises on the sides of my neck (I made adroit choices to my clothing, accessories), and with how I styled my hair until the purple striations faded.

We are happy. If you ask Ben, I suppose he would say we were always happy; but I have invested energy and understanding to validate that statement.

In the ensuing months following my final entry into the Motley House, I approached my discipline of interior design with a renewed sensibility. I revamped not only the website but the mission of my niche business venture. I run nearly every day, in the early mornings, just like I used to.

I've made friends, colleagues, and progress. Brooke is taller now.

The Motley House goes through its phases. Often, it is serene, and voicing chit-chat observations proves unnecessary. Still, months go by when a FOR SALE sign shows up in the front yard before abruptly disappearing. I watch the daily postal carriers place items in a mailbox which is apparently empty upon each visit. The lawn is neat and fastidiously maintained.

I've never again seen the dark-blue Mercedes in the driveway, though from time to time I snag a glimpse of a shriveled old man creep through the opened gate to the backyard.

More than anything, I try not to dwell on it.

But as I run by on my morning route, I consider the façade, doing my best to avoid making undue eye contact with the second-story window. There are moments, though, when I fail. Sometimes there is nothing.

Yet, frequently, behind the reflective murk, there is a figure. On those occasions, she is distinct behind the pane, her grave-gray pallor contrasting with the gloom behind her. Tightening my focus, there is a smaller, darker shape that is her mouth, and I've remembered the residue of that howl, the rugose scales of the ouroboros that is her lips.

Still, she has the meaningful view from her second-story aspect.

It's a perspective they can both accept.

ZWILLINGSLIED

———•———

Patricia Lillie

I WATCH HIM. One hand slides up and down the neck of the National Tricone, his fingers settle between the frets, and I know a twelve-bar progression colors the air. Dirty blond curls flop on his forehead and fall over his eyes. He looks like something out of a BBC period piece. The 1920s or 30s. The quintessential androgynous boy.

I watch him, still and lost inside his own head. He plays until his fingers bleed. Maybe the blood on the strings sweetens them.

I watch. Red streaks the fingerboard of my mother's guitar and splatters its gleaming belly. Lost in the music, he doesn't notice.

I watch, but I don't feel. I know the music hangs dead in the air. My pretty little man-boy has no soul. I close my eyes and search for my own. I find it, crumpled and stuffed in a box, locked away, right where I left it. It is safe.

HE TRAILS HIS fingertips across my cheek. I imagine streaks of red, burning my skin. I take his hand in mine and raise it to my lips. No blood, only hard, rough callouses.

"Wake up. Come to bed."

I watch his lips and wait for more but get nothing.

IN THE NIGHT, my mother comes to me. I get out of bed, and together we stand at the window and enjoy the night. She doesn't speak, yet I know her sounds.

"Your mother could have sung the phone book and people would have fallen at her feet," my father said. "You look like her."

He didn't add *too bad you don't sound like her*, but I heard it in the spaces between his words.

I IMAGINE MYSELF in a red satin dress. It clings to my curves and matches my lipstick. I wear it to a smoke-filled bar, crowded with people lost in music. I float on the soft, slow rhythms of whiskey, cigarettes, and longing. Bessie Smith. Billie Holiday. Etta James and Big Mama Thornton. Janis Joplin. Bonnie Riatt and Carolyn Wonderland. My mother.

Smoking in public places is illegal, red is not my color, my curves are practically nonexistent, and it's only open mike night at Be-Bob's Lounge. I put on black jeans and knee-high boots and stand in front of the closet unable to make up my mind. He pulls out a silk shirt, blue as a summer sky, and hands it to me.

I watch his mouth.

"For luck," he says.

The shirt has a red wine stain on the front and a small hole, the edges charred, on the sleeve. Smoking is not yet illegal in private. I put it on. It is the one I wore the day we met.

He wears black jeans and a shirt in the same clear blue. His is unblemished. Unscarred.

I WATCH HIM sing my words, the ones I wrote for him. *Alice belled the cat.* Not all my words. He changes a few. The cat is not a cool cat. Not with those gleaming teeth and that mocking voice, but maybe he knows. Maybe he takes the madness from my head and softens it. *We're* *all mad here whispers the cat.*

I don't look at anything but him until the song is over.

"Hey." A woman in black from the roots of her dyed hair to the toes of her Doc Martens plunks herself down across from me and blocks my view. "Is he your brother?"

"No," I say. Her voice grates. He is the only one I can't hear and the only one I want to hear.

"You could be twins. What's his name again?"

"Zwilling." He hadn't given a name when he took the stage, so I come up with one on the spur of the moment. My high school German classes don't go to waste.

She doesn't get it. "Like the actress?"

"No. Just Zwilling."

"Does he have a first name?"

"Maybe." I lean to the side and look past her.

"You don't need to be a bitch." She leaves me and heads for the stage, a harpy zeroing in on her prey.

I'm not worried. He's not my brother nor is he my lover, but he belongs to me.

THEY SAY THAT Robert Johnson had the music trapped inside. Desperate to set it free, he met the devil at a crossroads.

I understand.

Johnson died at twenty-seven. My mother was twenty-seven when I found her in the bathtub in a room in a cheap motel near Dockery, Mississippi. The water colored her white satin dress a lovely red.

THE HARPY STANDS at the side of the stage. The Wednesday night crowd, such as it is, is hushed.

He hunches over the guitar, his head bowed. I can't read his lips. I watch his hands. I know the chords. He is playing one of my mother's songs.

He finishes, looks up, and finds me at my table. His eyes are empty, cold. A smattering of applause ripples around me.

"Not bad, but something's missing," a man behind me says.

The story of my life.

MY FATHER DRANK himself to death listening to my mother's music. I played those same vinyl records over and over, wearing them out as the music crept inside me, filled me, fed me. I bought a beginner's guitar. Took lessons. I was mediocre at best.

My voice was worse than mediocre.

Before he died, my father gave me my mother's guitar. We both knew I wasn't worthy of holding it let alone playing it.

"A legacy is more than just the things," he said.

I never asked what he meant.

HIS SET IS over, and the audience is polite. A few are more than polite, but there's no encore. I'm not even sure one is allowed under Be-Bob's open mike rules. He stands, flips his curls out of his eyes, and hops off the low platform that serves as a stage. His new fan tries to speak to him, but he doesn't let himself be waylaid. He joins me, reaches across the table, and takes my hand.

I was wrong.

His eyes aren't empty. They're hungry.

ON THE EVE of my twenty-seventh birthday, I returned to Mississippi. I'm sure a lot had changed over the past twenty-three years, but the Riverside Traveler Motel was still there. I checked into a Holiday Inn.

THE HARPY APPROACHES us. She drops a business card on the table, ignores me, and speaks only to him. "You need work, but your technique is excellent and you're almost as pretty as that guitar. Call me."

She stares at him for a moment before turning to me. "It's uncanny. Separated at birth or something."

When she's gone, I pick up the card. *Miriam Bishop. Blue Delta Agency.*

I NEEDN'T HAVE bothered with the Holiday Inn. I turned twenty-seven at a crossroads in the Middle of Nowhere, Mississippi with only a pack of Marlboro Light 100s and a large bottle of pinot noir for company. Neither lasted long. No one showed up to make an offer for my soul. If Papa Legba was anywhere near, he was laughing his ass off at the silly little white girl drowning in self-pity. I fell asleep in my car.

HE CALLS MIRIAM Bishop. He gives her his name. Frankie. It is my name.

She talks about getting him into the studio but first books him a couple of shows at a small club. He proudly shows me his name on the poster. He is opening for the opening act. *Introducing Frankie Zwilling*, reads the tiny type. I don't remember telling him about "Zwilling." I assume it was Miriam's doing.

She asks—tells—me not to attend.

WHEN I WOKE up, my mother sat next to me in her white-red dress, staring out the car window at the stars.

"What did you do to your hair?" I said. Her long blond mane had been replaced by a mop of short ringlets.

She turned to me, and I saw my mother's gentle, benevolent expression but not my mother.

"Go away," I said and closed my eyes and went back to sleep.

I blamed the cheap wine. No one meets themselves in the front seat of a third-hand Buick somewhere in the back of beyond outside of Dockery, Mississippi.

It was the cut-rate red or a bad dream or both.

When the sun came up she—I—was gone.

HE PLAYS OUT, and I stay in. I am miserable. A headache. Vomiting. Worse, I feel as if a part of me, the deepest part, is being ripped away and shredded.

When he returns, he is sullen. Miriam is with him. She is not pleased.

"A tin music box would have had more heart," she says.

We agree I should go the next night.

"Get some sleep," she says. "You both look like hell."

When she is gone, he takes my head in his hands and forces me to look into his face.

"Please," he mouths.

I know what he needs, but I am not ready to give it. Not yet.

JOHNSON TOOK HIS guitar to the crossroads and the devil—or Papa Legba, depending on who's telling the story—tuned it. In return, Johnson freely promised his soul.

The rest is history.

The hotel had my credit card. My unused overnight bag contained nothing I couldn't live without. There was no need for me to return. Except—

My mother's guitar. Her beautiful shining National, unplayed since her death. I'd brought it to Mississippi but couldn't bring myself to take it to the crossroads. That would have required a leap of faith I didn't possess. Still, it was the one thing I owned that I couldn't live without.

MIRIAM DISCOVERS WHO I am, who my mother was.

"There's a PR angle there, if I can just figure out how to use it," she says.

"No," I tell her. "Don't you dare."

She books him farther and farther away from home, and I am always seated front and center. His following grows with every show. Miriam doesn't think I know she calls us "Tweedledum and Tweedledee."

In a crowded bar in Baltimore, I think I hear him, but the music fades, muffled by the fog in my head. I decide it is only my imagination.

People stop asking if I am his sister. Instead, they ask if I am his mother. The answer to each is neither and both.

AT THE HOLIDAY Inn, I found him in my room. Hunched over my mother's guitar, he caressed the warm metal. The room was silent, but I recognized the pattern his fingers made on the fretboard. *Alice met the Jabberwock.*

He finished, put the guitar down, and stood before me.

My nose. My mouth. The small space between my front teeth. I reached out and pushed his curls off his forehead and out of his eyes.

My eyes.

I wasn't frightened. I knew him like I knew myself.

"We'd better go home," I said.

Miriam books studio time.

"Forget the record companies," she says. "We'll do it ourselves and go independent." She knows there is still something missing, but hopes to fix it in post-production. "A good engineer is a magician," she says.

They argue over what songs to record. They agree to include my song, the one I'd written for him without knowing it. Miriam asks me to write another. I agree but fail to produce. I have the words, but I can't put them in the right order. I hear the chords, and I know what needs to be said. The song battles to get out, but stays trapped in my head. Locked away in its box, my soul begins to crumble.

Disgusted with me, Miriam suggests he cover at least one of my mother's songs. He is reluctant. The idea terrifies me.

He goes into the studio tomorrow.

I wake to the sound of a guitar. The guitar. I recognize it from the vinyl records I haven't touched since I returned from Mississippi.

This is not a recording. It's my mother's guitar. My guitar. The melody is the one I failed to write.

I find him in the living room. My mother sits beside him, glowing with maternal pride.

He sings the words I failed to write. I want to stop him, but in my mother's eyes I see myself.

"You're almost there," she says.

I hear every word, every note, and know he is everything I need. I give him what he wants.

ALL BLUES REVIEWS

Jabberwocky Blues, Frankie Zwilling
Red Dress Records

If the legendary Alice Charleston had given birth to a son rather than a daughter, that son would be Frankie Zwilling. In fact, the title track of Zwilling's stunning debut was written by Charleston's recently deceased daughter, oddly enough also named Frankie. The Charleston-Zwilling connection doesn't end with a shared song and a shared name. Rumor has it the 1938 nickel-plated National Tricone style guitar Zwilling plays belonged to Alice and was given to him by the other Frankie. And then there is the startling—some might say creepy— physical resemblance between the two Frankies.

An unearthly backstory has never hurt any blues musician, a fact that Zwilling is likely not unaware of given his included covers of Robert Johnson's "Cross Road Blues" and two Alice Charleston classics. Luckily, he lives up to the potential hype with his superb guitar playing and a voice like the aural equivalent of an arrow to the heart. The undisputed gem of the album is the final and only self-penned track, "Twin Song." Zwilling performs the dark ballad with a driving passion and heartbreaking depth of feeling well beyond his years. Frankie Zwilling is a worthy successor to the Charleston legacy, and *Jabberwocky Blues* may just be the debut of the year. A+

STATIC

———◆———

Chris Shearer

I DIDN'T KNOW what he would become then. None of us did. Had we known, maybe we would have done things differently. I'm sure we would have done it differently, but that's the curse of hindsight: you see what could have and possibly *should have* been, and yet, for all the power of imagination, you can't change any of it. You can live fantasy after fantasy in daydreams and during the hours of sleep when you are most vulnerable and honest with yourself, but whatever it is you want to change—a soured relationship, a broken marriage, a last goodbye—is always as it has always been. This is life.

My father came home in 1987. He came home carrying a green sack full of the makings of his life in the service and nothing else. I remember the sack because he left it in the front room, where it blocked the TV, which played *Teenage Mutant Ninja Turtles* at the time. My mother was in the kitchen, cooking, something she did rarely, but well, when he came into our home in a cloud of cigarette smoke. I was reflected in his sunglasses, along with the lamp. My brother crept downstairs when he heard his voice; he stopped at the bottom stair. He held the bannister.

I can still see the way Mom's lip turned and the late-morning sun broke through the window and flared in her loose curls. She didn't have the words. None of us did. Dad, as eloquent as he ever was or would be, scraped the top of my head with his calloused hand and then went to her. His heavy steps were muffled by the carpet. He hugged her, but it wasn't like the hugs you see in old movies; it was plaintive. Mom didn't push away, but she didn't hug him back either. She just let him take her in his arms. But then she looked at my brother, and when she did, she put her arms around the man I would come to call Dad and smiled for him.

Sharing a room with my father was awkward at first. Something inside of me, something instinctual, told me he didn't belong, and I wouldn't be alone with him. But it was clear by the way he changed the TV to a baseball game during my cartoons that he didn't care one way or the other if I was there or not, so it worked out. I'd only seen him a handful of times, and that handful consisted of slipshod memories of a birthday at McDonald's, a dark movie theater, a loud conversation in the kitchen, and one kiss on my forehead from hard lips and a rough, bristled chin. He ignored me that first day, something I'd eventually get used to.

That night at dinner, we waited for Dad. Mom wouldn't let us start without him, and he wasn't in a hurry to eat. The food cooled on the table, and my stomach rumbled. Mom called him for the third time. As the late-summer sun tossed bars through the fence beyond the window and the bars merged with ever-widening shadows, he dragged his hairy fist against the floral kitchen wallpaper to keep his balance as he stumbled in. He set his beer on the table before he sat; a cloud of cigarette smoke surrounded him. Mom had cooked six chicken thighs, enough for the three of us—Mom, my brother, and me—that day and the next. Dad took two of them. He didn't say Grace, and he ate greedily, so that chicken grease slicked his cheeks and chin.

My brother took two pieces, too, and he ate the same way. Mom dished mine and then took her own. She gave Dad a look that I hadn't seen from her before. She looked tired and a little like she'd lost something.

Dad burped when he finished and slugged his beer. Outside, the sun had set and lightning bugs flicked on and off constellating the sky framed in the window behind him. He lit a cigarette.

"I wish you wouldn't," Mom said.

Dad grunted in the rough way I would come to know as his.

"The boys don't need it. You can take it outside."

Dad inhaled slowly and then blew a plume of smoke over the table. It hung and curled. Mom grabbed my plate—I hadn't yet finished—and clacked it against her own. She took my brother's and Dad's, too.

"I'm not going to do this again," she said as she turned on the water to wash them.

My brother still had his utensils and he traced a shape onto the tablecloth with his butter knife. Dad stood, took his beer, and went to the window. He stared into it for a tension-slowed few seconds. I didn't want to move, and I didn't want to stay in the room. The air felt heavy and dangerous in a way I'd never before known. My brother smiled at me, but it was a smile brought by discomfort. Then Dad left through the back door. The screen smacked closed behind him.

Mom let out a heavy breath, and that was the end of it. As I went to the front room, where the TV already played the theme of Disney's Sunday Night Movie, I looked through the screen at my father, a shadow darker than the night around him, and the red tip of his cigarette trailing sharp, short movements. We didn't have air conditioning, and the night air was warm and still, but I grew cold.

That night Mom kissed my forehead as she always did before bed, but she didn't read anything. My brother—in the bed across the room—had a reading light and read his own books, usually comics but sometimes novels like Treasure Island and The Outsiders. Sometimes he shared parts of them with me after Mom left, but not that night. His light was off, and when she left the room and closed the door, it was as dark as my father's shadow through the screen had been. I shut my eyes and tried not to think about anything.

But as soon as the door closed, they started. Their voices came muffled through the walls and wood so that the words were all but lost and only the feeling of the words remained. I rolled to put my back to the sound, but it didn't go away. It only grew, not louder or sharper, but heavier. I felt a tear on my cheek.

My mother's distorted voice came, followed by my father's, which rumbled its way through the still house. The gruff sound of his voice put me on edge, and despite the heat, I had gooseflesh. I tried covering my ears so that all I heard was my own heartbeat, but that didn't help. Although I could no longer hear them, I felt what they said. Each time my mother spoke, tiny pins pricked my chest and stomach, and when my father growled back, I shook.

Their argument moved from the bathroom to the hall and then to their bedroom. When they closed the door, the house trembled, and I uncovered my ears. I could still hear them, and more than that, I could still feel them. The tension in the house was like a pall, and I felt trapped, unable to move or get away from it.

Across the room, my brother lay in frozen darkness. I didn't hear the deep, rhythmic breaths he made when sleeping, so I knew he was awake, but silent. I said his name once, and he didn't respond. At that moment, with my brother less than six feet from me and my mother and father fighting only two closed doors and a short hallway away, I felt the most alone I would ever feel.

I went to the window between the beds and opened it. The smells of dirt and night and summer sneaked through on a weak breeze that set me shivering. Outside, the stars were clouded over so that all I could see above was the hazy outline of a smothered moon. Distantly, cars rumbled. The lights in the neighbor's house were on, and I wondered if they would do anything to stop them. They would have had to have been deaf not to hear my parents' fighting. It was on the breeze too.

I often had a dream, both before and after that first night with my father, of flying. I dreamed that I would open that window and step outside into that same summer-scented night and be free of all that was and all that would be. I thought of that dream then, and I leaned closer to the open window, listened to the soft sound of the wind in the backyard tree and the jangle of my mother's wind chimes. I imagined what it would be like to fly. To be weightless and completely free. To soar above the clouds and over the dark pools of lakes and rivers and the ruffled forests and lurching hills. I wondered how far you could go and how long you could go before flying, too, became a normal part of life, part of the routine of getting up, going to school, coming home, and watching a late movie before stories and sleep. Until it, too, became routine, and it, too, lost its excitement, lost its sense of freedom. I closed my eyes and imagined the soft breeze coming through the window lifting me. My parents still fought, and I still heard them, but their voices and the feelings of their words were distant, like a midnight train whistle from the next town over.

"What are you doing?" my brother said. He was up on his elbows watching me.

"I couldn't sleep."

"No shit." He wasn't allowed to swear like that. If Mom had heard him, she would have washed his mouth out with soap. I wouldn't tell her.

"Do you think they'll stop?"

"Eventually." He turned on the light by his bed. The room seemed to ignite, and I had to squint to look at him.

"Do you think he'll hurt her?"

"No," he said, but I didn't trust him. Mom had never talked about Dad much, and she'd never told me that he'd hurt her, but somehow I knew that he had.

"Think it's something I did?"

My brother wrinkled his nose.

"Dad doesn't like me. I can tell."

"He doesn't know you. Give him time." My brother rubbed the end of his nose and sniffled. "Why do you think he's home?"

I didn't know. Part of me wanted to make up a reason. He was a hero, and he was returning home with medals and accolades. We'd see him in a day or two on the local news, and the governor would shake his hand. They'd both be smiling. But I couldn't picture my father smiling. Not then and not later. It wasn't in him to smile. "I heard Mom say something about dist-honorable dist-charge, but I don't know what that is. She said it again and again, though."

"Yeah," he said. He picked up an X-Men comic with Wolverine and Cyclops on the cover glaring at each other. Wolverine's claws were out and his teeth showed like a mad dog's. Cyclops's visor glowed red and smoked. "Come here."

I climbed into his bed with him, and he read to me, and when he did the night went away, and my parents' voices went away, and only the story remained.

My brother was asleep when I crawled out of his bed. The night outside had grown still and silent. The weak breeze that had come through the window earlier was gone and only the sounds of distant insects occupied the night. In the hours I'd spent in my brother's bed, the clouds had passed and the stars had found their separate ways into the dark sky. I wanted to touch them, but they were too far away. My brother made a noise in his sleep, something between a whimper and a snore.

I went to the door, holding myself, because I had to pee. The hall light was off so that you couldn't tell where the door ended and the wall began. I felt around for the knob, and when I found it, I turned it slowly. I listened as best I could with my heart thundering in my ears. I didn't hear anything, so I edged the door open.

The hinges made a small noise, not a squeak or squeal, more like a soft scrape. I didn't open it much, just enough to squeeze myself through. Out in the hall, the sense of something wrong, something indescribably off, blanketed everything. The shadow that led to my parents' room seemed to stretch into infinity, and I imagined that if I went into it I'd be lost forever, taken to some place far away from home, alone. I stared into it the same way I'd stared at car accidents on the road. I was looking for something, but I didn't know what.

Then I heard a noise. Nothing loud, but something that didn't belong. It sounded like radio static. I moved toward it before I knew what I was doing, and the closer I came, the louder it became, moving from a hint of sound, almost as if imagined, to a soft whisper of white noise. With it came a gradual brightening. It was loudest and brightest at the top of the stairs, and when I looked down them, I saw the flickering of the TV in the front room, that sharp white jump of a station with no reception. My father was down there. I had no way of knowing that for sure, but I knew it. I felt it. And everything wrong in the house was down there with him.

For a second I thought about climbing down a few stairs so that I could see what he was doing, but then I didn't. I didn't want him to see me, and he would. I knew he would. I tiptoed toward the bathroom.

The door was almost closed, so that only the width of the door itself stood out from the flat of the wall. Inside, the moon came through the small window over the shower, so that a hint of light silvered everything inside and leaked into the hall through the cracks around and under the door. The hairs on the back of my neck and on the tops of my arms were up. I took slow breaths.

I tiptoed closer to it, close enough to see the silvery spill inside, the way it stained the sink and my toothbrush and the shower. The way it made the fluff carpet in the middle of the small room look like a die-cast model. Mom was in there. She sat on the toilet with her hands covering her face. She was absolutely still, and for a second, before I recognized her, I thought she might have been a ghost that my father had brought back from the service with him. I stood to the side of the door, knowing I should leave and go back to my room, knowing that I shouldn't watch this moment, because it was private, it wasn't for me, but I stayed. I kept myself off to the side of the crack so that she couldn't have seen me if she'd looked, but she didn't look. She just sat there, a moon-smudged statue in the still of a hot night toward the end of summer. I have never seen anything as painful or as beautiful.

DAD LOADED MOM'S station wagon with a couple of suitcases, three brand new sleeping bags, a brand new tent, and a couple of lanterns. I didn't want to go. He'd been home for two weeks and wanted to take us camping, a word I didn't know, and an idea that, when my brother explained it to me, didn't sound fun at all. But it's what Dad wanted, and if the past two weeks had taught me anything, it was that Dad got what he wanted. In that short time, Mom had grown thinner and older, somehow, and she didn't talk or smile like she used to. I missed her, and I missed my family. And I didn't want to spend the next few hours trapped in the back seat of the car with this one.

"You sure you have everything?" Mom said. She moved her fingers through my hair. "You'll need a haircut when we get back. Before school."

I told her I had everything and asked again if I had to go. She leaned against the wall by the front window and watched Dad and my brother close the car's hatchback. My brother brushed his hands on his shorts, and Dad came toward the house. Before he stepped inside, he lit a cigarette. I looked at Mom, and her face didn't change. There was no expression.

"Come on. I want to get on the road so we get there before dark." He all but shoved me through the door. Mom followed.

My brother was already in the back seat by the time I got there. He had a small pile of comics set in the middle. I got in and grabbed the one on top. It was a Fantastic Four. He snatched it from me before I could open it. He had a wide smile.

I started to say something, but when I saw Mom's face reflected in the rearview mirror, I couldn't. She looked drawn and pale, and though her mouth was set, her eyes looked like they were holding back tears. Dad put a map on her lap. "If we get lost it's your fault," he said. She squeezed the top of the map.

As we pulled away from my first home, I leaned into the door. The leather was hot with sun and stuck to my arm. Outside, our house faded away the way I would come to know all things do, and parked cars, neighbors, and the houses of the neighborhood slipped by one after the other until there were no more neighbors and no more yards and no more cars or houses, until there were only empty fields with rickety fences and the occasional cow hidden under a small, solitary tree.

We pulled into the campground at dusk, just as the sun settled like a dollop of blood atop a bruised sky over the mountains to the west. There was a large sign and a ranger that Dad spoke to for several minutes. The ground was dirt and pocked so that the car jumped and shook as we rolled into a dark wood where the branches reached so low that they scraped the windows and the top of Mom's car. There hadn't been much talking during the ride, just the occasional word or two, but in that moment, we were all utterly silent for the first time. You couldn't even hear breaths.

Dad took a left and then another left, passing one group of campers with a neon-colored tent who were seated around a fire eating dinner. He pulled into our lot, which was marked with a wooden post, and turned off the car. As it clicked and settled, we all struggled out, stiff from the drive, and Dad began to unpack.

"Boys, your mother and I are going to set up the tent. You go find some wood for the fire." I didn't know what wood would make a good fire and started to say so, but then my brother grabbed me by the shoulder and pulled me toward the pocked dirt road and the line of trees beyond it.

I pushed a low branch away and ducked under another. My brother followed a walking path, and I followed him. As we walked, he pointed out the three leafs of poison ivy and the poison sumac. He handed me sticks and wider bits of grey bark. The path edged slowly downward for a bit and then grew steep. At the top of the steep part, I could see the lake beyond the trees. The sun had stained it an awkward red that glowed between low-hanging branches and leafs. I slowed to keep my footing. Only then did I feel cold, even though the temperature had dropped as soon as we'd rolled into the campground. I heard a thousand sounds around me: scuttles, birds, people's voices, shifting leaves, a scraping wind. My brother had moved a distance ahead of me, had grown small and almost hidden by the trees, and I called after him and ran to catch up.

Out of breath, I finally caught up to him near the lakeshore. He held a long stick in his hand and stared out toward the darkening water. I dropped the firewood and pressed my hands to my knees and gasped for air. Between breaths, I said, "Why'd you go running off like—"

He put his hand up to stop me and took a cautious step toward the lapping, reddened waves. The ground they touched was covered in smooth, flat stones and mud. My brother took another step. He held the stick in front of him.

"What is it?" I whispered.

He poked the mud to the side of a larger, squarish stone. He stepped back when he did, watching the mud. I scratched my elbow, which itched a little, and crept toward him. At the place where the ground changed from shrub and underbrush to smooth rock and mud, the rocks made a noise under my weight. He turned on me.

My brother's lips pulled back from his teeth, and he shoved me. I fell into a bush with sharp branches that scraped my neck, back, and arms. "Get back," he said.

As I struggled to stand, he poked the mud by the stone again. This time the mud moved. Not much, but enough that I saw it. Liquid black life slid away from his stick, curling into the shadow cast by the sun and the stone.

"What is it?" I said again.

My brother moved closer, and when he did the sound of a distant boat engine gurgled to life. I stared at the muddy shadow by the stone, waiting for it to move again. My brother poked it, and it did. The shadow slid out toward the white-topped waves that the boat had kicked up. It was long and thin and black. My brother chased after it, getting his feet wet.

"What was it?" I asked when he came back.

"Snake," he said.

DAD AND MY brother dragged our rented boat into the lake, and I mostly hung onto the back of it to keep up. When the water reached Dad's knees, he jumped inside. My brother struggled in at the same time, but I couldn't. It was at my waist and when I tried to pull myself in, nothing happened. Dad cracked open a beer from his cooler. For a second, I feared they'd leave me behind, maybe to drown, but then my brother came and helped me in.

The water smelled stale and stung some of the cuts on my arms and neck. Dad handed me an oar and said, "You two better get started if we're going to get anywhere." He had the cooler between his legs and sat on the front boat bench. The fishing rods stuck out from under it and hung over the water like three silver antennae. Beyond them, the pale lake stretched out for miles in every direction. A good distance to the right, the shores of a lone island broke the uniformity. Straight ahead, I could just see the rise of the far shore. I wondered why Mom hadn't come.

Rowing was harder than I thought it would be and after only a few strokes, my arms and chest ached, but I tried not to show it. I didn't want Dad to see that I was weak. He watched the two of us row and kept his back to the lake ahead. He stared at me, and the sun set shadows on his face that seemed to stretch too far, casting his eyes in black and elongating his cheeks and chin. He looked devilish.

"Head to the left," he said.

Sweat dripped from my forehead, stinging my eyes and the cuts on my neck. We headed toward nothing, into the sun-bleached plane of the still lake. A soft breeze twisted around us and soothed some of the sting. We passed another boat, and Dad tipped his beer at them. When I felt like I couldn't row anymore, he told us to stop. I was so tired that my hands shook when I lowered the oar into the boat. Dad handed me a fishing line, which he'd already baited with a worm and a bobber. I watched my brother cast to see how it was done, and then I tried. Dad laughed at me, but my brother told me to reel in, and then he helped me do it better.

Dad popped another beer and asked my brother if he wanted a sip.

He took one and made a face. Dad never offered one to me.

"You boys know what this used to be, right?"

I shook my head. Dad reeled in his line and cast it again.

"Look down."

I wasn't sure what he meant, but my brother pointed into the lake. I did, but all I saw was a white plate of reflected sun.

"Sure is something," Dad said. "They just filled it in. There were still people here, you know. Some people wouldn't leave when the county told 'em to." He took a long slug, crushed the can, and tossed it into the water. "Some people are stupid. But there's good fishing here now. Carp down there. Water's cold though. That's why you're not allowed to swim." My brother stared at Dad the way people on those Sunday shows stare at their slick-haired pastors. "Your mom and me came out here after we were married. Watched a kid dive from a boat right about this spot. The kid went down, but he never came up. Water froze him. You get that cold it paralyzes you. There was nothin' no one could do. Heart probably stopped soon as his head went under."

I didn't know what to say, so I fiddled with the hem of my shorts.

"Your mom won't come out here. She's scared of it." He laughed and cigarette smoke billowed from his mouth and nose.

As he laughed, a cloud passed over the sun and laid a shadow on the lake. I didn't want to look at him. There was something animal in his gestures and the way he talked. He smirked at my brother, and my brother smiled back. I let my gaze drift off to my bobber and saw what he was talking about. A distance below my line and below the boat, in the grime of the lake, sat a barn. We floated over its roof, which was still intact. It looked like a toy submerged in dirty bath water. I searched around the barn for other buildings or cars or tractors, but I couldn't see that far into the lake. Only the roof was visible. I imagined that there were bodies, skeletons by now, beneath that sick-green roof, maybe on the barn's floor, mixed with sediment and sodden bales of hay, picked clean by catfish, or maybe still floating but caught under the roof, until the day the wood rotted and came loose of its rusted nails and they'd float to the top.

I slid an inch away from the lip of the boat, as far as I thought I could without Dad noticing. I wondered about the boy he'd seen drown and imagined his corpse down there, flesh torn and picked at by hungry fish, maybe the carp Dad had mentioned, clothes still clinging to him, floating in the currents. I imagined the boy's body moving with them: still, but seemingly alive because of the lake. I imagined the boy beneath the boat listening to Dad's story—his story—and remembering. Maybe angry that Dad hadn't done anything to help him, that no one had. That they'd left him alone in the cold and wet to drown and then never found his body, never buried it. Something lurched in my stomach. Dad laughed, but I didn't know what he laughed at.

"What did you do in the service?" I said. The words came out stilted and weak. I stumbled over *service*, breaking it into three parts. My brother kicked my shin lightly and gave me a look that told me not to ask that. Dad just sat there. He was no longer laughing, but he didn't answer me. His lips were thin and white, set. "Were you in a war? Did you win any medals?" This time my brother kicked me harder. He also apologized for me. Said I was too young to understand. Dad reeled in his line and tossed it out again. It went farther than any of his other casts. He turned his back to the two of us. There was sweat on his neck that glinted in the sun that came when the cloud passed. I reeled in my line, too. When I brought it out of the water, the worm was gone, and I imagined that the boy had taken it, because he was hungry, too, down there with the fish and the barn and all the people the county had flooded all those years ago, longer than I'd been alive, longer than my parents had been married.

Mom was cooking something over the fire when we got back. We hadn't caught anything large enough to keep, but that didn't matter to her. And Dad hadn't said one word to either of us the rest of the afternoon, but he'd finished at least eight more beers. Mom met us on the road and touched my forehead, which felt hot and a little sticky.

"Got some sun," she said. She ruffled my hair. "Hungry?" Until that moment, I hadn't realized how hungry I was. My stomach rumbled. Dad plopped down on a wooden bench, and my brother sat beside him. I looked at the two of them and noticed for the first time how similar they were. My brother and Dad had the same nose, the same forehead, the same wide-set eyes. One was a smaller version of the other, less weathered, but the same. Dad lit a cigarette, and I imagined that one day my brother would light a cigarette the same careless way. "Did you have fun?" Mom asked me. When I didn't answer right away, she let it go.

"Damn fish weren't biting," Dad said. He sounded angry, and I moved so that I was behind Mom. "Your kid there don't know the first thing about fishin'. Cast like a girl."

Mom went back to her cooking, but before she did, she touched my shoulder and smiled. I sat on the top of a tree stump near the fire and near Mom. My legs, arms, back, and chest ached, and my whole body felt hot and sticky, and itched. Gilded towers of setting sun stretched between branches here and there, piercing the shadow of the wood, and I imagined climbing one into the clear sky and flying away. There were the same thousand sounds as the night before, but they were all drown out by the pop and snap of the fire and the sizzle of whatever Mom had put inside the tinfoil she'd suspended with sticks over the flame. The fire jumped and rolled. It colored everything around it orangish-red and threw seemingly random, deep shadows. One of these lay on Dad, who said something to my brother. The dark only touched my brother at that moment, but as I watched, it smothered him, too, before I turned away because the heat hurt my eyes.

I tried to picture my brother, then, as he'd be when he was Dad's age. He'd look like Dad, I had no doubt, but he'd smile. I was sure he'd tell stories, because he was good at stories, and I knew he'd have a family of his own. He'd probably take them fishing and camping, because he liked it, and I'd see him on weekends sometimes. We'd laugh about the past and talk about all those things grown-ups talk about, and it would all be different, because he wouldn't be my brother anymore. When we were older, he'd be his own man, and I'd be mine, and we wouldn't be connected, not in any real way, only through memories and blood, and he'd be gone. A great sudden sadness flushed through me, and I looked at my brother again, still lost in the shadow cast by the flame. I hoped that day would never come.

Mom told me to be careful when she set the ball of tinfoil on a plate and handed it to me. Dad and my brother were already eating on the bench. Mom stayed with me. She sat on the ground next to the fire and next to the tree stump where I sat. The fire colored her hair and cheekbones. She was beautiful. She pulled her tinfoil apart by its crinkled edges. Steam rushed out, and she took her hands away and stuck two of her fingers in her mouth for a second. "Let me do yours," she said, and she took my plate and did the same. The food, which she called a hobo pie, was a mixture of corn, hamburger, potatoes, and bread, all soaked in butter. My mouth watered as soon as the scent hit me, but I had to wait for it to cool to eat it. "Grandma used to make this when I was a girl." She took a bite of potato. "It brings back memories." I tried to picture my mom as a girl, but I couldn't.

MY BROTHER TOLD me to circle around and cut off its path. He tossed another rock, this one bigger than the last. The snake's curls twisted and rolled on top of each other like a roiling black sea, or some kind of ancient evil you'd only find beneath it. Nearby, the midday, yellow-topped waves of the lake lapped the smooth stones and mud. My brother took a step toward it, and the snake lashed out. Its head darted for him, and my breath caught. My heart hammered in my ears, and there was sweat on my back. It missed, and I tossed another rock to distract it.

The muscular tube of its body shifted; still curled, the black mass slid toward the lake. My brother blocked its path by striking the rocks at the edge with a long stick he'd pulled from a nearby tree. His fishing rod lay not too far from the snake and mine not far from it.

The snake's forked tongue slithered in and out tasting the air. Its dark eyes didn't move. In the distance, some partiers on a boat played a Van Halen album, and the compressed sound of Eddie's guitar soared on the soft breeze.

I threw another rock, hoping to draw it away from my brother. It was dangerously close to him, within striking distance, though it seemed unaware of it. The snake jumped toward me. Just as Eddie's solo reached its climax, my brother grabbed the larger, squarish stone and hefted it. He raised it over his head as the snake recoiled. Then he let it fall on the creature.

The stone make a dull thunking noise when it hit the snake and the rocks. It tumbled off to the side, leaving a bloody mass where the snake's head had been. Some of its long body was flattened and still, and the part that wasn't continued to move. My brother poked the mess with a stick. I wanted to run back to camp and hug Mom.

When my brother was sure it was dead, he kneeled by the snake. This didn't feel right to me. We were playing with it. He didn't have to kill it. It wasn't like him. Dad would have killed it, not my brother. He lifted the body. The snake, stretched out, was at least six feet long. My brother draped it over his shoulders. Blood reddened his hands and shorts and ran down his leg in dark rivulets.

He pushed past me and moved up the hill, carrying the snake back to camp, back to Dad. I didn't follow him. I didn't want to be part of whatever would happen when Dad saw his kill. On the ground where the snake had been, a red stain glistened the rocks. I felt ill and turned toward the thick underbrush and dark trees and branches that the sun hadn't touched. If I could have, at that moment, I would have flown away. I would have flown far away and never come back.

"Come on," my brother said.

I trudged after him, my stomach sick.

THAT NIGHT, AFTER packing the car, a long ride home, and a late dinner, Dad hugged my brother, the first he'd been affectionate with any of us. He didn't look at me when I said goodnight. Instead, he stared at the TV, which was stuck between channels, showing only snow. He always ignored me. I followed my brother up the stairs, but before I reached the top, I looked back down at Dad. The TV cast awkward shadows on his face, which gave him a devilish look.

Mom did her usual bedtime routine. She tucked us in, kissed my forehead, read a story, but I could see in her movements and hear in her voice that something was wrong. Her hands shook the smallest amount. Looking back, I know that she knew what I was only then discovering and it was too much for her. Part of me thinks she had known since the moment he walked into our home, his steps muffled by the carpet.

I fell asleep before she finished reading that night's story, the last story she'd ever read to me, and woke sometime after midnight. The house was still and silent and dark. Outside, wind scratched the roof and moaned. Clouds blocked the moon, and the air was electric with a coming storm. I climbed out of bed. I looked at the thing that lay where my brother had once slept and began to cry. Tears blurring my vision, I opened the door and moved toward the hazy, faint light flickering at the top of the stairs. The whispered sound of static.

I wiped my eyes and took the first step down.

STUCK WITH ME

———◆———

Shannon Lawrence

SHE'S DEAD WHEN I awaken.

At first I panic. Sobbing, I seek movement in her chest, a quiet breath. She can't be gone. I call for help, but there's no one else here. We are alone.

I am alone.

After some time has passed, I calm. I feel weak, and mourning takes too much energy.

Her mouth is open. So are her eyes, staring blindly at the ceiling, head tilted at a slight angle. I wonder what she was thinking when she died. Whether she knew this was her time. She certainly didn't when we went to bed last night. We were having an argument. Something about a guy we both like.

Liked, I mean. I guess she doesn't like him anymore.

It seems petty now, but it doesn't matter. I feel fragile, like I'm slipping away with her.

A thin line of saliva snakes its way across her cheek, puddling into the tangled black hair that nests behind her ear. I yearn to clean it off her face, but my arm doesn't want to move, resisting my attempts to lift it. With all the focus I can muster, I will my heavy hand to rise.

It does so, slow and shaky. I maneuver it to the ruffle around her neck, lifting the soft cotton. The saliva comes off with ease, and I even press it to the puddle for a moment in order to soak it up. Still wet, though it has lost its warmth. How long has she been gone?

A press of my fingertips to her throat tells me my first impression was right. No pulse. Her flesh is still warm against my fingers, though maybe cooler than my own. It hasn't been long. Perhaps I awoke at the moment of her death. It could be that her soul reached out and touched mine before drifting away.

Pain overtakes me. My chest aches. Maybe there's still room for mourning. My sister is dead. She died lying beside me. Did she whisper my name before she left me? Did she try to say something, to tell me something? Maybe some part of my brain heard it, and it will come to me in my dreams, snake in and out of my ears.

Oh god, I hope she didn't suffer. Surely I would have awakened had she whimpered or called out. If only I could lift my head enough to see the expression on her face. Whether it looks blissful, like one of our loved ones visited her and asked her to come away with them. Or frightened. The visitor might not have been a loved one. What if, instead, it was a wraith? The reaper himself. Something scaly and demonic. Skeletal. Her soul may have been ripped from her body unwillingly. Painfully. All while I slept peacefully beside her.

It's probably best that I can't see anything but her profile. From this angle, it doesn't look like she was in pain. Surely her mouth would look different. It wouldn't just be gaping open like that of a fish or an imbecile. Her lips would be pulled back, teeth clenched. A rictus of pain, they call it, right? Her eyes might be squinty if she were in pain, but I see no lines, no squints. They are wide. The lashes I was always so jealous of thrust outward, the sun lacing its way through them, casting a lacy shadow on the cheek nearest me.

Her skin is pale. The veins are visible, especially in her temple.

The blood pumps through my own veins in a sluggish manner. I can feel it pushing, shoving. The poisons are seeping through me, as jealousy once did. My own sister will be the cause of my death. Weakness already makes my limbs limp and hard to move. My breaths are slow and jagged, like knives slashing my lungs. Her last act will be my murder.

You may wonder if I killed her.

I didn't. At least I'm fairly certain it wasn't me. We fought, sure. What sisters don't? Especially sisters who are forced to be around each other all the time, her presence always by my side, body pressed to mine. We are—or were—mirror images of each other. Both with raven hair and hazel eyes. I share her pale skin. Even now, my veins may be as visible as hers, only mine still pulse with life. What life remains to them. The poison might even be visible as it moves through those pulsing veins. A different color. Does tainted blood pump as red as normal, healthy blood? Does it look bluish green through layers of flesh? If I could move better, I could check, look in a mirror.

In a test of my freedom, I attempt to lift myself up on elbows turned to taffy. The bed is soft beneath me. Too soft. But it's how she preferred it. Our life was a succession of acquiescences. A ballet of consent and resignation. "You first," "No, you first." We may have shared space, but we shared little in the way of tastes and preferences.

Mark is the exception. The guy at the supermarket. Always friendly to us. Handsome. His eyes a deep, chocolate brown. Dimpled cheeks. A smile to fight over. I wanted to be the first to kiss those lips, to feel them against my own. To taste them. But Emily said he looked at her first, smiled at her first. I was just the luggage she had to carry to grab a bag of apples. I was nothing to either of them. A skin sack of inconvenience.

She's wrong.

She *was* wrong. Death is the ultimate fight winner. There's no arguing with a corpse, even one nestled against your side. She always did have to have the last word, but this is a new low, even for her.

"I'm ugly, Melissa?" she had said. "Look in a mirror."

But she was my mirror. This argument never made any sense to me. She was ugly inside, but she missed my meaning when I said that.

"You know what I mean, Emily. You're a despicable, hateful person.

How could you say these things to me?" My voice had gone higher than I wanted, slipping into a whine. It was never good to whine to Emily. It hardened her. Sometimes it made her laugh, but it wasn't a pretty, tittery laugh, like her flirt laugh. Or low and melodious, like her happy laugh. No, this was her mean laugh, accompanied by a grimace, a baring of teeth. Cruelty in her narrowed eyes.

She was like a wild animal at times, dragging me with her on bursts of anger. I didn't want to go, but I had to. There was never a choice; I was her shadow. One time I even got punched in the face because of my proximity to one of her fist fights. Even when I wasn't the one being punched, I felt it rocketing through my body. We were one.

My backside is starting to get sore. Mostly around my tailbone, but it's begun to radiate out. I turn my head to look at her, a tear sliding out of my eye. I'll miss her. I don't know how I can go on without her. Not that this is an option. However long I have, I will be filled with this longing for her, this hollow feeling in my chest. It aches. She should be looking back at me. Her hand should be reaching over to move this stray lock from my face, to smooth it back. She'd laugh, kiss me on the forehead like she did sometimes. Be my everything, as she always has been.

The lacing on her nightgown has loosened. This time it's even harder to move my arms, but I lift them and reach over to tie the laces into a crooked, silky bow, my fingers clumsy. Her face is almost the same shade of cream as the nightgown.

Her open mouth is starting to bug me, so I press two fingers under her chin and push. Her teeth clack together, and I wince. At least she didn't bite her tongue.

When I remove my fingers, her mouth drops open again, but not as far as before. If she were alive, she'd be snoring. She always did. A snore I could feel as much as hear. Sometimes I couldn't sleep because of it. It's not like I could move to a different room.

I study her profile. The shape of her nose, her chin. Unbidden, my fingers touch on me the places my eyes touch on her. They're warm against my nose, sliding up the curve, over, down to the cleft in my upper lip. I allow my middle finger to drift over my lips, which part at the touch. Then two fingers over the line of my chin, so similar to hers. Index finger along my throat, the swell of my breast. I curl my fingers under, let the knuckles follow the curve around to the side.

Then my fingers drift farther, farther, down and over to my side, to the flesh that connects us. The bridge of skin, of muscle, that has joined us together since we developed in the womb. It's soft to the touch, yet firm underneath. We share not only flesh and muscle, but an artery that cannot be severed. An artery that pumps blood between our bodies, one heart to another. I suspect the poison I feel in my veins is her dead blood. Red and white cells with no further mission, shoved toward my heart, circulating through my veins alongside my own healthy cells.

There's no telling how long my body can perform on this mixture of cells, dead and alive. How long it will be until her body kills my cells and pushes them back through our link to overpower the living ones. How outnumbered must mine be before I die?

The rhythm of my heart has changed. The beat is inconsistent. Quick then slow, quick-quick, slow. Like a ballroom dance. Every little once in awhile it even feels like a twirl or dip has occurred. My breaths are more of a struggle when this happens. I gasp for air, feel like no oxygen is coming in.

It passes.

Now that there is only one of us, could a doctor sever that artery inside of her and curl it into my body? It would be beautiful if I could live, though my body probably couldn't handle it. After twenty years of being anchored on one side, I would fall over sideways. Flounder. My heart might not know what to do without that counter pump from Emily.

My clothes would have to be remade without that hole in them. All my shirts, my dresses. There would be no one to advise me on what to wear. What colors look good with my skin tone. What patterns make me look sallow. No one to talk on the phone to a man, to flirt, to say naughty things. I've never been good at that, but it was fun to listen, to choke back giggles so I didn't give us away.

She wouldn't want me to give up. It's odd that she went first, when she was the strong one. Always so hearty and boisterous. She's nothing now. She's not funny or charming or mean or smart. She's just dead. I'm not. I'm still here. Barely.

If I can just get to the phone. Drag her dead weight far enough. It's on the table in the corner of the room. Only a few feet away. My salvation of coiled cording and telephone wires. Three numbers, and someone will come help me.

I strain to my left, away from her body. Just a little bit more and I'll be able to grasp the side of the mattress to get some leverage. Her body pulls at mine, keeps me from moving as far as I need to. My muscles feel sluggish. I'm tired. A nap would be nice, but I can't fall asleep. Not now. If I sleep, I die.

When I attempt to take a deep breath in, it ends up being a pant. My chest rises and falls so fast, yet my lungs feel as if they're stuffed with cotton, with no room for oxygen. A cough shoots out of me, and it hurts. Everything hurts, with a dull ache that seeps outward from my chest. Sand is filling me, weighing me down.

I begin to rock my upper body from side to side as much as our connection allows. More. Faster. Farther. Rock, rock, rock, rock. The bedsprings creak. I rock until the motion is enough to help me swing my arm over, and this time I do grasp the side of the mattress. It's not a great hold, but it's good enough. I heave myself over, despite the resistance. Despite the pain that makes it feel like the shared flesh between us will rend. Sharp and tearing, the sensation makes me scream. But I roll, anyway, and she comes with me.

When I peer over my shoulder, her eyes are fixed on mine. She has fallen to the side and lifted a bit off the bed. I can't look away. Her eyes are vacant; they don't really see me. But they're so familiar. These are the eyes I have looked into more than my own. These are the eyes that have cried, glared, stared, and squinched up into laughter. Eyes that have looked through mine and seen everything I bore. My deepest inner thoughts.

It would be so easy to turn toward her, embrace her, drift away with her. I could melt into the sweet oblivion that calls to me. They would find us facing each other, arms wrapped around each other. The pain would stop.

Instead, I blink and break my gaze away. I continue to pull until I'm at the edge of the bed, and all I have to do is fall. There's a brief moment to brace myself before gravity takes me, and then I'm falling.

I'm pulled up short, hovering somewhere between bed and floor. When I open my eyes and look up, I see that it's her anchoring us to the bed. The pain between us is nearly unbearable. It feels like I'm bleeding out inside, like the artery must have burst open. It pulses, throbs.

She begins to shift. The mattress is compressed at the side, and she's sliding. Now so am I.

I hit the ground, pain bursting across my shoulder and hip before my head strikes the carpeting and explodes in agony. Then Emily lands on top of me. Her head slams into mine, and I realize what I felt before wasn't agony. This is.

Her body rolls forward off of mine and hits the floor, pulling me over with a shriek. My side aches so horribly that I question whether we're still attached at all. This could have done it, severed our connection.

It only takes a second to reach for the bridge between us and confirm we are still one. The skin there is cooling, and I move my fingers to her stomach. Her skin is no longer as warm as it was upon my waking. Ice is spreading from my sister into me, frozen tendrils that tease at my insides.

I'm lying on my stomach with her on my right, between me and the phone. This is manageable. I can do this. The carpet is thick, and I stretch my fingers out, wrap them in the fibers. More pulling. One of my nails tears down into the quick with a sharp pain, followed by burning, but I ignore it and move forward. Dust fills my nose, and I resist the sneeze. A sneeze would surely finish me.

My head feels heavy. Maybe just a brief rest.

The carpeting feels cool against my cheek. Soft, yet scratchy. My hurts drift away. My brain feels squishy, malleable.

Melissa.

"Mm?"

You have to keep going.

"Tired."

Move.

"Nuh-uh."

Don't be an idiot. Go!

An idiot? Only Emily would try to wake me up that way. I force my eyes open, blink against the gumminess. All I can see is taupe carpeting and black hair. When she fell, her face landed away from me. It's for the best.

I'm cold, my whole body shaking. My breaths are now so shallow I don't know how they can possibly sustain me. But I reach forward, grab a hold of the carpeting again. Drag myself forward. Emily's head shifts sideways, not moving with the rest of her body. Each pull arches her neck more.

By the time I reach the spindly legs of the table, her entire body has folded in half, pulled by that last anchor of flesh between us. It stopped hurting a little while ago. Now it burns. I am fire and ice.

The table leg nearest me is smooth, save for one small, rough slot of missing wood. Pulling myself up it turns out to be impossible—I'm too weak, and she's too heavy—but my attempt does make the table wobble. I rest my head on the floor again and shake the table until a scrape tells me the phone has shifted. Shaking harder, I strain away from where I think the phone will fall. It scrapes again, again, again.

There's a final scritch on top of the table then a moment of silence. The phone hits the carpeting next to me with a muffled slam. My lungs are screaming from lack of oxygen now, and I try to pull in a deep breath, which only makes me cough, a weak, yet painful, expulsion of air.

I grab the receiver and depress the button on the top. It was my idea to have an old-fashioned landline instead of a battery powered cordless phone in here. I'd heard they were more dependable, especially in emergencies. Unfortunately, it came with a short cord, forcing us to keep it over here instead of next to the bed.

A dial tone greets my ear, a welcome purr. 9-1-1, and I wait as it rings.

"You've reached emergency services. How may I help you?" The man's voice is low and soothing. Calm and professional.

When I open my mouth to speak, no sound comes out. Only a rasp. My breaths puff against the mouthpiece, my own sour morning breath bouncing back into my nose.

"I can hear you're there," he says. "I'm tracing the call. You're going to be okay."

He's a reassuring presence on the other side of the phone. His fingers tap out a staccato rhythm on the keyboard. Tappita-tappita-tap.

"I show your residence as 6932 Oak Lane. An ambulance has been dispatched. Try to stay with me."

Another rasp escapes my chest. I'm suffocating. Darkness is setting in.

Emily's arms slide around me, pull me close. The scent of her lavender face lotion fills my sinuses, and I relax into her. She's warm again. How odd.

"The ambulance is five minutes out," the dispatcher says in his soothing voice.

You don't have five minutes.

I'm sure she's right.

I nuzzle my cheek into the carpeting. It no longer itches. Nothing hurts anymore, either. Or burns. No more fire and ice. No more anything. I'm floating in a liquid sea.

I'm just so tired.

I was first again. She's always so competitive. *You even lose at dying.*

What a bitch.

THE FIFTH SET

----◆----

Charles Wilkinson

In Memoriam Witold Gombrowicz

JAMES PEWCRAFT BECAME aware something was wrong when presented with a bill for a tennis racket he'd never bought. It happened on a day when summer's deepest secrets seemed on the verge of disclosure: the lawn leading up to the Club House—an ideal green perfected from all the past season's previous finest hours: the sky faultless, the best minutes of daylight mixed to make an incomparable blue; the temperature beneficently adjusted; the sun warm on his brown arms—the subtlest of breezes cooling his forehead. To move from this to an intimation of an underlying discord was at first no more than a minor irritation, a misunderstanding soon to be resolved.

He'd almost reached the Club House door when he saw the professional waving to him from the shop entrance. Widgery kept a stock of essential equipment: rackets, peaked caps, shoes for clay courts and grass, tennis whites for both sexes and tracksuits with the club logo, as well as a wide range of leisure wear and energy drinks. When he wasn't coaching, he was to be found behind the till.

"Mr. Pewcraft! You're order's in," he shouted.

"What order?"

"Your racket. Steel-framed."

Pewcraft changed direction and made his way along the cinder path to the shop, which was housed in a white painted wooden building with a pantile roof and weathercock.

Inside, there was a smell of new clothes; fainter scents of rubber and cardboard boxes. Light glimmered on chrome-colored tubes filled with tennis balls. Widgery was a tall man who wore a sleeveless pullover on top of a white shirt. His tanned features were ruined by a downturned mouth and the thin-lipped disappointment of a talented, unsuccessful player. If it hadn't been for the back injury, the uneven bounce at the major tournament when he was a set up, he would be polishing the trophies on his shelf, opining on prime-time television.

"I'm sorry. There must be an error."

Widgery frowned and shuffled several pieces of paper. "That's not what I've got here. One steel-framed tennis racket for Mr. Jim Pewcraft. Payment on delivery. It's all written down, see," he said, flourishing an invoice in Pewcraft's face.

"Did you take the order?"

"No, the wife was in that day."

"There will be a perfectly straightforward explanation. I've seen the name Newcraft on the notice boards. And I don't answer to Jim. I'm James Pewcraft, always."

Shaking his head, Widgery inspected the invoice, as if somewhere there was a reference that connected the order to James beyond conceivable doubt. "I'll look into it," he murmured reluctantly. Then to himself: "Shouldn't have happened. The system's clear enough."

"Well, I'll leave you to your investigations," said Pewcraft.

Once outside, his irritation subsided. *At least no one had me down as a Jimmy*, he thought, as he made his way towards the Club House.

It was two months since he'd taken the lease on New Town Artists Supplies and bought a small detached property on an estate nearby. He'd not regretted leaving the capital. This part of Surrey seemed to have its own microclimate, one perpetually sunnier than the bedraggled north London suburb, congested and crime-ridden, he'd left behind. Every street and square in the New Town had a just-built sheen, a sense of having been recently erected to the exact specifications of a planning genius. There were no post-modern architectural idiosyncrasies, only a sense of a harmonious whole. The Club House sat sedately in the landscape, its design closer to New England clapboard neatness than grandeur, though there was a modest cupola that added a collegiate feel.

Pewcraft walked into the hall. Instead of going straight to the bar, he stopped in front of the green baize notice board. John Newcraft had just been elected treasurer. Pinned beneath this announcement was a sheet of paper asking for entries to the club's squash competition. A scribbled signature in black ink caught his eye. He'd never played a single game on the court and had no intention of doing so. Yet the name J. Pewcraft headed the list. He inspected it. Was the handwriting his own?

THE BANTINGS LIVED next door to James. Their long narrow gardens, both with summer houses at the end, were divided by a low wooden fence. At six o'clock every evening, if James was on his terrace, he heard the sizzle of a barbecue, soon succeeded by the aroma of meat cooking, the chink of ice cubes, the crack and whoosh of ring-pulls as cans were opened. At weekends, there were guests, and later in the evening James could hear the party moving off in the direction of the summer house, which had a pitched roof identical to his own.

It must have been in early September, with an Indian summer still holding, that Reg Banting's round red face appeared above the fence.

"Come on over for a beer and burger, neighbor! The missus is complaining it's too quiet here."

Pewcraft had thought to keep his distance, having long been wary of oppressive friendliness too close to home. But Reg's guileless cordiality and a reluctance to cook for one after a long day decided the matter.

"Thanks. I'll be right over."

Seated on the deck of the Banting's summer house, which apart from the presence of some potted plants was identical to his own, he accepted a drink in a tall smoky glass streaked with condensation; no doubt, in the American manner, it had been chilled in the refrigerator.

"How long have you been here?" asked Pewcraft, having taken a grateful sip.

"Not long. Nobody's lived here for more than a couple of years or so. That's part of the charm of the place: new people in New Town. Ah, here's Muriel."

A plumpish woman with a bird-like, freckled face was making her way across the lawn. She was holding a tray.

"You know the other half, don't you?"

"We've waved at each other, haven't we? More than once," said Pewcraft.

"I saw you one evening at the fundraiser. I was going to come over, but it was so crowded," said Muriel. She spoke in a precise, well-educated voice, although without a hint of social pretension.

"Where?"

"At the Tennis Club. They're trying to raise funds for an indoor swimming pool. Remember?"

"I don't know why they bother," Reg put in. "It's always another fine day in New Town. I've only ever heard it rain at night."

"It must have been someone else. I didn't go to the party."

"But you're a member, aren't you?" Muriel persisted. "I'm certain I've seen you there."

"Yes, but I'm only there at weekends. I've a lot to do at the moment."

"Oh," said Reg. "What's your line?"

"I've just taken over from Andrew Milcom at New Town Artists Supplies."

For the first time that evening Reg's habitual half smile vanished. He exchanged fretful glances with Muriel before getting up to turn over the sausages on the barbecue. Muriel began to rummage in her handbag.

"Although having said that, it was Andrew's sister, Lucy, I dealt with in the months before completion. Apparently Andrew went on holiday. An odd thing to do in the middle of an important property transaction, and a pity because there were a couple of matters concerning the business that I wanted to consult him about. Do you know him?"

"Yes. My Muriel used to paint, didn't you, love? Watercolors."

Muriel shut her handbag with a snap. "We might as well tell him, Reg. He'll find out anyway."

"Oh," said James, looking from one to the other, and surprised to see something close to dread written across their faces.

"Poor Mr. Milcom died," said Reg, ignoring the sausages and a blackened pork chop.

"He was murdered," added Muriel.

"Great heavens. How on earth did that..."

"Now we can't be sure of that, Muriel. The inquest..."

"Yes, we can!"

The smoke thickened above the barbecue. Once the culinary crisis was brought under control and further drinks served, the topic of conversation changed and was not renewed until Reg escorted James to the front door. "You must forgive Muriel," he said. "Andrew Milcom became a good friend. Gave her tips about her paintings. She stopped when he died."

"Was he..."

"There are some that say so. And by his own twin brother. But the verdict was left open."

WEEKEND SUNSHINE ON the tennis courts: a heat haze bringing a false fluidity to the base line. James felt the glare rising from the hard surface, scorching his face and the back of his neck. For the first time, he wished to play on grass. His opponent, Douglas Wake, had a game similar to his own. They were both tall right-handers and evenly matched in terms of pace and physique. The long rallies proved exhausting. Without his water bottle, James was dehydrated; his dry mouth longed for a cold beer. Then an ill-executed lob sent the ball spiraling way out of the court and into the pine trees. They stopped. James felt his shirt stick to his back; his socks were sweaty. A watery smudge hovered between them, blurring the net cord.

"Nice one, Douglas. What do you say to a break? A drink in the Club House. We can finish the game later."

"Why not?"

There were twenty courts and today most were occupied. As they walked along the cinder path, it struck James that there were no children or adolescents playing, even though it was Saturday. At a guess, he'd have said the players' ages ranged from the late-twenties to the mid-forties. Years ago there'd have been wasps on a day like this and midge-speckled air. Now there was no sound apart from the thwack of racket on ball, a sizzling off the surface—the metallic report as a smash rattled the wire fencing; the cries of the competitors.

"We don't seem to have any junior members. But come to think of it I haven't seen any schools in New Town."

"Who needs schools if there aren't any children?" said Douglas with a smile; he wiped his forehead with his wristband.

"Yes, but I still don't understand why there are no kids. Not so much as a single teenager. Statistically you'd have thought..."

"Have you seen any old people?"

"No."

"And what do most people in New Town do?"

"They work for the Institute. Or so I'm told."

"Exactly. Of course, there are a few people in the service and leisure industries. A handful of professionals—doctors, lawyers. But the majority of them work at the Institute, which needs mature, capable people without responsibilities. That means no children. And if you have any, why would you come to a place with no schools?"

As they walked up the incline, Widgery emerged from the shop and waved in their direction.

"I'm sorry," James said to Douglas. "I'd better see what this man wants. There's been some confusion about an order I'm alleged to have placed. See you in the bar."

As James walked over the springy turf, Widgery advanced towards him. The man appeared no more discontented than usual.

"Morning, Mr. Pewcraft. I'd just like to thank you for settling up."

"When was this?"

"The wife said you popped into the shop yesterday morning. 'Paid up without a murmur', that's what she said."

James had been at work all Friday. But what was the point of making an issue of it now the matter had been resolved?

"If you're happy, let's leave it at that."

Inside the Club House, there was no one at the bar apart from Douglas. Two beers waited on the counter, tiny bubbles rising in amber, heads of fresh white froth. James anticipated a sharp tang on the tongue, a taste of hops.

"Thanks, Doug. Sorry about that. Something weird is going on with Widgery. He's convinced I came into his shop yesterday to pay for a tennis racket. I'm never at the Club on weekdays. With the business in its earlier stages, there's too much to do."

"But I saw you yesterday. You were coming out of the squash court."

"Not me. I don't play squash and, as I said, I wasn't here."

Douglas stared at him. Then he took a thoughtful sip of his beer before replacing it carefully on the mat. "I suppose I was some way off." He glanced at his watch. "Look. It's still bloody hot out there. Why don't we start again later? I'll book us a grass court."

James nodded. They drank in silence for five minutes, then Doug gave him a pat on the shoulder. "Say five o'clock."

"Fine. I've a few things I need to do at home."

Outside, it remained oppressive. James decided to walk the long way back to the estate, a route that took him past the Institute. On more than one occasion he'd asked Doug what went on there, only to receive an unsatisfactory answer: research. Yes, but what sort of research? His friend didn't know. James had never met anyone who worked at the Institute, but practically everyone in New Town aspired to do so. None of them could explain why. Their answers were either imprecise or unconvincing.

The pavements closest to the Institute were lined with shady plane trees. Although it was September, no trace of brown or yellow had touched their leaves. The campus was set in parkland, clearly visible through wrought-iron railings. Copses of mature deciduous trees surrounded by tall grasses, a landscape crafted from the remains of a forest; buildings, white or in pale honey-colored stone, superlatively proportioned—examples of an order of architecture unknown to James, beyond Palladian in its perfection; sleek lawns, their green of great depth and vibrancy—a color never captured by a camera or on an artist's canvas; winding walks lined with dwarf trees, laden with pink and white blossom. As he paused to contemplate the scene, the apprehension that had disturbed him earlier evaporated. His perceptions now possessed an exquisite lucidity. All the inessentials of his existence had been expunged; he was left with mind and sensation alone. The afternoon was now defined by an unfamiliar clarity, an absence of care that left him free to experience the world with absolute attention and wonder. Why would anyone not want to work at the Institute?

COOLER ON THE late-afternoon courts; the pines just a shade darker against the cloudless blue sky. James's opponent had already arrived. A collection of yellow tennis balls nestled at the bottom of the fence. Had Douglas been practicing his serve? Now James knew he wanted to work at the Institute the question of whether he won at tennis seemed trivial. The lack of anxiety soon fed into his game. A delicate drop shot paid off; his services were firmer, his returns pinned Douglas to the baseline. He took risks: a fierce crosscourt backhand raised a plume of chalk dust. Between sets he understood that he'd always loved tennis because it demanded total attention. Ordinary worries were dissolved by the need to anticipate one's opponent's every move. The moments of most heightened awareness were when he was free from reflection; the past and future rendered irrelevant as body and mind bent themselves to winning the next point.

With the start of a new set, it became plain Douglas was determined to prevent the match from slipping away. He was moving with redoubled energy, forcing James to scurry back to return lobs and passing him several times down the line. At first, the games went according to serve; then, just as James felt his supremacy fade, he began to play with unexpected ease. Barely conscious of his body, he flew from one side of the court to the other. Several times he stretched to flick back shots from near impossible angles. Yet something in the nature of the game had changed; it was as if their every move was preordained.

The pine trees beyond the fence were almost black green. Afternoon dwindled to evening; the colors were dying away, and yet both competitors continued to see the ball clearly, its yellow now strangely luminous. Then James realized he could no longer see Douglas's face, but his opponent's physique exactly matched his own. Their style of play was identical; the drop shot and lobs, the quick movements from the base line to the net. Just before they were due to change ends, James became convinced he was playing himself. Douglas had either disappeared or succeeded in commandeering enough of James as to become an alternative version of his friend. And why had his opponent been so silent since the beginning of the set? Perhaps he would not want James to hear his own voice. There was no option. He must speak to the terror that was his substitute self.

"It's getting rather dark. Are there some floodlights we can turn on?"

Whatever it was did not reply. Instead there was something walking, holding a racket in exactly the way that James had always held his, to the back of the court. In a second, would he see himself? Then the court was flooded in yellow light and a figure, jaundice-skinned but indubitably Douglas, moved to the base line.

"How long do you want to go on for? Shall we just finish this set?" asked Douglas.

"Yes, let's do that. If we're level, we can play the decider another time."

That night James dreamt he was once again on the court. Twilight and a slim pale moon in the sky. Burnished black grass. Somewhere an owl. At the end of a set, he passed his opponent as they changed ends. His double stared at him but did not speak. The game resumed. Once he had lost to himself, he woke up.

JAMES WAS IN the office at the back of his shop when the door bell rang. He went through to find Muriel Banting inspecting the prices on sketch pads and pencils. Perhaps she wished to make a few drawings as a way of getting her confidence back. On the walls were original oil paintings, watercolors and line drawings in black ink, some depicting the town, particularly its central piazza; the rest were views of the Institute. Andrew Milcom had told him these were the only marketable kind. James had tried stocking posters and reproductions of Braque, Renoir, and Paul Klee, as well as black and white photographs of Parisian scenes and railway advertisements from the 1930s. There'd been not a single buyer. Tastes in postcards were also limited to local scenes; even these sold slowly, for the town had few visitors.

"Hello, Muriel. Have you found what you're looking for?"

"I haven't decided. Andrew Milcom was my mentor. I'm not sure I could produce anything worthwhile without him. Do you paint?"

"Unfortunately not. Andrew must be a great loss to the town. I'm but a poor substitute. He was particularly perceptive about what kind of work appeals to people here. Foolishly I neglected to ask for the painters' contact details," James said, waving an arm at the walls. "Once these have gone I've no way of commissioning any more. Unless you happen to know any of the artists."

Muriel moved slowly round, considering each picture with care. Without her husband, she appeared uncharacteristically severe. No doubt she relied on him to generate the geniality.

"Some of the signatures are far from legible, I'm afraid", said James. "It's odd that Andrew left no list, no paperwork of any kind. I've had to price them myself; no one's come in to claim a cut."

"I knew these artists. I was hoping to find one who might still be around, but none of them are with us anymore."

"They can't be all be dead!"

"No, I imagine they're all very much alive—and working for the Institute."

"So I can reach them there."

"No, of course not!" She looked at him with something close to contempt.

"So once people start..."

"The jobs are always full-time. That's one of the reasons Andrew didn't want to be employed there. It was why he fell out with his brother."

"Oh?"

"Although they were identical twins, they'd been separated at birth; at least that's what Andrew supposed. They found each other when he set up shop. His twin was already in New Town. Once they'd met, his only ambition was for them both to find work at the Institute; Andrew didn't want that. He said he'd have to become less like himself."

"You mentioned the inquest. But what happened to the twin?"

"He vanished. That was partly why an open verdict was returned. It was as if he'd been waiting all his life to find Andrew and when, despite the physical resemblance, they proved to be remarkably dissimilar..."

"Hardly his Platonic other half..."

"What he sought was something more than...completion."

"It sounds as if he wanted a double not a twin."

She looked at him closely and with a little respect. "Yes," she said. "There are some people who would put it like that."

Once she'd left with a sketchpad, it was quiet in the shop. James stared up at the paintings of the Institute. The views were always from the outside and every one had a sense of longing to enter a place from which the artist had been excluded. But was it somewhere they'd known before banishment, perhaps a prenatal paradise, or were they painting themselves towards the hope of a perfection never previously experienced?

At lunchtime, James decided to shut the shop for an hour. He walked down to the piazza. Another sun-saturated day: people sitting at tables outside cafés or walking in pairs, almost at peace with themselves; a scene of profound contentment. Yet James knew no one here could understand the transcendent joy working for the Institute was said to bring. Even now, in a place nearer to paradise than he'd ever been, there were days that were a degree too hot, fear of what seemed inexplicable, the necessity for rain, uneasy twilight, the black facts of night.

He'd almost reached the restaurant where he'd decided to take lunch when he saw Douglas coming towards him.

"Well met! How about finishing our match this Saturday."

Douglas stared at him, confused and surprised.

"Sorry?"

"The fifth set. At the tennis club. This Saturday!"

Every shining speck in the man's eyes spoke of unrecognition. He shook his head. "I'm sorry, you've mistaken me for someone else. I'm not playing tennis on Saturday and my name is certainly not Douglas."

James watched the man go, walking the way Douglas always walked, though dressed in a style—white linen suit and brown polished brogues— that was unlike his friend. The voice had Douglas's timbre yet not his manner.

When James returned to the office, there was a message from Douglas asking if they could play on the Monday morning. An acquaintance had arrived unexpectedly and would be staying the weekend. Trade was always poor on Monday and the suggested time was early enough not to intrude too much on his day. He left a message on Douglas's answerphone accepting. As he was about to go back to the office, one of the pictures caught his attention. It was a watercolor of the Institute. In places the ghostly white of the paper showed through, giving the scene an otherworldly quality. Without shadows, the trees floated above the lawns, their greens less vibrant, leaving the sky's untrammeled eternity and the stone buildings with nothing solid beneath them.

AS JAMES STROLLED along the cinder path towards the Club House, a woman he'd never met before waved at him from a window of the sports shop. It took him more than a moment to realize it must be Mrs. Widgery; by then it was too late to return her greeting. Inside, he saw Reg Banting standing by the notice board, his face florid beneath his tan, shining like mahogany. The legs beneath the oversized tennis shorts were thin and pale and led down to a pair of scuffed deck shoes. He was holding an old-fashioned, wooden-framed tennis racket.

"Good morning, neighbor! I see you're first on court."

"As a matter of fact, I am. How did you know that?"

"It says so here, doesn't it. You're down to play in the New Town Foundation Cup."

James peered at the notice board. He'd been drawn against Douglas. Had his friend been aware that they'd been taking part in a competition?

"Ah, I see! It's all very odd. I'd no idea I was involved in anything so important."

"Let's hope you get through to the next round. But if you don't you must drop in for another drink and a barbie. Muriel's always one for intelligent company."

"Thanks. I'd like that."

It was only once he'd reached the locker room that James wondered why he'd only be invited if he lost. As he'd arrived early and there was no one else changing, it was not until he was about to leave that he saw a white linen suit hanging from one of the pegs reserved for guest players.

In spite of himself, he was nervous. No one had ever mentioned the New Town Foundation Cup. What sort of reward could a winner expect? A battered silver trophy to take home for a year? Perhaps there was a cash prize as well. Outside, the day was not a degree too warm or cold. It was good they'd agreed to continue on grass. He wondered if switching from a hard court was allowed by the rules. It would be a shame if the result had already been invalidated.

To his surprise there were spectators sitting on the wooden benches on three sides of the court. Only the end overlooking the pine trees was free of them. As he came closer, he saw they were mostly men and women in their forties. Nearly all of them were dressed in long white coats; a few in shabby black suits carried clipboards. Was this a convention of cricket umpires unaccountably electing to watch tennis? Did tennis referees always dress in white? Anyway there was no need for them to descend in such numbers.

Peering around, James saw the adjacent courts were similarly blessed with spectators.

At least some sense of occasion was being conjured up. Douglas was practicing his serves. James waved but received no acknowledgement, a lack of cordiality that was discomforting. It was also unlike his friend to be so scrupulously turned out. James slipped through the gate and onto the court. Even as he approached the net, he received no signs of recognition.

"I see you're taking this very seriously," said James.

"Of course," replied his opponent.

"Who are all these people? I've never seen any of them at the club."

"They're assessors."

"Oh."

"Or researchers at the Institute."

"What? Are they going to keep the score?"

"No, they have no interest in who wins or loses. They're hoping to witness at least one perfect shot today."

A second Douglas came through the gate on the far side of the court and raised his racket to greet Jim. The first Douglas made his way back to the latecomer. The two appeared to be engaged in some argument, although neither raised his voice. Just as James had decided to join them—he'd have pointed out the second Douglas as his opponent—he was tapped on the shoulder. He swung round to find an exact likeness of himself smiling his own smile.

"I'm Jim," said the other. "Sorry you've had to wait. I'm your partner for the doubles today. No need to knock up. They're ready."

Were they precisely the same? Some things were different. Then James recalled he was more used to seeing his face in the mirror than in a photograph. Of course, he heard his voice in his head. So this was his other self, as if it had stepped out of a film. Now James was less singular in the world he felt a terrible loss.

Whatever the dispute between the Douglases, it had now been resolved. One was bouncing the ball, waiting to serve, the other had moved to the net. James opted to receive. The ball fizzed straight past his flailing racket. At first, the Douglases played with great control, both using the lob to good effect. But they seemed to be competing to be the quickest around the court and more than once they almost collided. It was just before the end of the second game that the clash occurred: two rackets attempting to return a drop shot; a tangle of arms and legs. And somehow an unplayable return. Then only one Douglas rising from the heap, rubbing the grass off his knees.

"Where's my...the other..." cried James.

"It's often this way in doubles: one player disappearing into his partner when things are tight. You always lose something to win games like these," said his other self.

Two to one should have been easy, James thought, but the amalgamated Douglas played with twice the power and speed of his predecessors, returning balls from every angle, propelling himself to the net to deal with a lucky mishit. But then the single man tried a lob right to the very back of the court. Both Pewcrafts scurried back and for a moment the yellow ball seemed to hang, a second sun in the sky. As James fell, his racket had vanished from his hand at the very moment that he slithered smoothly into Jim. He'd shed his old skin and become a new man. Now he saw the ball with twice the clarity, he found himself rising to smash it to the far side of the court, a shot of such celestial finality that it took him out of the game and straight to a desk at the Institute, where he found himself sitting next to a single Douglas.

MURDER SONG

———•———

Craig Wallwork

STANLEY NITHERCOTT HAD spent too long in the presence of ghosts. The old family home where he lived with his sister, Iris, had become a point of reflection, one where he would recall the tones of periwinkle and mulberry in his father's cheek the day he found him face down on the kitchen linoleum following a heart attack. Toward the end of his mother's life, the family couch had been relegated to the garage, and a bed erected in the living room to help restrain her as she succumbed to dementia. Following her death, Stanley would often hear her labored breathing, and on occasion, smell urine within the fabric of the carpet whenever he entered the room. He and Iris tried to remove all traces of their parents. They replaced the flock and Anaglypta wallpaper. They removed the Formica work surface in the kitchen and furnished it with granite. They opted for contemporary colors instead of the magnolia, but found that shades of neither Jasmine Shimmer nor Fuchsia Lily could transcend the coldness of each room. Following their parents' deaths, Stanley and Iris began to live in isolation, choosing to stay in their bedrooms as a means of sanctuary. They shopped for their own food and had separate shelves within the refrigerator. Utility bills were halved, and Stanley would firstly tackle any repair work needed before contractors were brought in. They became accustomed to their existence but hardly registered it. Neither chose to move on with their lives, nor find a partner to share their time with. Stanley regretted this more so than his sister and filled the cavity of loneliness with annual subscriptions to adult magazines. The day Iris found a lump in her left breast she confined herself to her bedroom, refusing to seek help or treatment. She did not lament or feel dread, but welcomed the tumor as one may welcome spring after a cold winter. Stanley waited for the day he would knock upon her door and receive no reply, and eight months later, on a cold morning in October, his rap was met with silence.

AS A YOUNG boy an extra tooth had formed on the roof of Stanley's mouth. It had caused malalignment of his front teeth, forcing them to jut and overlap like roof tiles after a hurricane. Their appearance was so crooked that Stanley refused to smile and would often keep his mouth closed even under moments of shared hilarity. For this, he was often referred to as morose, cold or introvert, though no one cared to find out differently. A modest appetite left him rawboned and wearied-looking. Age slowly thinned and grayed his hair. In warm and extremely cold weather he would suffer with urticaria on his hands, and could be found rubbing them in a manner not too dissimilar to a man warming himself by a fireplace. When Stanley decided to sell the family home following Iris's death, he was only thirty-three years old, but many would estimate him much older.

The estate agency had sent Stanley three viable properties in the post, all of which were within his budget. They were modest, suitable for a bachelor with no commitments. He had passed on the first two without visiting them, but booked an appointment to see the last; a small cottage made of limestone described in the brochure as self-contained and quaint. The young woman from the agency who met him at the property was called Katherine. She was small, petite. Her skirt was cut above the knee. A satin blouse remained unbuttoned near the neck, revealing a small crucifix nestling between the cleft of her breasts. Katherine explained that the cottage, and the neighboring property, was once part of the same dwelling but had been split down the middle and converted into two separate homes. The one for sale, the one Stanley was being shown, had fallen into disrepair by the previous owner. The only means of heating came from wood burners in each of the main quarters. Consequently, as Katherine guided him through the property, her words were swaddled in clouds of breath, and in reply, Stanley rubbed his hands.

"As you can see the property has a lot of potential. Rare do you see traditional fireplaces and original cornicing in a cottage of this age. Here, I have some history in my notes..."

Katherine checked her paperwork before continuing, "It dates back to around 1890. There used to be an old mill at the end of the road. The owners built terrace houses for the workers but the family were given cottages. I believe this was owned by one of the sons before it was divided."

Keen to hide his teeth, Stanley moved casually toward one of the windows in the bathroom they were in, and with his back to her asked about neighbors.

"A widower from what I'm told. Quiet, keeps to himself. He's probably in his late sixties, maybe. I wouldn't expect much noise, if that's a concern."

The window overlooked a narrow yard. Fists of wild grass punched through the asphalt. A small boarder, which may have one time accommodated flowers or vegetables, was now teeming with Dandelion and Cat's Ear. Stanley had never seen such neglect in a home. Damp had compromised the inner walls. Cracks tore through its plaster as thick as vines. Plumes of cobwebs fogged every corner and crevice.

The following day Stanley put an offer in for the full asking price.

THE LIVING ROOM had been stripped of carpet by the previous tenants. Floorboards now bore the scars of heel and the moving of furniture. A large fireplace with working flue gave a central point to the room, and it was here that Stanley lay recumbent on a mattress each evening.

Candles lit the room as the electrics were more a liability than a blessing. During the day he spent the mornings stripping the walls of woodchip and hacking back plaster. He hired a skip and disposed of the debris appropriately. At dinner he would eat in the local pub called The Nag's Head, hair flecked with plaster, face powered with dust. To the casual observer he resembled a ghoul, and though desperate for the company, no one ever sat near him, nor made enquiries to his work. In the afternoon, he would turn his hand to irrigation and the mapping of electrical wires. In the evenings he would rest upon his mattress, reading, or staring toward the vast void of blackness above him where he would render the frame of Katherine.

A small chimney breast beetled from the central wall of the main bedroom. The fireplace had been battened using an off-cut of plasterboard. Chalk marked the hearth where it had been pushed with some force to cover the opening, and as Stanley stood there appraising the provisional guard, he heard a sound like that of a mouse scuttling from behind. He knelt before the fireplace and offered his ear. In his mind he pictured tiny claws scratching at the plasterboard for freedom. He measured the sound more closely and realized it moved in a rhythm similar to the wind traveling down the flue. He deferred to logic and arrived at the conclusion it was the wind teasing the edges of the plasterboard on the opposite side, inciting them to flap and flutter. That night he comforted himself with a quart of whiskey and watched shadows born of the candlelight dance along the walls, and fell asleep sometime in the early morning dreaming of a rat gnawing at his face.

The noise within the fireplace presented itself to Stanley the following day as he stripped the outer sheath of a core mains cable. It was late. Outside the street was bathed in tones of orange and amber under sodium lamps. There was no wind, and so Stanley's attention was ruled by what was causing the noise. He placed a candle on the hearth and tapped the plasterboard with a hand-stripper. He gently pulled at one corner until it crumbled, creating a small gap. Candlelight ventured into it, revealing the stained-black stone of the flue behind, and not much else. He proceeded to remove the rest of the board until a cavernous recess yawned toward the light entering precariously into it. To his surprised the space reserved for a stove had been cleared, leaving a barren area wide enough to contain a human body. He crawled gingerly into the bay and turned the candle toward a hole which had been punched through the left hand flank of the alcove. A crude passageway stretched out into darkness, and on haunches he shuffled clumsily along the route. The hem of cobwebs grazed his neck. Grime collected along the fringe of his boots. The candle struggled to brave more than a few feet in front, leaving him unsure to where the tunnel's end may be found. He was about twenty feet along the route when wax trickled down his hands, igniting the tender skin and forcing him to jerk until his grasp slackened and the flame was quenched as it fell to the ground. Blind to what surrounded him, he decided to navigate back to the fireplace and enter the tunnel again in the morning with a flashlight and a good night's rest under his belt. Had a faint beam of light squeezing through a gap in the mortar not caught his attention, or the soporific tones of a woman's voice singing the lullaby *Rock-a-bye-baby*, Stanley Nithercott would have done just that. Instead, he crawled toward the light and pressed his eye to the hole. Beyond, Stanley saw a room with burgundy walls alit by a small bedside lamp. The gap did not allow for a full appraisal, and he did not see the singing woman until she walked into his view. She moved with awkwardness, as though avoiding floorboards that may groan if touched. Her long nightgown absorbed the lamplight giving form to the naked body beneath. He watched her lean over the edge of what he interpreted to be a cot, and recalled what Katherine had said about his neighbor living alone. There was an intimacy about the moment that unnerved him, but the warmth in her voice held him captive.

"Rock-a-bye-baby on the treetop. When the wind blows the cradle will rock..."

The strain of her position became more noticeable toward the end of the lullaby, her shoulders hunched.

"When the bow breaks the cradle will fall..."

Stanley could not see her face but pictured it in his mind as lowly but appealing. Her hair was the color of dying leaves, the skin on her arms virginal as the pages of an empty journal. As she neared the end of the song, her volume ebbed, making it difficult to hear the final words. Then, quite suddenly, a shadow moved against the wall behind her. A door being drawn back roused her attention and she quickly turned. Stanley mutely bade her eyes to find him, but she did not. Instead the woman looked with resignation at the person who entered. Now he could finally see her face. Freckles punctuated a dainty nose, and elliptic eyes summoned light from the room. Her youth was so pronounced that Stanley felt the gathering of all his years suddenly upon him. His skin furrowed in her presence. His bones ached. And as he contemplated how much time he had wasted in his own company, something struck the woman across her head. It came quick and unexpected. Blood mottled the lamp until the room was furnished in a reddish hue. Her body struck the floor so hard it could be felt beneath Stanley's feet. Then the shadow withdrew from his sight, leaving behind a portrait of murder. Stanley canopied his mouth with one hand, and with morbid curiosity searched the room until the arrival of a man's eye from behind the gap appeared before him. He wanted to yell, to scream, but he could not. The eye had robbed him of breath. Within a few seconds, Stanley had shuffled back down the tunnel, his heart a judge's gavel beating incessantly against his chest.

WHEN STANLEY ARRIVED outside the cottage, his chest was broiling and sweat soused his back. A dim light shone through the transom above the neighbor's door. He rapped his knuckles on its cold wood and pictured the old man with face speckled with blood. There came no reply. Stanley took a few tentative steps toward the door, leaned in and shouted, "Hello?! Hello! I live next door! I would not normally bother anyone at such a late hour, but it's very important that I speak to you."

A moment of silence, then the light bulb in the hall went out. Stanley heard a door slam and the low rumble of a television being turned up. He appraised the exterior of the man's house with the curiosity of a cat burglar. The upper floor was in darkness. Net curtains clung like ghosts to the windows. He crept and stumbled along the narrow path that led toward the back of the cottage, and like the front, every window there was veiled in the darkness. He walked to The Nag's Head and used the public telephone to report the incident. No sooner had he returned home, a police van arrived outside. He watched sneakily from the upstairs window and saw two police officers knock on the neighbor's door. The burble of introductions and purpose ebbed as the police entered the property. Though he tried, Stanley's ear could not breach the thick walls to hear what was said thereafter. He deliberated returning to the tunnel to see if the officer had arrived in the room, but before he could his door was struck with force. The police officer that met him was officious in tone and appeared too small for the uniform allocated him. It came as a surprise to Stanley when the officer explained that the neighbor had been very accommodating to their enquiry, and considering the hour, allowed him and his partner full access to the property. They had searched every room and found nothing that would suggest any foul play had occurred. There was no blood upon the walls. No mother or baby present. The man lived alone and enjoyed the privacy. The officer offered his closure by remarking upon the ill state of the old man and how shaken he was by their arrival. There was a moment when the officer paused, as if he saw something in Stanley's face, like that of familiarity or marvel, but he did not explore it, nor make comment. He then left, and again, Stanley returned back to his mattress, enveloped by night and the mystery of the murdered woman.

THE NEXT DAY Stanley returned to the bedroom. His bones chilled as he looked at the fireplace, which presented itself more as a mouth caught in shock than a place for flames and burning ember. He spoke to himself quietly.

"Fear is living in the mind, not within life," he assured himself. "Fear is not real. It does not exist."

He lit a candle and once again made his way to the hearthside. He directed the light toward the tunnel within the opening. In a faint whisper he heard the woman's voice singing her lullaby again.

"She does not exist," he hesitantly muttered as he crouched and moved forward.

The walls were ashen in color. Water oozed from fractures that coursed its smooth veneer, and minerals had decomposed the brick leaving them petrified and cold to the touch. As the woman's voice stretched out from beyond like the Siren song, sludge gathered around his feet, slowing his movement. He extinguished the candle's flame when he reached what he assumed to be a halfway point. A scintilla of light in the darkness presented itself once again. Finding the gap, Stanley looked into the room, and like the previous night, the woman was dressed in a white nightgown. She approached the cot with clumsy gait and sang to her sleeping child. Stanley blinked and reminded himself he had yet to truly grieve the loss of his sister, that time spent among mould spores and fungi may have adversely contributed to some cognitive behavioral change. He could not deny that the same woman who had been murdered the previous evening was standing in front of him again, alive and mimicking the same routine as before. Stanley watched as she turned toward the door to acknowledge her murderer. It was clear from her expression she knew this person. And so Stanley did something that he did not plan or expect.

"RUN!" he screamed. "RUN!"

As much as he tried to promote his voice, she did not hear him. Stanley Nithercott witnessed again the shadowed hand of her assailant strike her down, her blood misting the bedroom, the demonic eye presenting itself before the fracture of the wall before him. And like before, he ran back to the sanctuary of his home.

EVERY NIGHT WAS the same. Evening fell and the lullaby leached from the fireplace, pulling Stanley down the cold tunnel to observe the young mother get bludgeoned with cruel intention. His meagre appetite worsened as a result. He could barely hold anything to his lips without waves of nausea swelling from his gut. A small Pakistani doctor prescribed Klonopin to subdue his anxiety and spoke extensively of the benefits of rest. Stanley was assured that bereavement precludes the need for brain scans or cranial biopsies, and that a few nights sleeping in a warm bed would do him a world of good. That night he returned to the fireplace, watched the woman die for the eighteenth consecutive time, and returned to his mattress bereft of hope and sanity. He began to withdraw from his domestic responsibilities. Paint cans were left opened to allow a thick skin to form in colors of lavender and duck egg. Plaster hardened to rock. Dust sheets gathered its flock. Days were shortened with long naps that furred Stanley's tongue and numbed his mind to the world around him. He had not showered or bathed in nearly a month, and as much as the cottage had leaked into his skin, likewise the fetid stench of Stanley Nithercott lingered in each of its rooms. In silence he heard the echo of her voice hushing that baby, and so he would walk up and down busy streets where heavy goods vehicles and the bedlam of modern life drowned her out. Pedestrians would sidestep him. Young mothers would pull their child's arm to avoid them brushing against him as they passed. If Stanley ever lifted his eyes from the pavement, he would see the woman standing among the swarming crowds dressed in her white nightgown, skull cleaved and the pallor of her face veined with blood. He was never without her, shackled by misfortune. For years Stanley had wondered what it would feel like to be with another person, and now he knew.

IN THE HARDWARE store Stanley appraised the axe with an interest reserved when selecting a stone to skim across the surface of water. His fingers brushed the smooth veneer of its head, and there was an emphasis placed on its weight and fit within his hand. In the end, it came down to noise, which given its normal use would draw too much attention once swung. A short stroll along the aisle found his hand gravitating to the curved, slender neck of a 15-inch pry bar. He picked it up and scrutinized its teeth.

"Much better," he quietly commented, and purchased the item along with a box of latex gloves.

It had been six weeks since he first saw the woman die, and not one day had passed where she was not born again, only to die before the night's end. He had tried to resist the urge to attend the small bedroom, and had gone so far as to spend one evening in The Nag's Head to avoid hearing her voice. But upon returning home, prostrate and eyes searching for counsel in the ceiling, he could hear her lullaby skulking down the stairs toward him. With no respite, and lack of enthusiasm toward involving the police for fear they would arrest him for harassment, Stanley's conscience settled on breaking into the old man's house. It was the only way, he believed, to end the cycle.

THE DOOR THAT led to his neighbor's kitchen faced a preened garden. Hedges were trimmed and roses cut back to the crown. A cloche enveloped a small bush like a pupa, and where once bedding plants thrived, the soil had been tilled ready for the spring. As Stanley forced the teeth of the pry into the doorframe, he drifted briefly to the architecture and arrangement of his own garden, and wondered if he too could mirror the use of space there. The kitchen smelt of cooking oil, refuge and economy detergent. A small stove was flanked by work surfaces the color of oatmeal. A cream refrigerator gurgled and whined in the corner. Stanley noted it was the same make and model he and Iris shared at the family home. He crept to a small hallway that gave access to a staircase, and the noise of a television behind a closed door went some way to settle his racing heart. A warm light stretched out from the landing above, and cautious of how volatile the floorboards beneath his feet could be, Stanley considered every step as he ascended toward the bedrooms. A pale wooden door left ajar revealed to him a room with walls of burgundy. It was the bedroom where he had seen the woman tending to her baby. He felt something like a pinch and the gathering of bumps along his skin as he realized the man may already be in the room, and that his hesitancy had already put her in danger once again. With his grip affirmed around the pry, he peered into the room and stepped forward.

The air was charged with a linseed poultice. Stanley didn't know it then, but the smell of its gruel mixture would never leave him thereafter. He studied the bedroom more closely, searching for the murderer in the shadows. A mirror nailed to the wall reflected a dimmed image of the woman as she sat alone at a small maple vanity. The soft bristles of a paddle brush being raked through her hair produced a sound similar to footfall over virgin snow, and briefly ushered in memories of Stanley's family home in winter where he and Iris as children would leave deep impressions in the shape of angels. The woman replaced the brush upon the vanity. Stanley forecast her turning to find him in the mirror's reflection, and he considered retreating back to the landing. But as she turned slowly and with grace, her expression was beatific and serene. She could not see him, and so he kept his position near the threshold of the door, watching her. She then approached a wooden cot where two infant feet shifted and stirred. Stanley could just see inside the cot and estimated the child's age at around two years, a boy. The child did not protest, wail or moan when she placed a pillow over its face, and as the boy's legs thrashed as its tiny lungs searched for air, Stanley fell into a state of shock. It probably lasted only a few seconds, but as her back arched, and the muscles in her arms tensed as she applied pressure, Stanley broke out of the numbness and advanced forward. On hearing his footsteps the woman turned quickly, and as Stanley's shadow shifted across the back wall, his hand raised the pry, and down it came. Its teeth cleaved her skin, peppering the white cotton of her nightgown red. Releasing the pry from his hand he rushed to the cot and gazed down at the pillow from where beneath two kinked legs lay inert. The boy's bloated belly did not rise or fall. A marble pallor had settled over the infant skin, and when he removed the pillow, Stanley found the boy's head reclined and mouth slackened, the weight of his mother too much for the fragile neck to bear. Without forethought Stanley rushed to the fracture in the wall and pressed his eye to the hole. He wanted to warn his other self to take the woman's life before she could take that of her child's, but before any counsel could be delivered, the eye from within the tunnel recoiled, leaving an empty space. Stanley pressed his mouth to the hole and raised his voice, "It was the woman! She killed her boy! She killed her boy!" But he knew he would never hear it.

FROM THE HALLWAY the low mumbling of a television could be heard from within the living room. Stanley turned the handle to its door. Inside the walls wore a coat of textured felt the color of rotting pomegranate flesh. The carpet presented like that of asphalt, yet was probably more a bluish-red in daylight. Photo frames stood erect upon a mantle, and within them faces were painted in shades of black, grays and ochre. The only vibrancy in the room came from the flames that blazed within the belly of a fireplace, the spitting of smoldering logs homely and inviting. It was a room untouched or modernized for many years, preserved, Stanley believed, to possibly reflect a time where its owner was more content. The only other color in the room came from a green leather armchair facing the television. Stanley approached the chair slowly and circumspectly. He walked around to the front and saw a spindly cadaver sat peacefully with mouth agape, eyelids receding to expose eyes pearled by age. The man's hand, festooned with liver spots, held a pry bar identical to the one Stanley had struck the woman with. Examining the old man's face, Stanley realized why the police officer hesitated when he looked at him. Before him was a mirror of himself, aged and dry as parchment. Stanley ran quickly to the mantle and picked up a photo of a young couple. The camera's long exposure had cleansed the woman's face of expression, but it had not removed the freckles on her nose, nor her youthful countenance. Beside her stood a rangy-looking man with thinning hair and lips that sheltered rows of uneven teeth. The man's arms swaddled a boy no more than two years old dressed in a cream doublet paired with breeches. The remaining pictures were similar compositions, some showing the child in its first year swathed in silken robes, many others within the arms of its father. To any observer, casual or otherwise, it was evident the man had rehearsed holding the child before it came—a man who had longed for the love of another person, and whose only fear was to spend his life in the presence of ghosts.

THE FINAL DIAGNOSIS OF DOCTOR LAZARE

David Peak

AT FIRST THERE was nothing, and only in his awareness of this nothingness did something emerge. There were two identical rooms—two sets of four white-tiled walls gleaming with light—suspended over a black void. He saw them as if from above, these two identical rooms, miniature glass cubes, and within each room he saw a bed and a chair facing the bed. He felt himself drifting toward the two rooms, worried at first that he might slip into the depthless space between them, becoming lost forever in the black void. Yet as he drew closer, still caught in the drift, the two rooms pulled together and became one, sharing the same light.

He felt the warmth of the light upon his face. Air filled his lungs. He opened his eyes.

The man lay in a twin-sized bed tucked tight beneath white sheets. Sunlight filled a wire-reinforced glass window. Nearby an empty wooden chair faced him. The walls of the room were white tile, gleaming and sanitized. He heard a sound like the rattle of an alarm and saw a steam radiator in the corner where before there had been nothing.

A doorway appeared and a man wearing a white lab coat and brown pleated pants walked through it. He sat in the wooden chair opposite the bed, crossed one leg over the other, and balanced his clipboard on his thigh. Then he removed a retractable pen from the breast pocket of his lab coat, clicked it, and offered a sterile smile.

"Good morning," he said. "I am Doctor Lazare."

"Where am I?" the man in bed asked, surprised by the sound of his own voice, the way it rattled around inside his head, tinny and alien. He cleared his throat.

"You're here with us," the doctor said, scribbling notes as he spoke. He paused a moment, then met the man's eyes. "Before we continue, I need you to promise me that we won't have any more violent outbursts— not like yesterday." He smiled again. "Can you promise me that?"

"Yesterday?" the man said.

"You don't remember," the doctor said. He seemed to consider this for a moment, then uncrossed his legs and stood. He wheeled close a metal table—which somehow the man had not previously noticed— and used the controls on the side of the bed to raise the man into a sitting position. Finally he removed a ruled notepad and a yellow pencil from the side pocket of his lab coat and placed them on the table.

"I'd like to administer a test," the doctor said. "Don't worry—there are no right or wrong answers. It's merely a method of measuring the progress of your recovery."

"My recovery?" the man said.

"Your recovery," the doctor repeated. He removed a sheet of paper from his clipboard and laid it on the table beside the notepad and the pencil. The paper contained four diagrams drawn with black lines. "Please take a moment to familiarize yourself with these diagrams. After a few moments, I will ask you to re-create them."

The man studied the diagrams. The first diagram showed a single square, and then below that a set of four equal-sized squares, and then below that a set of nine equal-sized squares. The second diagram showed four sets of two overlapping circles. The interior of each circle was shaded differently, as were the overlapping regions. The third diagram showed yet another circle. From that first circle two arrows pointed to two additional circles. From each of those second two circles, two arrows pointed to two additional circles, resulting in a total of seven circles. And the fourth diagram was a simple octagon, which resembled a stop sign.

Doctor Lazare took away the sheet of paper that contained the diagrams. "Now," he said, "please re-create what you saw using the pencil and the notepad. I'll leave you alone to concentrate. When I return, we will review your work and discuss the results." He crossed the room and quietly closed the door behind him.

The only sound in the room was the radiator rattling, which the man did his best to ignore. In doing so the sound disappeared. He made to reach for the pencil and saw that his right arm had been handcuffed to the bed rail. The handcuffs were connected by a silver-link chain, which afforded him extra range of motion, exactly enough to reach the pencil on the table.

He looked to his other arm and saw that it was wrapped in pressure bandages. When he attempted to move the fingers on his left hand he found that they did not respond. A plastic oxygen sensor was clamped over the tip of his left index finger. He traced the plastic tube from the sensor to a monitor on an extendable rolling pole. The monitor beeped at a regular rhythm, and a small green light on its face held constant.

All of these things he accepted as truths, facts beyond manipulation.

The man picked up the pencil in his good hand and started to re-create the diagrams as he remembered them. When he was done he set the pencil down on the table next to the notepad and looked over his work. With his mind free, the sound of the radiator returned.

Dr. Lazare came back into the room. This time he did not sit in the chair but rather stood next to the bed, looming over the man in the bed. "Let's see how you did," the doctor said, once more laying the sheet that contained the diagrams on the table next to the notepad.

The man looked at the diagrams on the paper and then looked at what he had drawn on the notepad. He looked back and forth from one to the other several times.

"But these aren't the same diagrams you asked me to re-create," the man said, angling his line of sight upward to better see the doctor's face, which now appeared distorted. "You've switched out the first piece of paper with another."

"I'm afraid that's not true," the doctor said. The expression on his face was difficult to make out, somehow disproportionate. He crossed his arms over the clipboard, holding it close against his chest.

"You've tricked me," the man said, looking back to the diagrams, tapping his finger against the doctor's paper. "These aren't the same."

"Most peculiar," the doctor said. He scratched a few notes on his clipboard. "There's nothing to worry about. You're merely exhibiting the symptoms of your illness."

"My illness?" the man said.

"Your illness," the doctor repeated. "I know that your recovery has been difficult for you, but I assure you that we are making progress. I'd like you to continue reading from the diagnostic manual." He gestured to a thick hardcover book on the end table beside the man's bed, both of which the man had failed to notice earlier. "Take notes on anything that takes your attention, anything at all, and we will discuss your notes during our next meeting."

After the doctor left, the man lay in his bed and continued listening to the radiator rattle, the steady beeping of the monitor, the beating of his heart. He tried to move the fingers on his left hand. He wondered what kind of illness he had, whether or not it was serious, how long he had been here, and who had brought him here. He wondered who he was—and in this he felt eerily adrift.

Eventually he picked up the book on the end table. It was quite heavy, and difficult to manage with only one hand. The book was titled *A Diagnostic Manual of Illnesses* and its author was Doctor Lazare. He saw a dog-eared bookmark tucked within its pages. The man opened the book to where he could only assume he'd previously left off and began to read.

Without recovery the severity of the patient's suffering is likely to increase until it becomes unbearable. A patient with an illness whose suffering becomes unbearable will find relief only in death. Only the recovery process can prevent the death of the patient.

The patient suffering an illness cannot begin the recovery process without first understanding the "root" of the illness. When referring to the root of the illness we refer not only to the "cause" of the illness, but also its Thanatotic drive (see Appendix II for more on the various drives). Identifying the cause of an illness is helpful in classifying its symptoms; it is true. In isolating the pure function of its Thanatotic drive, however, we are able to best understand the behaviors of the illness, and only in understanding those behaviors—or "behavioral inhibitors"—can we begin to address and correct them, thus relieving the suffering of the patient.

The root of the illness must first be pinpointed through a process of elimination. By writing down the symptoms of the illness, and subsequently discussing these symptoms with a licensed medical professional, the patient can then consult the diagnostic constellation chart found in Chapter 18. The diagnostic constellation chart offers a visual representation of the shared symptoms of all catalogued illnesses, i.e., those illnesses officially diagnosed by licensed medical professionals. Once a list of the symptoms of the illness has been compiled, and subsequently cross-referenced against the diagnostic constellation chart, the patient can then eliminate inapplicable behavioral inhibitors. Upon completion of the elimination of inapplicable behavioral inhibitors the patient can begin the recovery process, which can prove long and painful, fraught with frequent pitfalls. Therefore it is of the utmost importance that the patient learns to rely solely on the guidance of his doctor.

LATER THAT DAY, or perhaps even early the next day, an orderly dressed all in white—white shoes, white pants, white shirt—entered the man's room. His head was shaved and gleaming. Using a small key attached to a ring full of other keys, the orderly unlocked the man's handcuffs, removed them from the bed rail, and then slid them around the armrest of a nearby wheelchair, tightening the single strand with a metallic ratcheting sound.

After the orderly helped the man out of his bed and into the wheel-chair, he reattached the plastic sensor to the end of the man's left index finger. "You have a visitor, lucky duck," the orderly said, rolling the monitor with one hand, and guiding the chair with the other. "She's waiting for you in the courtyard."

The orderly's white shoes were silent on the tile floor, the movement of the chair smooth—everything in motion. Caged light-bulbs hung from the arched hallway ceiling, passing in a procession. They entered a large room where a television set blared empty, indiscernible noise. A few people in plain white clothes, robes, and paper gowns milled about aimlessly. Then the shrill sound of an electric buzzer hung stubborn in the air, a set of double doors opened as they approached, and a rush of daylight overwhelmed the man's senses.

He shielded his eyes with his good hand and saw the light through the pale skin of his fingers. Everywhere still he heard the sound of the electric buzzer. He closed his eyes and saw black spots, negative impressions of the sun, drifting.

His chair came to a sudden halt and the man felt the orderly set the footbrakes. He opened his eyes. The sky was limitless, the air clean. In the distance he saw a mountain range, chunks of dark stone dusted white. The rest of the scene soon fell into place: a placid black-water pond, stone walkways, wide lawns. He saw women and children dressed in their finest clothes. He saw couples walking hand in hand, sitting on benches, feeding ducks in the pond. He heard the sounds of laughter, murmurs of distant conversation.

"Malcolm?" It was a woman's voice, echoing as if through a long tunnel. He heard it again, more insistent this time. "Malcolm, can you hear me?"

There she was, sitting on a park bench beneath the partial shade of an old tree. She wore a wide-brimmed hat and an overcoat. She wore stylish, oversized sunglasses. Her slender hands were folded in her lap and the sharp lines of her diamond ring caught the light of the sun.

"Are you talking to me?" the man asked, turning to look over his shoulder, as if she might be talking to someone behind him. No one else was nearby; apparently the orderly had elected to give them privacy, sneaking away soundlessly. The monitor softly beeped.

He turned to the woman and saw her face change in a manner he couldn't quite understand. "Of course I am," she said. "Who else would I be talking to?" She paused. "Malcolm, please, we've come all this way."

Next to the woman sat two boys in school uniforms, identical twins. They had the same tousled blond hair, the same blue eyes, the same small noses and ruddy cheeks.

These sudden intrusions of things and people he hadn't previously noticed were surely a symptom of his illness, he thought. He would have to remember to write that down.

"Hello, Dad," the boys said in unison.

Malcolm stared at the two boys in silence.

"Darling," the woman said, "don't be rude. Say something to your sons."

"My sons," Malcolm repeated. The two boys looked at him, expectant, waiting for their father to speak to them like fathers speak to their sons. He didn't know what fathers said to their sons, so he decided to tell them what he did know. Perhaps, he thought, it would mean something to them. "My name is Malcolm. I have an illness. I'm working on my recovery."

Malcolm was unable to discern whether the boys were bored or terrified. He searched the eyes of the boy closest to him, looking for a clue. He saw that the boy's eyes resembled two glass cubes. Looking deeper he saw that within each of those two cubes stood a bed and a chair facing the bed. He settled back into his wheelchair, thinking about what this might mean. Then he took out the notepad and with his good hand wrote down all of the things that took his attention, just as the doctor had instructed.

When he finished writing, Malcolm looked around the courtyard. Two of the ducks rose from the black waters of the pond as if levitating, motionless, and then darted off into the sky. He watched the ducks shrink down to the size of black dots, and when he blinked they disappeared.

They had escaped, he thought. They must be the lucky ones.

"Darling," the woman said, her voice thin, nervous, pulling him back from his drifting thoughts. "Have your doctors said anything about your release?"

"My release?"

"When you'll be allowed to return home."

"Return home," Malcolm repeated. He folded and unfolded these words in his mind, repeating their sound until they seemed to lose their meaning. "How long have I been away from home?"

The woman shook her head. "Darling, I don't..." Her lips were pressed tight together, a crooked white line, and her pitted chin quaked. "I don't understand."

"How long have I been away from home?" he said again, insistent this time.

Nobody answered him. The woman started sobbing. The two boys had turned away, looking in opposite directions. One rested his chin on his closed fist; the other slouched with arms crossed over his chest. He saw now that they weren't twins at all, brothers perhaps, but certainly not twins. One of the boys was clearly older than the other, his facial features more pronounced. One of the boys had hair that was darker than the other's.

Malcolm wrote in his notepad that two things that initially appeared to be the same will sometimes reveal themselves to be different. He wrote that he should not be fooled by deceptive appearances. He tapped the rubber pencil eraser against his lower lip. Then he continued. If two cubes appear in place of a person's eyes, then the black void must be the space inside that person's head. He remembered what it felt like to drift above the black void, the fear of the gulf between two things, where there was nothing at all. And if there was a place where there was nothing at all then surely no person could exist there.

"I don't believe that you're real," he said calmly to the woman. He looked at the two boys. "All of you. None of you exist."

From behind her dark glasses tears slipped down the woman's face. She didn't say anything as she stood and went to the two boys, gently touching each one on the shoulder. They rose and she guided them down the stone walkway until they had disappeared like the ducks in the sky.

The monitor beeped, signaling that everything was normal and that nothing had changed.

The patient's illness will ultimately define the patient's reality. "Symptoms," by definition, are subjective evidence of the illness itself. Additionally, these symptoms may indicate the existence of something hidden, such as a previously undiagnosed illness, or a trauma buried in the unconscious. Just as the body serves as a representation of the goings-on within, that-which-is-real occurs in a "submerged" reality beyond the surface level. Therefore, the reality of the patient can never be fully understood by the patient. This circulus in probando *is known as the "dilemma of rings." After all, what is a circle if not a line that has lost its way, doomed to repeat the same course of action again and again?*

As previously noted, conducting an investigation into the illness at its root can occur only after the symptoms of the illness have been catalogued and cross-referenced against the diagnostic constellation chart. With this process completed, and with the recovery process underway, the patient—working under the supervision and guidance of the licensed medical professional—can peel back the surface of reality and reveal that which is hidden: the "event" of the illness. The event of the illness is the underlying cause in its primary state. Such an event can only be witnessed under the skin, so to speak. By peeling back the patient's skin, the subjective nature of the illness will be revealed as an objective reality, where it can then be studied and better understood.

The dilemma of rings states that nothing can be proven to be real unless it has been correlated with some other person, place, or thing already present in reality. Some of the most difficult-to-diagnose illnesses are "nested" in this very idea. The danger here, of course, is that the patient should lose their way during the diagnostic process, therefore losing their grip on reality, as well as the thoughts and memories from which their identity is constructed.

FROM THEN ON Malcolm spent his mornings in bed reading, his afternoons watching television in the common area, his evenings back in bed correlating his symptoms. He worried that he wasn't making sufficient progress in his recovery. All of the notes he wrote, the handfuls of unmarked white pills he swallowed, the time he spent reading, cross-referencing against the diagnostic constellation chart—and still his recovery seemed as elusive as ever. He worried that he had lost his way. He worried that he was turning in circles.

One day the orderly used the key attached to the ring full of other keys to unlock Malcolm's handcuffs, removing them from the bed frame. He then fastened the strand around the monitor's rolling rack. "The doctor would like to see you now."

When he arrived at the doctor's office, Malcolm asked about the purpose of the monitor, and why he must remain attached to it.

"It assures us that everything is all right," the doctor explained from behind his wide desk. "That beeping noise you hear every so often? Well that tells us that your vital signs—your heartbeat, breathing rate, temperature, and blood pressure—are as they should be. The signal is monitored from a control room. At any given moment on any given day, each and every patient is accounted for. We must ensure that everything is in its right place, so to speak."

"In its right place," Malcolm repeated. He folded and unfolded these words. Was everything in its right place? Or was everything—objects, people, shadows—placed in such a way so they only appeared to be in their right place?

He took note of the things found within the doctor's office, in case something might be out of place, in case he had missed a clue. There was a full-body model of a skeleton propped up in the corner. Various academic degrees in glass frames had been carefully arranged on the far wall. On another wall there was a laminated poster that explained first aid for cuts and scrapes. Malcolm decided that this second poster was meaningful.

"What is taking your attention?" the doctor asked.

Malcolm explained his concern that he was turning in circles.

"It's your paranoia," the doctor said, writing all of this down. "Perhaps it's worsening as a result of the anxiety you feel regarding the speed of your recovery."

"Yes," Malcolm said. "It's worsening—the anxiety."

"But that's wonderful news," the doctor said, smiling. "Not that you have anxiety, of course, but rather the fact that you've identified and diagnosed your paranoia. This signifies that your recovery is on track. After all, acute paranoia is one of your symptoms. Remember?" He gestured to Malcolm's notepad. "See for yourself."

Malcolm opened his notepad and thumbed through the pages until he found what he was looking for. There, in the middle of a page full of other symptoms, he saw the words "I am paranoid."

"Did you write this in here?" Malcolm said, turning the notepad so the doctor could see.

"No," the doctor said. "But that you think I did is a good sign. Your accusation correlates your emotions with a thing outside of yourself."

Malcolm watched the doctor's face closely.

"My advice for you," the doctor said, "is to change up your routine. You've become too set in your ways and it is interfering with your discovery process. Get outside your comfort zone. Do something un-expected."

The next night, still handcuffed to the beeping monitor, Malcolm decided to heed Doctor Lazare's advice and explore the halls beyond his room—to change up his routine. He went wherever his attention took him. He rode an elevator down to the basement, passed by signs that said Do Not Enter. He went down a hallway lit with dim, flickering light, where puddles of rust-colored water had formed on the floor.

Exposed plumbing snaked along the ceiling, steam coursed loudly through the pipes, and industrial machines pounded away in unseen rooms. Eventually Malcolm found a metal door with a placard that said Control Room. He tried the door handle, expecting it to be locked, and was surprised when it opened all on its own. The room was dark; the only source of light was a work lamp on its side on the floor. An audio monitor hidden somewhere in the shadows warbled a stream of static in which he discerned faint weeping sounds.

"Hello?" he said. "Is anyone here?"

Malcolm shut the door and locked it—in case anyone might be following him. Then he carefully made his way to the overturned lamp, picked it up, and set it on a nearby desk. Angling the light, he saw a bank of television monitors, all of which had been turned off, the dozen screens smooth as black stones. Countless sheets of loose-leaf paper, each one covered with sequences of numbers and codes, were strewn about the floor.

A crack of light was visible on the opposite wall—an open door leading to yet another room. This second door had a sign on it that said Danger: Power Supply. He pushed through.

The pounding of the industrial machines had grown louder. Malcolm found himself standing at the foot of a long hallway. A florescent light hung flickering from the ceiling, suspended by a coil of thick wire. More exposed plumbing—the twisting tubes and pipes like so many veins exposed beneath stripped-away skin—covered one wall. Opposite the steam pipes he saw a wooden desk and an empty chair, not dissimilar from the one in his room, the same wooden chair he had seen reflected in the eyes of his son.

The end of the hallway was obscured by shadow. He felt drawn to the darkness. His heart pounded in rhythm with the unseen machines.

Malcolm's progress was halted by a rusted fence that spanned the width of the hallway. He laced the fingers of his good hand through the cold chain link. There was no going past this point; there was no gate, no entranceway, no way to pass through. Beyond this fence he saw only darkness, endless hallway. He turned around.

He saw the body from some distance—wearing the unmistakable

uniform of a security guard—slumped forward in the wooden chair behind the desk. The handle of a surgical scalpel protruded from the smile-shaped wound in the body's abdomen. Malcolm maneuvered around the darkly shimmering puddle of blood on the floor, careful not to get any on his white shoes, the wheels of his monitor's rolling rack. Then he leaned forward to get a better look at the guard's face, which was turned sideways in the low light, resting flat on the desk. It was a mess beyond recognition. A series of deep cuts dragged along the jawline, across the hairline, and around the eye socket. His lips had been mutilated; one of the eyeballs had burst.

Malcolm slid free the scalpel and put it in his pocket; it might yet prove useful.

He closed the door to the dark hallway behind him, muffling the sound of the industrial machines, and returned to the familiar light of the hallway. From there he easily found his way back, as if guided by an invisible hand.

The primary danger of self-diagnosis stems from a lack of objectivity. If the patient self-diagnoses as nyctophobic, for instance, they will then justify any decision made to avoid darkness as a means of not worsening their illness. Yet an avoidance of this nature does not aid recovery. Perhaps the event of the illness occurred under cover of night? Such an event, allowed to lie dormant, protected by the patient's self-diagnosis, shall remain occulted. And if these occultations are not interrogated rigorously, the recovery process will be impeded.

The very nature of the recovery process—frequently painful, discomfiting— is likely to result in self-diagnoses that "insulate" the patient from identifying the most insidious symptoms of their illness. Here it is the responsibility of the licensed medical professional to guide the patient to confront the bias of their self-diagnosis. A patient who lacks the guidance of a licensed medical professional is statistically far more likely to experience a variety of mental breaks, including dissociative amnesia, dissociative identity disorder, or delirium.

Patients near the end of the recovery process are most at risk of a biased self-diagnosis. Despite the recovery of the patient being of utmost importance, as previously stated, the patient on the verge of full recovery will seek to remain within the "embrace" of the illness, rather than experience the unknown. It is a truly dangerous time, and one in which the patient could potentially lose touch with "knowable identifiers"—or the very objects that tether the subjective nature of the illness to objective reality. Identifiers such as feelings, thoughts, memories, and impulses can become "enstranged," resulting in horrific acts of violence.

MALCOLM SAT ON a paper-covered medical exam table, his slipper-covered feet resting on the retractable step. The room was small, brightly lit. Several glass jars lined the counter along the wall, each containing an unrecognizable mass of flesh suspended in green-tinged liquid. The steel sink was spattered with dried blood, and the walls were littered with laminated posters that detailed first aid for cuts and scrapes.

A woman wearing a white lab coat and a pleated skirt entered the room. "Good afternoon," she said, heading straight for the sink. "Are you ready to have your bandages removed?"

The doctor washed her slender hands, seemingly undisturbed by the bloodstains in the sink. When she was finished she retrieved a pair of scissors with a ribbon handle from one of the cupboards. She asked Malcolm to extend his arm with his palm facing the ceiling. He tried to look her in her eyes—to get a glimpse of her hidden self—but she did not meet his gaze, remaining entirely focused on the task at hand.

"Seeing a newly healed wound for the first time can be quite unpleasant," she said. "Please be prepared for unwelcome thoughts."

Cradling Malcom's hand in hers, she snipped through the bandages from his wrist to his elbow. The severed strips fell away, revealing a network of jagged incisions neatly stitched together with dark thread. With his good hand Malcolm traced the scabrous tissue with the tips of his fingers. He felt nothing.

"Now we need to remove your stitches," the doctor said. "You may experience some slight discomfort."

Using tweezers, she gently plucked at the thread, sliding the sutures up and out of the skin, and snipped each knot with the scissors. When she was finished she cleaned the wounds with a cotton ball soaked in cool rubbing alcohol.

"All done," she said. "Can you wiggle your fingers for me?"

Malcolm tried to do as she asked but his fingers did not respond.

"Close your eyes," the doctor said. "I'm going to touch the tip of each finger in no particular order. Please tell me if you feel anything." She paused. "What about now?"

"No."

"And now?"

"Nothing."

Malcolm opened his eyes, felt the world spin away from all he had known. The posters on the walls were gone and the walls themselves had been replaced by unadorned concrete. A small barred window near the ceiling let in slanting beams of cold blue light.

He turned once more to the glass jars, seeing now that the smallest contained a pair of eyeballs, the next largest held what appeared to be a severed hand, and the largest contained a human heart.

Malcolm studied the doctor. "Where am I?"

Ignoring his question the doctor pried open Malcolm's eyelid with her thumb and forefinger, shined a small flashlight into one eye, then the other—blinding him. When the light clicked off Malcolm saw black suns drifting. The black suns dragged darkness over the walls, and the darkness was like an infection spreading through the room. A jagged fissure ripped through the concrete wall, a cracking noise as loud as thunder, beginning near the floor, and then extending like the branches of a tree.

He tried to stand, to flee the expanding dark, but he was stuck in place. He was strapped to an emergency restraint chair. The straps bit into his shoulders, his forehead; another strap spanned his lap. His wrists were strapped to the armrests, his ankles to the chair legs.

"Tell me," the doctor said. "What do you think happened to your arm?"

"I don't know."

"Think, Malcolm."

He felt himself drifting once more, weightless. "I can't."

"For the sake of your recovery," she said, raising her voice, "it's important that you remember. Can you recall anything about the day before you woke handcuffed to your bed?"

He closed his eyes and let the black void swallow everything outside himself, joining with the spreading infection of the room, the drifting black suns ringed with light.

A single still image took his attention, unfinished and dark around the edges, like a great room lit by crooked fingers of lightning. He saw himself sitting behind Doctor Lazare's wide desk, in the room with the model skeleton propped up in the corner, its hollow eyes gaping.

More images followed, only these were not merely still, but moving—vivid with sound and color. He saw wide-eyed patients dressed in white disappearing behind locked doors, dragged kicking and screaming through the tunnels deep beneath the building. He saw men and women strapped to gurneys wheeled down darkened hallways. He saw bone saws and large-gauge needles held up under blinding lights, the mouth of a furnace lit up like an inferno. And then he saw a security guard roaming the empty halls, making his rounds, stopping at each door, each individual cell, to peer through the viewing panes.

Malcolm took in all of these sights as he watched the wall of closed-circuit TVs in the control room. He wore a white lab coat and pleated pants. He twirled a retractable pen in one hand, nervously clicking its button. On one of the screens he saw the security guard descending the steps into the basement, sweeping the beam of his flashlight across the hall. In a fit of rage Malcolm swept the contents of the desk onto the floor—the reams of paper that contained readouts of each patient's vital signs, the small radio that piped in sound from the nearby operating theater—and the light of the work lamp angled toward the ceiling. He turned off the TVs, plunging the room into darkness.

He stalked through the shadows, coming up behind the security guard and plunging the scalpel into his side. He watched himself slashing frantically at the security guard's hands and fingers as he attempted to protect himself. And then he was back in his room, in his office, pacing back and forth, his hands pressed to the sides of his head.

Another flash of lightning lit up his office an electric blue. The life he had built himself, the knowledge he had accrued, the accomplishments and laurels that stacked like so many cadavers—all of it would soon be gone.

There was only one thing left to do. He sat down, opened a drawer in his desk, and removed yet another surgical scalpel. Then he took off his lab coat, rolled up his sleeve, laid his arm flat on the surface of his desk, and with his good hand—his operating hand—pressed the cold blade against his flesh.

He held his hand against the wound, tried to hold in all the blood, but it forced its way through the spaces between his fingers, escaping. He felt dizzy, his vision fading, lights drifting. Always he felt like he was drifting.

Malcolm opened his eyes. The female doctor stood before him, watching him, taking notes.

"Tell me, Malcolm," she said. "Tell me what happened."

The whole room trembled, as if it might collapse. He tried to read the doctor's face, to get a sense of what she was thinking, but her features had gone smooth, a single continuous surface. She could be anybody at all. And if that were true, then nobody was anybody.

"I can't be who I think am," he said. "It's just a symptom of my illness."

The cracks in the wall ripped open. Great slabs of black stone crushed the light out of the room. In the newly hatched darkness Malcolm drifted, rushing toward the limitless black beyond. Wind whipped at his face, the rush of sound all consuming. He opened his eyes.

If the state or quality of the patient's reality is fractured—if the subjective reality is wholly isolated from an objective context—then, with no other recourse, the patient will unerringly search out that which best "mirrors" what is real. The patient does this unknowingly, seeking only to maintain some semblance of the status quo, a reflection or echo of the safe and the known.

Anything beyond the known, in the patient's limited perception, will constitute a continuation of the illness, and result in further suffering.

In cases of extreme fracturing, the patient may become fixated on the fracture lines themselves, rather than the so-called pieces of reality. To illustrate this point, imagine the patient staring into a broken silver glass mirror, and believing that the material behind the reflective surface is their reflection. Such fixation is likely to result in a total loss of the thoughts, memories, and feelings that constitute the "self" (further elaborated upon in the diagnostic constellation as "identity delusion disorder"). This disorder is typically the result of violent trauma spurred by an accumulation of paranoia. Essentially, the patient who believes that they are being invasively investigated or pursued by unknown or faceless entities will lash out at any real or imagined investigators or pursuers.

Malcolm, if you're reading this, if you've made it this far, then surely you realize these words are intended to release you from the grip of your illness, to relieve you of your suffering. Surely you realize that these words were written only for you—by you. You're in the final stages of your recovery. As such you must be careful when making your diagnosis. Think of all the evidence. Remember what it means to be a person with a name and a family, with memories and feelings, and the freedom to live a life of your own choosing. Do not give in.

MALCOLM STOOD IN the center of the room and turned in a circle. When he came to a stop he saw a bed and a chair facing the bed—just like before. Still he was unsure if this was his room or if it was merely meant to resemble his room.

Things emerged from nothingness all on their own. He saw a steam radiator in the corner, a wheelchair beside the bed, and the diagnostic manual lying page-down on the floor, its cracked spine displaying the name of its author: Doctor Malcolm Lazare. He saw his monitor on its rolling rack, its constant green light, the silver gleam of the handcuffs, the plastic sensor clipped to end of his finger. He searched out anything that was not in its right place, and one thing took his attention immediately. Where once there had been a wire-reinforced window there was now a full-length silver glass mirror.

He studied his reflection in the mirror: a faceless man in a white hospital gown. He remembered something he had once written down. Two things that initially appear to be the same sometimes reveal themselves as different. Likewise two things that appear to be different can reveal themselves to be one and the same.

There was nothing—he was nowhere, drifting—and only in his awareness of this nothingness did something emerge. Where he should have seen the man who was Malcolm, he instead saw a body with its secrets exposed to the world, a skeleton poorly disguised by a suit of skin. His skin hid who he really was. It was his skin that buried the root of his illness. He must emerge from beneath this deceptive surface once and for all.

Malcolm pressed the blade of the scalpel against his forehead, just below his hairline, felt the cool metal come up against bone. He felt nothing as he pulled a line down the outer edge of his face, the blade gliding cleanly along his ear, below his chin. He made an identical incision on the other side of his face. Then he traced a circle around one eye, the other eye, drawing so much blood he could no longer see.

He worked without aid of sight, snuck his fingers deep beneath the lip of skin at the top of his forehead and began to slowly peel away the featureless mask, the deceptive thing that hid his true self.

There was blood everywhere. His hospital gown was completely soaked through, clinging to every contour of his body like a second skin. A shudder of dizziness sapped the strength from his legs, his knees rubbery. The monitor released a frantic high-pitched whistle, the unmistakable alarm of fading vital signs. He meant to silence the machine somehow, in case they came running for him, in case they tried to save him, and slipped in the puddle of his own blood. The weight of his bones pulled down his body, pulled down the monitor. He dropped the blade, heard it clatter against the floor.

With a final effort he ripped free the clinging mask. His vision returned, and with it the light of the room. He saw everything as it truly was, the sunken world beyond the blinding illness. The light was everywhere all at once, and as he pulled away it became smaller, smaller still, until it split into two gleaming glass cubes. He saw them there, as if from above, felt himself drifting away into depthless space, free of the fear of losing himself.

ENDANGERED

———◆———

Jason A. Wyckoff

FAXES RECEIVED AT Len's office fell reliably into three categories: correspondence from doctor's offices, spam vacation offers, and endangered child alerts. Len checked the machine's output tray when he passed by, but never got out of his chair just because he heard the beep announcing a new arrival. He couldn't recall the last time anything business-related had come via fax. Whenever anyone stopped by to send a fax to a doctor's office, he was always asked, "Does anybody even use fax machines anymore?" Yes, he'd reply, doctor's offices did. No, he didn't know why they insisted on using the archaic technology.

On Thursday morning, there were two faxes waiting—a rarity. The first offered, in bold 36-point Comic Sans, a trip for two to Acapulco discounted to astonishing off-season rates. The fireworks in the margins promised irrepressible festiveness regardless of the date.

The second fax, under the caption, 'Missing,' reported the vital stats of Jassmyn Rogers between two pictures of the fifteen year-old. Len winced at the girl's name, and then felt bad about it. A person's name wasn't a choice. Perhaps her parents hoped the creative spelling of their daughter's name would encourage her to become similarly unique. He

114

had no right to judge any name born of love. And besides, maybe she hated her name. Maybe she went by something else. Still, he couldn't help but tally how often such non-standard monikers appeared under the 'Missing' banner.

She was white with long brown hair, juvenilely thin, four-foot-eleven. Len tried to think if he knew anyone else that height. It seemed such an indeterminate height—a 'burgeoning' height. He noted another commonality Jassmyn's 'Missing' flier shared with others: the two photos could have easily been two different people. The one on the left must have been a selfie. It was a close-up, shot at a downward angle; she was wearing a baseball cap and pouting playfully. The picture on the right might have been a class photo. She had on heavy shadow which changed the shape of her eyes, and she was smiling uncertainly, possibly self-conscious about a chipped tooth. She wore a (presumably) gold chain around her neck with a pendant spelling 'Love' in cursive. Doubtless, anyone who knew her could identify the girl correctly in either picture, but of course the point was to make her identifiable to strangers. Len supposed it made sense to show different looks to widen the possibility of someone recognizing her in person, but to him it only created an element of doubt. If he saw a young woman whose ex- pression matched exactly the face of a single photo, he would not hesitate to contact the authorities. But if he tried to remember both, and observed the 'subject' long enough to be sure, she would likely show a range of expressions and angles sufficiently diverse to under- mine his confidence.

Not that he would ever see her. Len was sure of that. Of course he knew it was possible—he worked downtown, after all—but he couldn't imagine how their worlds would intersect. He travelled in closed circles. Still, he felt obliged to study the flier, just in case he could help. He wondered if that was really why he looked. He hoped it wasn't only morbid curiosity which drew him. He wondered if anyone could help her. He hoped she was a runaway who would turn around when she realized what she'd left behind, or that her home life was so bad that she was better off with a similarly-desperate Romeo with a pure heart and a fast car.

Len knew the latter was not likely.

He flinched when Joe, an architect, burst into the mailroom. He folded the flier hurriedly and held it between both hands.

"Hey, Len!" Joe waved several sheets of paper. "I have to send a fax to my little girl's pediatrician, believe it or not." He nodded towards the object in question. "Does anyone even use fax machines anymore?"

ON SATURDAY, LEN drove two hours to his father's house. He hadn't been there in a decade. His father had recently married for the third time; this Len discovered upon receiving a wedding announcement after the fact. The event had been a 'destination' wedding in Stowe, Vermont, during ski season. Len had never known his father to ski. Probably his father had decided it would be rude not to invite his eldest son to at least meet his new bride, and since he was unlikely to have any reason to pass through Akron anytime soon, invited Len to return to his childhood home. Len doubted there was much enthusiasm behind the invitation, or if there was, it was borrowed; he cringed at the thought that 'Kat' (six years his elder) would try to be uncomfortably chummy with him the way wife number two did (eleven years his elder; he wondered briefly whatever happened to Cecile). Regardless, Len thought it would be rude not to accept, and so, just before noon, found himself pulling into the drive of the egregiously oversized house where he grew up.

It irked Len that his father, Harlan, had been right. The neighborhood had turned around, in part because of people like Harlan buying up the grand but dilapidated properties and restoring them to their original splendor, and partly because of new developments of 'McMansions' set in the drained wetlands surrounding the original estates. Len was five when they had moved into the large house from their cozy cottage near his grandfather's church, and he hated the grotesquery at first sight. The many rooms and hallways and crawlspaces to explore which should have thrilled a young boy (or so Harlan repeatedly scolded him) he found off-putting at best, and terrifying at worst. His few school friends he would not invite over, though of course they knew where he lived, and so took their impression of his home life exclusively from the mammoth size of the residence. In truth, Harlan was not rich. Extensive groundskeeping work and restoration of the exterior were done quickly, which depleted Harlan's available funds; rehabbing the gutted interior proceeded thereafter at a trickle as the money became available. So Len grew up with the appearance of being rich, but he never felt privileged. He usually felt cold.

The worst part of the house was the basement. The house was wide, or 'broad-fronted,' as though the original builders placed the same value on the importance of presentation as did its current owner. The basement ran the length of the house; stone walls dividing it into sections provided structural support. Interior stairs on the north end (the house faced west) spilled into the main area which contained the utilities. There was also a storm cellar door at the back of the house, at the end of a spur jutting from the main rectangular block, but it was kept padlocked, as the antechamber was cluttered with earth and broken stone, debris from the disintegrating lime plaster on the clay foundation. An open space ran along the back of the house. At the southern end was a chamber more decrepit—and to Len, *viler*—than even the 'dirt' room. Here the ceiling had crumbled inward. It was supposed that the room above had been the original kitchen, as the mound in the chamber below was comprised not only of mud and plaster and stone, lathe, and daub, but also of chipped brick and shattered grey tile. And the dirt component was truly *mud*; there was a noticeable slope to the floor of the basement which carried seeping water to the southern end, which never dried, even in summer. And the slope of the floor meant also that the ceiling there was higher, strangely high, before even accounting for the wooden-toothed, yawning hole above. The 'old kitchen' was cordoned off and locked for the duration of Len's childhood. This area not even Harlan would encourage him to explore. Nevertheless, Len had seen the room both from above and below, probably very few times. Few enough that he could almost forget the room existed until it reared in his nightmares. In those dark visions, he could not identify any *specific* evil lurking in the rot and ruin. But while no ghoul crouched in the filthy shadows and no horde of insects writhed over the sodden clutter, yet the room held its breath, and its breath was not only the fetor of stagnant dampness but the very spirit of dread, so that the stillness itself was ever fecund with menace. And though Len wanted nothing more than to avoid that foul pit, when his nocturnal wanderings led him through locked doors and solid walls to the derelict room above, he had no choice: he had to look at the awful wreck below, and he could not turn away, and he would wake up sick and afraid. Len grew up wanting to leave.

Harlan's prospects improved in consonance with the neighborhood, such that by the time Len left for college, he had approximated the wealth he imitated, though even then—and Len suspected even now—his fortune was tied almost entirely to his house. The other residences in the neighborhood had been restored by investors who flipped them, living in the houses only briefly, or not at all.

Between moving in at five and out at eighteen, his mother had moved back to the cottage, his father had remarried, his mother died, and the first and second floor were just about finished.

Though it appeared restoration was now complete, yet, as it always had, the house bridged two eras unconvincingly. The wide, symmetrical layout indicated a neoclassical sensibility, but the upper section, separated from the austere bottom third by an elaborately-patterned frieze, was capped in the Queen Anne revival style by a skirmish of gables. There was, perhaps fortunately, no room for a turret. The house was yellow, the shutters white; the clouds above were dabs on blue canvas, serene and stationary.

Len parked on the brick circle in front of the separate garage. As he opened the back door of his car to retrieve his soft-case 'spinner,' he heard his father call his name.

The slowly-closing screen door behind him indicated that Harlan had emerged from a side entrance to the house which hadn't been there before. Len realized with a start to which room that entrance must lead—the 'old kitchen.' He was so unsettled by the idea that his father had to repeat his name before he saw the proffered hand. He felt the dampness of his own palm in his father's grasp.

Harlan noticed the bag in the back seat. "Were you planning to stay?"

"Oh! Oh, that," Len said. He hadn't known what was expected of him; the invitation was unspecific in that regard. The tone of his father's question was much more definitive.

"It's just with you being only two hours away, I figured you'd probably want to head back," his father said. "Of course, you're welcome to stay, if you want. We have some out-of-town guests right now, but there's...there could be room if we move some things around."

"No, no, that won't be necessary," Len assured him. "That's just my travel bag. It's for—I take it whenever I'm on the road, you know, in case of emergencies. I, uh—I just needed to grab my phone charger. I noticed the charge on my cell was low," he lied. "If that's okay."

Harlan laughed. "Well, sure! My juice is your juice!" He clapped Len on the shoulder. After a second, he asked, "Well?"

Len looked at him, unable to parse the reference. Then he remembered his lie, said, "Right!" and retrieved the charger from his bag, blocking his father's view with his body so that he wouldn't see the clothes and toiletries inside. He turned back and presented the fat, white plug and twist-tied cord triumphantly, like the heart from his first kill.

His father nodded. "All right, then!" He turned and beckoned, flipping his left hand forward. "Come on in."

They crossed the lot and approached the side entrance. Len felt vaguely nauseous. Harlan opened the screen door. The door beyond was already swung inward.

Len muttered, "This is new."

"Oh, yeah, sure. I guess you haven't been up since we've finished the rehab. *Lots* of changes to show you."

Len followed inside, but only took one step further as he surveyed the combination laundry and 'mud room.' The washer and dryer were set along the wall towards the rear of the house. Two hampers, their lids bulging up, rested underneath long shelves on the interior wall beside a centered doorway. On the wall towards the front of the house were coat hooks like bronzed roebuck skulls, staggered in alteration, low-high, over tufted mats. Matching shelves on this side of the door were cluttered with hats and plastic tubs.

"What's the matter?" his father asked.

Len looked down at clean vinyl sheeting in a terra cotta tile pattern.

"Oh, *that* nightmare." Harlan laughed. He stepped from the far doorway back to the center of the room. A wave of panic nearly toppled Len as he watched his father hop up and down.

"All fixed, buddy. Good as new!"

When Len went to follow his father into the main house, he couldn't help but trace a wide arc. He knew he must have crossed over what once was empty space, but he allowed himself distance enough to leap clear if the floor suddenly collapsed once more.

They passed into the dining room, which was adjoined to the kitchen in a modern, 'open' floor plan. Two young women in white, pleated shirts and red bow ties were stretching their arms over their heads as they removed stubborn swaths of cling wrap from large platters.

"You picked a great day to come up," Harlan said.

Len didn't make the choice; only one date had been suggested.

"Like I mentioned, we have guests staying. Marty and Billie. They're sort of me and Kat's 'cruise buddies.' We met them last year and hit it off so well that we planned our vacations together again this year. So I thought, hey, let's make a day of it and have some friends from work and the church over to meet them. You remember the Hillsons? They'll be here."

Len didn't think it was a coincidence he'd been invited that day. With so many guests, Harlan wouldn't need to 'keep him entertained'— or spend too much time with him at all.

Harlan stopped and lowered his voice to speak confidentially. "It's a bit of bad timing for Kat, unfortunately. She slipped on the stairs and broke her wrist."

"I'm sorry to hear that," said Len. "Is there anything I can do to help?"

Harlan laughed. "Not unless you've taken up catering as a side-line to...to your job. No, Kat can still order people around, and that's all that's necessary."

A melodic but quavering voice called, "Harlan!"

Harlan winked at Len and nudged him with an elbow. "Speak of the devil and she appears."

Kat entered. Len thought she looked younger even than her supposed age, though her eyes were sunken. "Oh!" she piped. "You must be Lenny. I'm so pleased to meet you." She extended her left hand in greeting, which Len took. Her right hand was unavailable. Len had expected to see a cheerful pink or purple cast below Kat's elbow. Instead, the bulky white plaster cast extended up to her shoulder and was fixed upright by an elevating support rod connecting from elbow to hip. Kat tilted her head to indicate the encumbrance. "You'll have to excuse the crumpled wing. I guess I'm not the accomplished skier I thought I was!"

Len was so rattled by the extent of her injury and the discrepancy between its stated causes that he didn't correct the abandoned juvenilia, 'Lenny,' and didn't shoot a questioning glance towards his father until long after the elder man had time to dismiss any tell in his expression.

Harlan said, "We should have just had you plug that up in the other room."

Len looked at the adapter in his hand as though it might answer the question of why he hadn't done just that.

"Lenny needs to charge his phone," Harlan explained to Kat. "Do you mind, dear?"

"Oh, not at all!" She pivoted to stretch out her open hand once more. When Len hesitated, she said, "It's no bother."

He felt obliged to hand her the charger. He worried about the awkwardness of maneuvering his phone into her already occupied hand before realizing he hadn't brought it in with him.

"There you are, Kat. Billie's been looking all over for you!"

A stout, balding, ruddy-cheeked man appeared from behind her. Harlan introduced Len to Marty as Kat excused herself and scurried back through the living room.

"How's it feel to be back in the ancestral homestead?" Marty asked.

Harlan snapped his fingers. He said to Len, "Remind me before you go that I've got a box of your old stuff for you to take."

Marty noticed Len glance over his shoulder in the direction where Kat disappeared. He leaned towards Len and winked. "Something to do with the *drinks*, I think." He chuckled. "Knowing my Billie!" He slapped his stomach heartily as though he'd just finished a big meal.

As they seemed to be waiting for him to say something, Len responded to Marty's question obliquely. "I haven't been back since the house was finished."

Marty winked again. "Wondering what your old man's turned your old room into, eh?"

No, he wasn't, really. His was the first bedroom to be abandoned, so Len knew it was the one most likely to be repurposed. Whether it held exercise equipment or canvas-laden easels or two yoga mats and a candle had nothing to do with him. He would have been more surprised if Cecile's boys' bedrooms had been converted.

But Len realized he should have taken the bait when Harlan instead suggested, "Well, you haven't seen the basement. We know that for sure."

"How's that?" Marty asked.

"He used to be afraid of the basement," Len's father said. "Well, I'm *assuming* the past tense."

"Afraid?" Marty chortled and chucked Len on the shoulder. "You should have locked him in one night. 'It is the strike of the hammer which straightens the blade.'"

Len's first thought was that he had no desire to see the basement, but his hesitation to object belied that conviction. Apprehension ran cold through his arms and legs, but his fear was curiously softened by nostalgia. In truth, there was nothing that tied him to his childhood home more than the enduring-yet-vague images insinuated into his subconscious. If that horrid chamber had been erased from waking life, perhaps seeing it thus might negate its existence inside his head. While he deliberated, he felt the controlled panic of the ground falling slowly away as the roller coaster train climbed the lift hill, that thrill which amplified the shudder accompanying each clack of the chain with the dual threats of the possibility of failure and the assuredness of success.

"Sure," he assented meekly, though neither of the other men heard, as they were already halfway across the living room.

The basement access was still at the far north end of the house. The old stone stairs had been removed; black rubber safety pads covered the middle two-thirds of the new white oak planks; the green paint on the rail felt tacky beneath Len's hand. In view to his right as he descended were the tangle-crowned furnace and water heater, their pilot lights hissing steadily.

He stopped on the bottom step. His heart beat faster. Though swept free of the old debris and generally clean besides, little else had changed. The cement floor was the same; the layout was the same—the same walls partitioned the west side of the basement into the same stall-like chambers and the same open space 'hallway' ran the length of the back of the house. Len had expected more development. He had hoped for a carpeted, finished basement to obscure its primitive origins. There was still inadequate lighting. Naked bulbs hung from sockets in only three crossbeams.

Marty clapped his hands together exuberantly and exclaimed, "The prize attraction!" He stood at the opening to the 'spur' outgrowth where at the end Len knew there was once a pair of locked storm cellar doors.

"Hands off, you greedy bastard," Harlan playfully chided his friend. "I've paid enough already for today's libations."

Len joined them. The mounds of dirt and plaster scabs had finally been scooped up and removed, presumably through the new, metal doors at the top of the short, wide stairs. A narrow table stood off-center on the deeper side of the room. Along both walls large racks of small, diagonal cubbies had been erected and stocked with wine bottles.

Marty protested, "But surely you can spare a Pinot Gris before the feast. Are we not civilized men?"

Harlan chuckled. "Speak for yourself. But if you can find a white in this house, you're welcome to it. I only have a taste for reds. And I'm totally lacking in compassion for anyone who feels differently!" He turned to Len. "What do you think?"

"It's quite different than I remember," he answered, almost cheerful with relief. He pointed towards the end of the room. "I've never once gone through those doors."

Harlan shrugged. "No reason you should, I suppose. They're still locked from the outside, anyway."

"Got to keep these babies safe," Marty said, cradling a Chilean Cabernet Sauvignon.

"Put the baby back in the crib," Harlan said flatly, and though the phrase was glib, he watched until the act was accomplished.

"I'm afraid the rest won't mean as much to you, Marty," Harlan said as they re-entered the main area. "From Lenny's perspective, it has more to do with what's *not* there than what is." They moved into view of the first chamber. Harlan made a limp motion with one hand. "It's just storage," he said.

Shelves lined the walls. On one side, they were stuffed with the full-color display boxes of products likely found within the house proper: a vacuum cleaner, a ceiling fan, a laptop computer. Len wondered if most of the boxes were empty. As if in reply, Harlan commented, "You never know when you're going to have to send something back."

On the other side, Len was surprised to see a wide assortment of electronics. He identified tube televisions, VHS players, telephones, stereo components, game consoles, and even a ham radio by their function, but not their origin. Though their age indicated they had long sat idle, he didn't remember any of the objects in use while he was growing up—nor the three aquariums on the bottom shelf, stuffed full of plastic plants and coiled, clear tubes.

Len was startled by the sharp rapping of hard-sole shoes on the cement behind him. He spun around just in time to see a man moving purposefully into the wine cellar. He was clad chin-to-toe in black; only white hands and head were visible outside of his turtleneck. The fantastically loud clatter of his heels stopped abruptly once he was out of sight.

Len stood frozen in place, staring at the space which the figure in black had crossed. The man had borne a startling resemblance to Len. His carriage was different, his strides were purposeful and his posture was straight, his shoulder blades flat. And, if such a thing could be, his identical features cut a sharper profile. Len started and gasped, late after the fact. Fresh oxygen brought elucidation: the shock of seeing someone *nearly* like him caused him to ignore the differences and refine the similarities. His sudden appearance jarred, his abrupt disappearance precluded closer inspection. Mystery solved. Still, Len felt unsteady.

He guessed the man must have been one of the caterers, even though he was dressed differently from the women in the kitchen. But if it was one of the caterers, then what was he doing? His father had mentioned that they had brought all the wine required. He waited to see if the man would emerge back into the basement, or if he would hear the creak of the storm cellar doors—despite Harlan's assurance that the doors were locked. Notwithstanding the grand appearance of the estate, Len didn't think his father had any household staff; even if his fortunes had continued to improve, there was even less reason for the expense now that the children were gone. He was about to ask, but realized he'd yet to call his father 'Dad' since his arrival and the word stuck in his throat.

"This one here is mostly construction materials," Harlan said, further down.

Len glanced over his shoulder as he turned, and then joined his father by the second stall. Similar shelves here held stacked lumber, boxes of screws and nails, a vent with an exhaust fan, square-foot tiles still in their shipping boxes, and other such things. On the far side, the lumber was darker, and long nails were collected in mason jars; Len thought he saw a wrought-iron fireplace grate.

"We salvaged what we could from the original house as we tore into it," Harlan explained. "Waste not, want not."

"You won't find materials made like that anymore," Marty added, to which they harrumphed their agreement in unison.

"Well, take a gander, bucko," Harlan said. "It's all you." He waved Len forward. Neither he nor Marty moved towards the final chamber.

Len's eyes traced the ragged edge of the wall which partitioned the last stall. Shallow breath wheezed in and out of his open mouth. He felt the slope of the floor leaning him forward. The weight of *imminence* drew him on. He nearly lost his nerve—he *did* lose his nerve, but his feet propelled him forward unbidden. In turning to look inside, it seemed as though the house instead rotated to meet him.

There was nothing to be seen—not even shelves to match the other stalls. The horrid heap was gone, the rough shadows it protected, chased away. The floor near the wall looked like it might be clammy, but there was no black mud pooled in the corners. The oppressive sense of weight dissipated with Len's routed expectations, ill-formed as they had been.

Behind him, Harlan said, "See? Nothing there."

"Should we see what mischief the ladies are up to?" Marty called.

They turned and started away from the empty chamber. Len glanced again at the old construction materials as they passed those shelves. They moved on to the next stall.

The clap of hard-soled shoes on cement sounded from behind him. A chill shot through Len and goosebumps swelled on his arms. He shrank away as he turned back. The man appeared—*he* appeared— from around the corner of the last wall and stormed down the hallway towards them, seemingly oblivious of their presence. It was him! Yes, there was no denying it now; Len looked at Len, clad in black, the same, yet different—vigorous and resolute: the model of a man. Len couldn't speak to alert the others, who seemed not to hear. He knew it was impossible that his double had gotten behind them—he would have seen him in the chambers as he passed by. The man could only have come from the far end, from the empty chamber—where there was no other way in. His father's and Marty's blather continued, uninterrupted, as they strolled; Len suddenly understood that the two men did not see the other approaching. Five—four—three strides away: the familiar but expressionless face loomed; unblinking eyes stared forward, but would they turn? Len flinched and covered his face, afraid the man's gaze might shift to meet his own—it would be his doom, he knew. Each bone-snap clack of the heel rapped like a pick on the brute stone blocks. In the black of his hands Len yet saw his stark, pale face, eyeless, and then *his* eyes alone in the blackness staring back, the eyes of the mirror with the force of a terrible mind behind them which *should* have been alien but which shared much too much in common.

The sound was gone. Len lifted his gaze and saw that the man had disappeared.

From the foot of the stairs, Harlan and Marty stared back at him quizzically. Len brushed his nose as he let his hands drop. "I'm allergic to mold," he squeaked. He tried to sniffle convincingly, a difficult feat for a breathless man.

LEN TRIED TO shake off his experience in the basement, but he found it impossible to concentrate thereafter, which made him uncommunicative (whether to his father's consternation or his relief, he couldn't tell). He tried to rationalize the man's presence, tried to force himself to accept the only possible interpretation: his exact double was in fact one of the caterers, whose movements Len had failed to note because he was focused on the peculiarity of being once more in the much-changed, much-the-same basement that had terrified him in his youth— the influence of which caused his overly-sensitive reaction. The man had been moving quickly and purposefully and did not 'disappear' but simply moved out of sight while Len was covering his hands. The other men did not react because of their conceit of their station—why should they notice the help? (And why would his father bother to note a resemblance?)

But he knew what he saw. The constraint 'you *thought* you knew what you saw' held no vigor. How could one think otherwise of what one sees? Therefore, only contrary visual evidence could serve to soothe his psychic perturbation. So, as the broad back patio filled with people he did not know—and the Hillsons from church, whom he recalled only vaguely—Len scanned continuously to see if his doppelgänger would reappear with a platter of canapes or some such. He snacked, absentmindedly grabbing hors-oeuvres from passing trays and consuming them uninspected, looking only at the servers and not the food. Perhaps inevitably, he positioned himself to look back diagonally across the crowd in the direction of the former 'old kitchen' and the wretched (be it cluttered or clean) chamber below.

His gaze drawn repeatedly thus, he yet failed to note that Kat was centered in his survey until Marty clapped him on the back, leaned in close to his ear, and with wine-sour breath slavered conspiratorially, "It must be hard to have a stepmother like that, eh?"

Len watched Kat laugh along with her guests at her awkwardly jutting appendage as she provided once again who-knows-what explanation for her injury.

"What wouldn't you like to do to *her*?" Marty purred.

The lingering pomace of various sharp and rich tastes curdled at the back of Len's throat. Suddenly, he burped, but, in trying to keep from vomiting, somehow the stifled belch came out sounding like a giggle.

Len didn't bother to say goodbye to his father before he left. He'd forgotten to retrieve his phone charger, but sometime in the interim the promised 'box of your old stuff' had materialized next to his luggage in the back seat of his car. Box and contents never made it inside his apartment. He'd been given his youth soccer participation trophies, nothing more. No photos. He tossed the box in a dumpster. His apartment was small; Len was vigilant against unnecessary clutter.

Long drives typically exhausted Len. And though he felt limp upon his return home, he thought it would be difficult to sleep after the events of the day—or perhaps it would be bad to do so, welcoming nightmares. So he sat on his sofa and watched the late news. His head bounced several times as he caught diminishing snippets of the broadcast, before he finally fell into a fast and dreamless sleep just after seeing a face on the TV he thought he might have recognized.

THE NEXT DAY, early evening, he went shopping at the grocery store. In the vestibule where the grocery carts were kept, there was a video rental kiosk, around which several teenagers were huddled, squawking. His hand on the crossbar of a cart, Len happened to glance over at them, and he froze. He could have sworn that one of them, with long, brown hair, was the 'missing' girl Jassmyn, from the fax he'd received at work on Thursday. He couldn't be sure—he thought she looked very much like the school photo Jassmyn, but nothing at all like the candid selfie version. Then he remembered he'd seen her picture on the news the night before as he was dropping off. Or at least he thought so. They'd said her body had been found in a drainpipe. But had he dreamed it? He awoke that morning with the fresh relief of having dreamed nothing at all, but it was possible the vision had come before he had properly nodded off. Had he dreamed her dead?

"Dude!" The teen boy's voice, meant to be confrontational, cracked. "Stare much?"

"Oh, my God!" one of the girls breathed and giggled.

Len looked at his hand clutching the crossbar, and then looked back up. "I'm sorry," he said, "I was just thinking how funny it would be to take one of those carts there with the yellow and red toy kiddy car on front, and—without a child inside, of course—to push it around the store, weeping openly."

A curly-haired redhead guffawed and then caught herself short, clapping her hand over her mouth.

"What?" asked 'Jassmyn.'

A girl with glasses backed towards her tall, Indian friend.

"Or, if you did have a child—a son, preferably—you could work up an act where you pretend to be embarrassed while he yells and screams the whole time, 'Somebody help me! This man is not my father!'"

"Dude, what the shit," the boy breathed without any bravado.

The tall girl stepped around her bespectacled friend and warned in a heavy accent, "Stay the hell away from us, freak!"

"Pervert!" the redhead spat. "Come on, let's get out of here."

The boy and the tall girl corralled their friends protectively through the sliding doors.

"Is your name Jassmyn?" Len asked, and though the long-haired girl, understanding the question was meant for her, turned back to look at him from the sidewalk, no answer was forthcoming.

THE HALF-LIFE OF PLASTIC

———◆———

Esther Rose

I PROPPED UP my small, flat breasts with a push-up bra and then pulled on a skin-tight black dress. My control-top fishnet stockings sucked in my modest belly almost enough for comfort, but I chose tall high-heeled shoes to make my figure look more slender and to bolster my deflated bum. I could hardly believe what I was intending to do— go out? In public? Normally I only left home to go to my mother's house, where I would climb steep rickety stairs to her bedroom and turn on a light to see the shadows under her eyes.

I pulled out the bottom drawer of my dresser and rummaged for the war paint that had once given me the confidence to face the world. I carefully placed pots of makeup on my bedside table, pushed myself up against the mirror on my bedroom door. With a soft applicator of flesh-toned cream I filled in the deep bags under my eyes, and then I lined the rims of my eyelids in heavy black liner. I drew my lips in large and full, patted and pinched and prodded my tired face to bring blood circulation.

I took a taxi to the only club in town I'd ever gone to, the bright neon sign in the window flashing with the words "Dark Energy." The light inside was so low and soft that your eyes would play tricks on you here, hiding the commonplace deformities that people bore until the inevitable after-party at the twenty-four hour diner. There was always something glaringly wrong with everyone—an implacable way that they were ill-at-ease in their own bodies, something that was only revealed when they turned their heads or laughed. The only perfect people were the ones you saw on stage, the ones you never got close to, or the ones who got fixed.

I saw her standing at the booth where the musicians sold their CDs and graphic T-shirts. I hadn't spoken to her in six years, not since she'd told me I was a selfish monster and she never wanted to talk to me again. Soon after that encounter, she'd moved away with Mark.

She'd gotten some work done since I saw her last—her breasts now dwarfed her thin waist.

"Mira?" I said, ducking a little so that she could see my face in the red light that flashed from the stage. When she looked at me I immediately felt that I had done something wrong, saw the fear pass over her features. But then her face contorted into sadness and she pulled me into a tight hug.

"Mary," she said into my neck. "I missed you so much." I felt her shaking in my arms, her huge breasts pressed into the bony wall of my chest so that I couldn't hug her any closer.

MIRA LED ME by the hand to the basement and pulled me into a bathroom stall. She placed one of my hands on the curve of her breast and told me to squeeze a little. I could feel buoyant resistance, like a water balloon just under the soft tissue.

"Do you like them?" I asked.

"I love them," she said. They really looked amazing, perfectly round spheres. Nature had never made them this beautiful. She lifted them up so that I could see where the incision had been but I couldn't see any scars.

A week later she was by my side at the doctor's office during my consultation, showing the surgeon her breasts so that he could sculpt mine to look just like hers. And two weeks after that she was with me after my surgery, cooking for me, feeding me, letting me rest my head against her stomach. She moved into my house and took care of me for that whole week when the nerves in my chest would spasm and shoot pain into my fingertips. At night I would fall asleep in front of the television while she stroked my hair.

My incisions became infected, the space underneath my breasts red and inflamed. When the infection subsided I was left with thick, pink scars.

"It doesn't matter, sweetie," Mira said to me. We were watching one of those dating game-shows where a woman has to choose from three men based only on the sound of their voices. The audience could see the men shifting awkwardly in their seats, trying to project as much charm and bravado as they could muster. We were both waiting for that moment when the man she chose came around the curtain and the woman's face registered that split second of dismay.

I rubbed the puffy skin on my chest. If I pushed I could feel the scar tissue sliding around over my ribs. She pulled my hands away from my skin.

"We'll find a way to fix it. Anything can be fixed," she said.

OUR MOTHERS HAD died within a week of each other.

"I can't stop thinking about her smile," I said, tears dripping into my diner coffee. I pictured my mother's long teeth gone yellow from a lifetime of nicotine and coffee, with thin stretched lips that exposed the gum. Towards the end of her life she would make these bulk-orders online, buy ten cheap dresses from China at a time and then call me to come over so she could model them for me. Every time she would pull the excess fabric from her bony frame and toss a dress my way saying, "this would look better on you," her eyes shiny and hungry and her teeth gleaming like half-buried treasure. She loved the way her illness had wittled her down.

Mira leaned forward across the table and captured my hands in hers, looking at me steadily. The feeling of skin-to-skin contact with another person made a sound escape from my throat, hot tears streaming down my face. We both had brown, almond-shaped eyes with long eyelashes. I had never noticed how similar our faces were before.

"I know what we have to do," she said.

GETTING THE TEETH was not easy. I had years of practice breaking and entering and I knew how to pick locks and find the easiest and most discrete point of entry, but the hard part was the way that my mother's mouth had clamped shut. It took so much effort to pry her jaw open, and then more to pluck the teeth. I fell backwards a few times with a tooth in my pliers and my shoulders were sore with effort.

I collected her sharp canines, her large front teeth that had poked over her lip sometimes when her mouth was closed.

Mira's mother was already buried in a remote suburban cemetery. She somehow got the groundskeeper to agree to help her dig up the body; she had to convince him that no one was going to come see her mother so there would be nobody concerned about the churned up earth. Mira was like that, now—alluring, convincing.

Harder than acquiring the teeth was finding a doctor who was willing to implant them for us.

"Maybe I can do it myself," I said. I had been a plastic surgery resident in what felt like another lifetime, though this had nothing to do with dentistry. I spent some time researching how to implant teeth, had dreams about taking a sewing needle and threading them to the inside of my cheek. Finally Mira found someone who was willing to compromise.

"She'll make a porcelain mold of our mothers' teeth and then implant them as veneers." It was almost as good as the real thing.

After our teeth were done, Mira's mouth was perfect, her gums fresh and pink. I wasn't so lucky; I would spit a mouthful of blood into the sink every morning.

A LONG TIME AGO Mark had been in love with me. It was before he was in love with Mira. I didn't even know he existed until one night when Mira whispered into my ear at Dark Energy that she was setting me up with him. I would have done anything for her; the next day Mark and I went out for dinner. He was as handsome as a male cover model, with smooth poreless skin and perfectly symmetrical features. I couldn't understand why a person as beautiful as him was interested in me.

"You're a biomedical engineering student," he said over a plate of rich Tikka Masala. I gulped my red wine and nodded, nervous to be reminded of the exams that I had yet to study for.

"I'm pre-med," I clarified, "but I'm interested in plastic and reconstructive surgeries, and implantable devices."

He pulled his sleeves all the way up, exposing thick, well-muscled arms.

"So when you're Dr. Mary, you will be able to replace both of my arms with robot arms."

I laughed. "I guess I could, but usually there has to be some kind of medical need..."

He frowned. "So I have to get into some kind of accident first?"

I realized that he was serious. I tried to end our date quickly, but when he walked me back to my car he pressed his beautiful mouth against mine and I thought for sure that this would be my only chance in life to sleep with a perfect ten.

I brought him home with me. After we made love in the dark, his head resting against my pillow and the soft light from outside illuminating his unnaturally perfect face, he said, "Both of us have a lot of room for improvement, but the sky's the limit. We can be anything we want to be." I was young, then. I told him I wasn't really interested in another date.

The next day Mira called me, screaming her outrage that I had hurt Mark, that I was a monster. And two weeks later, they moved away together.

Why couldn't I have loved Mark, too, I asked myself. Why had I been too stupid to fall in love with him.

MY MOM'S ILLNESS had been severe since I was five years old, the doctors giving her a one-year prognosis over and over again while she clung tenaciously to life with one thin hand wrapped around a pack of cigarettes.

We lived in a typical middle-class neighborhood, complete with two car garages, white picket fences, and carefully manicured lawns. We were the white trash of the neighborhood, our unkempt yard strewn with half-dismantled appliances, our car held together with duct tape. My mom would smoke in the yard in her bare feet, walking the perimeter of her overgrown garden. When he was alive, my stepfather would roast entire pigs on a spit in the yard, filling the neighborhood with the smell. The neighbors looked at us like we were pitiable at best, and I hated them for it. I did what I knew they expected me to do; I developed a criminal hobby. I learned to pick locks so that I could steal from their refrigerators whenever I was hungry.

Mira was the one who taught me how to break in. She grew up on the opposite side of the same neighborhood, where the houses weren't so nice, where no one looked twice at two scrappy girls in tube tops with stuffed bras, wearing a thick layer of makeup and platform heels.

At first we tried to get my mother to stop smoking, to start walking a little, to eat full meals. Instead she built a fortress of delivery boxes around her bed, taped a sign to her door that read "Do Not Disturb." When she was in a good mood, it was because she was draping a necklace around my neck or carefully applying a new shade of lipstick to my lips.

"It's hereditary," she said, with both promise and apology in her eyes. She wanted me to know what I was in for. I didn't believe her.

"You're so beautiful, Mary," she would say. "It's like you got all of the beauty that seeped out of me." Once I was older it became obligatory for me to go to her house every week and cut open her packages, to pose and model for her.

"When you're a great surgeon, promise you'll fix this," she said to me the last time I saw her alive. I never could bring myself to tell her that I had dropped out of my medical program.

Without my mom around, I wasn't close to anyone except for Mira. Everyone else would try to tell me that the things I saw weren't real. "There is nothing wrong with you," they promised. But Mira would never lie to me. She knew that my life was a urinal cake, the black sludge at the bottom of the trash can. She didn't tell me I was perfect. She said, "We can fix this," and we did. Together.

We got our noses done like tiny upturned buttons. After that my mouth wouldn't move the same, because they had made an incision through my upper gum and it had cut a nerve. Nothing was more perfect than a face that could hardly move—frozen forever in time.

We had the mass of our bodies surgically shifted around, the protective fat over our organs sucked out and poured into our asses and over our silicone breasts. We had ribs removed, our feet reshaped. We both wore our mothers' teeth around our neck. We were in a constant state of recovery and it felt like it was the way things were meant to be.

ONE RESTLESS, RAINY day we decided to go shopping to dress our new bodies. Mira looked in the mirror and frowned, her strained smile painful for me to see. She ran her hands over her face. She traced the line of her huge breasts, examined the curve created by the Brazilian butt lift. We looked like the bikini-clad women who danced on set in music videos. "It isn't enough," she said.

"What more can we do?" I asked. I felt a desperate tug in my chest, like the tether between us was being pulled gently away.

She pulled her mouth apart with two fingers at each corner, so that the skin separated from the underlying tissue.

"I need a bigger mouth." My stomach turned.

"Like bigger lips?" I asked. "There are a lot of ways to do that. Fillers, fat transfer, injections..."

"No," Mira said. "I need my whole mouth to open bigger."

"We won't find a surgeon willing to do that," I said.

"We'll have to go somewhere else to do it then. Bangkok. Delhi."

I hoped that if I let the conversation drop she would just forget about it. I was a little bit scared after the rib removal; I started bleeding out on the table, and it was by sheer luck that Mira was right there and that we had the same blood type for a transfusion. Maybe she would think of something a little more practical, like permanent eyeliner or liposuction on that tiny pocket of fat we both had at the inside of our knees. A few days later I saw her poking and pulling on her cheeks again, her porcelain veneers gleaming in her mouth, and I knew that she was still thinking about it.

"What ever happened to Mark?" I said. It was my Hail Mary—I had been avoiding the subject, careful not to upset Mira, but I hoped now that it might upset her so much that she would forgot about everything else. Instead she just shrugged her shoulders.

"He kind of went off the deep end," she said. "He started working at a meat processor and got his leg caught in a machine, so they replaced it with a prosthetic. He insisted he didn't want to leave the company, and then lost an arm. I realized at that point that he was doing it on purpose."

I swallowed hard. "And where is he now?"

"Who knows. He just kept having his parts replaced with mechanical parts. At this point I don't think he would even pass the Turing test."

"I'm not sure he ever would have," I said. She flashed me a mean look, but then we both laughed.

"Do you remember that woman who got surgery to look like an owl?" she asked. I did remember. I cut that story out of the magazine, folded it and carried it around in my purse for weeks. She had changed her name to Hooty, replaced her hair with a mane of feathers and had the skin around her eyes pulled back and rounded out. She had tip surgery on her nose to make it look like a sharp, downward-pointing beak.

"I found her surgeon," she said. "He lives in Istanbul. He made me promise that we wouldn't tell anyone where we got our work done."

A FEW DAYS later we were in an airport in Kazakhstan, waiting for a transfer flight to Istanbul. My long, silky hair extensions draped around my shoulders and tickled the top of my huge breasts. Everyone stared at us, two beautiful women with our arms wrapped around each other's tiny waists. My ass kept bumping into things because I was not yet familiar with the way I took up space. Sometimes, a man would press himself against me on purpose, growing against my skin. I didn't mind. We were two goddesses gracing this earth, and soon our perfection would allow us to transcend it. It was only natural that, until then, our bodies would be coveted.

Our eyes were still the same eyes, though now that our noses were tiny and our chins had been scraped to a delicate point they looked exceptionally large on our faces. Our shoulders touched in our claustrophobic airplane seats and I drank in her heady perfume. I wanted to kiss her, to bathe in her. When she looked at me with sleepy, heavily lidded eyes I knew she felt the same. But there was no pleasure in the flesh that could compare to the pleasure of transforming it. We both understood that touch would never bring us close enough.

Still, I wondered—where does this end? Mira had the vision. Mira was the one who knew what we had to do. I tried to dispel the fear that was building up in my abdomen. Every transformation had left her more perfect, but my body was covered in bruises and scars, my organs were failing. For some reason she healed and I didn't. I carried a small handkerchief with me and coughed blood into it. She promised me that we would fix what was broken inside of me—this would be the next surgery, or perhaps the one after that.

SOON WE WERE in the operating theater, holding hands across the metal slabs of operating tables, heavy with medicated sleep. Our procedures would be done back-to-back, but we preferred to be put under at the same time. We had developed a routine; we would fall asleep together and wake up together, we would see our transformation in each other and that would make our progress feel real. Mira's surgery was first. I fell asleep before her hand could go limp in mine.

When I woke up some time later, it was to the sound of the doctor barking frantic orders. I could hear the heart monitor beeping erratically, and I knew that I had woken up to my own death. I clawed my way through the haze of sleep towards consciousness. I didn't mind that I would die here—I was sure in this moment that death would be just like sleep, blissful and perfect. But I wanted to see Mira one last time. When I turned to look at her, I realized that her monitor was the one flatlining, her body convulsing as the electric paddles were pressed to her chest.

"Don't get up," the nurse at my side said, pushing me down as I tried to lift myself on my elbows. The anesthesiologist must have given me another hit of barbiturates then because I faded helplessly into sleep.

When I woke a second time, I was alone in a hospital room. My entire body ached. I pulled my gown aside and saw the tubes protruding from beneath bandages—bandages everywhere, all along my chest and abdomen and in the clefts of my hips. I felt my face but there were no bandages around my mouth; they hadn't touched that part of me. I pressed a button on the wall to alert the nurse. A woman came in quickly, her eyes round with terror.

"Where is Mira?" I asked her. The nurse shook her head and frowned.

"Your sister was very sick. She did not survive the surgery."

I knew the nurse had to be lying. Mira must have decided that she didn't want to be with me anymore. She probably told them to put her in a different room. As I worked out this puzzle in my head, pieced together the signs that Mira was through with me, the doctor came into the room.

"You are going to live another day," he promised. "The surgery was successful. You should be grateful for every breath you can still take." I snorted. This was so typical of doctors—to hack you to pieces and then tell you to be grateful. I had known my fair share of men like this in medical school.

"You are very lucky," he insisted to the face that I had turned into the pillow. "If it wasn't for your sister, you wouldn't have much longer to live."

"What do you mean?" I asked.

"Your kidneys were completely shot. You had cancer of the ovaries and the womb. How could you not know? You must have been sick for a long time. Your sister was a perfect organ donor, of course."

I wanted to tell him that she wasn't my sister, but it didn't matter. He wouldn't be able to understand what we were.

"You might still have cancer," he said. "You'll need treatment."

A FEW HOURS later I pulled the needles out of my skin and wrapped myself in a blanket from my hospital bed. In my personal effects, tucked into a corner of a beige hospital armoire, I found my lock-picking kit and the device I used to crack key card entryways.

Finding the hospital morgue wasn't difficult. They were always in the basement and they had the look of a meat locker, with big metal doors and smooth metal flooring. I opened the door easily, I didn't even have to mess with the wiring.

The walls were stacked with shiny metal drawers and within each drawer would be a preserved body, no longer feeble or flawed, no longer struggling to survive. I searched for Mira's name on the interchangeable placards. I had reached nearly the end of the drawers when I saw it. My heart was beating so fast I could hear it in my ears. I ran my finger over the inscription on the card. Mary. Mary was the one who had died.

I pulled open the drawer and she was there, her mouth stretching from one side of her face to the other, thick black stitches holding her expanded lips in place. I felt myself sink down to the floor. And then, without a clear reason, I began to laugh. I laughed so hard that I thought I might disrupt the stitches in my abdomen. I ran my fingers across the scars on the underside of my breasts and felt nothing—no scars. I passed my finger over my teeth, where the veneers had made them bleed, but there were no cuts in my mouth. I remembered something that Mira had said to me: "Smile more. You're prettier when you smile." And I smiled like an idiot, tears spilling down my cheeks. I couldn't explain it. I was happy.

EIDETIC

———— ◆ ————

Steve Rasnic Tem

QUENTIN COULDN'T REMEMBER how long he had been awake, even when he made a concerted effort to count the hours and create a detailed record of his whereabouts and doings for the day. He wrote himself a series of notes with his calculations and placed them at key points in his house planning to return to this problem later. He noticed the living room curtains were still closed and needed to be opened, for reasons of health or sanity or for appearances' sake. If you kept your curtains closed your neighbors assumed something was wrong with you. Was it Vitamin D or C you obtained from sunlight? He had no idea, nor was he cognizant of the benefits of either. He wrote himself a note to conduct more research. But he figured sitting in a dark room for too many hours turned you into a bit of a dark room yourself.

The curtains snagged but after some effort he was able to stutter them open. He wondered if his neighbors noticed, but surely they weren't watching him that closely. These days he wasn't even sure who his neighbors were. Traffic on this narrow neighborhood street seemed unusually heavy. Perhaps there had been an accident elsewhere. A dangerous situation, he thought, for all the children and elderly with no say in the matter. No say in anything, it seemed. He wrote a rough draft of a note he would revise later and send to the editor. In fact he would make copies and send them to all the editors.

In his house accidents had not occurred in years. Everything that happened in his house, he thought, happened deliberately. Perhaps that should reassure him, but it made him sad.

In his head he could feel the high-pitched pressure of brakes being applied. He'd always wondered if he was the only person with the ability to hear such things as brake pressure, as joints stiffening and arteries hardening, as the thoughts of insects, mice, and other vermin. Not that he understood their thoughts; he simply heard them: a constant background of disintegrating activity happening at all hours of the night and day. He had written notes many times in the middle of the night attempting to capture as many of their thoughts as possible.

Quentin retreated from the de-curtained window, traveling deeper into the house where he kept the bulk of his possessions, jammed onto dust-laden shelves—some with identifying notes and some without, or packed into a variety of bins stacked on the floor, or in ancient graying laundry bags stuffed into corners. He'd once had a variety of "normal" furniture: cabinets and chests of drawers and sideboards and the like. He wasn't sure when, but at some point he'd disposed of them all.

Now his things were so loosely organized he had little idea of what he did and did not possess. He'd long ago realized he needed to get rid of much of it. Perhaps he needed to get rid of it all, if he wanted to move around freely and breathe again. You can't live in a space that's already occupied. And yet throwing away too much felt like a form of suicide.

As had happened so many nights before, someone was sitting in his favorite chair. No, not his favorite, and certainly not his "lucky" chair, but the one he was accustomed to sitting in. He'd sat in this chair after his daughter died, after his wife left him, after the news came about his brother and sister-in-law's tragic accident. After so many deaths of friends and relatives, people he had known or just admired, after so many times of shock and despair as the list of people he knew dwindled toward nothing. He sometimes wondered if he had been singularly cursed in this way, but knew this was simply the reward for living a long life. And once the last person he knew was gone, what then?

He recognized his intruder immediately, as he had every other time. He'd long believed that somehow he had accidentally stepped into the wrong life and become trapped there, and this was his evidence.

The other Quentin did not move, even when approached from a variety of angles, even when a hand was waved in front of his face, and his name was spoken. His own name. "Pardon me, Quentin?" Why did he always feel compelled to apologize to himself? It was his house, after all, even though other people had lived in it before him who were now dead or moved away, and other people would live in it long after he himself was gone. He had paid for this interval of time, for the privilege of pretending he understood his own life and his place in it and somehow this would last, leave any impression at all. You could rent some space on the planet—someone would always be there willing to take your money—but you could never truly own.

"Excuse me, Quentin. You're in my chair. You need to explain yourself or leave."

The other Quentin turned his head, and Quentin thought the face somewhat more handsome than his own, as if perhaps this other Quentin were accustomed to more sleep, better eating habits, or at least a bit of exercise, as if in general this other Quentin had had a much luckier time on the planet. What a difference a few percentage points in attractiveness might have made in his life! He preferred not to dwell on the implications.

He should have grabbed the intruder, pulled him out of his chair, but Quentin was a coward and always had been. He'd pretended to be otherwise, of course. It was a simple thing to proclaim you would take action in hypothetical situations as long as those hypotheticals did not occur.

Instead, as he had every other time, Quentin cleared a space on the floor beside the chair and sat down, thinking this Quentin would not be able to ignore him forever and eventually would feel compelled to respond.

In the meantime he wrote a series of notes to his other self, thinking any reasonable Quentin could not help but pick them up and read.

The other Quentin had his eyes wide open, but he had no doubt this other Quentin was fast asleep. There was an ill-defined anxiety about the face, a troubled aspect in the features that suggested he was otherwise unaccustomed to trouble. The other Quentin's lips were moving rapidly, but no sound was coming out. The Quentin intruder was apparently dreaming, and should he feel insulted that the nightmare this other Quentin was dreaming was his own, pitiable life?

He considered the possibilities of awakening the other Quentin. Would he disappear? Would they trade places, or would one or the other die?

But what happened was what always happened. He eventually fell asleep, and when he woke up the other Quentin was gone. He could not tell if any of his notes were missing or not.

He really needed to get out more. Regular exposure might blunt the harsh impact of change.

SOMETIMES QUENTIN WROTE love notes to women he had not yet met. Of course he could not mail these because of a lack of address. He emptied his heart out in these notes, and was not afraid to take on both sides of a hypothetical lover's quarrel. He considered them good practice until an actual relationship occurred.

He made no attempt to visualize these women. In fact to do so would have felt exploitive. But he always knew everything they might have to say, and how hearing these things would make him feel.

Sometimes he would watch the woman across the street walk her dog. The dog was a shaggy mutt and barely controllable, and Quentin liked to think this was her husband, or at least the only male currently in her life. Quentin liked the way the woman always had a few kind words and a head rub for the dog, even when he had behaved so poorly.

At night the woman's house looked like a miniature lit by hidden spotlights, although Quentin was confused as to where these light sources might be positioned. Even when there was no moon out, and with the streetlights some distance away, her house always looked the same. Quentin always felt as if he were watching that house on television.

One night the woman's house burned down. Quentin hadn't witnessed the start of it. He wasn't sure how he couldn't have noticed—the fire had been attended by multiple alarms and a large number of trucks. Everyone else in the neighborhood spilled out onto the sidewalks to watch. But there were always large swatches of time Quentin could never quite account for—times when he was busy searching through his possessions, writing notes, or falling asleep in his chair. When he finally realized what was happening he watched as the others watched, only he did so peering through his front window with all the houselights off. He stood far back from the glass so no one could see him.

The day after the fire a low-lying fog filled much of the neighborhood. It clung to the dark ruins across the street, sculpting faces onto the few burnt posts still upright, then later when a breeze came, all these were swept away as if in recognition that whoever had once lived there now was gone.

That night he watched as a tide of insects eased out of the black grass and over the flagstone patio of the house that was no longer there.

Quentin did not know for sure if the woman had died. He didn't get the paper or watch the news, and of course he never asked anyone. But he never saw this woman or her dog again. In any case, she no longer felt like a real possibility for him.

HE DISCOVERED THE other Quentin soaking in his bathtub with eyes fixed in an unfocused stare. When was the last time he'd taken a bath, drained the tub? A scum of leaves, twigs, scribbled notes, and unidentifiable debris floated on the top, clinging to the other Quentin's skin. Had he left the bathroom window open at some point?

His other face was freshly shaven, eyebrows trimmed, indicating some pride in appearance. It made Quentin embarrassed to look. At least his chair was now available and he could go sit there if he wanted to.

But he wasn't sure if he should leave this Quentin in the tub unsupervised. As before, this Quentin appeared to be asleep with his eyes open. What if he drowned? What would that do to him? Was it even his responsibility? He didn't want to just dismiss the problem—there had to be some reason for all these repeat visitations.

If he was going to remain in the bathroom he could at least take the opportunity to groom himself. Quentin couldn't remember the last time he'd paid any attention to his looks. If any of his neighbors did bother to stop by what would they think? There seemed little point after his wife left him, but this other Quentin was proof he could look better.

Hair filled his bathroom sink, along with dirty coffee mugs, a couple of plates, and a few pieces of silverware. Had it really been that long since he'd washed? The hair wasn't even his—too long and of different colors, smelling vaguely of perfume. He might have had company over, invited or uninvited, or perhaps a woman or two had spent the night. He had imagined such events many times, but seriously doubted they'd actually occurred. Cleaning the sink took almost an hour, even when throwing all its contents into the already overflowing bin.

A decline in personal hygiene was one of the first indications of mental distraction, or so he'd read. He'd fix himself up and prove those so-called experts wrong.

He sensed the other Quentin watching him as he washed up, brushed his teeth, combed his hair, shaved. Yet when he turned around his better twin appeared inattentive, leaning forward as if waiting for something to rise out of the filthy water. He returned to his shaving with some apprehension. In the mirror he looked strange to himself, vaguely different from before. Perhaps it was the angle, but he appeared to have lost some weight. Then he noticed the faded note taped to the edge of the mirror: "Always look behind you." Had he written it, or his other? In his nervousness he nicked himself deeply below the jaw.

Frantically he searched for something to staunch the blood, heard splashing behind him, and twisted around with a stiff, sour-smelling towel pressed to his neck. The bathtub was empty, the other Quentin vanished again.

He'd gotten blood on his clothes, and changed them quickly. Already this seemed like a big improvement. The old Quentin would have remained in those clothes, content to put up with the stain.

Deep within the garage Quentin's car rumbled to life. He went out there to check, and indeed the Chrysler's engine was running, the car laden in a thick layer of dust since he hadn't used it in some time. He couldn't remember the car's original color anymore. He slipped into the driver's seat to turn off the ignition but the key was missing. He listened carefully—the engine was no longer running.

Climbing out of the car he became aware of a thick stench of sour vegetation. He looked around the concrete floor and when he reached the garage's back door he discovered that numerous fibrous vines had grown underneath the rotting door and through the swollen jamb. He found a crowbar and used that to pry the door open. From there he pushed his way into the backyard through a sea of green and brown, sweetness and rot.

He'd stopped weeding the back garden years ago. He could see that it had multiplied in size, pushed itself under the back porch forcing the entire rear of the house to rise. Now he could make sense of that unpleasant aroma that had permeated many of the rooms for so long—it was a fainter version of what he smelled out here.

The house itself was obviously not in the same position in the lot as it had been when he first moved in. The east yard was narrower, the west yard considerably wider.

Something moving through the chest-high weeds caught his eye. He recognized one of his old red-checkered shirts and part of some familiar black jeans hanging from an obscured figure as it made its way toward the now unsecured garage. He remembered how he and his wife had used these items years ago to outfit a rickety scarecrow in the middle of their vegetable patch.

Quentin attempted to catch up with it, fearing he might be locked out of the house. But his worsening arthritis made it impossible to move quickly. Sometimes when excited he forgot how old he actually was. He needed to be more careful. A fall at his age might prove fatal. He vowed that once inside he would write himself a note containing the necessary cautions.

Back in the house again he tried to locate the shirt, or the scarecrow, the other Quentin, whoever or whatever he had pursued. But try as he might the only footsteps he heard were his own. Now and then he would hear a throat clearing itself in another room, but he always arrived too late to catch the intruder. He had a notion that the other Quentin might try to communicate with him through writing, but there were so many notes now—and all in the same or similar handwriting—he could not tell which had been written by someone else.

Sometimes he would see himself outside the windows looking in, but the windows were so dirty he couldn't tell if it was the other Quentin, an invading memory, or simply his own reflection. Sometimes he would try to communicate with this outside self, but he was sorely put off by the way it would silently mouth his words as he spoke them.

After a few hours he completely lost track of the time. With each passing week it seemed he became a little bit smaller. He took up less room in his bed and the rooms themselves seemed larger and increasingly empty. On the other hand the few times he saw the other Quentin he seemed quite a bit larger. A mentally unstable person might believe the other Quentin had stolen some of his essence in order to nourish himself. But Quentin believed that all creatures meant only the best for each other, and that any apparent advantage was only a matter of coincidence.

In a desperate try for coherence Quentin went through the house gathering as many notes as he could find. He sat down and read each one, organizing them into piles according to particular themes or threads of thought. Many of these messages seemed to be hasty attempts to catch fleeting notions, reminders, plans, grocery, and to-do lists. In the past he'd tried various systems for capturing such things—computer programs, beautiful journals, once an audio recording system—none of them ever worked. Every time he went back to the notes, scattered on flat surfaces, taped to walls, layered in drawers. He was always spilling food on them, having them snag on his clothing, stuck to the bottom of a glass or plate. The attrition rate was brutal—he'd lost fully a third of what he jotted down. But wasn't that how it was with any aging brain? Ideas and memories were always leaking out, erased, or rubbed away simply as part of life's daily wear.

The content of these notes was invariably disappointing, full of trivia and not one word relating to the true concerns of his heart. Had he been a good person? He wasn't sure. Nothing recorded here illuminated that question. And people lied to themselves about such things all the time.

Completely exhausted he trudged up to bed one night only to find it already occupied by the other Quentin and one other. It was a woman, and from her hair and naked back he felt sure it was his ex-wife. She appeared to be asleep. The other Quentin slowly rolled his head over and looked up at him.

If anything, this other Quentin looked younger than he ever had before. He appeared to be the approximate age Quentin had been when they'd first been married, or so it seemed. But Quentin knew he had never looked this good: skin so smooth, and somewhat androgynous with the scarce body hair. His ex-wife moaned softly, and Quentin realized that somehow, impossibly, he had lost her name. The other Quentin smiled ever so slightly, and she rolled over face-up. Her entire body was covered with small love notes in tiny, indecipherable handwriting. But Quentin didn't need to read them, because he had written them.

The other Quentin said nothing, but he kept smiling, and that was more than enough to enrage him. He glanced at the bedside table, and saw the box cutter there, grabbed it without much consideration, and set to the task of erasing that oh-so-satisfied smile.

There was nothing to it really. No blood, and so no reason to stop. The blade wasn't even an inch long, and so he had to press hard, but the other Quentin quite accommodatedly lay still. The bits of him floated off like transparent gel which floated into the air before rapidly dissolving. The skin bearing his appearance was nothing more than sham, drying up and vanishing as his contents emptied. By the end of his labors Quentin was hovering over an empty bed, no worse for the wear and tear. His sheets appeared only slightly moist.

He searched the room thoroughly, and was satisfied that he had been left safely alone. Again he examined himself for blood, and found no stains or other indications.

He went into the bathroom and looked at himself in the mirror. He wasn't sure what he had expected, hoping perhaps to have taken on that younger aspect. But he appeared unchanged.

When the red lines began to appear he actually thought them quite beautiful. As they expanded he thought they resembled a sort of bloody topography, before the bits of him began sliding away.

THEY ARE US (1964) :
AN ORAL HISTORY

———◆———

Jack Lothian

ISSAC PETERSON (PRODUCER)

At the time I was working out of an office on the Paramount lot. This would've been a few years before Gulf & Western bought them out in '66. Everyone was feeling the pinch; we'd been strongly advised to look for films that could slide in with lower budgets.

My secretary Sheila would type up reports on books she'd dug up, quick one-paragraph summaries, and she'd highlight any that she particularly recommended.

SHEILA WELSH (SECRETARY)

I'd probably have a proper title now—development assistant or something. But back then I was just 'a secretary,' no matter what my actual role was. It really was a different time. I was young, and I suppose relatively naive, thought nothing of spending my weekends on the porch with a stack of dime-store novels, trying to hunt down the next big thing. It felt glamorous just to be connected to the industry.

I still remember the first time I read *They Are Us*. It was a relatively simple story—a couple move to the city, and their marriage disintegrates as they renovate a crumbling townhouse. Partway through they start to suspect each other of all manner of affairs and infidelities, and there's a suggestion that maybe they aren't themselves all the time.

It was a little hard to follow, but the basic concept—a couple, a townhouse, a marriage in crisis—felt like the kind of thing Isaac was looking for.

CARL MONKTON (AUTHOR)

It was the only novel I ever finished, and the only one I ever had published. I wish I'd never written a word.

ISSAC PETERSON (PRODUCER)

It felt like an easy sell. Small cast. It had potential to be one of those 'prestige projects'—get a renowned director on, a couple of stars who don't mind slumming.

I didn't read the book though. That's what I have staff for.

SHEILA WELSH (SECRETARY)

Isaac tried to read it. He stopped halfway through. He said it disturbed him, but wouldn't elaborate. At the time I thought he was just being lazy, spinning an excuse not to finish it, but looking back I'm not so sure.

The book left me feeling oddly unclean. Do you know what I mean? When you read something, and it feels like it's sunk into your pores. There was a cruelty to it like the author enjoyed tearing this couple apart, and by extension, I suppose the reader becomes an accessory to that. We're watching their lives unravel, and we could choose to stop reading, we could close the book, but we read on, and so their pain and misery continues.

It was me who suggested Laurent Loubet as director, although Isaac took credit for that at the time. He doesn't take credit for it now, obviously. I was in love with Loubet's movies, I was pretty much crazy for any French cinema I could see back then. I never thought Isaac would go for it, but apparently Loubet was looking to break into Hollywood, so he was willing to work for scale.

LAURENT LOUBET (DIRECTOR)

I'd never made a movie outside of France. To me, American film was mostly popcorn and soda, but that was a canvas I felt I could work on. I knew that it was unlikely that Mr. Peterson would give me the kind of control I wanted, so I insisted on writing the script as well, at a reduced rate. I understood fairly quickly that his real interest was profit and loss, and that I should lean into that.

CARL MONKTON (AUTHOR)

I sent them a letter, politely asking them not to make the movie. They didn't respond. I had no control over the rights, I foolishly signed them away to the publishing company in the first contract. It's a strange feeling, to hope that your words and sentences aren't popular, that your novel doesn't sell, that it won't do the very thing that stories exist for—to be read.

ISSAC PETERSON (PRODUCER)

Monkton was a bit of a kook, truth be told. Letters, phone calls, even showed up at my office. The guy had no idea of how the business worked, he didn't seem to understand that the publisher had sold us the rights. It got so that I told studio security not to let the guy onto the lot.

Then it escalated.

ARTHUR KAY (HEAD OF STUDIO SECURITY, 1962 - 65)

I got a call, around 1am, from Mr. Peterson. He was saying Monkton was outside his house, hammering on the windows. I got there as fast as I could. It was quite the sight. Monkton had cracked the glass with his fists, which were all cut and bloodied. He turned as I approached, and he just bolted straight at me.

I served in Korea, even saw some action. He wasn't easy to drop though. First punch should have taken him off his feet, but he kept coming.

I don't want to speculate about the guy, whether he had personal problems, or whether he was involved in narcotics. He was lucky—Mr. Peterson decided not to press charges, concerned about bad publicity.

I'll always remember though, grabbing him by the collar, trying to force him to the ground. He was laughing like I was doing exactly what he wanted me to, like it was all some sort of game.

You meet all kinds in this job.

CARL MONKTON (AUTHOR)

I did show up at the studio, yes. But I never went to Isaac Peterson's house. Never.

LAURENT LOUBET (DIRECTOR)

I don't think any of them really understood the book. The characters at the start aren't always the characters you're reading about later on. It's about a fractured reality. Can any of us truly know ourselves? If memory is a construct, how can we believe anything that has happened? What if you had to see yourself as you really are, not what you pretend to be, stripped bare of your delusions and self-justifications? To me, that was a terrifying concept.

ISSAC PETERSON (PRODUCER)

I hated Loubet's screenplay. It made less sense than the book, and that apparently made no sense either. I gave him my usual notes though— *find someone we can root for, keep the romantic sub-plot on the boil, remember this has to play in Poughkeepsie.*

I've had a pretty decent career. Most of my pictures stack up, maybe not always with the critics, but at least at the box office. I understand the business is all about entertainment. We're getting people out of their houses, to hand over their hard-earned cash. That doesn't mean every movie has to be empty and vapid. It's just gotta be worth the trip.

I signed up Bruce Mountford for the lead, and Jayne Southern to play his wife. People forget now, but they were big stars. Maybe not all-time hall-of-famers, but they were on the magazine covers, and they both had some decent hits under their belts. Bruce wasn't the world's greatest actor, but he had charisma, and sometimes that's better.

And Jayne? She was beautiful. She was like a more homely Ava Gardner or Veronica Lake, and I mean that in the best way possible.

I'm still angry with Loubet for what he did. But maybe he was right.

All I know is that *They Are Us* is my biggest regret. Not just in the business. Biggest regret period.

TERRY MORETTI (1ST ASSISTANT DIRECTOR)

The first few weeks were as smooth as any I've had on set. We'd maybe slipped two or three days behind schedule—there were a lot of hold-ups with the lighting; Loubet wanted it to look like the projector bulb was faulty, so that the audience would really have to peer and squint for some of the scenes. It was very French, and I don't think Mel (Mel Rayner, director of photography) was really getting what Loubet wanted.

There was one day, about a week in, when Loubet went around the set and just started removing bulbs from Mel's lights. I thought Mel was gonna go for him. I had to step in and explain to Mr. Loubet that we didn't really do that sort of thing here. There were unions and what not.

This was all pretty standard fare though. It was around the third week though that things started to go wrong.

SHEILA WELSH (SECRETARY)

I was friends with some of the people on the crew—make-up, costume. We'd meet for drinks, swap stories. I had an inside line to Isaac and his various shenanigans, so that made me popular, especially after a few cocktails.

I heard there were problems with Jayne Southern on set, that she was becoming increasingly erratic. They were having issues with her in the mornings—she'd be partway through getting her face done, and she'd suddenly get up and walk away. Diva-like behavior, I guess, or that's what we thought.

I remember Karen (Karen Chanter, make-up artist) saying that she thought it was the mirror. "She can't stand to look at herself."

KAREN CHANTER (MAKE-UP ARTIST)

I have no recollection of saying that, but that doesn't mean it didn't happen.

There is one thing I've never told anyone. I got to work one morning, and the makeup trailer was trashed. There was powder and blusher everywhere. There was all this writing scrawled across the mirror in lipstick and eyeliner, but the words were all jagged and backward. I didn't know what to do, so I just dug in, cleaned the place up.

I'm pretty sure Jayne had done it, but there's no way I could confront her. I asked security if they'd seen anyone, but they said I was the only person who'd been to the trailer that morning, although they seem to think I'd arrived an hour before I did.

It didn't really matter who was responsible—it was a hell of a mess, and I was worried I'd lose my job, that they'd blame me for not locking up properly the night before.

LAURENT LOUBET (DIRECTOR)

Bruce and Jayne were romantically involved off set, even though they both had other partners. You could see it at rehearsals—they had a spark like there was no one else in the room. It was destined to go wrong, as all affairs of the heart do, but back then I shot chronologically, so I was not worried. If they grew to hate each other, it would help the verisimilitude of the piece. And it did go wrong, but maybe not for the reasons we all thought at the time.

TERRY MORETTI (1ST ASSISTANT DIRECTOR)

It was a simple kitchen scene, about two-thirds of the way through, where the wife becomes convinced that she's not talking to her husband, that he's somehow become someone else. Not physically, I guess, emotionally. They argue, and she throws the pot of water at him.

LAURENT LOUBET (DIRECTOR)

Jayne struggled on the first few takes. I told her to play it naturally, to let the words do the talking, but she kept 'acting'—raising her voice, throwing her arms out, all very melodramatic and American.

Something switched on take five though.

Karen Chanter (Make-Up Artist)

I remember sensing something was wrong. Even before Laurent called 'action,' she seemed stricken. I was trying to do my final checks, and I could see the panic in her eyes. She was like a trapped animal, looking for a way out.

Issac Peterson (Producer)

She just went for Bruce. Physically attacking him, clawing at his face. Then she suddenly stopped, staring beyond him, through the windows of the kitchen set. She staggered back, and let loose the kind of scream I hope to never hear again. I swear the set walls were vibrating with the sheer force of it.

Of course, you wouldn't have to take our word for it, you could view the footage yourself, if Loubet hadn't lost his mind later on.

Laurent Loubet (Director)

I stand by everything I did.

Bruce Mountford (Actor)

I've never spoken about *They Are Us* and I never will. I'm sorry. I'm just not comfortable discussing it.

Issac Peterson (Producer)

Bruce had his agent and manager on my back constantly after that 'kitchen incident.' Things just got worse between him and Jayne—and it wasn't just her. There was one take where Bruce just stood there, staring right down the camera lens. We had two weeks left of the shoot, so it was my job to rally the troops, keep them going, get us over the finish line. I think Loubet enjoyed the chaos, but none of the crew did. Even the set we'd built, a replica of an old townhouse, started to fall apart. They'd come in for work in the morning and find a door hanging off the hinges, or the windows smashed.

We made it to the end though. Almost.

We had enough in the can to complete the movie if we had to. It didn't matter, though, not after what happened.

SHEILA WELSH (SECRETARY)

I still remember getting the call, like it was yesterday. Jayne had driven her car into a brick wall, just off Hancock Park. She died instantly. We were in shock. Utter shock.

LAURENT LOUBET (DIRECTOR)

My last conversation with her weighs heavy on me, even now. She told me that she wished she could be who she was before she was her. I assumed she meant stardom, the pressures that came with being in the public eye. Later on, when I viewed the rushes of that day on the kitchen set, went through them inch by inch, I understood what she really meant.

BRENDA SOUTHERN (JAYNE'S YOUNGER SISTER)

They said she was on drugs, but for Chrissakes, everyone in the movies was on something. The studios would hand them out like candy. Uppers, downers, whatever it took to get you to work.

Do you know how it feels, to stand there at the funeral, for the person you love more than anything in the world and have those vultures outside with their cameras like she's still part of their damn sideshow?

I tried to get the police to re-open their investigation, but they wouldn't. There was an eyewitness to the crash, though, who said he saw two people in the car, just before it struck that wall. He said he wasn't sure which one was my sister because they both looked the same.

ISSAC PETERSON (PRODUCER)

One eyewitness out of three or four. My heart goes out to Brenda, but she was looking for answers to a question that didn't exist.

I thought the best thing would be to release the picture, after a respectful period of time, as a tribute to Jayne's wonderful career. There's precedence—Jimmy Dean, Monroe, Jean Harlow. It never happened though. Loubet stole the negative and destroyed everything—all the footage, all the work. The whole damn lot.

LAURENT LOUBET (DIRECTOR)

Jayne is standing in the kitchen, and she attacks Bruce. Then she steps back, and she stares off. The camera was on her, but there's a moment where it shifts to the side, an almost imperceptible move before it racks into a close-up on her face. I'd encouraged Mel to do that—to give an uneasy, dreamlike feel to the proceedings.

I sat there in the editing room, staring at the frame. You could just make someone out, beyond the kitchen window. It looked just like Jayne, staring back at herself, only this other Jayne has her mouth wide open, and it's like the jaws have unhinged, so there's this impossibly dark fissure spreading across the face. Move forward one frame, and it's grown even wider as if it's going to keep going, obliterate the features. In the next frame, the camera has already moved away, centering on Jayne as she prepares to unleash that horrifying scream.

I replayed it over and over and over. Then I loaded all the negatives into my car, drove out to the desert, poured gasoline over them and lit the match.

CARL MONKTON (AUTHOR)

I wrote the book while I was holidaying in Prague. I was staying at a hotel on the edge of the city, and I'd contracted some kind of nasty fever, the sort where you wake up, drenched in your own sweat, shivering hot and cold at the same time.

I don't remember much about the actual writing process. I'd wake and find myself hunched over the desk, my pencil scribbling away on the paper. I was surprised that the whole thing was coherent as it was. Three or four days, and it was done. It wasn't a long book. It wasn't particularly good, but I felt I'd unwittingly captured that sense of affliction, where you're not quite sure what is real or isn't, where it feels like reality is bending around you.

The night before I returned home, I woke up some time past three, aware of someone else in the room. I could see their silhouette, by the window frame. I remember being unsure if I was still dreaming or not, even more so when I realized I recognized the figure; I knew I was looking at myself, but that it also wasn't me. I reached for the light, but understood, on some level, that if I turned it on, I would never recover from what I saw.

So I lay there in the bed, staring at that window in the half-light, at this figure who may or may not have been there, at the way the dark outline of their mouth seemed to stretch and fall forever. I was paralyzed by the fear, by the waiting, sure that something terrible was about to happen, and then I blinked and the sun had risen, and the room was empty. My fever was broken.

I wish I could say I have never experienced anything like that since, but even now there are times when I wake in the dead of night and have to force myself to keep my eyes closed, so that I will not see that figure by the window, the one who is watching and waiting.

I couldn't help feel that I brought something back, hidden between the lines of that manuscript.

I'm not even sure now that it was me who wrote it.

SHEILA WELSH (SECRETARY)

She was such a sweet girl—even though she was older than me at the time, she'll stay the same age forever now. There will always be a Jayne Southern, caught in an eternal celluloid world, never growing old, never changing. She's still smiling somewhere, eyes bright on the silver screen, unaware of what lies ahead, of the end that waits for her.

I still stop by and put flowers by her grave every so often. It's been years, of course, but it feels like the right thing to do. I saw Isaac there once, hunched over, staring at the inscription on her stone. I didn't approach. I suppose her death must have stayed with him as well. I ran into him, a few years later, over on Melrose as he was exiting a restaurant, and I asked him about it, but he denied ever having been there.

The worst thing is I believed him. I don't know why, but I did.

I believed him.

BIRDS OF PASSAGE

—◆—

Gordon B. White

IF I DIDN'T inherit my father's natural instinct for adventure, it was drummed into me steadily enough by the time I was a young man that you wouldn't have been able to tell the difference. If you don't go looking for adventure, he would say, adventure will come looking for you. Over the years, I got so used to the counter-programming against my inborn tendency towards the comfort of safety that I wonder—if left to my own natural limits—would I have turned out differently? Are there other dimensions with less driven, but perhaps more content, versions of me? I've thought about that a lot since my father died.

My father and I had plenty of what he would call "adventures," even though we sometimes disagreed on what qualified. Road trip to the mountains and across state lines? Sure, that counted. Pushing his broken car to the dealership and walking home? Not in my book. Nowadays, although I would not trade any of them for the world, the years have smudged away most of our individual adventures. However, I will never forget Cotner's Creek.

I was ten years old and it was Labor Day weekend. I remember that clearly because there are only two real sections of my life: before that trip and after. If I ever were to return, I wonder if there would be a third fork, or if this is it? My father would have known, of course, but he's not likely to tell me now. It's not impossible—nothing truly is—but it's very unlikely.

We'd spent the week before preparing for the trip. In retrospect, I realize now how much of it had been planned in advance, but the way that my father involved me made it seem like as much my trip as his; it was as if we were equal partners stocking up for the expedition. From the way he consulted me about which canoe to rent, to the excursions up and down the supermarket aisles shopping for two days of river rations to fill the cooler that would sit between us, I seemed to have a say in every part. Finally, I thought, I was a man and my opinion mattered.

We excavated my mother's garage until we rediscovered the musty relics of sleeping bags, poncho liners, and other accouterments for camping. These were leftover things that had been squirreled away after he'd gotten married and stayed buried after he'd gotten divorced, but even their stale smells were akin to the yellowed pages of an old atlas—a reminder of adventures past and the empty spaces where still more hid. Although we had a tent, too, we agreed that we wouldn't bring it because the forecast was clear and we wanted to sleep beneath the stars. What was the point of two men heading out into the wild only to hide from it all? We wanted to experience everything.

Because I was an equal partner in name and spirit, if not in stakes and logistics, a brackish current of trepidation and excitement swept me along. What if we got lost? What if we capsized? Where would we go to the bathroom? Were there wild animals? Would it be cold? My father laughed at all of these questions but gave me straight answers, although most of those scenarios never came to pass. What did happen, though, was something that I could never have understood how to ask. Even after we went down Cotner's Creek, I'm still not sure I can.

MY MOTHER DROVE us down to the bridge over Cotner's Creek, out off the interstate between Statesville and Wallace, which is near where my father grew up. The highway crosses through long fields of cash crops slit by the occasional meandering river and further hemmed in by fingers of undeveloped forests. In the summer those fields are heavy and green, swaying under fleshy tobacco leaves or tight-lipped bolls of cotton. By the fall, however, they're in the process of being stripped bare and harrowed through for the next year's planting. It was Saturday, and she planned to pick us up further down the river the next afternoon.

She watched as my father and I off-loaded the rental canoe, our camping gear, and the Igloo chest filled with provisions. It was only years later, when she was moving in with her next husband that I came across a snapshot she had taken that day when I wasn't looking. There I was in a bright red cap and bright orange life preserver, a figurehead on the bow of the canoe like a little ornamental torchbearer. Behind me, my father is caught in just the slightest profile, forever frozen in the act of pushing off along the winding path of water and toward the veil of trees beyond. I've looked at it many times, but I still can't read in that sliver of his face if he knew what was going to happen.

As we set out, though, in the full of morning's light, it was a grand adventure. Paddling with the river gave the sensation not so much of leaving the world behind, but as if we were pushing further inside it. Our surroundings changed along each bend of the river, as if the banks were contorting themselves to show off every aspect as we moved deeper into its coils. Open fields gave way to trees, but then a broken-ankle turn would reveal a fenced-in yard. At times, the creek thinned out to barely a stream, but then another turn opened up to cataracts of near-whitewater rapids. No matter how many stories I'd heard from my father, watching the world switch from inhabited to primeval, from narrow and cultivated to wide and bursting with wild energy, it was seeing the shift with my own eyes that brought an understanding no story ever could. As we moved through these unfolding aspects, all united by the almost arbitrary cut of the creek through their disparate dimensions, it was as if I was moving backwards past my father's stories and into a deeper, stranger imagination.

There is one part, in particular, that sticks out to me more than any other. We had just come through a peculiarly narrow pinch of the creek and opened up into a wide, glassy pool. The water was brown but transparent for about a foot down before it clouded over, resisting the sun that punched through the grasping branches and into the shallows. Beneath us, as if the shade of our canoe was obfuscation from a higher plane, long-bodied gar swam up from the clouded depths and followed beneath us. In our shadow a new layer of their world was presented and so they rose up, their needle-noses and armored flanks primitive and unintelligible in this thin layer. I wondered if they knew that my father and I could have held gig hooks to spear them or nets to ensnare them, but that to us, in particular, they were curiosities. They had lived for decades in this river and their ancestors had for millennia been kings of this simple cut of water through the deep red banks, but even though they knew nothing of us, we could have—had we wanted—been a danger. Still, they swam and basked. They dove back deep into the blackness, and if they saw us—if our canoe and our unused armaments registered to them at all—it only gave them more freedom, allowing them to rise higher in our shadow before descending back into their depths, unable to ever properly describe to their fish wives and fish children what marvels they'd seen.

Is it any wonder, then, that as the whole world of the creek grew so gradually stranger and stranger the further we travelled—as new creatures swam up and the banks bleached from red to gray, as the trees grew crooked and vines hung like witch's hair—that I failed to appreciate the full extent of how different things truly had become?

As the day ended and the palimpsest of sunset colors and evening sounds settled around us, we found a bend in the river with a wide open field next to it. Because it was so vast and clearly unused by other people, we set up camp further off the bank, up on a little rise. The canoe stayed below, wedged into the grey clay at the waterline and lashed to a few saplings. We spread our tarps and bedding over the dead leaves and gnarled roots, but the ground's chill still permeated up through the layers.

The night was cool and a thin film of clouds swept back and forth across the wide, hungry sky. We were just at the point where the ground opened up into the field and the trees overhead still clung to the modesty of a few leaves, but beyond them the silver teeth of stars were starting to nibble through the bruise of the evening. Looking up, the night felt cooler to be that bright with distant fire.

We made our own fire of the thick branches already littering the ground. Although it hadn't rained in days, those long arms of wood had soaked up the moisture from the cool ground and the water below. Their bark hung like damp skin, hissing and whistling before taking the flame. Still, once we had the fire going, the cocoon of light it wove was enough to make me feel safe within its embrace.

After a day of paddling, our provisions of box juice, peel-top soup cans, and King's Hawaiian Rolls was practically a feast. As usual, we talked about small things—my school, our plans for a tree house once he found a new place—but all of it took on a grave importance there by the river. It was as if we were discussing ancient things, as if our lives outside the woods had become myths that occurred centuries ago or perhaps that wouldn't occur for centuries yet. Maybe it was that dislocation that unmoored my father, which sent him back down that silver thread of memory outside the firelight. Whatever the reason, he then told me a story I'd never heard before.

"When I was a boy," he began, "I grew up about fifteen miles from the bridge where we set off. You know how I've told you before about my best friend Gary? Well, he and I did this same trip that you and I are doing. Gary and I put in at the same spot—although it was a different bridge back then, an old one made of bricks that they tore down when the highway came through."

The thing about his stories, I've come to realize, is that I never could quite tell when they were true and when they just felt that way. They all felt real enough then and, in time, all of the past takes on that same grain that blurs true and untrue, so the only thing I guess that really matters is who remembers it and how it felt to hear it.

He went on: "When Gary and I made this trip, though, it was summer. It was so humid that year, so damp in the air, that do you remember that little waterfall in the rapids we took after lunch? Well, he and I did the same thing, but we got a good foot further past the edge before we tipped over because the canoe was paddling through that steamy air."

"Was it the same as it is now, though?" I asked. "Because it feels, maybe, strange?"

I couldn't quite put what I felt into words, but from the slight drip of a frown that escaped him, I could tell he knew what I meant, but that he hadn't been planning on taking his story down this path. At least, not yet.

"Yes." He swallowed hard and looked at me with the steel glint that meant that this was man talk. No anger, no fear, but still deathly serious. "I think that's why I brought you here."

"This place is," he fluttered his hand for a moment, trying to conjure the right word out of the fire. "It's a soft place, I think. It isn't quite here, and isn't quite there. There aren't people and there aren't roads, but you can feel that something more surrounds us."

It took me a moment to respond. I held a paper towel napkin in my hands, which I balled and unrolled to an unheard rhythm. He was right, or at least it felt like he was right. Because there I could also feel something under that black dome of sky and all the million fly specks of distant light above us that peered through and then were swept away in the current of clouds. Some enormousness that seemed to both pull me up and press me down at the same time. Out in the distance, the soft yellow bruise of light pollution over far-off cities seemed like dapples of light on the river bottom, obscured by layers of some other medium that my father and I were now suspended in, just like gar in the river.

"I feel it," I said, although the description of it wouldn't come to me for years. But the way I said it, my dad knew. He nodded.

"I don't know what you'd call it," he finally said. With a slender stick, he prodded the embers on our low fire and sent the shadows skipping like water bugs. "Maybe the bigness of nature, or a great spirituality. Something, though, you don't feel at home."

He looked out for a moment at the darkness, at the stars above. "Sometimes," he said, "I think about all the possible worlds we could have lived in, but that we're in the one that makes you my son and me your father and brings us here. It sounds stupid," he paused, "but sometimes I look at you and I think, 'Are you real?'"

"Yeah," I said. He laughed and I smiled, even though I don't know if he saw me do it, there in the shadow just beyond the fire's light. For a while, we just sat and listened to the world.

"Do you feel it everywhere?" I eventually asked, meaning the thing he had talked about and meaning everywhere outdoors, but even though I didn't clarify, my father knew. He and I shared a wavelength like that.

"Maybe if you try real hard, but I've never felt it quite like I feel it here." He leaned back, caught between the orange light below and the silver light above. "Just think," he went on, "that outside of our fire light, it's miles to the nearest town. Straight up and out above us, for millions of miles is nothing but empty space. Beneath our skin, hidden from sight, run rivers of blood and cells and atoms and, deeper still, the empty space between them. You and I and everything else are just thin layers between space and distances, just skins between mysteries we could never know."

He stopped, probably wondering if he'd gone too far or said too much. Then he looked and me and asked, "Are you scared?"

"No," I said, "but it is a little scary."

"Yeah," he nodded as he spoke, "but it's also kind of awesome."

As if to underscore the end of that thread, I threw my crumpled napkin into the fire. I watched, however, as the edges caught the ember, glowing and curling up at the tips like wings. It must have been shaped just right by the chaotic worrying—a broken bird accidentally birthed through dirty origami—because the folds caught the warm air beneath them and it was buoyed up, burning, into flight. Up over the fire, we watched it rise, catching feathers of flame as it rose, shrinking and consuming itself from the outside in as it drafted up towards the stars. All told, it couldn't have taken more than a few seconds, but it my mind there is a forever-playing slow motion shot of the paper phoenix, rising up into the blackness and fading from view—too far, too small, too burned—until it seemed to be swallowed into the night beyond us.

We sat in silence for a moment after it vanished, listening to the wood whisper in its combustion and the crickets sing along. Behind us, the water chuckled softly and, on the other side, the great open field lay quiet in the starlight. Everything just beyond the fire was bluer than the deepest water and, beyond that, only black.

As my eyes grew accustomed to the gloaming, however, a single point of light emerged in the distance. Seeing it, too, my father stood up and pointed across the field. Despite the stars above, the darkness was like a curtain of black wool pulled from the ground to the trees, but across from us, near where I remembered the opposite tree line being, there was a glow. It was faint, but pushing through the cover like a hot vein beneath night's scales.

"Is that a fire?" I asked, but I knew it was. Immediately, I recalled the rising flame from our fire and had visions of a soft coal falling across the field, catching hold there on the ground. "Did we do that?"

"I don't think so," my father replied. "It looks too big, and it's too damp for anything to catch from that little spark."

"Is it other people?" My imagination again went to the other side, now peering around at the possible figures surrounding that distant beacon. I had thought that we were far from town and it seemed un-likely that anyone else would find the same adventure here that we did. I didn't have the capacity then to conjure up a full parade of horribles, but dim shapes around a greasy fire were enough to set my hairs on end.

As we watched, though, across the field a single flake of fire rose up into the air. From our distant vantage, it was just a speck, like a star falling upwards in bad gravity, but I knew what it was. The fragile paper wings of a crumpled bird, rising and vanishing in the air. I knew that ours had looked the same at this distance.

My father moved from the fire's edge to the border of the darkness. Eyes ahead, he leaned down to probe the shadows, returning with a long, broken branch. The branch's tips were still clotted with leaves, which my father then dipped into our dwindling fire. They smoked, but the flame caught hold and soon gripped the branch in full. My father stood, holding the fiery flag before him like a bright red wing. Then, turning to face our far-off friends, my father began to wave the burning branch—back and forth, back and forth, then pause. Then again.

It felt like hours, but must have only been minutes, because my father's makeshift torch had only just burned itself out when we received a response. There it was, across the field as if in the black mirror of a river light years away. The response, or the perfect mimicry, in flaming semaphore—back and forth, back and forth. Then again. Then nothing.

My father was many things over the course of his life, but what he was that night was calm. While images of monsters crowded my head, haunting visions of dark-eyed reflections of a black-eyed father and son waving their flaming lure across the no-man's land between us, my father remained sanguine.

"Okay," he finally said. "Well, it must be people like us. Probably just passing through." I wanted to believe him, but what gave him away was the stoic deadness to his voice. He was a man of large passions and bold humors, so to hear him modulated was even worse than silence.

Still, through his strength and my own dogged impersonation, we managed to ignore our sister camp for the rest of the evening. We let our fire dwindle and die, and then waited as the one across the field similarly faded from sight. As the night wore on, though, if I borrowed my father's strength to set up camp and eventually crawl into the sleeping bag, then actually falling into sleep was my own weakness. I'm fairly certain that even though he lay down, too, my father never truly slept because otherwise he wouldn't have been awake when it happened.

"Are you awake," he asked, but loud enough that it was a question that contained its own answer. It was still thin night, not yet tipping towards morning, and if the sky was a war between black and silver, black was still the clear victor. In fact, as he shook me gently and I first opened my eyes, I wasn't sure it wasn't a dream.

"Are you awake," he asked again, but he saw that I was because he put his rough palm over my eyes. "Just stay like that," he said, "but you remember where the boat is." It wasn't a question. "If I say so, you go and push off and don't stop, understand?" I nodded by instinct more than awareness, but he must have known, because he said again: "Even if I'm not there, you go alone to the bridge. Do you understand?"

There, beneath the clasp of his hand, I knew that he was serious. I took a moment to let it sink in and visualize myself running from whatever unknown horror lay in the space beyond my father's protection. I could do that, I thought. It would be an adventure.

I nodded.

"Okay," he whispered, and drew his hand away. I rose up, though whether on my own or under his power, I can't quite say. I looked out into the distance across the field, expecting to see the neighboring fire rekindled, but instead of illumination all I saw was the roiling dark.

The night itself moved, and the earth itself unrolled.

What at first I had thought to be distant trees moved and swayed, revealing themselves as great long appendages slick with the faint starlight. They towered above us, falling and rising in time to a rhythm that we could not hear. Neither my father nor I could speak to interrupt that moment.

High above, the clouds parted and the bright yellow moon, now full, gazed down on us. Then it rolled its pupil around and the sheer gravity of the thing's attention pinned me to the ground, then slid off me like a wave.

"Does it see us?" I meant to ask, although I don't know if I did or if the way I gripped my father's hand asked for me. But he just shook his head as the giant eye looked away. He hugged me close.

What we saw was awesome, in the truest sense. It was gorgeous and grand and terrible all at once.

It was like the Northern Lights, but of darkest black on a layer of black.

It writhed like the coils of giant snakes in the hands of boundless night.

In the distance behind, a mountain shrugged its shoulders and began to move.

And then it was dark again, as if a veil woven of a new kind of darkness had fallen. One that wasn't the absence of things, but rather the richest depths of possibility. A darkness from which anything could emerge.

In the years that followed, I've theorized but abandoned all theories on what we saw. Something ancient from beneath the earth that sunk away again without a trace? An echo of a form on a different dimension, cast like a shadow onto our world? A god? A demon? In the end, I don't know what to call it, but seeing it made me—joyful? In a flash, I had been gifted indisputable proof that there is strangeness in the world that we may never know, but that this universe is an amazing and infinite place. Even if our roles are smaller than we could have ever imagined, to be a part of such a grand machine made me ecstatic.

But even in the twists and turns as my mind reshaped to accommodate the possibilities of what could be born from the fertile dark, something more tangible emerged. Across the field, two globes of light rose up from the ground. Steadily, they began to move, bobbing and undulating like nodding Cyclopes across the field. My father and I both looked down at our hands to make sure we weren't doing anything that these lights were now mirroring, but no. They were moving on their own.

"Shit," my father said. It was a rare curse that slipped past his lips, at least when I was around. What he did when I wasn't around, however, is something that no one but the dead can answer.

At some point, I suppose, he must have planned what he did next, but I don't know when he could have. Maybe, as you get older, you have a store of actual or imagined experiences to draw from as needed, some stock built up in worries or dreams. Maybe when he thought his son was in danger there was suddenly a bloom of possibilities that he had seen all once as if in a giant knot and, from that, he picked the thread that ran out our cord for the rest of our days. All I truly know is that he moved without hesitation.

He picked up a stick and shoved our remaining roll of toilet paper on it. He handed it to me and grabbed another stick, repeating the process with the roll of paper towels. Two sprays of lighter fluid and a light-anywhere match stuck against a rock, and suddenly we both held torches. Although the burst of light blinded me, washing out the rest of the world beyond that blast of illumination, in the distance I could make out giant shadows crawling across the empty fields toward us. The bulbs of their illumination still gleamed even in my swollen eyes, but I wonder what possible horrors or beauties the glare had spared me.

"Wave your torch up and down with me," my father said. We did, like the beating of a bird's broken wings out of unison. Out across the field, although still drawing closer, the iridescent spheres held aloft by the long, dark things did the same.

"Run out ten steps, wave it, then run back to me."

I ran, every step away from my father pushing deeper into the viscous night. I waved my flaming beacon and saw him do the same with his.

Across the field, the appendages—for what else could they have been other than some intelligent part of that great mass?—mimicked our motion. I ran back to my father, the torch swaying up and down as my distant double did the same.

Reunited by the ashes of our dead fire, in our makeshift torchlight, I saw a look in my father's eyes that I had never seen before. I knew love and I knew dedication, but until that moment, I did not know sacrifice.

He grabbed my torch from me and swung them both up and down, up and down. Across the field and drawing closer, the two lights did the same.

"Stay here," Dad whispered. "Close your eyes and count to one hundred. If I'm not back by then," he nodded towards the river, "you take the canoe. Got it?"

"Yeah," I managed to say.

He smiled. "It's an adventure, isn't it?"

Then he ran, out into the empty field and away from me, swinging the branches of fire like a bird flapping its wings, drawing a path across the dark sky. Across the field, the two lights did the same. They followed him out into the void, towards the wall of the woods on the far side of the field.

I closed my eyes and started counting. Surrounded by the silence, every number in my head was an explosion. At ten I was brave, by twenty I was frightened, I was sucking back tears by thirty. But the night seemed to swallow my sobbing and by sixty I had stopped. I made it to one hundred, because that's what my father would have done. In part, though, I think I wanted to give it as long as I could, to see what might happen.

Most of what occurred next, I can remember, but all the details are so wound together that even now I lack the perseverance to fully untangle them, so I instead decisively cut through it with only a glance at the pieces. How I opened my eyes in darkness and stumbled over roots back to the banks. How I shoved the canoe out into the black road of the river. How blobs of light seemed to follow me along the shore even as the current pulled me away, fading in the growing dawn until I realized that I was starting at patches of the rising sun coming through branches over the smoking silver ribbon of water.

Hours passed. When I finally got to the bridge, I leapt from the canoe. Feet sucking into the red clay bank, I wrestled the boat up into the switch-thin reeds to wait beneath the very literal and mundane crossroads. Over the hours from gray dawn to robin's egg blue morning and on to golden noon, my terror ebbed. In its wake, however, I could feel there was a new high water mark drawn onto my soul—a place where the fantastic had reached up to and left its thin, but indelible line. I didn't know then that I might always be searching for that level again, but in the bright light of day—and later, too, even in the darkest night—I knew that there was nothing in this world, or any other, for me to truly fear.

As a result, when the forest wall down beyond the bend began to creak, I again felt that equal mixture of excitement and trepidation. As the skin of the woods trembled, as the knots of branches began to spread, as something emerged, I was open to the full possibility of what might be emerging.

But, still, I was surprised to see my father stumble out of the brambles.

My father, his face ash gray and his beard much longer than it should have been. My father, staggering beneath some unseen weight, looking gaunt and haunted and as if he was surprised to find himself in the space that he now occupied. He must have seen the canoe or the movement of the weeds, though, because even before I could call out to him, he broke into the closest thing he could manage to a run, bending and tripping through the deep mud and the high grass.

"Gary?" he called out as he approached.

"No," I managed to say. At the sound of my voice, even though every movement was already falling over the top of every other, he moved even faster. He crashed through the last few feet, almost collapsing on top of me, but then wrapping me up in arms that felt thinner than I'd remembered from the night before.

"Is it you?" he asked, pulling me close. "Are you real?"

"Yeah," was all I could say.

He hugged me then, hard, and I'm not ashamed to say I cried. With my face buried in his chest, I could smell the river, but also his sweat and the fire's smoke and something that tingled like if magnets had a smell and you spun them north to south beneath your nose. I never loved anyone more.

"Let's not tell your mom, okay?" he said.

At the time, I thought it was the standard seal of the adventure—that we keep it to ourselves. It was only much later that I realized we wouldn't have been able to adequately describe it. It was better, I now understand, to hold the knowledge of an unlimited world in silence than to make it smaller by trying to explain it.

WE ONLY SPOKE of it once afterwards, years later, when he was in the hospital for the last time. His wife and my sisters were outside talking to a doctor and the whole coterie of aunts and cousins were waiting in the lounge like a conspiracy of ravens, so I was the only one by his bedside when he opened his eyes. I leaned in close, because his throat was parched and his voice was breaking.

"I'm not afraid," he said. He hadn't said what about, but there was really only the one thing—the big Other that hovers over most of us.

"That's good," I said. "Because I might be." I was used to his trailing off by then and was glad of the silence that bubbled up, but then he spoke again. His eyes got suddenly clear and his voice was strong, like we were back on the river and talking serious man talk again.

"Do you remember Cotner's Creek?"

I nodded.

"I'm glad we were together to see it," he said. "Now, though, there's something else."

"I know."

"I'm not afraid," he said again. The way he looked at me but beyond me, I don't know what he was seeing or if he was fully with me, but it's the only thing that I would give anything not to truly know. Then he said it: "It's an adventure, isn't it?"

He squeezed my hand, his taut sinews closing in like a bird's talons or the long mouths of a school of gar. Then he closed his eyes and fell back into something like sleep. Beneath his thin covering, deep blue rivers of veins pumped slowly along and I could hear his breath rattling beneath the paper of his skin and in the great empty space behind his ribs.

I never spoke with him again.

As I myself grow older, I often think back to that night on the river. About how there's a world around us, but beyond us, too. A world that takes things, changes them, but sometimes gives them back. All of it— all of it is ripples.

I think back to the flaming wings of paper, rising up and vanishing into the darkness before the thing came to us. Even though my father has since passed on and I, too, am getting old, I have no fear, because I know that in the sky above, in the water below, past that thin thread of night, there are mysteries that we can never know. There is more to it all than you or I could ever fully comprehend and, while that terrifies me, it also brings me comfort.

I know that even if the universe has no thought or regard for our existence, we can give it meaning through our own actions and our love for one another. Instead of hiding in the darkness, we take to wings of flame that bear us on like birds of passage, beating bravely out into the great unknown.

THE HALF-SOULED WOMAN

———◆———

Nina Shepardson

LOOKING BACK ON it, Carrick was amazed that no one had ever tried to bribe him before.

He had been carrying people across the border river for a little over ten years now. As was customary, the client's family paid him whatever they could. Most often the payment took the form of coins. Silver was the most common, as the majority of people in the riverside country were neither rich nor poor, but a few paid with copper and fewer still with gold.

Some were so destitute that they didn't even have copper to pay Carrick with. These unfortunates offered him food (which usually meant they were missing a meal) or cloth (which usually meant they wouldn't have a cloak come wintertime). Carrick tried to accept these meager gifts with as much gratitude as a pouch of gold coins handed over by a wealthy merchant. That was how his predecessor had trained him.

He had never outright refused a client. Once or twice during his tenure, a criminal had been executed for crimes so vile that even his own parents would refuse to pay for his passage across the river. The corpses of such men rotted away on the near bank until nothing was left. Legend had it that these trapped souls were the origin of the things in the river.

Sometimes, a family would beg Carrick to allow them to accompany their loved one across the river. They wanted to see their spouse or parent or child sit up in the boat and step onto the far bank. They hoped for a chance to say goodbye, or reassure the client of their love, or ask a question they had been afraid to pose during the person's life. Carrick refused these requests as gently as he could. He reminded them of what law and custom dictated: that only the client and the boatman could cross the river.

These unconventional situations were few and far between. Most crossings were uneventful. (Carrick mentally scolded himself for even thinking the word "boring." It wasn't a word that one should apply to so solemn and important a duty.) Even in the strangest circumstances, though, no one had ever tried to bribe him.

Until Risia came, looking for her sister.

RISIA'S SISTER HAD died the previous winter. A sickness had crept down from the mountains like the scout of an invading army. Many had died, so many that Carrick didn't remember them all individually.

"Sini was my best friend," Risia said. Her eyes were downcast. Carrick couldn't tell whether it was from sorrow or respect for his calling. "More than that, really. She was the other half of me." She held out a tiny wooden box. "There's cinnamon inside. Please."

If the box was full, the value of this gift outweighed anything else Carrick had ever received. But he closed his hands over Risia's and pushed the box back toward her. "I'm sorry. I know you want to see Sini, but I can't take you."

Risia looked up at his face for the first time. "I don't want to just see her. I want to take her place. I want her to live again. Please, I'm sure no one there will notice any difference. She looks just like me."

CARRICK BOWED HIS head as the old man climbed out of the boat. During the last few years of his life, he'd relied on a cane to walk, but now he stepped confidently onto the shore and strode away into the fog.

Bracing his pole against the bank, Carrick pushed the boat back into the river. As he did so, movement on shore caught his attention.

He'd never seen the dead bathing or washing their clothes in the river. He assumed that, like the living, they performed such chores in the smaller streams and lakes. This place of transition was sacred, and besides, he could imagine that even the dead wouldn't want to encounter the things in the river. Sometimes those who had predeceased a client would come to meet him, but this motion was well downstream of where the old man had disembarked.

The movement resolved into the figure of a woman dressed in the traditional gray-blue robe. She emerged from the fog and stood on the very edge of the bank. As Carrick pushed off, the water lapped at her toes.

When he saw her face clearly, he almost dropped his pole in the river.

He had seen the same face looking up into his eight days ago. The same green eyes meeting his gaze, the same black hair cascading around her shoulders, the same slender fingers holding out a box of cinnamon.

"Risia?" Carrick drove his pole down into the riverbed, anchoring the boat in place. The woman stared at him in silence for a few moments before stepping back and receding into the fog.

Carrick sat in his boat for some time after reaching the near shore. How could Risia have gotten across the river without him? No one who hadn't been trained as a boatman would brave the river. And swimming across was out of the question.

"Master, you said that if someone asks to be taken across with a client, we must refuse. But what if they try to cross on their own? The river isn't that deep, and the current isn't very fast."

Carrick's mentor had deep crows' feet at the corners of his eyes from his frequent smiles, both the gentle ones that comforted the grieving and the raucous ones that came with the celebration of his continued life. Now his face shifted, as if he were an actor replacing one mask with another. His brow furrowed, his lips turned downward, and a shadow seemed to pass through his eyes. "I saw someone try to swim the river once. A man whose son had broken his neck falling out of a tree. He couldn't see the shapes moving toward him,

NINA SHEPARDSON | 181

because they were almost the same color as the water."

Carrick leaned forward, resting his elbows on the table. *"What did you do?"*

"I turned the boat toward him."

"Even though we're not supposed to delay in taking the client across?"

Carrick's master nodded. *"I've been our country's boatman for over forty years, and that's the only time I've ever broken the rules. I couldn't bring myself to believe that the boy would want me to let his father drown."*

Carrick knew full well that drowning was an optimistic guess at what would happen to anyone who swam the river, but he refrained from pointing it out.

"I hoped to beat the things to him, or maybe that my presence would scare them off. After all, there's enough of them that they could capsize the boat if they wanted, but they've never done it. I thought maybe there was some pro-hibition against them harming the boatman, and that they'd leave me alone if I came to the man's aid."

Carrick's mentor had already been old when they met. Now Carrick imagined him as he must have been in his youth, with a vibrant red beard and broad, straight shoulders. He wouldn't want to tangle with such a man, especially when he carried a stout wooden pole in his hands. *"Were you able to save him?"*

The shaking of a lowered head gave him his answer.

THE THINGS IN the river had never crawled up onto the shore, but most people were still wary of building houses too close to the bank. Carrick spoke with those few who might have seen someone stepping into the water. According to them, no one had approached the river but the fami-lies of Carrick's clients, and they had stayed where they were supposed to.

A few days later, Carrick transported a woman who'd died in child-birth. As she clambered up onto the opposite shore, he saw Risia again, standing on a rock that jutted out into the water. The next week, she watched him ferry a middle-aged craftsman whose heart had given out.

Carrick hadn't known Risia and Sini, so he had to ask around to find out where they lived. Their abode was a two-story house, with a shop on the ground floor and living quarters above, like many in the riverside country. Carrick leaned against a wall across the street, watching. The shop was clearly open: people entered and left with boxes or wrapped parcels. The silversmith whose shop was next to the sisters' glared at him over a bristly mustache, but his face softened when he recognized who Carrick was. Then his lips pressed together again, the fear of thievery being replaced by a far more serious one. Some of the townsfolk whispered that the boatman knew in advance who was going to die.

The silversmith looked up and down the street, made to reenter his shop, stopped with one foot over the threshold, turned around, and walked across the street to where Carrick stood. "Good day, boatman," he said.

Carrick offered a reassuring smile. "Good day. I'm afraid I don't know your name, sir."

"I'm Pelman," said the silversmith. He held out a hand for Carrick to shake.

"Our meeting enriches me," Carrick answered. "Is there any particular reason you wished to speak with me?"

"Well, boatman, I can't help noticing that you've been standing across from my shop for several hours. Is there...ought I to be worried?" His upper lip was twitching a bit, making his mustache look like a restless animal.

"I'm sorry to have worried you. It isn't your shop I was watching."

The color drained from Pelman's ruddy cheeks. "It's not Miss Aubergine, is it? Risia?"

Carrick opened his mouth to answer, but Pelman cut him off. "Is she really to be taken so soon after her sister? Isn't there anything you can do?"

This, too, was an idea some people had about the boatman, that he could sometimes prevent a death. Some said he could only do it if the would-be decedent was pure of heart; others claimed that a kinsman had to volunteer to take their place.

"No, no! It's not that, either. I have no reason to think either of you are in danger." Carrick searched for a way to explain himself without telling Pelman what he'd seen. The last thing he wanted to do was start a panic by making people think something was wrong with the land of the dead. He finally settled on, "She just seemed to be hit especially hard by Sini's death."

"Oh, she was." Pelman looked less frightened now, but far from happy. "She didn't open the shop for a week, said she couldn't bear to run it without her sister. Now she seems to be even more dedicated to it than she was before. I suppose she's trying to stay busy and keep her mind off things."

Or she was trying to make enough money to pay for a good bribe, Carrick thought.

"You have to expect it would be especially difficult, though, what with them being twins and all," Pelman continued. "My wife's family came from the mountain country, and they say there that one twin can't live long without the other. She was afraid that Risia would follow Sini across the river."

Of course! Carrick would have jumped in the river rather than admit it to anyone, but his memory of taking Sini across had blurred together with the other trips he'd made during that plague-struck winter. When Risia said that Sini looked just like her, he'd assumed she was referring to the close resemblance often shared by siblings. If they were truly identical, it was Sini he'd seen on the opposite bank, not Risia at all.

His shoulders slumped in relief at this easy explanation, but it was short-lived. Sini's behavior was still unusual. *Why is she waiting for Risia? Is she expecting her sister to join her soon?*

CARRICK LEANED BACK in the armchair, his feet resting on an embroidered footstool. The book resting on his lap was written in a precise, steady hand that matched Carrick's memories of its owner. His predecessor had told him most of the things he'd need to know in person, but there had been obscure cases over the course of his tenure. These, along with more general records of the people he'd carried across the river, were described in the book.

There was no mention of twins, but Carrick noticed that as time went on, his mentor used more and more words to describe the brief glimpses of the other side he'd caught through the fog. From what he'd been able to see, it seemed very much like the riverside country. There were cobbled lanes, houses of wood or stone, even farm animals. (The latter had caused him some consternation. Animals weren't carried across by the boatman, so where did the ones on the other side come from?)

After he closed the book, Carrick spent a few minutes recalling the fleeting images he'd spied through the fog. He wondered about how his clients spent their new lives and whether his parents ever thought of him.

PELMAN'S WIFE, MARIS, had the tall, thin build common among the mountain people. Like Pelman, she had been nervous about a boatman's interest in her, but Carrick reassured her that he was just curious about her people's traditions. "There may be wisdom we don't have, and it could help me serve my clients better." *One in particular.* He sat down at the dining-room table with Maris and Pelman, turning a cup of tea around and around in his hands while she spoke.

Given his profession, she naturally talked first about the sky burials. She reminisced about the woman who'd been bird-caller in her youth. Carrick had never liked birds: they were too fickle, never content to stay in one place for any length of time. It was strange to think that if he'd been born in the mountain country, he would have had a different calling.

He guided Maris to stories of people whose final journey didn't go quite as planned. Most of these tales didn't end well, and he could tell Maris didn't like telling them, so he thanked her with a bowed head.

"If you'll pardon me, may I ask you just one more thing? I notice that the stories of things going wrong all feature people who've had some contact with the deeper truths. A shaman's apprentice, a woman who was dead for a few minutes and was returned to life, a man cured of the wendigo's touch. Do your people believe twins have such access to the deep truths? Are there any stories about them?"

Maris and Pelman shared a look. "My people say that twins share one soul between their bodies," Maris said. During her recounting of abnormal events, she had looked anywhere but at him. Now she met his gaze with determination. "When one twin takes to the sky, the other follows soon after."

"But," Pelman jumped in, "it doesn't look like that will be the case with Miss Aubergine."

Carrick held Maris's stare. He knew what she wanted to ask. *Does it?*

SCRAPS AND BOLTS of cloth surrounded Carrick. He felt like he was in God's palace in the days before the world, with half-finished bits of Creation on every side. *Here's the sun, and over there's the moon, and that thing on the chair will be a wolf.*

"I can't finish anything," said Risia. "Not since I used up all the material Sini left behind."

Looking closer, Carrick could see some pieces that were quite near completion. A pair of midnight-blue gloves, a lavender dress with a print of delicate snowdrops. "You seem to be doing all right to me."

Risia shook her head. "They should have lace, but Sini was the lace-maker. She was half the reason people bought my clothes at all. More than half."

"But your work is beautiful! Any lacemaker in the country would be happy to work with you, I'm sure."

Risia just stared at him, and Carrick wondered if this had been the wrong thing to say. He was good at comforting people when they brought clients to him. He assured them that he would get their loved one to the other side safely, that he would watch the client take their first steps on the opposite shore. "That's what they need most," his mentor had admonished him. "They have to know they can trust you to do right by the client. They need to know that their family member or friend or comrade is starting a new life, that they haven't become one of the things in the river." He had never sat down and talked with someone after their kin had been delivered.

"It's like..." Risia looked around, as if hoping to find something in the room she could point to by way of explanation. "She was like a mirror. I could look at her and see my own thoughts and feelings and...she helped me understand myself. Now I feel like one of the *strigoi* the mountain people fear, who can't see their own reflections. I feel like I don't know who I am anymore."

Carrick thought about what Maris had said. The strigoi were the mountain country's equivalent of the things in the river; they were what happened when a dead person was denied passage to the next life. They were trapped souls whose bodies had rotted away. But what of a body with only half a soul? What of a person left behind on this side of the river, while half their soul had gone on to the other? Was that a monster too? He remembered Sini standing on the shore, as no other person had ever done after passing on. *My duty is to help the dead start their new life, but what if she can't? What if the next life needs a whole soul too? What is my duty now?*

THE PROW OF the boat bumped against the shore. Risia looked up and down the bank. "Where is she?"

Carrick was wondering that too. *The one time I actually bring her sister, and she isn't here!*

The mist that shrouded the land across the river shifted, and Carrick saw a slate-blue shadow within it. *A shroud inside a shroud.*

Sini stood at the edge of the fog, peering at Risia as if she couldn't quite believe her sister was really there.

"Sini!" Risia shot to her feet, making the boat rock.

"Sit down!" Carrick grabbed Risia's wrist and pulled her back down onto the bench. "If you fall in the water, it'll be worse than staying on the other side, believe me!"

Risia sat down and cast an anxious look at the river to either side of the boat. There were a few ripples, but nothing broke the surface. "You said you'd take me across."

"I said I'd let you see your sister. I can't break the rules to pieces; who knows what would happen! But I couldn't leave things as they were, either. So I found another solution." Carrick raised the pole out of the water and laid it flat across the palms of his hands. Water dripped from both ends into the river as he held it out to Risia. "Every time you bring someone across, you can see her."

"And what will happen to you? Do I take you back across?"

Carrick shook his head. "No. I'll get off here. That's how the calling is passed from one boatman to the next. You'll find plenty of books and journals in the cottage that'll teach you what to do."

"But your family—"

Carrick shook his head again. "Surely you've heard the rumors." This was another thing people said about the boatmen: that the other shore of the river drew them, like insects to a pitcher plant. Anyone who got too close to them might be drawn in too. A few boatmen had married and raised families, but not many.

Risia bowed her head and took the pole. "Thank you." She shimmied over on the bench so Carrick could get by. As he passed, she said, "Good luck in your new life, boatman."

Carrick paused with one foot on the boat and one on the shore. "I'm not the boatman anymore."

Risia smiled. Carrick didn't know it, but it was the first time she'd smiled since Sini's death. "Good luck in your new life, Carrick."

"May you guide the dead well, boatman." Carrick stepped onto the farther shore. He breathed in, and the fog spiraled into his lungs. He wanted to say more to Risia but knew he could no longer speak in the presence of a living person. He walked into the fog and was surprised to find that it wasn't cold and damp as he expected. As he moved through it, he heard sounds coming from beyond. Voices and footsteps, the lowing of cows and clucking of chickens, the rattle of wagon wheels on a road and the thunk of a hammer pounding in nails. They were the same sort of sounds that one might hear upon entering any living town.

Then he was through the fog, and the land of his new life spread out before him.

RELEASED

———◆———

Timothy B. Dodd

WHEN HE PULLED up the first time I was walking away from town on the straight stretch of Clinton Street, the vacant warehouses lined up between me and the Conemaugh. I didn't even notice what kind of car he drove. I just watched as the automatic window slowly rolled down.

Plain white T-shirt and a construction worker's tan. Hair slicked back. Thin mustache that looked slightly crooked. Tiny, ferreting eyes.

"Give your legs a rest. Let me give you a lift." Front teeth gap. Skoal.

I jumped back, scraping my shoulder against the building brick, and kept walking. It hadn't been more than a couple hours since I dropped off the Greyhound into town. Did I look drunk or high or homeless or vulnerable?

I'm supposed to be staying now with my old high school friend "Terry Thacker" who works at Gautier Steel. Spent weeks getting that "confirmed." I had only one free ticket coming to me, which meant one chance, one choice. I chose here because it was the only place no one on the staff got excited about.

"Seen better days," my case manager, Jane, said.

"Yeah, kind of a dying place," Lina added. She was day manager at

188

the center.

"I never heard a good thing about it," Charles told me a few times. He was one of my doctors. His only interest is fancy dining as far as I can tell.

So they got me my ticket grudgingly, took me and my bag to the bus station in Clarion, and sent me on my way with a "You sure you don't want to go back to your brother's instead?" They got me a position at Sheetz too. Part-time grunt work. I'm supposed to report there this week, but I don't know. I probably won't go. Well, truth is, I know I won't go.

Johnstown's only known nowadays for the flood that roughed it up over a hundred years ago, and you walk around these old steel towns never expecting to come under threat. Sure, you might hear an argument on the street over child custody. "Come on, Terrence. Catch up with Mommy." You might hear drunks and loud belches from alleyways or an occasional brawl. And sometimes obese men three times larger than anyone I ever saw in Iraq can appear out of the dust behind the old buildings—walking, but only barely. You'll hear a few honks that might mean, "You don't belong here." Or, "What the hell are you doing walking around this place?" Or, "Cut your hair, you bum." But you shouldn't really ever experience anything that puts you in danger. Nothing that puts your already shitty health at risk.

It's Sunday afternoon now, so streets are even emptier. Church services are done: Lutheran, Catholic, Methodist, whatever. The NFL games and engine tinkering and Sunday brunch with buttery mashed potatoes, or the sleeping after taking your church clothes off—it's all done somewhere else.

When no one's around, you tend to notice the ugly sculptures on the city's sidewalks. Rusted metal put together for no reason, not even to praise God. Some of these sculptures cost a city millions of dollars. You can get numb looking at them. Morley's Dog is also spread around town. The original was some sculpture or piece of ceramic, I don't really know, that was rescued downstream after the flood. They returned it to its owner, but upon death he donated the dog to the city. Now it's displayed in a little green space near City Hall, standing proud like it knows it defied the odds of survival. The dog became so popular that they started replicating it. Now you'll keep running into them all over town: in front of the fire station, the library, at the edge of the Kroger's parking lot.

I sit down on a bench on the square, Central Park. On the ground at my feet I see one of those familiar blue pens. I pick it up and twirl it around. Sure enough, Clarion Psychiatric Center is written on the side. I push the top of the pen down and watch the little head pop out of its sheath. It works. Beside the pen there is a necklace made of silver, a double crucifix. On the inner crucifix hangs an emaciated, twisted Jesus. I glare down at the tiny face—looks like Vision from the Avengers. I set the necklace on the bench beside me and put the CPC pen into the small pocket of my book bag. Do you know who placed them here? Were they forgotten? Lost? Missed? Will someone return to pick them up? Or are they dead? Or was it me?

I take out a twenty-ounce plastic bottle of Coke, a third of it left. It has lost its fizz since bouncing around in my backpack all morning. With the soda I have a little plastic bag of three mini-muffins filled with tiny, hard purple bits they say are blueberries. This is lunch. But breakfast was decent—sausage links and those instant eggs they serve at the continental breakfasts of mid-level chain hotels. They were having a little fiesta this morning at the reddish, Neo-Romanesque cathedral on the corner two blocks from here. Orange juice, a banana, little plastic cup of yogurt—and got to sneak these muffins into my bag. I ate so well that I shook the church members' loving hands afterward. When I exited the building, I was so full I just leaned against the shop next door for fifteen minutes—Gus's Guns.

The muffins are super soft, but there's something phony about the freshness—something that makes them slide down your throat like liquid. But I swallow them all in less than five minutes. I'm not going to complain about food. The Coca-Cola is nearly warm, but I finish it in one long swig, leaving me only with plastic.

I need a rest. I've been walking around since my Catholic feast a few hours ago. Even though I carry the bare minimum in my bag—an extra pair of pants, three T-shirts, a few pairs of socks and boxers, toothbrush, toilet paper, a bar of soap, pen and paper, my pocket alarm, and then any food I can preserve—it still tires my neck and back.

The good thing is I'm left on my own here. Still I know he's watching me. When we used to sit out on the central squares in Garmisch or Munich, you always knew someone was watching you. That's what people do on squares—watch each other. Here, you look around and see no one, but you're never as free as you think. That's why they send him out to follow me.

Johnstown's got at least five old-age homes that I counted while walking around, three no-named taverns that might or might not be serving drinks. Eyes come from there. From the places that only halfway exist. From the people and places that are half-asleep. Not completely alive. Not completely dead.

There's a brand new football field near the river. Imagine ten thousand people sitting around inside on a Friday night, cheering while kids knock each other silly. I knew when I walked by there that he was inside, watching me as I passed. I felt him again when I walked past the Goodwill store—in an old, red, two-tiered British bus camped nearby. Why else is something like that here? Or the pile of old fire hydrants, hundreds of them, in someone's backyard? You think they're a part of some sport?

How about the parking lot behind Johnstown's Flood Museum? Or on the wooded banks that climb the mountain alongside the "world's steepest inclined plane?" There are eyes there, too. I've learned to recognize. Let them say I'm crazy. All their tests and hypotheses break down at black holes.

After a two-hour nap I stand up and stretch, take a look around. No one bothered me. A couple cars drive by the east side of the plaza. Probably just the restless types. Guys who need to gun up their engines. I pick the cross up from the bench, examine it more closely. Look into its eyes. Inanimate object, you think?

The third car drives by. It's him again. He's cruising slowly, window down, arm hanging over the door. And a hot dog in hand, most likely from Coney Island; "Famous Hot Dogs," its storefront says. Makes me hungry, but he's got those beady little eyes that I know are peering dead at me. He sees through the trees, halfway across the plaza. He's been circling the plaza these two hours while I slept. He's not going away. Richard Ramirez was like that. Driving around, stalking. You think he's really in jail? All the phone calls the last two weeks, and Jane repeating over and over again: "No, I'm not going to answer that question, sir." "No, we can't divulge that information." "That is not your concern."

I grab the cross and put it around my neck, put my backpack on, and head off across the far side of the plaza. I take a left and walk a few blocks, circling back around, thinking maybe I'll look for an early dinner and a place to sleep. It's quiet, the shops all closed—either permanently or until tomorrow. There's "Ed's Smoke Shop," another old age home they call a "community." There's a used clothing store, a T-Mobile office, a couple Cambria County government service buildings, and then I'm at the Franklin Street bridge, yellow ribbons stretched across it because the concrete on its underside is crumbling and probably there's something more structurally deficient too. I duck under the ribbon on the bridge's sidewalk and see the narrow, four-story, turn of the century office building built just to the side of the bridge. The "No Trespassing" sign is flapping off its wall and a few windows are busted. I walk to the rear of the building, away from potential eyes, and find a spot where the window is cracked. I pick up a large brick on the ground and bust the window open, climb inside, careful not to cut myself again.

The rooms on the first floor are vacant except for old newspapers, cardboard boxes, and a few crates. No office furniture left behind, no makeshift spaces for my kind. In the corner of the building the stairwell is obscured, and I take out my flashlight to climb. Piles of leaves have accumulated on the steps. At the top of the stairs there is light, direct sunlight coming through the windows. Still, the second floor is much the same as the first—dusty and empty. A few raggedy pieces of carpet litter random parts of the wooden floor. Several pigeons have taken up roost. I go to a distant room, the one with the least light, and set my bag down. This will suffice for at least a few nights. I take a small towel out and put it in a dark plastic bag to carry with me—everything else can stay here.

I make my way back down and exit through the same open window, hop back on the bridge and cross over, greeted by an advertising billboard for Ben Franklin Plumbing, a caricature of the founding father carrying a wrench. I can't think how bifocals, the flexible catheter, or electricity relates to sinks and toilets.

A couple blocks more and I reach Sheetz. It's one with a little sit-down area off to the side, and I find some leftovers still on the tables: a couple of onion rings, half a burrito, the last ounces of a Mountain Dew. I sit down and gather the items together at a table as if I'm a paying customer. An older man in a wilting John Deere cap sits with his back turned to me, and when he ups and leaves I've got what's left of his iced tea and French fries too. It fills me up.

I go to the restroom with my towel to wash up and use the loo as the Brits say. Entering, I see the back of a white T-shirt hulking over the urinal. The head above it looks back as the door creaks. We make eye contact. His hair is patted down, slick as ever. He doesn't give up. He speaks, but the words come out unintelligible, a fire surrounding his lips. I retreat and leave the store altogether.

I walk back downtown—no reason not to explore more when you're new and need to pick up whatever you can. Back off the plaza, one block north, I pass a new age spa and medical weight loss center. The storefront is painted in a tacky black and gold with a thematic design that looks like strands of seaweed. Plants rise from a bed of quartz pebbles laid near the sidewalk. The company name is lit up in fluorescent pink—YU, an acronym for "You're Unique." I wouldn't know so well, but the whole set up feels like part Chinatown takeout, part new age gift shop, but one hundred percent scam: weight loss, medical Lipolaser, diet pills and plan, led teeth whitening, cold sculpting, facials, Botox injections, and jet peel. I would not step inside. I would not want to see their eyes. I would not shake their hands.

I walk down Washington Street past the Flood Museum, parallel with the Conemaugh, and then pass over the bridge on Johns Street. They've constructed what they call a city park, riverside. It's little more than a quarter-mile line of elms alongside a concrete walkway with a steel railing overlooking a clean highway and the confluence of two dirty rivers. Plus a lot of signage that praises the benevolence of the companies and individuals that made it all possible. On the walkway there's really no one who could see you unless they're walking at your side. Nothing wrong with confined, but this isn't going anywhere. The trees are not thick, but prevalent enough to conceal JWF Industries' building complex, a metal manufacturing company on the other side. There's nothing much to view on the muddy river, and you'll lose count as the cars zip by.

I hear four sounds while walking. There is the sound of the Conemaugh flowing, but it's limp, like the sound of water gurgling in a slow-draining bathtub. Just as constant is a low, background hum coming from the countless vehicles skirting by on the highway, like the sound of the ocean at low tide. There are also the caws of the crows—loud, distressing, cantankerous. Smart and cautious birds, I'm told, but I hate them, wish Noah hadn't placed two of them on the ark. Last is the screech of wheels, the railroad cars on the tracks floating across town every couple of hours as if on a string.

By these sounds, truly, you shall know us, I say. Not by the sounds in church or in our homes. Not by the singers on our radios or the stories on our bookshelves. And I am tired of knowing.

Dark clouds have moved in, and I turn back. Growing up, Mother always expressed hatred for rain. She'd complain that she would have to bring in the laundry drying on the line. Or run out to get the mail so it wouldn't get soaked. Overreaction? An indication of her OCD? Or maybe just another example of people wanting to control their environments. No hair out of place, Solomon. Don't dirty your shoes.

We had our three-bedroom, middle-class house in the Pittsburgh suburbs, but it's never enough. I'd sit in the pew every Sunday morning and night, most Wednesday evenings too, my body tense, hoping she wouldn't testify. Hoping she wouldn't talk about her burdens. Hoping she wouldn't tell them about me. "I don't know what else I can do with him. He's not like the rest of us."

I return to the abandoned building. There's no reason to risk getting caught in the rain. But when I cross through the broken window this time, he's there. He's found my place for the night. Sure, his head is a little smaller and he's not smoking or eating or urinating now. He's just knelt down on his haunches, grinning. I know it's not just me. I know he's fighting all the people going to work in the morning.

But I hate him. He's more my family than my own mother who is dead now. I have tried my hardest to lose him—from refusing him, to drugs, to therapy, to the cross, to trying to lead that "normal" lifestyle. But still his lips move and he's got a smirk on his face like my father's when he ate pickles or watched a Clint Eastwood movie. He's always pleased, always content to find me. When he talks, I understand not even a word: just sounds and vibrations and heat that shoots out at me.

I drop to my knees and start to crawl to him. I am tired, and he can't be beat.

Slowly, I move closer. I feel shards of glass below my knees. I feel shards of glass cutting into my brain. I see my past, my life, in blurry waves—broken, fractured, incomplete.

He reaches out his hand and his smirk becomes the smile of a pastor, a crook, a salesman, all the advertisements, doctors with sweetly colored pills.

I know he has found me for good this time. If I can't escape him now in this new place forgotten by everyone, I never will. He touches, grabs, suffocates. I am done.

He has found my crucifix on the floor, my pen, my bag upstairs. In a building where I can't speak. And soon they will find me, too, my en-larged tongue dangling from my mouth. They will find a body lying down on an abandoned floor, its spirit cut out, blood moving no more. He takes all that's left of me, leaving a shell, and the day of the Lord does not come. Like a thief in the night.

AS WITH ALEM

———◆———

Farah Rose Smith

THEY WERE HEAVY days, when I knew him. Dark blue eyes, the warmth of his mouth, the tightness of his skin against me. Simple breath, simple movement. The dead parts of me bursting out—no longer painful.

He had come to my husband's studio in a frenzy of anxiety, the dark glamour of his eyes piercing into me. A portrait, he requested, for the paper. Our dear friend, Marid, having recommended me to him, after sharing tea over solemn volumes and the new fragmentary oblivion of my husband's nearest breakdown.

I positioned him before a broken mirror, the shards splitting up his face into a thousand persons. He liked the surreality, the suggestiveness. "Like a panther," he said, as I climbed the stool, the couch, the ladder to find him in the most appealing light. I knew him beneath this mess to be handsome and alone. The fullness of expression was in the spirit. I absorbed every bit of this man. A feathery, familiar feeling.

"Closer," I said, directing him towards the mirror. He stepped in, his pale face becoming wider, less obliterated, among the shards. His gaze took to floating in a dream of velvet. I stepped in with him.

"Closer," I said again, his being almost one entirety, split only in half

197

at that proximity. I stepped in. His hand moved atop the camera, lowering it away from my face, my features.

"Closer," he whispered, pressing his lips against mine.

I could see the reflection of my husband's beach landscape on the far wall, through the mirror. My eyes closed, fathoms of passion flowing into me, his dark blue gaze cradling a broken boyhood. He would come again in these abandoned hours, seven or eight times that year. Upon the ninth, his shadow lurking outside the door, I would not let him in. I never said goodbye.

"When did you last speak to him?" My expression dips, a concealment of wonder, phantom scents of Alem's black coat, his solemn notebook, slipping under my nose.

"He wrote me a letter to say he'd taken up lodging here, at the estate."

Marid walks with me on the shore, looking of another age in his black corduroy suit and cane. His spirit still hums with the melancholic wit of our former acquaintance. What he knows of my dealings, there is no surety. Only speculation, and the microsmile upon witnessing my unease. He insisted that I come here.

The water is sickly grey, like watered-down gasoline. It ebbs with an elderly hesitation. The earth has swallowed my heart, but it has not been fatal. Not yet. I raise a hand to my temple and wince.

"Forgive me, the headaches have returned." Marid nods, and continues.

"So tell me of this woman he has taken in." I twitch at the eye, the mouth, wrists twisting towards the ground...a dancerly defiance.

"She looks exactly like me." A fit of laughter breaks out of him.

"Fear of similarity is a desperate humor, my dear."

I track the dying sunlight with beats of the heart. The house is white, sullen. The cupola is blue-green. I did not mean for such a thing to come up. All that he says, signaling to the sky with his book, is that some people have forever dancing about them. Perhaps she was one of these miraculous creatures. He won't admit to me that he introduced my husband to the girl, as with Alem.

"But she looked like me," I say.

"You will come to enjoy your privacy here, I think, my dear," Marid says, dismissing my brooding with a sweep of the hand against the sea, the bulk of his coat billowing behind him.

"Far away from all that nonsense."

"What did Alem make of his time here?"

"Oh, a bit of writing, a bit of reading, as was in his character."

"I'm surprised that he would seek out your company, after all."

"It was penance, the offer. But even a favor cannot save one from being consumed from within."

"What became of him?"

My tone is feverish, but he is not thrown by it. A curious grin curls left, then right, measuring madness.

"He drowned. Swept out by some misfortune. Drunkenness, perhaps. Or a lack of will to begin with."

A BLUE BEETLE spits on my leftmost hand. I am the beneficiary of buzzing and bleeding in this dreaded house. There is a large colored portrait in the lower room. Gentle limbs painted by gnarled hands. I pull old books from the shelves without titles. They are written in languages that are unknown to me. There is a certain sense of fullness in the house. Something that comes to me in the absence of a crowd. Cold rooms, creaking doors, the stink of the sea hangs in the air. There are no birds but bugs, salt, and memory. One must imagine themselves immobile at the end of the world—miserable, as miserable as I have become.

It is not without merit, this horror of mine. His words and thoughts were my tender companions once, against a tide of violent paint. One might hear infinity in the language of beasts, should they put aside their designs and listen. Each a stranger among another's oppression. The senses become inflamed in the widest throes of guilt. What can it be, this blue spell of anguish? He wept in my hair, still erect, streaming out new life into me. His body was beautiful and violent.

My husband never discovered us. But like the familiar wilting of my passion years before, his eyes and heart turned elsewhere. He became accustomed to a particular pretension, a vulgarity of the mind, that undoubtedly would have set him against me, no matter who wandered in or out of his arms. But why must it be her? She, who looks so like I did, all those years ago?

I turn down the moth-eaten covers, take off my clothes, slide my nude form into the musty sheets. I have not strength to change. My black hair has grown back, as tough as wire. I don't wear make-up anymore. My cheeks are sunken, eyes rimmed with thinning skin. I run a wooden brush through when sitting. Dust falls. I tremble and watch my long fingernails—red, gold, white. Page after page of this life, I encounter deep dark things. My capacity for wonder has exceeded reason and the essence of myself. I will be a shut-in for many days and nights. For months, perhaps, listening to the trickling tide coming closer—ever closer.

He left me for her. I slow my tears, mock the hope within my chest, come to in the arms of sleep.

The light coming through the windows is green. Ungodly color spins over the bed sheets. It beats like a beacon for me. I do not know whether to feel threatened or at home. I am immobile—rich with the bodily responses of fear. A form approaches from the infinite night—a form of man blurred out at the sides, in a long shiny black coat. The mask of green is cobbled together by broken wood and weeds. This person towers over me, setting in the deep urgency—a dream in the waking world. These are the touches of ancient things.

What is a worm but a nightmare of passion in small form? I have had dreams before of water. Streams of whispers. Spindles of black smoke. Alem. The outburst of memory sets me against the world again. Irritated with an excess of heat creeping up my spine, I glare to the absence of life through the window, a willful mysticism lingering. There is no governing body to this madness. There is something to the eyes... a familiar look. Painful, and fiercely engaged.

Suddenly, what lies outside the window is quite different. Signs are here of a tropical phantasm. The red eclipse crosses the ocean and a sky as delicate as the old world. I feel myself before this dark element, walking up and down in confusion, my heart tight with the pulsations of passion, of regret. I get up, step as lightly as a bird to the edge of the floor, heart racing. Do I know this man? Have I known him, or do I recognize the emptiness, a spectral projection of my most fragile self? In the disenchanted evening, I will collect these dream projections, but not write of them. If I write, turning page to page of these horrors, this impure poetry, I will bring to myself only travel into time, unbearable— time that towers over me in the heart.

At the center of all things, silence pops. There are no bright rooms in the house. All the lanterns have gone out. I walk into the hallway, down the staircase, towards the parlor. Every step is matched by this figure—black bird of night. The endless, empty worry breathes into me. I feel him behind me. I feel him within me. On the shore, I reach down. My hands are weak, unable to grasp the sand.

I see from here, all of the changes of the landscape. The grey of the water is now green. The richness of color, the clarity of the sea, the cliff rock, sharply lit by the pale yellow light of dawn. One can discover new avenues of frenzy, of regret. Dreaming torment under cobalt skies, drunk with the reality of my human heart. Vitality plucked away with the permission of God. Dead birds fill the beach. Shadows stand still, rocking at times, effortless in their indifference. They are not a manifestation of worried dreams. They are, in fact, quite real. All look at me, silently. I would not entrust my guilt to such images. The faces are shapeless. As dark as vantablack on canvas. And then I see the machine.

It is a great metallic thing, like a giant screw in situ, bearing down on a nearby cove from the zenith of the cliffrock. Its shadow obscures the beach. Energy pulses from there to here. I'm a spectator to the rot, the horror hidden by shadows on the beach, but I will not hold my lantern up to their faces. Not yet.

I go back into the house without respite, hands twisting madly against myself. Days will pass now, longer than before. Evenings of hours trying their part with shame. I cannot remove this trickery of time, eyes half-closed. I remember his suffering after the last time. Had I known the pain of it, I may not have done such things.

I tremble, in expectation of madness, consumed by this compulsion to chase, to abandon. I would rather stretch out, sleepless and alone, then gaze into the infinite light beams of the past.

I LOOK OUT the window, wrapped in a blue sweater, cup in hand, phone in the other. Waking life. The shore has returned to its original form.

Minx is on the line. She tells me the girl is a cunt, a usurper. I don't use these words. Among the stories that took root in the mouth was that she was like me. It was not until I saw her that I knew this to be true. Have I not earned this horror through a fatal mistake of my own? The irony is inconceivable. It is in the worst of things that I recognize in myself. I write this down, but later in the morning, the pages will be stale. Green and indescribable, and I will remember nothing of them.

Marid returns to deliver the papers. I sign away my partner, my life. I free him up for his pleasure, for my discontent. But was I not unhappy with him, always?

"Without rest, I take it?"

"A troublesome dream."

"Oh?"

I tell Marid of the light, the man, the great machine in the cliff-rock. I tell him of the shadows. He is struck, though his expression maintains its rascality, its reserve.

"Your visions are worrisome, Samirah. But did you not mention having a terror of a headache upon entry to the house?"

"I did, yes."

"My uncle had similar aberrations of the head, not unlike yourself upon entry. I imagine the stress of coming over seas under such circumstances has driven your dream world outward." There is something of an understanding in him, behind these words.

"You sacrifice sleep for an army of dream spirits. Damn them, curse them, get them out, that's what I say. But tell me...did it feel as though it were an evil thing?"

"No. Familiar." He stands, gathering the papers, grabbing his cane from the nearby wall.

"Such things are a child's concern."

HER BEAUTY STRUCK a victory against my intelligence. It is all not as simple as that. We only become what we have acted towards. I have had my perverse enjoyments. My glimmers of happiness in a body that was not mine. It is the doom of natural life, to see your eyes on another face.

He left me for her.

I reach a hand to my sagging breasts. A clumsy, failing gesture to grasp, to understand. It is absurd, this spasm of hatred. Granted, one may protest violently, loudly, but Marid had offered his home as sanctuary. I must be grateful. Maybe it was the thought of Alem here that brought me on. He was stealthy in his decomposition, wasn't he? He had always known that he wanted to soar above the indignities of men, in the silent spheres of waiting art. How can one cherish such moments of deceit against another? Is this not the definition of evil? I take what I deserve, as one is inclined to do on occasion, with only slight remembrances. I hate her, and cannot hate her. There will be something of my trials in her fate, something of hers in mine.

But did Alem not look like some dark angel's illustration of my husband?

THE UPPER HALLS gleam, a cavity of silent sound. The night has come again, and this wave of green light. A shiver in my spine guides me out of the bed. My heart beats to a universal clock. Wind rustles my hair. I become flushed, lips dry from the salt of the air. I am alive in a song of great magic. Wind blows over the beach, through the cliff rock. The strange machine twists down, a permanent shape among the stars. The great booming sound lives through the senses.

He stands with me, this man of night, concealed by metallic cloth and fractured nature. A chill strikes my cheek, and I know myself to be inches from him. In this proximity is the fear of everything. Of death, of discovery. I ask without thinking,

"Why does Marid bring us to the house?"

Alem rests his hands on my shoulders before pointing a hand to the shore. Froth and loam flow up closer to the porch. The shapes are undisturbed. They watch gently in the darkness of borrowed night time. An urgency boils up into me—the vastness of my guilt. I walk down to the beach, towards the shadows, the distinctive edge of madness brewing. I suddenly feel bolder, cluttered up, degenerate. Quiet tides of silence build in me. I take to running towards the shape, the person. I see on the far side of anguish, all of them. Through a deep laugh, the tones of Marid in his collective genius, I am pulled into the infinite contemplation of passion and regret, into these apparitions of myself.

THE FALL GUY

———◆———

Tom Johnstone

WHEN I WAS little, like many small boys of my generation, I watched a hell of a lot of action shows on TV. It never occurred to me at the time that the actor who played the rugged hero wasn't the one actually slugging it out with the villain, jumping off tall buildings, and so on. I hadn't fully taken in that what was happening wasn't real at that point anyway. Not really. And yet I somehow knew deep down that no one got hurt.

Apart from the stunt doubles.

The risk of injury is part of the job. They're trained in how to take the falls with minimal risk, so the A-listers don't have to, but that doesn't mean there's no danger. It wasn't until I was a little older that I became aware of this profession. One of my favorite childhood TV shows was *The Six Million Dollar Man*. It starred Lee Majors, so naturally I tuned in to *The Fall Guy*, a later show in which he played as a stunt artist who got into all sorts of scrapes both on-and off-set. I was a bit older by then, a bit more sophisticated, enough that it tickled me, the irony of him playing a stunt man, when he probably didn't even do his own stunts himself. That was when I started watching more closely during the action sequences, to see if I could spot the blurred, anonymous face in the Lee Majors wig, wearing Lee Majors' clothes, fleetingly visible for a few seconds, deceiving the viewer with a conjuror's misdirection and sleight of hand. When the network showed reruns of *The Six Million Dollar Man*, I'd amuse myself by trying to see the face above the collar of the iconic red tracksuit. It got better when home video came in, and you could slow it down and freeze-frame it.

Even then, however, the faces of the stuntmen were elusive. Sometimes you could make them out briefly, but mostly the directors took care to make sure the doubles were only visible from the back. Sloppy editing occasionally allowed you to glimpse a comically mismatched face, but only briefly, in long shot, and the primitive nature of the analogue technology meant the features were indistinct, shot through with the fuzz of interrupted tape. By the time DVD came in, I'd grown out of this obsession anyway, and it seemed a little morbid looking for the faces of the dead or maimed.

All right, that's perhaps a little melodramatic, but when I said you couldn't eliminate danger, I wasn't exaggerating. As I grew older, I began to look closer into the behind-the-scenes histories of the TV shows I'd loved as a child. I discovered the hidden casualties of slipshod safety standards among those unsung heroes of the industry, stunt doubles killed or horribly injured in accidents on set, like Roman convicts killed for real on stage, their exemplary punishments serving the audience's bloodlust. Of course, you hear about these things when a leading actor dies performing his own stunts. I'm thinking of *The Crow* of course.

At the time, learning about these lives sacrificed to entertain me affected me profoundly. It was something of a loss of innocence.

LIKE MY FATHER and uncle, I was born in January, and have often wondered if there was some significance to this. The month is of course named after the two-faced Roman god Janus. Maybe that's why I became fascinated at a young age by the tale of Edward Mordake in the 1896 encyclopedia *Anomalies and Curiosities of Medicine*. I first read about it in one of those books of 'true mysteries of the unexplained' that were all the rage when I was growing up, though I've since dis-covered the story was apocryphal. According to Gould and Pyle, the authors of this tome, Mordake was born with a rare condition, a second-ary face on the back of his head.

Of course, such things are not unheard of in medical science—Craniopagus Parasiticus, Diprosopus, Polycephaly. Most specimens are stillborn. There's little chance of reaching adulthood with such con-ditions. Mordake, we are told, survived into his twenties, and took his own life and presumably that of his 'devil twin.'

This brings me to the more lurid aspects of the tale.

According to the *Anomalies*, Mordake is said to have begged his phy-sicians Manvers and Treadwell to "crush it out of human semblance," so tormented was he by the second face's nightly gibberings and mutter-ings. He even took the trouble, before he poisoned himself, to request its posthumous destruction, fearing its "dreadful whisperings" might pursue him beyond the grave.

One other notable feature of the case was the sex of the reverse head. In keeping with its general demeanor—that of opposing every action and expression of Mordake, smiling and sneering when he wept—the parasitic twin-face's sex was the opposite of his, that of a woman "lovely as a dream, hideous as the devil." In one of the more lurid accounts I read in my 'true mystery' books, there was another twist of the knife. Towards the end of his life (it claimed), Mordake was further plagued by nocturnal visitations, knocks on the door and windows of his country house by an intruder in the grounds. He was unable to make out the face of his tormentor because it wore a cloak, a cowl hiding its features.

But after his death, the bobbies found a corpse in the woods nearby: a woman, naked under her cloak, her face a featureless blank, her hand clutching a scalpel.

DESPITE MY BIRTH month, there was, I hasten to add, no secondary face on the back of my head. Yet I did wonder at times if there was someone watching over me. During my childhood, I had a habit of wandering off on my own when we were on our long summer holidays in the Hebrides. I'd get myself lost in the glens, get stuck in peat bogs, climb vertiginous cliffs and almost fall into crevasses hidden by banks of ferns, oblivious to any danger around me. The scents of heather and seaweed filled my nostrils, the far off bleating of sheep and screech of gulls the only sounds to reach my ears.

On one occasion, I lost my nerve while climbing, my eyes gazing first down the sheer drop below, then above at the seemingly insurmountable climb ahead of me. I became paralyzed with terror. I thought of the dead sheep one of the local crofters had shown me, dried blood tangled in its porridge-like wool. The animal had panicked, he explained, and hurtled off the edge of cliffs like these. My own panic hung over me like a great black cloud, smothering me, stopping my breath. As consciousness started to fade, I felt a strange dislocation, a disbelief that this could be happening to me, a feeling that I was watching the event from outside myself.

I came to myself at the top of the cliff, my face wet with tears as if I'd woken from a dream awash with overwhelming grief. I must have blacked out. But how had I completed my ascent? There was no one about in this wilderness to ask. All I could do was try and find my way back to the cottage my parents rented, which was owned by the aforementioned crofter. As I stumbled through bogs and over rocks, I wondered at the perversity in my nature that made me seek out these dangerous situations in lonely places. It was the first time I became aware of this quality in myself, and indeed of the charmed life that allowed me to indulge it without repercussions.

When I returned just before dark, there was little drama about my disappearance. Father was out fishing with his brother. Mother was in the cottage meditating. This setting allowed them both to pursue their separate interests, and increasingly, separate lives. Perhaps Mother's transcendental state was so total, she had been oblivious to my absence. Yet she seemed convinced I had been around, or at least surprised that I hadn't been.

THE BLACKOUT ON the cliff was not the last of such episodes, but later ones had a different cause.

As I grew older and approached manhood, it was universally assumed I would follow in my father's footsteps into the surgical profession. But I went off the rails, developing an excessive and precocious attachment to alcohol that led to lost hours and alarming lapses of memory. This threatened the bright future my father had mapped out for me.

In the most frightening of these incidents, I found myself dancing on the track at a tube station in front of horrified onlookers. I could see rats scurrying about under the platform. By some miracle, I managed to climb back up without touching the live rail, before the train hit. As it screamed into view, I briefly thought I glimpsed a charred, smoking thing disappear under its wheels. A rat perhaps, but it looked far too large for that. Another time, I lay down in the middle of the street near my parents' West London home. I might have been crushed by an unsuspecting motorist, had a neighbor not spotted me and dragged me to the house. I only know about this because my mother told me of it afterwards. I was fifteen at the time. Whatever death-wish spurred me to these self-destructive acts, it remained unfulfilled.

IT WAS DURING a later visit to the cottage that one of these shameful incidents revealed the true nature of my situation to me, in all its putrid, gilded, blue-bottle glory. It so happened that my sixteenth birthday fell during this particular vacation, and my parents in their wisdom organized a party for me. The guests consisted of my uncle, my mother and father and me, and our landlord and his family.

The crofter, Willie MacKinnon, filled the kitchen with his presence, his ever-present smile of polite contempt for us widening the square face under his tweed cap. He leaned proprietorially against the sink, as well he might. He'd built the place after all, and I mean with his own bare hands, not in the sense the phrase is often used—to mean so-and-so paid someone else to build such-and-such a place. His nose was hawk-like, his lips fleshy and carnal, his blue eyes watchful behind his glasses, his feet spaced wide apart where he stood.

"Ah, the birthday boy," he said as I shambled in, his voice sardonic. But then his voice always sounded sardonic. My father and his brother, standing there like Tweedle Dum and Tweedle Dee in their matching tweed jackets, muttered something to each other in French, something that's puzzled me ever since, something like "*Doigt du Seigneur*." At least that's what I thought it was at first—"finger of the lord," especially since my uncle was waggling his plump index finger suggestively. Then I remembered the stock phrase was "*Droit du Seigneur*," a feudal lord's right to enjoy the favors of his tenant's bride, which could have been a bitter joke at my mother's expense. As I listened to their sibling chuckles over their jest, I did wonder if their laughter might be a kind of whistling in a graveyard. MacKinnon made them uneasy. They'd always communicated in one kind of secret language or another, and French was as good as any in this situation, allowing them to flaunt their supposed educational advantages in front of their host, even as my father hosted him.

But their view of him as a pig-shit thick man of the soil was seriously misguided. When I'd visited the croft's main building, sent on errands to fetch jugs of sour milk from the herd or exchange notes for bags of fifty pence pieces for the electricity meter, I'd seen shelves groaning with books, including a copy of my mother's pop-feminist bestseller, *Apes versus Angels: a Brief History of the Sex War*.

"That's the wife's," he said when he'd come in with the coins or jug or whatever it was this time, and caught me staring at it.

"I'm more of an Ed McBain man myself," he added. But though there were plenty of well-thumbed paperback thrillers, there were numerous other, weightier tomes, on subjects as varied as economics and animal husbandry—even three large volumes of Marx's *Capital*.

"What he wrote about the Highland Clearances was a real eye-opener," he said, enjoying my shocked expression. "You thought I just had it for show, didn't you? It's the wife who's got the degree and all, but I've done a fair bit of studying in my own time. You've got to pass the time somehow during the long winters here. There's only so much drinking and fucking and playing cards a man can stand." Again he grinned at the look on my face.

I'd heard my mother talk of Morag Mackinnon as some sort of suffering martyr. Maybe it was she who'd given Morag the book as a gift, some sort of spur to domestic rebellion perhaps. Morag now stood with her husband in the kitchen my parents rented from them. Actually, she stood some distance away from him, chatting to her daughter Sarah, while he exchanged guttural words with his two sons, both at least as heavily built as their father, the older one Donald at his right hand, the younger Billy at his left. Morag was a wiry, fox-like woman, with a dry wit to match her husband's constant air of scorn. Anyone less like a martyr you couldn't imagine. The way my mother told it, she'd abandoned a promising academic career in favor of a life stoically battling the peaty soil and the dour elements, and turning a blind eye to Willie's infidelities. But I do wonder if there was an element of guilt to the manner in which the author of *Apes versus Angels* viewed their relationship. Well, perhaps not guilt exactly. She was a believer in free love, a creed my father was only too happy to honor in his way, but which sometimes came into conflict with her advocacy of the mystical Sisterhood.

Finally, there was Sarah, a vision in stone-washed jeans and mousey perm. She was tanned and freckled like her mother, but not so weather-beaten, a faded maroon and white-striped rugby shirt ballooning to accommodate her burgeoning womanhood. She'd inherited her father's mocking blue eyes and sensual lips. I remembered my father's briefing earlier that day when he'd caught me gazing out of the window at her as she traversed the small-holding on some errand. He'd decided to impart some of his Experience of the Fairer Sex.

"I've seen the way you look at her, old sport. There's no fooling this old dog! But there's no point being bashful, the way you usually are. Take it from me, faint heart ne'er won fair lady. You have to show her who wears the trousers—you understand?"

I nodded wearily.

"And don't forget, you're quite a catch, you know!"

"Yes, such a handsome young man he's grown into," my mother agreed. She'd just floated into the middle of our father-son chat in her kaftan. "Just be yourself, darling, and she'll be putty in your hands," she purred. I groaned inwardly. If there was one thing I hated more than anything, it was both of them fussing over me.

"I don't mean that, Gloria, though it's true of course. But he's not just a handsome young man. He's a handsome young man with a bright future. Young Sandra would be a fool not to want to land this one!"

"Miles!" Mother protested. "Her name's Sarah."

"Well, whatever her name is, don't be fooled into putting all your eggs in one basket, old sport."

I looked back at him blankly. My mother huffed out of the room.

"Look, just make sure your old man's covered up," he said, ruffling my hair and handing me a foil packet containing something I'd never seen before. Through the crackling material, it felt like a ring with a piece of skin stretched taut over it. As I examined it, turning the mysterious object over and over in my hands, I could hear my parents arguing in the next room.

It had all sounded so easy when he'd said all that. But now, standing there with an expanse of granite floor between me and her, the room felt simultaneously a vast, intimidating cavern and a tiny, cramped cupboard. I felt my father and uncle's identical pairs of beady eyes boring into my back, wordlessly egging me on. Something in me balked at the 'droit du seigneur' he'd urged me to exercise. On the other side of the divide, the presence of Willie and his sons added to my anxiety. They pretended disinterest, discussing the price of sheep dip and the like, but the occasional shrewd glance in my direction told me otherwise. Morag had gone over to chat with my mother, leaving me painfully aware of Sarah standing alone. My mouth felt parched. My father was on hand with a whisky tumbler.

"Bit of Dutch courage, old sport," he whispered.

"Are you no going to top us up too, Miles?" Mackinnon called over.

Finally, feeling a little lightheaded, I found myself at her side, exchanging mumbled pleasantries about the weather as she smiled shyly back at me. Was there genuine warmth there that might have translated into something deeper and sweeter, or was it the polite attentiveness required of her in her role as the daughter of the croft? Now, I'll never know, but it's fair to say the McKinnons weren't known for making a big song and dance about the social niceties of making their guests feel welcome, beyond providing basic amenities. Perhaps Sarah was the exception.

"Sorry the weather's not been better for you, David," she said, her voice soft as milk, but not the sour sort I'd often fetched from the croft.

"Oh, I don't mind," I said magnanimously. "It's not like we come here expecting the Costa Del Sol."

Her laughter was like music.

"Now you're going to say if we'd come a month ago it would have been blazing sunshine, right?" I added.

"Well, it's funny you should say that…"

We both laughed then. It sounded too loud for the stony room where our respective families stood expectantly, making halfhearted small talk amongst themselves. I felt a deadly silence spring up between us, heavier and more impenetrable than lead. My skin felt prickly, itchy, simultaneously dry and sweaty.

"Quite a party," I remarked drily.

"Better than *my* sixteenth," she replied.

"That bad, eh?"

She didn't seem to want to go into details, so I didn't press the point. She quickly changed the subject.

"I'm surprised your uncle stops so far away—what with the two of them being twins."

I muttered something about my relief the cottage he rented was on the other side of the island.

"Aye, I could see how it can be a bit much sometimes—both of them together and all…"

Then she asked: "Do you ever get them mixed up?" This in a low voice that seemed to draw me closer. I could see the golden down on the side of her face, smell her hair.

"No, but I think my mother does sometimes," I whispered.

She let out a shriek of what could have been laughter, so piercing it shook me away from her.

My mouth felt horribly dry, the silence unbearable.

"What are you two whispering about?" my uncle brayed. "Something improper I hope!"

I made a beeline for the Macallan bottle, my father muttering "Well, all right, but don't blow it by getting plastered, old sport."

When I turned back to my quarry, I saw her father had moved towards her, saying something I couldn't quite hear. Once he'd left her alone again, I lifted my glass to my lips only to see it was empty. Before refilling it, I went back over to her, offering to get her one too.

"Not for me, Miles. Actually I'd best be going soon. Some of us have got work in the morning."

"Cows to milk?"

"Aye, those heifers won't milk themselves."

"Are you sure? Not just one for the road?"

"Well, it's no but a short distance, David."

Things begin to grow hazy around this point. I remember babbling about everything and nothing for a while—anything to ward off that terrible leaden silence, pretending not to notice Sarah's increasing surreptitious interest in her watch. At some point, I grabbed the almost empty Macallan bottle from under my father's nose and tried to fill her empty glass, but her hand quickly covered it. "All the more for me," I observed gallantly, as I poured the last of it into my own glass, oblivious to her eyes flashing a look of dismay towards her mother standing nearby. I remember nothing else after that.

I WOKE UP to a knock on my bedroom door, then my father stepping smartly in bearing a tray laden with a full English breakfast. The smells of it made my stomach church with nausea.

"Eggs frae Oor Wullie's ain hens," he began in a mock Scots accent. "Not as curdled as the milk I trust," he went on in his own voice, "but I imagine you'll be needing a bit of a pick-me-up, old sport. How are you feeling, by the way?"

"Oh, a bit hung over," I said, my head beginning to pound. Then I remembered. "Look, Dad, I'm sorry about the Macallan..."

"Not me you need to apologize to, old sport. Shame about the whisky. Still, if you can't down a bottle of Macallan on your sixteenth, when can you?

"But you need to learn to hold your drink before you pull a stunt like that again..."

I struggled to digest his words as I contemplated the glistening food arrayed before me. My head swam in grease along with the fried bread and bacon and square sausage.

"Stunt?" I repeated. "What... stunt?"

"Ah, you don't remember. Thought as much. Never mind. Still, least said soonest mended."

I had no appetite whatsoever, but my fork slipped from my fingers, puncturing the runny yoke, saturating everything nearby in a daffodil-yellow avalanche.

"Dad, what happened?"

"I'm rather afraid you over-bounded your step, David."

Despite the facetious jumbling up of the words, the way he used my name instead of "old sport" alerted me to the seriousness of the situation.

"What do you mean?"

"Well, when I told you to be forceful, I didn't mean...well, that."

My stomach lurched, in much the same way it had when I'd got stuck climbing that cliff and stared back down the way I'd come. The black pudding on my plate resembled an abyss.

"Well, what?" I asked. "What did I do? I don't remember what happened!"

"Right. I see. Perhaps that's just as well."

No, it bloody well wasn't. A picture of me was emerging from my father's dark hints, a portrait he'd only let me glance at sideways on, one I didn't recognize, or didn't want to, though it looked and spoke like me. My evil twin perhaps? But I had to know what I'd done, look at my other self squarely in the eye.

Suddenly, maddened by his evasions, I reached out and grabbed him by the wrist, overturning the breakfast tray and scattering its contents all over the quilt, demanding that he tell me what outrage I'd committed.

"All right! All right!" he said, freeing himself from my grip. He wiped a splatter of egg yolk from his tweed jacket with the handkerchief he kept in its top left-hand pocket.

I sat there propped up on the bed, listening to the sound of my hard, labored breathing roaring in my ears, the steady drip-drip-drip of the overturned coffee cup lying on its side near the edge. I was dimly aware of the scalding heat of its spilt contents soaking through the counterpane.

Eventually he spoke.

"Got to watch that temper of yours, old sport. Might be your down-fall one day, though what poor, young Sharon had done to provoke you is beyond me. Mind you, she can give as good as she gets. Kick like a mule, that one. Hope you're not too sore down there..."

I shook my aching head. I couldn't feel a thing 'down there.'

"Well, it was the only way she could get you off her, once you'd... wrestled her to the ground like that. In front of everyone in the room too! You're lucky her old man and his brothers were outside at the time, or you'd have got worse than a pair of sore sacks..."

Again I mentally checked my groin. Nothing. Numb. Everything felt numb apart from my head and my gut.

"Well, when they heard her cries and rushed back in, saw you like that, I just said you must have lost your balance—as we all do, in our cups. They just laughed and nodded. Probably think I've sired a son who can't hold his drink. And they'd be right, I suppose..."

He let out a bitter little laugh and began rubbing at the egg yolk stain again. I wanted to slap his hand away.

Still, it didn't sound so bad, now he'd told me what had happened. Did it...? From what I could make out, all I'd done was fall over drunk.

It was just that the landlord's daughter had been underneath me at the time. But I was less than convinced by this spin on it. Thinking of her trapped underneath me like that, the 'sex war' suddenly seemed a very asymmetrical one.

And my father's face still looked grave.

"They seemed happy enough with this explanation at the time, but I don't know what she's said to them since...

"Of course she'd be a fool to start blabbing about a schoolboy error like this to the authorities, risk ruining the life of a young man with such a bright future ahead of him, over a bit of clumsy, boorish behavior brought on by one too many, eh? But who knows what the fairer sex is capable of once they get a bee in their bonnets!

"Anyway, let's not worry about that just yet. The police are a ferry-journey away. Not that she'll press charges if she knows what's good for her. Let's clean this mess up, and go downstairs to face your mother."

She was sitting at the kitchen table smoking a cigarette. At first, she refused to meet my eyes with hers, much less speak to me. I suppose you could say this had hit her quite hard. For her, I'd always been the exception to the rule, the angel embedded behind enemy lines with the apes.

Though I tried to put the tray down on the sideboard quietly, a slight clatter of crockery caused her eye to jerk my way.

"Well, that's a waste of a dead pig." She blew smoke out to drive the point home.

"Look, Mum, I'm sorry about what happened."

"What *happened*?" she repeated, her voice shaking with cold fury.

"What I did."

"It's not so much what you did, but what you said." Another puff of smoke. "Those obscene, degrading things you spat out at that poor girl as she lay there helpless..."

Not entirely so according to my father, but he hadn't mentioned any verbal abuse.

"What...things?" I asked.

"Do you need me to spell it out? Do you think I can bear to sully my mouth by repeating them?"

She turned her face away and took long drags from her diminishing cigarette, as if to mask herself in its haze. I fiddled aimlessly with the cutlery on the tray.

I opened my mouth to speak, to tell her it all felt like a forgotten dream that had happened to someone else, not me, but the words stuck in my mouth like the sickening remnants of half-digested food. *What was I going to say?* I reproached myself in an internal spasm of self-loathing. *It wasn't me, Mum, it was my evil twin? He poured those foul thoughts into my mind and put those vile words into my mouth. What a convenient conceit! What a wonderful cosmic get-out-of-jail-free card!*

But in spite of her anger, which with characteristic entitlement I knew would abate in the end, probably already was doing, Mother was already on hand with a get-out clause of her own.

"And you didn't help, Miles, plying the boy with booze."

"Boy? He's a man now, my dear." He addressed me, desperately. "Anyway, it wasn't me doling out most of it, old sport, it was your Uncle Matthew." He turned back to my mother with a sneer on his face, which he pressed close to hers. "I sometimes wonder if you can tell us apart, my dear..."

I stared at the breakfast debris so I only heard the slap, followed by "Don't you dare make this about me, you prick! You set this up with him to get at me. I heard what you two were saying about the *Droit du Seigneur*. I suppose you thought he was doing her a favor, asserting his ancient rights, spewing his *noblesse oblige* all over her! What were you saying to him when I walked in on your little pep-talk—something about how all the nice girls love a bad boy, was it?"

"Well, you'd know all about that, wouldn't you, darling."

"Just what are you...? You bastard."

Her voice was dangerously quiet, and followed by the kind of silence that heralds a thunderstorm. His eyes gleamed as he stroked his reddened cheek, as if caressing a badge of honor, tilting his head as if daring her to strike him again, on the other side. I don't imagine it was what the Bible had meant by turning the other cheek.

But I'd heard enough. I listened to their voices as if through a fog of tobacco smoke and lies, continuing the increasingly bitter recriminations. I crept out of the kitchen and stood in the porch, staring at the mist-shrouded farmyard where rocks crouched like shapeless beasts.

After a while, they finally became aware I'd left the room and followed me. They began calling me back, warning me not to go outside, as I stumbled out of the cottage to breathe in the cool, damp air. Their voices, growing fainter as I walked on, sounded almost fearful. I couldn't understand why they were so worried. Up to now, they'd been more interested in tearing strips off each other than addressing me. Far from making anything about my memory lapse clearer, they'd left me with more questions than answers. Thinking of my father's insinuation about his twin brother—and the way Sarah had shrieked with laughter at what I'd said about my mother confusing the two, as if she'd heard some whispered rumor I hadn't—I was beginning to wonder who I was. Who my father was at any rate.

I don't know if I was hoping to see Sarah, and apologize to her. Whether or not that was advisable, she was nowhere to be seen. When I did see her eventually, she seemed to bear me no ill will, was even friendly, if a little distant, so I said nothing about that lost evening. We passed the time of day, nothing more. Least said, soonest mended, as my father might have put it.

I wandered on, into the mist. Beyond me I could see the croft house, looming in the mist, sat atop its rocky perch. Nearby stood a wooden post, supporting one end of a washing line. It had always reminded me of a stake for a witch, or a whipping post. Now it seemed it was just such a thing. Three large men stood around it, a smaller figure lashed to it, sagging beneath repeated blows from each, as if they were taking in turns to land a punch on the face, or sometimes a kick in the groin for variety. It was difficult to make out the features in the fog, but I could see it was dressed in my clothes, or rather replicas of the ones I was wearing. The face might have been mine too at one point, but as I moved closer, I saw that any resemblance to me, or indeed to any human being, had long since disappeared beneath a mass of bruises, contusions, scar tissue, the limbs twisted, broken, set, re-broken...

One of the men broke away from the punishment beating: Willie Mackinnon's grim face emerged from the mist, leaving his sons to continue their bloody work in his absence.

"Off you go, David. You don't want to see this, son."

And for once, there was no trace of sarcasm or contempt in the way he addressed me. There was even a little kindness there, but none left to spare for the wretched creature wearing my clothes. I heard the wet sound of flesh splitting under another heavy blow.

As I walked away, the truth struck me. This was my stunt double, the one who took all the falls for the harm I did to myself, the punishment for what I did to others. I thought of those youthful brushes with death, getting stuck halfway up cliffs, then blacking out and coming to at the top. Though I'd made the mistake of looking down when I was climbing, I hadn't once I was out of danger. I might have seen a broken body lying at the bottom in my own clothes, shattered limbs writhing like a crushed but still-living insect.

Then there were the later escapades, often linked to alcohol, as I sought to prove my father wrong and build up my tolerance for drink. The time I danced on the tube track and yet managed not to touch the live rail. The time I wrote off my father's Bentley, yet emerged unscathed.

I began to wonder if my walking, suffering Dorian Gray portrait made me invulnerable. Was there any risk I couldn't take? Was there any crime I couldn't get away with?

AT THE AGE of twenty-one, I resolved to put this to the test.

By this point, I'd managed to restrain my more self-destructive tendencies enough to get most of the way through a medical degree. I overcame my penchant for self-flagellation, put that all behind me and learned to be at ease with myself, even the more unsavory aspects of my personality. Instead of feeling guilty about them, I embraced them. I learned to listen politely to my father's hearty nostrums. *Be discreet. If you can't be good, be careful. Always keep your old man covered up. And whatever you do, don't get caught.* I even took some of his advice on board. Stopped being such a wet blanket, as he might have put it. I was after all following in his footsteps, professionally speaking. Perhaps in other ways too. There were rumours of his conquests, sexual and otherwise, occasional bleatings of worse from the inevitable, grudge-bearing casualties left by a respectable man on the road to success. After all, the profile of such a man, according to popular wisdom, often mirrors that of a psychopath.

I even found time to extend my studies into my leisure time, managing to combine recreational activities with professional development. Fortuitously, the Mackinnons had fallen on hard times and had to sell the croft to my father. I imagine he relished the class revenge. He let me use it as a little hideaway, using the romance of an island love nest to my advantage, as well as my own status as a top pediatric surgeon. I built my own surgery there for my own private research projects. I don't remember much about what happened there. It all seemed to happen at one remove.

I do sometimes wonder though if part of me wanted to get caught, just to see how much abuse my other self would take, to see whether he might become mutinous if I pushed him too far. It was the same sort of perversity that made me tamper with the straps on my own parachute when I went sky-diving recently for a charity in aid of the children's hospital where I now work—a desire to test the forces that charmed my life. Maybe it was that spirit which made me slapdash about packing the right maps and climbing gear when I went mountaineering alone in the Cairn-gorms. Of course, in the end the instinct for self-preservation kicked in. I remembered how to release the emergency parachute. I managed to let off flares and mountain rescue got me down with only mild exposure.

The carelessness that allowed the young woman, a journalist investigating medical malpractice, to escape from the surgery I've kept secret for five years now, is one I may live to regret. But not for much longer I think. Somehow she made it to the mainland before I could stop her.

The police are a ferry journey away, but there has been no news that he has handed himself in in my place. It's only a matter of time before they come with a warrant for my arrest, and there will be no way out then. I cannot face the prospect of a trial, not after what they're likely to find buried near the *Viburnum davidii* I planted when I took possession of the croft. I'm going to find that cliff where I got stuck all those years ago. If I throw myself off it, I wonder if he'll take my place at the bottom this time.

SCORDATURA

———— ◆ ————

Jess Landry

ODETTE STARTS THE morning with Bach's Cello Suite No.1 in G major. There's something about the way the notes pour from her cello as the bow glides across the strings that makes her feel at home. The strings reverberate against the bow, fine strands of a Siberian stallion's hair, the cold metal vibrating on the cello's fingerboard, loose then tight, tight then loose. The way the acoustics in her empty room make her feel like she's happily suffocating, every stroke of the bow pressing tighter against her chest. The bass notes, the high notes, all filling the air around her, squeezing, pressing, against the tall windows in her room. The music holds firm against the stark, white walls, off her cream-colored bedsheets, perfectly made and ready to welcome her this evening. They bounce off the ceiling, off the herringbone-patterned hardwood floor, against the small door that leads to her bathroom. The notes reverberate through her: in her dark hair and into her pale skin. They seep into her brown eyes, the fabric of her grey dress, through her fingertips and into her bones. She knows this Suite, and many others, like the sun knows to rise and fall in a day. Somewhere in her room, likely in the locked chest at the foot of her bed, are hundreds of sheets of music, all inherited from her mother, all no longer needed.

THE BOW CURVES around the C string, a smooth bass note, closing out the Suite. The sun shines in through one of her windows in her bedroom where she faces while practicing. Their apartment sits on a corner block of Rue Saint-Martin, another apartment sitting adjacent with her own, a lush green park directly in front of her.

A few people walk the cobblestone streets four stories down, some hand-in-hand, others hurrying along by themselves. Small shops line the road, and as she sets her cello down and props open the window, the room immediately fills with the aroma of fresh bread from the nearby bakery. An orange tabby tomcat sits across the way in the adjacent apartment, sunning itself, his eyes squinted and content. One floor up, a man in a red shirt sits on his small cast-iron balcony, tiny cup and newspaper in hand.

Odette imagines what the cobblestone must feel like under bare toes. Would it be cold? It must be—though the sun is bright, it's no match for the tight Paris streets.

A tap echoes through the apartment, followed by two more in quick succession. Odette clears her throat, taking in one last smell of baking yeast, and picks up her bow, ready to spend the rest of her day practicing her debut concerto, the one she'll be playing in four days' time at the Palais Grenier. Kodály's Sonata in B minor, all three movements. The impossible piece.

ODETTE STARTS THE morning with Bach's Cello Suite No.1 in G major. Outside, people traverse down the cobblestone street. The cat across the way is in his normal spot, waiting for the sun to peak.

The cold cello strings fit snugly into the self-made grooves of her fingers like a second home. Down-bow, up-bow, she lets her elbow guide the stroke, the music spilling from her like a river of her blood gushing from an open wound. She wonders how that would feel, the blood pouring from her body, out of her shell and pooling at her feet. Would it seep through the herringbone floor? Would it collect in the unused space between her room and the room below, her mother's study? Would it pool and pool and press down on the intricate *fleur-de-lis* patterned ceiling until it broke through the plaster and onto her mother, covering her in a sea of red?

She's playing faster now, an eighth above tempo. Her brain tells her to slow but her hands refuse to listen. The cat across the way lays on his open perch, the man sipping his drink and reading the paper one floor above him. Odette longs to be that cat, to be free and lazy, to watch the world without a purpose.

Three quick taps sound from the room below—a stick to the floorboards—a first warning to keep tempo.

The cat's owners don't keep him confined. They open a window for him every morning. He wears a collar with a small bell, and sometimes, when Odette's window is open, she hears it ringing. The cat likely eats the freshest of foods; his dish is probably made of crystal. And at night, he sleeps with his contented look in the centre of his master's bed, nestled comfortably between sheets and legs.

Faster now, almost double its tempo. Three more taps, now with more force, more echo—her second warning.

To be that cat, Odette would walk off that ledge and onto the street below. If she jumped from the window, her fingers wouldn't ache, her hips wouldn't burn; she wouldn't have to practice anymore. Her room wouldn't echo with the taps from below, her mother banging on the floor. If she jumped, she'd be free. She'd feel the coolness of the cobblestone, the rush of air flying past her as the ground quickly approached. Would others rush to her aid, or would they leave her on the street, her body mangled, her bones broken, her blood spilling through the cracks forming a tiny red stream? At least her last breath would be one of fresh bread.

The cat's looking at her now, his contented gaze gone. Wide, alert eyes stare back as though it's spotted its prey. They lock on one another, nothing but twenty meters and the sweet French air between them.

He's sitting up, watching her, watching her play, watching her hands and fingers flail wildly across the cello. The cat takes a step towards her, toward the edge of the windowsill, as though an invisible bridge connects them, as though he wants to step off.

With a final stroke, she finishes the song, short of breath, cold with sweat. She rests her bow as one loud thud shakes the floor underneath her. Her third and final warning, one that always comes too late.

"Odette!" a muffled cry rings out from below.

She turns to the cat, and the animal gives his head a shake and takes a step back, into the safety of his home, into the warmth of the sun.

IT'S MID-DAY BUT the fireplace in her mother's room is alight, the room filled with the smell of burning wood. Her mother sits in front of the flames, her wheelchair placed within a few feet. The back of her head is always the first thing Odette sees. The woman's hair is pulled back in a tight bun, the wear of years staining its color: a once vibrant dark brown, similar to Odette's, now a muddy, bland display. She tries her best to hide the off-color, the wrinkles, the crow's feet, by pulling her hair back as tight as it can go. Her face—*is that how I'm going to look when I'm older?*—is a face full of corners and angles. Sunken cheeks and hollow eye sockets rest on a paper-thin neck. Underneath the usual black smock is a body diseased.

She's wrapped her shoulders in her favorite fur blanket—one that was gifted to her while on the Canadian leg of her last tour before the muscular dystrophy overtook her—pulling it closer to her neck as Odette approaches, her thin, wiry fingers attempting to clutch at the fabric. Next to her, her silver cane, the one she had made before the disease made her wheelchair-bound, the one that she still finds the strength to lift. Its wooden stem grows from thicker to thinner with a silver-plated head shaped like that of a crow's, its beak acting as a place to rest her thumb. Both the stick end and the crow's head have found Odette's skin at some point in time; both ends likely to find it again shortly.

"Sit," her mother says without looking up from the fire, her eyes fixated on the flames. Odette does as she's told, the area on the floor is warm underneath her from the long-burning fire. Odette hears the shuffle of anxious feet from the next room—the hired help scrambling away to avoid her mother's wrath, leaving Odette to take the brunt.

Mother and daughter sit in silence for a moment, like they always do. The flame's reflection in the crow's head catches Odette's eye, and she quickly loses herself in its world, a space of reflections.

In the reflected world, are the roles reversed? Would Odette be the former ingénue, a musical prodigy, bound to a wheelchair after an unavoidable disease took hold of her? Would her mother be the child, the up-and-comer with her début at the Palais Garnier in a few days time; the daughter of *the* Marguerite Wagner, world-renowned cellist and socialite? Would she stare emptily into the flames, her mind wandering much as it did now, waiting to inflict pain both spoken and forced upon her only kin? Would she sit in this very spot night in, night out listening to her daughter play in the room above her, catching her off moments with the thwack of her cane to the floor, her muscles and joints throbbing?

"I expect you know why I called you down here."

Odette nods, her gaze shifting from the reflection to the floor.

"Then I also expect you know what to do."

What if just once, this one time, Odette didn't do as her mother commanded? What if she ran, ran to the window, and let herself fall from the fourth story and onto the cobblestone street below?

"Odette."

Her mother's voice is stiff, hoarse, much like the woman's final weeks playing the instrument she loved. Before her body betrayed her with an infliction of which there is no cure, just a life of pills and pain and losing control of your own body. But Marguerite was a fighter. Even as her fingers curled and her knees bowed, as her muscle mass slowly wasted away, she pushed. She pushed until her body screamed back, confining her to this chair, this prison on wheels.

This would not be Odette's life. Not now, not ever.

"Odette!"

The woman slams her cane onto the floor, the vibrations shaking through to Odette's bones, rocking her back into the present. She feels her mother's frigid stare upon her.

Odette stands and moves towards the fireplace, the sound of the crackling logs relieving the room of an otherwise dead silence. She places a hand on the mantle, one devoid of any family photos, any mementos of a childhood. Instead it's lined with trophies, medals, keys to cities—material things that mean nothing except to that of the beholder. A mantle filled of ghosts, remnants of another life. Odette brings her other hand to the back of her neck and pulls at the button holding up her dress. The fire's heat burns at her face, drying up the tears before they reach her lips. The dress falls from her slender frame, and she shivers as the air touches her exposed skin.

"You should know better by now," Marguerite says, picking up her cane.

ODETTE RUNS TO her room, the fabric of her dress clinging to her back. She's never touched fire but the feeling drumming through her body has to be close to it.

Careful not to let her back scrape anything, she sits straight and grabs her bow and cello, the reasons for all her suffering. Below, her mother bangs the crow-headed cane against the floor; Odette sees a glimpse of her flesh still dangling from its sharp beak.

With her bow up, Odette begins the third movement of Kodály's Sonata in B minor, the venom inside her fueling every stroke. She would be better off jumping out the window. That would ruin her mother's grand plans, plans that were originally meant for Marguerite in her prime, now only up to Odette to follow through. *The heir to the cellist's throne*, she'd once read in a London newspaper. The article painted her mother in pastels and sunshine, and talked about how her MD diagnosis was a complete surprise, how it changed her life for the worse.

"But then I turned to my child, my sweet Odette," the article had quoted her. *"And I knew that my legacy would live on through this little girl."*

She looks out the window and sees the cat across the way, sunning itself in the late afternoon blaze. Odette's suffocating; the heat, her rage, the music pushing against the flimsy window pane. Her eyes fixate on the cat. She wills it to look at her, to feel what she feels.

As Odette plucks at the strings, the cat opens its eyes. He turns his head towards her.

The tempo increases, the bow movements more frantic than earlier, an organized chaos. Everything Odette has, everything she is, cascades from her wounds, from her hands, from her instrument. The animal sits up, as it had earlier, its eyes on Odette.

Go on. She wills it through the music. The cat takes a step toward the edge of the windowsill. *Do it. For the both of us.*

She reaches the finale. But she's on another plane now, another world where notes and music meld together, where rage and heat are two in the same. Mother's below, waiting for this moment, polishing her crow for another round.

Go on.

His little orange paw takes a step.

Go.

Odette's fingers glide over the strings, pressing and relenting in the exact moments where they need to. As her bow crosses the final note, the cat pitches himself off the ledge.

Odette stares at the empty windowsill, gasping for breath. She rushes to the window, nearly knocking over her cello. She throws open the pane and sticks her head out. Four stories down, the body of the orange tomcat lies, its little chest heaving, its hind legs twisted in a way that shouldn't be, its eyes looking up to the sky, to Odette. He takes his last breath on the cobblestone street as people step over him, not a soul stopping to help.

ODETTE PICKS AT her plate: coq au vin with scalloped potatoes and herb-garnished peas, a lukewarm glass of water. Wilhelmina, their chef, clinks away in the kitchen, washing and scrubbing dishes. Marguerite eats steadily, ferociously, as though the woman hasn't eaten in days.

The fork sits awkwardly in her curled fingers, a skill she refuses to give up. Her shoulders tight, her arms as pointed as the angles of her face, her contorted body hidden under a black shawl. With a full mouth, she still manages to speak, spitting criticisms at Odette: her tempo, the pressure of her bow on the strings.

"If I can hear it from one floor under you, how do you think it will sound in the Palais Garnier?"

Under the dim dining room lights, Odette's mind can only see the cat, its mangled body, the possessed look in its eyes as it stepped off the ledge.

Did I make him do that?

She pushes a pea absentmindedly across her plate, her mother's voice tuning in and out.

"I expect you not to make a fool of me. Do you know how many influential people will be there? Do you know how long it took me to achieve what you've done in so little time? You should be grateful."

Impossible. In her sixteen years of life, never once has Odette willed anyone to do anything. If she had any will, she would've kept it all for herself and certainly not forced a cat to jump to its death.

"Odette."

But what if she had? What if there was something inside her that made the animal end its life? Did it feel her heartache through the windowpane? Did it look into her eyes and understand what she wanted it to do, because she was too much a coward to do it herself?

"Odette!"

Her mother smacks her crow's head against the wooden table, rattling the dishes, shaking the water in her glass.

"Have you heard a word I've said?"

Their eyes meet, and in them Odette sees a faint reflection of herself.

"Yes," says Odette.

"Well then, enlighten me." Her mother stares her down, peeling back Odette's flesh and exposing her for the liar she is. Marguerite taps the crow's head against the table, Odette looks down at her half-eaten dinner.

"Upstairs. Now. Kodály's Sonata in B minor."

She thinks to protest. Today could be the day when she finally stands up for herself, when no comes from her lips and she stands tall, taller than her mother ever was, then she walks out the door and never looks back.

She gets up and pauses for a moment, parting her lips. Marguerite pays no attention to Odette as she walks by. Instead, she sets her cane down and feebly attempts to pick up her fork.

"Odette." She stops on the second step as Marguerite turns her head slightly, her profile aglow from the dining room lights. Wilhelmina's footsteps creak in the kitchen, the cling and clang from the dishes barely audible. "Play it until your fingers bleed."

BACH'S CELLO SUITE No.1 in G minor, that's how Odette starts her day. She looks out her closed window across the way to where the cat used to bask. Now that window's closed, the blinds drawn. She had checked last night before going to bed to see if the cat's body was still laying on the cobblestone, but it was gone. No doubt the owners had found him.

First position, bow up. Slack the wrists, and go.

Music spills from Odette's body. She closes her eyes, imagining the room filling with music in a physical form, like a warm down blanket covering every inch, every nook. Wrapping itself around her, over her tiny frame, her swollen back; engulfing her dark hair, turning it white, as white as her room, as white as snow.

Could I do it again?

Her eyes open, the bow nearly skipping over the strings. She corrects her posture while still playing, her mind now wandering to the place she didn't want it to go.

Fighting it, she turns her head to the window. The man in the red shirt one floor up from the cat's apartment is sitting on his small balcony, the paper in his hands. He looks to be mother's age, though his face seems warm. She pushes the ridiculous thought from her mind, trying to tell herself that she had nothing to do with the cat's actions; that she, Odette Wagner, daughter of Marguerite Wagner, famed cellist, on the brink of succeeding her mother in talent, soon to have her debut concert at the Palais Garnier in Paris, did not force any creature from its perch. No, she did not have the ability to sentence living things to their death.

But what if I do?

She finishes the Suite, letting her bow rest. Then, she takes a breath and brings her bow back to first position.

Second finger on B and first finger on A, second finger to F sharp, first to E, the impossible Sonata reverberates through the room. Her gaze sets on the man, sipping from his tiny cup.

The music pours, her fingers burning. The man doesn't budge.

She's stretching her fingers as far as they can spread, her whole body pushing against the instrument using as much of it to play as her hands. It resounds through her chest and into her veins. The man doesn't look up from his paper.

Suddenly her back spasms, causing her bow to jump. The pain flares through her skin, her muscles, she even feels it in her teeth. She stops, pulling at the fabric of her light dress that presses against her open wounds from yesterday. Below, the crow's head bangs once against the floor.

Odette fixes her posture and resumes from the last bar. The crow's head bangs twice more like a muffled metronome.

It echoes inside her as she gets near the end, the most intense part of the Sonata. *Tap tap tap.* It's all she can hear, drowning out the sound of her own instrument. It's all she can feel, the crow's beak tearing at her flesh. It's all she knows, the disapproving glare of her mother.

With everything in her, she plays the final note, her bow leaving the strings smoothly. She takes a deep breath and looks out the window. Her eyes meet those of the man in the red shirt right as he takes a step off his balcony.

Someone screams as Odette throws her bedroom window open. He's twisted like the cat, except this time, people have noticed. The din of the gathering crowd rises like the smell of fresh bread. People step back as blood spills from his body—as red as his shirt—out onto the cobblestone, dripping between its gaps and trickling down with the slope of the street. His body twisted one way, his face the other, looking up at Odette with a hollow stare.

But what if I could?

THE PALAIS GARNIER is full, every crushed velvet seat, every curtain-draped loge, all 1,979 seats filled with faces Odette's never seen before. Her cello sits centre stage in its holder, the bow hanging beside it. The stage lights run over its polished maple surface, illuminating it as though it were on fire. Marguerite Wagner's famed cello. A massive chandelier dangles high above the crowd, sparkling in the theatre's glow.

She peeks from behind the stage curtains, her hands steady and calm as the faces take no notice of her. They're not here for Odette, not really. They're here for Marguerite, they're here to appease her—perhaps some to mock her—the once famous cellist whose own body betrayed her, bound to a wheelchair, no feeling left from her ribs down.

The auditorium doors open and in comes Marguerite, commanding the attention of all those as she's pushed to her seat. Her black lace dress—the one she wore when she last played the Palais—squeezes her frail frame, her eyes looking forward, a thin smile acknowledging the admirers who applaud as she takes her place at the front of the venue.

The clapping subsides as the lights dim, and with a deep breath in, Odette walks onto the stage.

She takes her seat, and brings her cello into her arms, heavy against her body.

She brings the bow to first position, and begins.

Kodály's Sonata in B minor, the first movement. The acoustics of the theatre travel the music far and wide, into the ears of every soul in the building. She focuses on the strings as she brings the bow fore and aft, crescendo to decrescendo. The music flows from the Stradivarius just as it did at home, in her room with the window overlooking the park, the cat, the man in the red shirt. Where she looked down at the cobblestone streets, wanting to press her bare feet against them, avoiding the spots where dried blood hadn't been washed away. Would the street feel like the crow's head? Would the first touch be cold, then would it turn into fire?

She looks up from the strings, her eyes washing over a sea of unknowns. These faces, round and thin, man and woman; these eyes staring up at her, no feelings behind them. Her eyes find her mother's, the woman with the distorted body in the front row, her eyes burning holes into her, the crow's head in her palm. Under the dim lights, her face looks more angular than ever, a Picasso in the flesh. A tight mouth with tight eyes with skin beginning to sag at the jowls. Is that what Odette had to look forward to in her elder years? To look as though she hated every moment, no matter how big or small? Is that what she was to become?

She finishes the first movement and the audience applauds as they're supposed to. She begins the second movement. The faces in the crowd stifle yawns and fidget in their seats the more she plays. A cellphone rings; a deep chuckle echoes from somewhere. Her mother turns to the crowd in disapproval, her grip on the crow's head tightening.

At the end of the second movement, Odette cracks her fingers and raises her bow. She begins the third, the final piece of the impossible Sonata. The faces perk up as though she's just screamed from the top of her lungs. Their bodies stop fidgeting and become taut to attention— this is what they've been waiting for. This is what reminds them most of Marguerite. This is the last Sonata she played.

Odette's fingers pluck and press, her hand rises and drops, her body pushes against the wooden body of the cello, using it as much as her other extremities. Music spews from her fingertips, her eyes, her mouth. It fills the space in the auditorium, seeping into the skin of the faces watching her.

Odette's fingers feel as though they're moving faster than they've ever moved before; her bow movements making their own breeze.

What happens after this? she wonders. *Am I destined to live a life identical to Marguerite? To have others fawning over me, traveling the world to play in famous theatres night after night, to drink myself to sleep and eventually wind up pregnant. To have a child out of spite? To have an incurable disease take over my body? To force everything I wanted for myself upon my child?*

Marguerite smirks, her grip relaxing on the crow's head, her thumb flicking at its sharp beak keeping in time with the Sonata.

Odette looks to the crowd, she has their attention now. She has the very breaths in their chests. Their bulging necks that spill from their too-tight lapels, their stomachs that push and scream against the tight fabric of their dresses and suits one size too small. Their eyes hollow, their blank minds.

This is not the life I want.

The raw wounds on Odette's back swell against her organza dress, her chest heaves and heats up like she could melt the stage from her presence alone. She pulls the cello closer until her and the instrument are two in the same—two beings turned to one, one heart, one mind.

She plucks the strings as her mother starts to cough, bringing her hand to her mouth.

Odette plucks again, her gaze not leaving her mother's. The woman coughs and coughs, her other hand on her chest, dropping the crow's head. Other faces in the audience turn to Marguerite, a distraction from the performance.

Odette brings the bow over the strings hard, nearly snapping them. Marguerite pitches forward in her chair, falling to the carpeted ground. The faces stand up around her, rushing to the woman's aid, but Odette keeps on, the music is her and she is the music. She watches as several men rush to Marguerite, but they clutch their chests and their heads and their stomachs and their necks before they can reach her. They collapse beside Marguerite, near her, in the aisles, in their seats; blood spilling from their eyes, their noses, their ears. The women in the audience stand and scream as bodies from the upper balconies throw themselves off the ledges and onto the patrons below. Chaos erupts as the faces realize something is wrong. Men step over women rushing for the theatre doors, people shove one another in a chance to save themselves. But it's no use. Odette plucks the strings and the theatre-goers fall like dominoes in a row.

As she nears the final bars of the Sonata, she looks at her mother, a woman tangled on the floor amidst a sea of convulsing bodies. Marguerite grabs hold of her wheelchair, her gnarled hands finding the armrests. Using everything within her, she pulls her head up while her body remains on the ground, blood spilling from her eyes, tears of pride that Odette never knew. The two lock eyes, a blaze alit between them.

Still, Odette plays on.

For the first time in her life, Odette sees a look on her mother's face that she's never seen. It's not pride. It's not contempt or hatred or jealousy. It's not love—it'll never be love.

It's fear.

Odette drags her bow over the final note, a long, deep bass tone. And as she draws it out, as her fingers sizzle and the welts on her back throb, her mother's eyes widen. Odette watches in amazement as Marguerite's torso starts to curve backward in time with the note, crooked fingers grasping the armrest no match for the unseen force crushing her.

As Odette ends the final note of the impossible Sonata, Marguerite's bones snap, echoing through the theatre like they were two in the same.

ODETTE STARTS THE morning with Bach's Cello Suite No.1 in G major. The way the notes pour from her cello as she brings the bow across, as the strings reverberate against the Siberian horse-hairs, the cold metal vibrating under her fingers, loose then tight, tight then loose. The way the acoustics in her empty room make her feel like she's suffocating, every stroke of the bow pressing tighter against her chest. The bass notes, the high notes, all filling the air around her, squeezing against the open window in her room.

A few quick swipes and she finishes the Suite, the pressure in her chest releasing. She sits back in her chair, taking a breath. Outside her window, the sounds from the street below rise with the smell of fresh bread. Smiling, she sets her cello aside and grabs some loose change from the mantle in her room.

Odette steps outside, barefoot onto the cobblestone street, avoiding the cracks with dried blood still in them.

STRINGLESS PUPPETRY

———◆———

CC Adams

"Evil is whatever distracts."—Franz Kafka

NIGHT HUNG OVER St. Paul's cathedral like evening wear, the blue tinge of the dome itself looking almost ghostly against the darkness of the sky. Saturday night brought people out en masse to a number of bars dotted in and around the area, the night alive with sounds: chatter, and hard paving rang with the clack of high heels or the scuff of leather uppers. Philomena, arms folded and clutching her elbows, walked across the expanse of the square, taking in the scene around her. One Jaeger-bomb and her stomach had protested. Unlike some drinkers, not only did Philomena know her limits, she never argued with them. Deciding to quit while she was behind, she made her apologies to the girls, and hugs and air kisses later, headed back to St. Paul's Underground.

The balmy warmth of early evening had seen temperatures hold well into the night. And while it never got shoulder-to-shoulder crowded like Oxford Circus or in and around Liverpool Street, St. Paul's had too much foot traffic for Philomena's liking. *But, hey, small mercies.* She'd be back home within the hour, and 8-Ball would stop pacing the carpet and yowling once she'd—

Oh.

Gait slowing, Philomena inclined her head. Passersby drifted around her unfazed.

Wha-a-at?

She lifted a hand to her mouth, covering a smile of bemusement. "Oh, my God..." Some distance ahead, a woman cut through the crowd as she headed away from the station.

Now at a standstill, Philomena watched the woman, open-mouthed. Medium height, caramel complexion, blond hair with black roots, black dress with white T-shirt underneath. Philomena looked down at herself, and the wedge mules. Then back at the woman, now halfway across the square.

How the hell...?

How was this even possible? Philomena turned as the figure walked on, tracking her movement. Further away now, the figure came to a stop at the pedestrian crossing, waiting for the traffic to slow.

Philomena followed, as the traffic up ahead stopped and the woman crossed over to the other side of the road. Noting the beep from the crossing ahead had stopped, Philomena picked up the pace, and trotted across the road before traffic continued on behind her in a river of headlights and gleaming bodywork. A few yards down the nearest side street, the woman waited, bare arms folded as she leaned back against the wall. On seeing Philomena approach, she gave a smile of weary relief, her mouth falling open in a fatuous grin. Philomena came up to the woman until only inches separated them.

"Wow," she breathed. "You know I didn't want to believe it."

Philomena looked the woman over from head to toe. Both of them looked *exactly* the same, sounded *exactly* the same. Even the clothes were *exactly* the same—from the faded denim jacket right down to the shoes, and their creases and scuff marks. Philomena raised a hand to her mouth, stifling a nervous laugh, and the woman's gaze fixed on her hand.

"Are we twins?"

Philomena swallowed. "I...don't know. I guess we must be." How were you supposed to react to a revelation like this? As far as Philomena knew, she had two sisters and a step-brother (courtesy of Mum), but aside from that, no other siblings. Surely after a...a few years, (*try since ninety-seventy-eight*, she railed at herself), you would have found out that you have a twin. *A twin.* This was just unreal.

"What's your name?" the woman asked. Her eyes were wide: full of bewilderment.

Name?

Oh.

"Philomena. But everyone calls me Mena; Phil is a boy's name—but you probably know that, right?"

"Oh." The woman gave a slow nod, her eyes never leaving Philomena's. "I guess I can see that."

Another nervous laugh. "Okay, cool. What's your name?"

"My name?"

"Yeah. I'm guessing it's not Phil or Mena."

The woman licked her lips. "No, no, no. It's Amanda, sorry"—she shook her head—"this is just a little weird for me."

"You're telling me. Well, hello," she said, holding out her hand.

Amanda made to shake it, and fingertips from both hands met head-on. "Oh!"

Now, with more care and attention, they shook hands.

Shaking hands was the kind of thing that Philomena would only really do in the workplace, when she had to meet someone from another department. You observed certain etiquette when you shook hands with someone: gave them a firm shake, but not so damned strong that you broke every bone in their hand—it was a greeting, not a competition. On the other hand, you didn't want to be such a wet fish that it felt like shaking hands with a corpse. But in shaking hands with Amanda, it felt precise. No stronger or weaker than Philomena's shake, and released at the same time.

Odd.

"So," Philomena said, drawing her hand back and folding her arms.

"What are you doing around here?"

Amanda shrugged. "Same as you, I guess. Going for a night out, just to do a little drinking. Do you want to come?"

No, no, no. "I was just going home, actually," Philomena said. "I wasn't feeling too well earlier."

Amanda gave a brief smile. "Dizzy?"

"A little, yeah."

Amanda gave a little shrug of her shoulders. "I get it. Maybe it was a harbinger, maybe it was a sign, you know?"

"A sign? What was?"

"A sign that something different would happen. It's not every day that you run into your twin, right? Maybe this was the universe telling you that something special was going to happen."

"By making me sick? I think I'll stick to the boring and ordinary, thank you very much," she said, laughing. Amanda laughed as well, cupping her hands over her mouth and nose, wide-eyed. "You're okay?"

"Yeah," Amanda said from behind her hands. "This is just a little..."

...weird, is all.

Amanda tilted her head; gave a wan look of resignation. Of course it was weird. Both women sobered.

"Look," Amanda said. "As long as we're here, why don't we spend a little more time answering those questions? I'm sure we've both got them. Maybe we can figure out what the hell has happened, or what's happening. How does that sound?"

"Sure. Did you have anywhere in mind?"

Amanda jerked her head in the direction of the side street. "I was off to the Patch Bar. I think it might even be a red straw night?" She looked at Philomena, her expression expectant.

It didn't *quite* gel. As the two women made small talk, Philomena had done her best to shake a sense of unease, but was unable to. Sure, London was a big city, but that the two of them would cross paths after all this time seemed a little unlikely. On top of that, this woman was dressed exactly the same as Philomena. Was that what it felt like to have a twin? Philomena wasn't sure. And as uncomfortable as the situation felt, Philomena decided that time spent with her double would hopefully answer more questions.

The two women made their way down a narrow side street flanked by the occasional car and the occasional smoker until they came to the Patch Bar, a spacious cavern of wood paneling, dim lighting, and packed with a clientele of mostly thirty-somethings, dressed to impressed. Thirty minutes and two Singapore Slings apiece later, Philomena and Amanda sat on bar stools beside a pillar, and scanned the crowd. Conversation had been light, polite, but ultimately cagey at first. Amanda was down from Manchester with two days to kill before an Australian couple caught up with her in the capital. They would hit some of the markets—from Borough to Camden—and maybe take in something more scenic like The Shard Bar. Had she checked out the rooftop bar at One New Place? Which wasn't a million miles away from St. Paul's tube? Oh, yeah, Amanda said, but The Shard had a better view of the cityscape. You couldn't beat a great view now, could you? Philomena felt the same way but gave a nod, simply murmured her assent, and returned to her drink. With each sip and each gaze into her drink and its ice, Philomena could feel Amanda's eyes on her, as if she were hypnotized. Disconcerting, to say the least.

"Not much of the way of talent in here," Amanda said, scanning the crowd over her shoulder.

Philomena shrugged. "It is what it is. Still, it looks like there may be one or two attractive prospects in here."

"Excuse me." A male voice beside her, hand warm on her shoulder.

Philomena turned to the source. A dark-haired stocky man grinned at her, one hand still on her shoulder, the other hand on Amanda's shoulder. The Polo logo on the left breast was bigger than it had to be, like the curve of belly under his shirt. Still, he had an easy charm about him, and didn't stink of alcohol: all of this, Philomena computed in a fraction of a second. A glance at Amanda garnered a nod: *could be worse*.

"How come you're sitting, and not mingling with the rest of these good people? Enquiring minds wanna know."

Amanda frowned at the newcomer. "They do?"

"Oh, absolutely, they do. Don't worry," he said, clapping a hand to his chest. "I won't ask how you know each other. I can see you've got coordination down to a fine art. Can I at least ask your names?"

Introductions were made, the man revealing himself as Justin. Justin who made a living in property development. Justin who had only swung by the Patch Bar as he had finished reviewing a new property about ten minutes away and figured he might as well stop off for a drink before heading home. The more the two of them spoke, the more Philomena saw Amanda draw herself up: shoulders back, smoothing hair away from her neck. Conversely, seeing something so flirtatious, felt awkward. Of course, it wasn't Philomena—it just looked like her, but that didn't make it feel any more comfortable. Amanda showed her friendly and fun side: leading the conversation, fingertips skating across Justin's shoulder.

A casual caress of his upper arm.

Even touching a fingertip to his chin, at one point.

Wow...what am I doing? I? She?

To his credit, Justin gave them both his attention, turning to each one as he spoke to them, body language not overbearing, respectful but open. Philomena wouldn't have been quick to say he was her usual type, given that she liked the classic tall, dark, and handsome, and while Justin was dark-haired and handsome, he barely had an inch on her. The wedges weren't even her highest heels. So, no, hardly a dreamboat. Amanda, on the other hand, couldn't keep her eyes off him.

Attraction?

Amanda laid a hand on top of Justin's as she bit coyly at her lip. "Well," she breathed. "As charming as this has been, I feel I must head home for the night. A girl needs her beauty sleep." *Look at her*, Philomena thought, *a little alcohol and some man-candy, and look at her go. Priceless.*

Justin gave Amanda a look of mock reproach "Really? You're just going to abandon me?"

"Well, 'abandon' is such a horrible word. This isn't goodbye, think of it as a 'see you later.'" She leaned in and gave him a kiss on the cheek, before tilting her head past him to look at Philomena. "Don't worry about her. If I can tie a knot in a cherry stem with my tongue, so can she. Isn't that right, sis?"

"Ahhhh, I don't know anything about that." But that half-smile curving Amanda's lips proved unsettling; a smile that Philomena herself would use when her patience began to wear thin with someone. What she knew was that she should just make her excuses and leave. Then it would be snuggling with 8-Ball and watching—

"Really? I'm sure Jade Woolwich would disagree."

Amidst the bustle and loud music of the bar, Philomena's gut clenched in unease, and a wave of goosebumps ran across her neck. The Jade incident was years ago and witnessed only by two girls and the nine of diamonds from a pack of playing cards.

O-kaaaaay. Okay, play this safe now, nice and easy.

"Ooooh," she said, bringing her fingertips to lips forced in a smile. Justin, now in Amanda's embrace, looked over his shoulder at her. "One drink too many," Philomena said. "Back in a tick."

Philomena edged her way through the crowd, her mind racing. Beneath the veneer of social civility, there was an undercurrent of antagonism—*deliberate* antagonism. She could cut through the crowd and head straight up the stairs and leave, but if Amanda saw her, that would be bad. Worse, Amanda might come after her—and something about her twin seemed predatory, as if she were waiting for an opening. No. Best bet was to cut to the right, go to the ladies room, and then double back to leave. At least the bar was packed to capacity; you couldn't move more than a yard before you'd need to square your shoulders and sidle through the crowd like a playing card slid back into the deck. Loud music, chatter, full venue. It would be hard work to keep track of—

"Oh, my God," Amanda said, appearing at her shoulder. "Are you okay?"

Oh, shit. "Yeah, I'll be fine. Just give me a minute?" she said, her gaze hopeful. *Please, please, PLEASE go away.*

Her expression one of resolute benevolence, Amanda latched onto

Philomena's wrist. "Come on."

She shouldered the door open and led Philomena in, the door closing behind them and muffling the bar music.

Amanda turned back to Philomena, her eyes wide in excitement. She smoothed down her skirt and adjusted her bra, while Philomena finger-tucked stray hair behind her ear, her hand trembling. Lips curving in a thin smile, Amanda laid a hand on Philomena's ass and guided her to stand in front of her, facing the mirror. Amanda's chin came to rest on her shoulder and Philomena looked for her reflection.

Her breath caught.

"Wow," Amanda breathed. "How does something like that happen, eh?"

Overhead fluorescence or not, Philomena strained her eyes, but all she could see in the mirror was a line of cubicles on one side, along with a line of sinks on the other. She had no reflection.

Neither of them did.

How?

Philomena peered at the mirror, still seeing the same reflection—save for hers and Amanda's, which were still...missing. A sidelong glance at the cubicles, and the sinks, then back to the mirror.

Dead? Am I...dead?

No. No, that wasn't possible—if she were dead, her heartbeat wouldn't be thumping the way it was now. She didn't have a reflection, and neither did Amanda. But that didn't make sense, since the only thing that didn't have a reflection...

Oh, my God.

...was a vampire.

Amanda's hand, resting on Philomena's shoulder, now crawled up to the back of Philomena's head like some bony spider and shoved her. Caught off-guard, Philomena thrust out her hands to shield herself—and felt cold glass smack against her hands

...as Amanda's palms clapped against her own, although she couldn't feel them.

Weird.

Weirder still that she hadn't fallen over. Or smashed into the mirror for a faceful of glass. Disorientation rippled a wave of nausea, which Philomena fought to swallow down.

What happened? What happened?

Arms outstretched and hands still touching on either side of the glass, Philomena saw her concern mirrored in Amanda's eyes.

What happened? What did you do?

Efforts to open her mouth failed, her lips fixed in the same faint smile of bemusement on Amanda's face. Concussion? Amanda *had* grabbed the back of her head and shoved pretty hard. Was that why she couldn't feel anything? Lack of sensation was disconcerting enough, without trying to figure out how exactly she was still standing. Philomena fought to tug her arms back, to move her legs, anything.

Nothing.

Paralysis?

Oh, my God.

OH. MY. GOD.

Slowly, Amanda peeled her left hand away from the mirror, as Philomena did likewise with her right. Struggling to resist, Philomena's hand moved of its own accord, rising to her mouth and stifling a cough of bewilderment.

"Wow," Amanda breathed. Her eyes flickered. From the mirror, to the cubicles, the sinks, the ceiling, the floor. She clapped a hand between her breasts, her chest heaving. "So this is what it feels like."

And here was where the dreadful reality had sunk in: that Philomena was now her own reflection, and Amanda—Amanda who was Philomena's reflection all along had now come to life. Roles were now reversed, with Philomena consigned to the wrong side of the mirror, with her reflection (*fucking Amanda, Oh, God, that's not fucking Amanda, that's my reflection!*) taking her place in the real world.

Fingers trailing back from her mouth, Amanda leaned in closer (with Philomena compelled to follow suit), and prodded the flesh of her cheek. "This is unreal," she whispered. From the corner of her eye,

Philomena could see her own finger moving in tandem with that of her double (*that's not fucking Amanda*), but she couldn't move by herself. Not without her double's actions puppeteering her. Worse than numbness, she couldn't...feel anything. Here in the void of the mirror, the urge to weep, to scream, was overwhelming.

Which, thanks to her double, simply wouldn't happen now.

And on the back of this, what would happen to Philomena when her double stepped away from the mirror. *What would happen?*

Her double peered into the mirror, one fingertip under her eye as she pulled down the lower lid and Philomena responded in kind, helpless. The fingertip lingered before rolling forward on the pad.

Driving the nail into the skin.

Pleeeeease, no.

The nail bit deeper into the skin, with Philomena feeling none of it and powerless to do anything. When a line of blood appeared above the nail, her double drew her finger back with a wince. "Well," she said, panting a little. She wiped a bead of blood away on the tip of her little finger, and sucked it. "Mmm. That's different." As if in response, the toilet flushed from within a cubicle.

Help! Somebody, look! Please, fucking look! Just fucking look!

"I'll just have to give that Justin something extra," her double said. And then growing solemn, and backing away from the mirror. "At least I won't make you watch."

Turning on her heel, she strode away.

Noooooo! Don't leave me here! Don't leave m—

THE BATH HOUSE

———— ◆ ————

Tim Major

SCARCROFT LANE WAS so black with shadows that Mark had to squint to make out the two figures at its far end. He watched as his best friend, Oren, held out his hand to whoever it was that stood before the old gate to the primary school, the one labelled *Girls' Entrance* which was no longer used; Mark had always teased his two daughters about having every day to be dropped at the *Boys' Entrance* instead. Even his youngest girl had left the school now.

The stranger reached out and took the package from Oren. His head bent; he must be making sure the money was all there. He turned and waved in Mark's direction. His silhouette was warped by shifting patterns on the path behind him, a peculiar lattice caused by the leaves of the trees having almost swallowed the lamps up on their posts.

"All right," the woman beside Mark said. She had introduced herself as Anna. "We can go now."

She turned and strode away. Mark glanced back along the lane. Now there was only one man standing at the corner of the park, but he couldn't tell whether it was Oren or the stranger who worked with Anna.

He hurried to catch up with her. Her shoes made no sound on the tarmac; he was surprised that she wasn't wearing clacking heels to go with her fashionable dress and pale trench coat. She had good legs.

"It's all a bit cloak and dagger, isn't it?" he said.

Anna didn't reply.

"Sorry," he said. "I'm a bit nervous."

"Don't be."

At the end of the lane she turned to face him. Her smile seemed genuine. Mark felt a pang of familiarity.

"Are you sure you don't work at the university?" he said.

"I'm sure."

"I could have sworn we've met before. This isn't a chat-up. I'm married."

Her smile faltered, just for a moment. Mark cursed his error.

"I'm not a face from the past," she said, unruffled. Then she took his arm and led him along Nunnery Lane, parallel to the city wall and past the skeletal limbs of the cranes that towered above and behind it. He had never seen this road empty of traffic before, but he reminded himself that it had been years since he had been out and about after midnight. Despite the absence of any cars, Anna stopped at the crossing opposite St Thomas' Hospital and waited for the lights to change.

The tall plywood boards put in place by the construction crew still barricaded the road leading to Victoria Bar, which was the only access point to the Bishophill neighborhood from the south. Anna marched directly to the makeshift gates and, after some moments of tinkering with a padlock and chain, she pushed one of the heavy boards aside.

"We can't go in there," Mark said. "Can't you see the signs?"

Anna was already inside. "It's the only way in. You can come through or you can go home."

Oren had already paid the money, and in the circumstances it was difficult to imagine a refund being offered. Oren had been coy about the exact value of his gift. In the birthday card he had given to Mark in the Winning Post, under the pre-printed *Happy Birthday*, he had written: *42 deserves Life, the Universe and Everything.* Later, when the other people Mark had invited to celebrate his birthday had gathered around the karaoke, Oren had taken Mark to one side. He had sensed the trouble Mark had been having recently, he said, it was there in his eyes. Had Mark heard about the bath house? Did he understand that this was a big deal?

Of course, Mark had heard the talk. Surely everyone in York had. The details about the bath house changed from telling to telling—not least its supposed location—and nobody claimed firsthand experience.

Mark glanced along the deserted street, took a breath, then side-stepped through the gates. Anna had already set off towards the arches of Victoria Bar.

As he passed through the city walls he felt immediately the absence of the usual terraces of houses. He lurched to one side slightly, as one does when walking on the platform beside a moving train and the train abruptly ends and disappears. He had viewed the construction plans on the council website. The care home and apartment complexes were due to take up the entire area between Fairfax Street and the mound of Baile Hill, which necessitated the demolition of dozens of the old, narrow houses. But the lack of them still felt shocking.

"There," Anna said. She pointed to one of the few intact buildings alongside the Portakabins of the building site.

"There, meaning that's where we're going?" Mark gazed up at the building on the corner, with its conical roof that almost, but not quite, punctured the half-moon. He had walked past it many times before, but now, in the dark, it appeared imposing and unfamiliar. None of the street lamps were lit and so the three tall doors of the building—though Mark knew they were painted red—appeared black. "But that's an old church, not a bath house. Primitive Methodist, wasn't it?"

"Does it matter?" Anna said.

"It does to me." All that gossip about the bath house, all those rumors about rejuvenation, and it still didn't click. "I'm an atheist, Anna. I don't think this is for me." It occurred to him that he had never considered religion as a part of the solution to his various problems. His parents had instilled in him a deep mistrust. Perhaps it was partly their fault, his state of mind. Perhaps they had robbed him of a potential lifeline.

"It isn't a church now. It's a bath house."

"I suppose it does sort of look the part. Those three big doors. Men, women...and children, I suppose." He thought of his girls tucked up in their beds, and then shuddered at a wave of claustrophobia despite the wide-open space that surrounded him.

Anna shrugged. Nevertheless, Mark noticed her hesitation, as though she was uncertain about which door to use. She pushed the middle one and it opened smoothly. Mark followed her in.

The lobby was barely better lit than the street outside. Mahogany panels glowed dully under a single strip light. An obese man wearing a too-small waistcoat leapt up from his wicker chair. He glanced at Anna, then past her, as though noting which of the doors they had used, then fixed his gaze on Mark. His expression was a mix of surprise and skepticism. Mark turned to see that the choice of doors had been trivial; all three led into the lobby.

"You're sure?" the doorman hissed.

Anna nodded. Immediately, he rushed away, slamming a wooden door behind him.

"That's some welcome," Mark said.

"Come this way."

Another flash of déjà vu. Perhaps Anna had once visited him at his office at the university? He would have remembered if she had been one of his students, looking like that. Being on campus—his home turf— gave him a certain confidence.

Still pondering, he followed her through a different door than the doorman had taken. It led into a curved passage that must lead around the rounded outer edge of the building.

"Do you want to just point me towards the changing rooms?"

Anna didn't reply and strode ahead of him. Mark realized that the passage was sloping downwards. Soon it seemed to curve back on itself. They must be below surface level now. He reached out to touch the wall, which was rough stone rather than brick. It was cold and damp.

"Mind your head," Anna said.

Mark crouched to make his way beneath a rock outcrop that protruded from the low roof. Then the space opened out again. His eyes adjusted slowly. Stubby candles arranged on the stone floor lit a wide, circular chamber.

"What is all this?" he whispered.

Anna turned. Her straightened hair and neat appearance seemed totally at odds with the setting. She looked up and around; then, in the manner of a practiced tour guide, said "This chamber wouldn't have been discovered if not for the impending construction work. You were right about the original purpose of the building, and isn't its design glorious? Hence its Grade II listing. These sorts of things can be got around, but of course there must be due diligence and research."

Once again, Mark was distracted by the familiarity of her face. "I'm not sure I understand. So local historians came digging before the place was due to be knocked down, and they found a—what?—a cave?"

"Not only a cave. A well."

Anna stepped aside to reveal a hole in the centre of the stone floor. It was the width of a sewer manhole. Beside it was a large, freestanding copper basin, and inside that a wooden bucket with a rope coiled in and around it.

The idea that this was the same bath house that locals talked about in hushed tones seemed ridiculous. Oren said a friend of a friend had come away with her chronic anxiety cured. A couple of months ago Mark had overheard two pensioners at a bus stop gushing about someone at their retirement home having been granted a new lease of life. Had these people, and all the others, come here, to this dingy cave? Had they all sat in that same copper tub?

"This is all a bit hippy for me," Mark said. "And I've just realized I didn't bring a towel or anything. Plus it's a school night."

"Please," Anna said. "Lower the bucket into the well. It's all part of the experience."

"You're honestly going to make me draw water for my own bath? I wasn't expecting a full-on spa treatment, but this seems positively medieval."

"As is the water, I suppose. In fact, this chamber likely dates to before the Roman period. We don't know. We're not historians."

"Then what are you?"

"Please. Take the bucket. The water level isn't far down."

Oren would be disappointed when he found out what his money had paid for. Whatever the cost, Mark could have paid it himself; his savings were substantial. He'd been squirreling money away for years, for the girls. Just in case he ever decided he wouldn't be around to see them through to adulthood.

For the first time, it occurred to Mark to wonder how Oren had made contact with Anna in the first place.

Reservations aside, Mark had to admit that he needed something. And if it wasn't this, he didn't know what it might be.

He sighed. "In for a penny, I suppose." He removed his jacket, folded it neatly and placed it on the floor, then edged around the hole to the copper basin. Anna must be right about the depth of the well: the rope attached to the bucket was only a couple of feet in length. He wrapped its loose end around his hand twice. He leant over the hole but could see no reflection. He lowered the bucket. After a few seconds he heard a tinny, echoing splash.

He grimaced as he tried to raise the bucket. "Is there silt down there? It's heavy." He glanced up. Anna was watching him, expressionless.

He planted his feet wider apart and heaved. The bucket reappeared and he hoisted it up and onto the stone floor. He gestured at the copper basin and Anna nodded. When he poured the water he saw that it glistened clear without any silt residue. "It must have snagged on something on the way up," he muttered.

"Don't worry about it. You'll need more."

"And this is supposed to be a treat." But he felt an impulse to show Anna that he was stronger than he appeared, or perhaps it was simply an impulse to win this fight that he had begun. He dipped the bucket down again into the hole. If anything, it seemed heavier this time, once it had filled. He clamped his left hand over his right to ensure that the loose end of the rope didn't slip from his grasp. He grunted as he pulled the bucket up and then tipped the water into the basin.

"More, please."

This time it took all his effort to even begin to raise the bucket. It knocked against the inside of the well as he stepped backwards to pull at the rope. When he had yanked it free he fell to his knees, jarring his bones against the stone. He was weak. Forty-two and already decrepit. He looked up at Anna. He tried to arrange his face so as not to appear pleading, but then blurted out, "Isn't there somebody who can do this for me?"

"No."

He cleared his throat. "Is this going to be worth my while?"

"Yes."

"More?"

"More."

He lowered the bucket and then paused to summon the energy to lift it. Halfway up, the rope tore from his hands, scalding him with friction. With a gasp, Anna leapt forward and grabbed at the rope before it slipped fully into the hole. She pressed it back into his hand and helped him wind it around his injured wrist. Mark stared at her. The filled bucket hadn't fallen all the way into the well, and yet she had borne its weight easily. Her arms were as thin as his eldest daughter's.

He hauled at the rope. He might as well be pulling against a mountain.

"I can't," he said.

"This is the last one."

He noticed movement at the entrance to the chamber. A man and a woman stood there. Both of them wore black, formfitting outfits, like wetsuits or gymnasts' uniforms. They watched with interest, peering into the copper basin without coming any closer.

"This is the last one," Anna said again, quieter.

Mark gritted his teeth. He looped the rope around his elbow and grasped it lower down with his left hand.

He breathed in through his nose. He staggered backwards until the rope was taut.

His stomach muscles ached terribly.

He gulped a breath and stooped awkwardly to wipe his forehead on the arm of his shirt.

He saw the man and woman clutch at each other. Perhaps it was in shared mirth at his plight.

He refused to be beaten, not by this.

He roared.

The bucket pulled free of the hole. Its momentum sent Mark sprawling backwards. The bucket tipped and a cupful of water splashed back into the hole. Moving as one, Anna and the pair at the entrance lurched forward; the man succeeded in righting the bucket before it toppled back into the hole. He supported it at the edge of the hole with one hand, as though it had no weight at all.

"Take it," Anna said to Mark. "Tip it into the basin."

"I can't move," Mark groaned. Internally they were all laughing at him, surely, and he deserved it. "I think I tore something."

"Take it," she said again. She sounded far less calm now.

Reluctantly, Mark scrabbled upright and held the bucket in both hands. He grunted at its weight and tipped its contents into the basin clumsily. Some of the water splashed up and trickled over its edge. Mark heard a stifled groan from behind him that sounded like anguish.

He panted and wiped at his forehead. He stank.

"This had better be good," he said.

The three other people stood around the basin, staring into it. The water did look inviting, after all that work. Perhaps this is what had happened to the others who came to the bath house. After so much effort anybody would be grateful for a wash.

After several moments of silence, Mark said, "Look, would you mind all leaving while I strip?"

He started to unbutton his sweat-sodden shirt, but Anna stopped him.

"Not here," she said. "They'll take the water upstairs to the bath house."

Mark watched in bemusement as the man and woman in bodysuits took their positions at either end of the basin. Despite their excessive caution, it was clear that they were able to lift it without difficulty. They walked with baby-steps out of the chamber, shuffling to pass under the low rock outcrop.

"You did wonderfully," Anna said. "I know it was difficult."

Once again she took him by the arm. This time the action seemed more intimate. She really was quite pretty. Mark thought of his wife at home in bed, his daughters. He had made a promise to himself. What had Oren got him into?

They followed the black-clad man and woman along the sloping passage and into the lobby. Anna rushed forward to hold open a second door that led into the main building, the same one that the doorman had taken earlier. Mark followed obediently.

He was surprised to see that the church pews were intact, as were the seats in the gallery above. He had thought that the place had been converted into apartments long ago. The basin-carriers made their way slowly along the central aisle, as solemn as if they were carrying a coffin.

He was relieved that there was no altar. It was only when he had passed the final pew that he could see what was in its place. White ceramic tiles had been fixed where the floorboards had been prized up, an area around three meters square. The tiles had been arranged haphazardly, badly aligned and with protruding edges. The central part of the tiled area was lower than the rest. The edges of this shallow pit were sharp where the tiles had been snapped to fit.

Carefully, the man and woman lowered the copper basin into the pit. Then they both stepped back and stood in silence.

The doorman reappeared at Anna's side. He peered into the basin. The water was peculiarly still. The doorman ushered Anna away to one side of the room. Mark saw him nod gravely and then press something into her hand. An envelope.

"Hey!" Mark called out. His voice echoed strangely. "Anna—what the hell? Are you on commission or something? I paid you for this already, or at least my friend Oren did. That's not on."

Anna's face flushed. She glared at the doorman, then sighed. "It's a psychological thing. You wouldn't have believed it was exclusive if it was free."

No level of spiritual relief could be worth all of this idiocy. "Look, I've had enough of this," Mark said. "All this nonsense."

"You can take off your clothes now," Anna said.

"No. Are you kidding?"

"You've heard about the bath house. You know it will be worth your while."

"I hadn't heard it was a health-and-safety-nightmare sex dungeon. I hadn't heard you were luring people here for God knows what reason. I'd heard it was—"

"What? What had you heard?"

Suddenly, he felt he might burst into tears. "That it would be something wonderful. I don't know. That it would—" He didn't want to finish the thought, but he also couldn't bear Anna's raised-eyebrows expression, like a teacher waiting for a correct answer from a promising student. "—help."

"It will. What else?"

Her pleasant smile robbed Mark of his outrage. "Just what they all said. That it would be a transformative experience."

Anna gestured towards the basin. "Please. We understand that you are suffering. This will be what you need. I swear it will. We are here to help."

We are here to help.

Finally, it hit him.

"I know you! I know where I've seen you!" He could picture her now, in clothes as neat as these, but plainer. That same indulgent smile. "At the clinic. You were behind the reception desk. You're the receptionist for—" He lowered his voice, suddenly conscious of the others in the room. "—Doctor Rix."

Anna's smile vanished. "I worried that you would remember me. A younger woman. That's what you like, isn't it?"

"What on Earth do you mean by that? I'm not going to stand here and—"

He was about to turn and leave, but the black-clad man and woman each took one of his arms. They were strong.

Anna shook her head sadly, a teacher disappointed by a clumsy error. "Usually our clients are very grateful."

"Seriously? Grateful for this? Get the hell off me." Mark wriggled but couldn't free himself.

"Take off his clothes."

Mark writhed as the man and woman pulled at his shirt and trousers. The man eased Mark's briefs down and over his feet. Mark spat at him, then shivered, more from shame at his nakedness than from cold.

He saw movement in the upper gallery. There were people up there, too shrouded in darkness for him to make out their faces. They shuffled their way to their seats, craning their necks to look down to where the altar should have been.

Anna gazed up at them. She held up a blue cardboard folder.

"We have been making the same error continually," she said in a voice loud enough to carry across the room. "We have been misidentifying the criteria that are necessary. This man, Mark Higham, drew water from the well, but only barely. It was as heavy to him as lead."

A murmur rippled across the gallery.

"Any of the partial successes of our previous bathers were pure chance. Flukes," Anna continued. "They did not have the necessary characteristics. Their having experienced loss was not enough. Depression, not enough. Guilt—that was closer. But Mark Higham suffers from something that is subtly different."

Mark stared at the blue folder. "Is that my file? From the clinic?"

Anna turned. "Not that it contained everything I needed. You hardly divulged a thing to Doctor Rix. All that money spent on psychotherapy, and you squandered it by clamming up."

Mark had hated the experience from start to finish. All men got down in the dumps at the onset of their forties. Doctor Rix was a charlatan, just listening and saying nothing. He hadn't got to the root of anything at all. He hadn't helped.

He realized that his mouth had become utterly dry. He glanced at the water in the copper basin and licked his lips involuntarily.

"Help him into the bath," Anna said.

The man and woman in black outfits complied instantly, forcing Mark to take a step backwards, then another. He teetered on the sharp edges of the tiles. The woman moved to stand behind him. She took him by the shoulders and eased him down while the man pinned Mark's arms to his sides.

As he tilted backwards, Mark's vision filled with the dark figures in the gallery. Their eyes shone.

With detached interest, he realized that he had stopped fighting against his captors. Life had been a struggle for many years. There was something strangely comforting about having no choices left to make.

He gasped as he came into contact with the cold water. No, not cold, but as shocking as ice. It hardly seemed like water at all, more like something solid but still capable of enveloping him. It seemed to clasp his body and draw him into itself.

The pressure on his chest felt unbearable, even though he was able to breathe as usual; he could still feel his chest rising and falling. He couldn't speak. Another choice taken away from him.

"Guilt is only part of it," Anna announced, her voice coming from somewhere far away and out of sight. "What we required for this procedure was something greater and more toxic. An absolute loathing for oneself."

Mark wondered only idly about her assessment of him. Maybe it was true. Maybe he ought to have given Anna and Doctor Rix more of his attention. Maybe they were here to help.

Then Anna said, "Please, lower down the apparatus."

The black-clad man and woman disappeared from view. Mark heard a straining, creaking sound. Gradually, he became aware of something shifting far above. Whatever it was grew in size as it was lowered towards him. Like the basin in which he lay, it was made of copper. A concave dish with a rough surface, as though beaten with a hammer. It came closer and closer, then stopped, hanging only a few meters above him. It was enormous. In its dimpled surface Mark saw shimmering reflections of the water of the basin, and a distorted outline of his own submerged body. He did not want to see himself.

Anna's face hovered into view. She tapped the blue folder. "Libby Morel. You loved her." She stated it as a fact, not a question. "It's not such a crime. Yes, you were married. Yes, you had two young children. Yes, you were, and remain, a lecturer at the university where she studied. All of that is written in this folder."

Mark opened his mouth but couldn't force out any words. He closed his mouth again: the water threatened to seep in.

"She made you happy," Anna went on, "but you didn't make her happy. And then you made her miserable, once you threatened to break off your relationship. Professional reasons. But so much is missing from the account you told Doctor Rix, Mark! I had so much detective work to do. Now I know a little about Libby Morel, about her state of mind at that time."

Mark saw a change in the play of light on the surface of the copper dish. The reflections seemed to shift faster with each passing second, even though he was incapable of introducing any ripple into the water.

He thought he saw a face up there, alongside his own reflection.

He screwed his eyes shut.

"Libby Morel," Anna said.

He opened one eye a little. He could see her, Libby, as she was back then. Nineteen and prim and beautiful.

"Libby Morel," Anna said again, "was vulnerable. But that isn't it. She felt betrayed. But that isn't it. She was suicidal. But that isn't it, not quite."

Mark could no longer look away from the light on the copper dish. Libby Morel. Water tickled at the corners of his eyes; he was sinking bit by bit. He could no longer close his eyes.

"You found her."

He found her.

"You found her in her room on campus."

He found her in her room on campus. She had been facing away from him, in the dark, facing away from the door and towards the window.

"You found her hanging from a cord around her neck."

He found her hanging from a cord around her neck. An electrical flex tied around a beam.

"And you left her there."

It hadn't been a conscious decision, not really. He had run, though not before he had closed the door carefully behind him. He had run. While he was running he had wondered whether or not she had been alive still, and whether or not she had seen him in the reflection in the dark window. While he was running he had reasoned with himself: if he had not been there he could not have helped. He was not there. He was not there.

Anna's voice was almost too far away to hear. "It doesn't matter that she is still alive."

The girl in the neighboring room had found her, rescued her. She had heard the creaking and nothing else, had thought Libby was masturbating, had thought it would be funny to burst in at the wrong moment.

"It doesn't matter."

It didn't matter. Libby had lived, left, moved on to who knew where. Mark hadn't seen her. He had done what he had done and it didn't matter whether Libby had lived or died. He had done what he had done. That had been his choice.

"You loathe yourself."

It was a literal thing, a cliché. He hadn't been able to look at himself in the mirror. He loathed himself, and the kindness and indulgence of his wife and his daughters could only make his loathing deeper and worse, not better.

"You wish that you could crawl out of your own skin."

Yes, he did.

The light grew more intense. He could no longer see his own re-flection, though the second figure seemed to be growing more distinct, its eyes shining. But that wasn't Libby Morel up there, reflected in the copper dish.

Anna's voice was almost a whisper when she said, "He is beginning to dream."

Yes, he was. It was beautiful. He felt heavy and light and sore and he felt nothing at all.

"He could crawl out of his own skin."

It was beautiful. He could crawl out and he could slip away.

"It will be different this time. Whatever crawls in may be better or worse than Mark Higham. But it will not loathe itself. It will be differ-ent this time."

It would. The light was beautiful.

Narrow as the basin was, Mark felt something in there alongside him, nuzzling up against him, close as close could be.

PICKY YUUN

———◆———

J.C. Raye

CUPUN HAD BEEN hunting the bear and it had killed him. So, while Yuun was preparing hard bread on the oil stove, fully expecting him to appear at their tent, arms laden with the meat that would keep them and the thick fur from which she'd craft soft boots, her husband was being mauled and partially devoured. As the couple was alone in this part of the territory, without any family or clan remaining, when Yuun heard the team barking strangely and Cupun still did not return, she took a spear, the snow knife and a dog, and went out to look for him.

She found his body, not far from their camp, on a patch of rocks clumped with snow, and he was no longer living. His upper back had been changed into a row of fringe, and Yuun was unable to determine which of the tangled, slowly freezing strips were skin and which were parka. But, turning him revealed far worse. The meat of one thigh had been eaten out through the front of his trousers, exposing bone whiter than new snow. Cupun's chest, still freshly bleeding in the shielded warmth underneath his body, was a crisscross of deep slashes met by dozens of the distinct and large, curved puncture wounds inflicted by a bear who was more angry than hungry. It had taken its time in the kill-

263

ing. It was not honorable.

In other times, the body would have been prepared well, with a great mourning ceremony and feasting to follow. But Yuun did not know the purifying rituals the men would have performed, and there was no one to prepare food for, so she merely dragged the body to a flat place and washed it, while first removing those items which she might need for the ìxt'. Sadly, she could not spare the length of skin to make her husband a full shroud, and so only covered his head before burning the body. Yuun was only grateful that his last breath had not occurred *inside* the tent, for then the home would need to be abandoned altogether, and she would be much worse off.

When it was done, Yuun carefully placed the charred bones and ashes into a cut purse tied with sinew and buried it. Though she could not be cheerful, she knew she must be strong and turn towards life, though it would be a solitary one without her mate. Yet her greatest fear now was not the fast approaching change of season, and journeying to the winter hunting grounds alone. Helping the dogs pull the sleigh through ridges of ice pushing up from the sea. Testing the surface with her harpoon, making certain it would not break under the load. Even cutting the large blocks of hard pack to make her new home did not present worry. All this she could do herself. These things could be seen, felt, made, overcome. Like her people, it was the unseen which she feared most of all, and she was certain Cupun's death was the work of an evil spirit come to plague them. Perhaps one of the troublesome dead, or revenging animal soul from a dishonorable kill. But it was no matter. From this, she needed protection. This she could not do for herself, and it could not be left. It was not death she feared, only more suffering at the hands of an invisible ghost.

THE ìXT', THE shaman, the one who could see his own skeleton, made his permanent home in one of the towns along the coast, and it was there she took the kayak. Yuun and her husband did not travel there often, except to visit the trader, when a helping spirit decided to send them a good catch of white fox. It was a strange place, *town*, where many of her kind had long since moved, to live among the whites. A place of wooden houses and washing machines, and the white baby cribs painted with delicate flowers or animal crests.

The journey along the water was uneventful. No weather slowed her, and this was a good sign. But for the last part of her trek, Yuun needed to tie up the skin-framed vessel and walk among the houses, a part of the town she had not been through before. Though the initial sight of children playing and hooded women cooking in pots put her somewhat at ease, the many curious faces and hard stares were so unexpectedly powerful, Yuun almost lost her footing more than a few times. She was not used to walking on boards as it was. Navigating the wide planks, she acted as a baby caribou taking its first steps. Shaky. Unsteady. Lacking a confidence which all could see. The soles of her feet longed for the comforting scrunch of snow rising up to meet their shape and she was already homesick for the quiet sound of her camp, penetrated only by the slaps of lathery current hitting slick rock.

The shore town seemed so much larger than she remembered. The number of structures had grown beyond counting, and a few of these so great they blocked out the sun as she passed them. Mysterious symbols on poles and doors made her head cloudy. Strange calls made her jump. Many times, she needed to stop and ask for help, and Yuun found these to be long, painful moments, all. People with faces like her own did not always understand all of her words, nor she, theirs. Much of the time she would put her spear to the ground and draw, receiving in return, just enough instruction to travel a few structures further, before needing to stop once again. Whites would quickly wave her away, angrily it seemed, so she no longer approached them at all.

SHE FOUND THE shaman's home at a spot most inland, facing away from the rest. To look at its placement, it seemed to Yuun that the village itself was speaking, exclaiming that it would only tolerate such a one among them, torn between ways ancient and ways modern, *there*, on its very edges. Barely in sight. Easy to slice away, should he offend. Though she fully expected the elder, Nikalik, to possess one of the finer wood homes she'd seen, his was in fact the poorest. The front face consisted of planks and doorway as the other houses, but the rest was a mound-shaped dwelling dug deep into the ground, covered in a low roof of sod and bark. It looked in great disrepair, as if the man had abandoned it long ago, and Yuun felt fear to enter and look, as something might collapse inside. But immediately, the shaman appeared at the door. The sound of her steps had brought him. Wearing a crown of bear claws, white man's clothing, and tanned, salmon-skin boots, he was shorter than she, hairless, and very thin. An old man which a powdery snow-storm might have carried away.

At first, he thought to drive Yuun away with a stick. He had assumed she desired a forbidden ritual. The spell which would reveal the *name* of the *nakws'aatì*, the witch or sorcerer who had unleashed destructive power upon her family. For shaman who lived in the towns now, this practice was long taboo. Whites could take him away or hang him should he perform it or attempt to put any specific name to malicious works done upon some, whether the spirit world revealed it truthfully or not. Whites had their own laws, and to live with them meant having to obey the words that they lived by, at least in appearance. *Their* elders pro-claimed there were far too many medicine men, and woman, who falsely accused, labeling innocents as demons, to cover for their own lack of spiritual powers in curing illness or controlling weather. Here it was said that the *Christian god* alone could see clearly into men's hearts, and that *he* would justly punish those deserving in the *afterlife*, so there was no need for this magic any longer.

So Yuun explained to the shaman that she only sought protection for her long journey to the winter hunting grounds. No more than that. She also presented him with a parcel of *ts'ak'àawàsh* and a pair of mittens, and he seemed both satisfied with her intentions and her gift. He bade her come down into his home and sit on a small wood stool near a smoky fire. He put something into her hands. It was heavy and flat, one side like ice and the other like stone. Yuun had never seen her own reflection, but had heard tales of mirrors, though could never understand the purpose in their use. In the flicker of firelight, the heavy wrinkles on her bronze forehead moved, like the undulating waves under a kayak on a clear day. As she dipped her chin to inspect her brow more closely, her wide-set, dark eyes sank even deeper into shadow, to the point where they appeared to have fled! Nikalik gently touched her shoulder and she looked up at him. Smiling, he rapidly wrinkled his nose several times and indicated she should do as well. The change in her face when she did so made her giggle, and the giggle brought the perfect curve of her lips into the light, reminding her so much of Cupun's cleverly crafted hunting bow. The shaman then took the mirror from her and poured her a full tin cup of cloudberry tea, which warmed her and delivered a pleasing aroma. Nikalik treated her well, and this came as a surprise to Yuun. Her only other history with a shaman had been a terrible one and had forever changed the course of her life.

WHEN FIRST MARRIED, Cupun had taken Yuun to settle with *his* family, far from her own. This was as it should be, as women should marry from an opposite clan. But he had no sisters, and his mother and aunts had died from illness. And women can be a comfort to each other. There were none to share the long days, or play *katajjaq*, the holding of arms while huskily chanting the sounds around them, from nature, from tools, until someone could no longer breath and the game was won. Instead, Cupun chose to teach her all *he* knew. The knowledge his father had passed to him. All that he might pass on to a future son. How to fasten the sharp point on the shaft of an arrow. Kill a seal at the breathing hole, or caribou at the crossing place. Use the drill to make a bow out of driftwood and bone. Cupun would often make Yuun snow bears to test her skill with the spear, showing her how to strike in the vital place. They did these things, and soon her skill in hunting was as good as any of Cupun's brothers.

But Yuun bore him no sons, no children. Twice, a child lay sideways inside her belly and was delivered after the cord had already strangled it.

Cupun, full of grief, and at the urging of his father, visited a shaman, said to be most powerful in seeking the source of this pain. The man had taken a full armload of precious driftwood and many skins to perform the ritual.

The shaman told Cupun his family had been cursed by the spirit of a jealous witch. That women were not meant to live among his family, and that every child would come out in this way. But the man did not stop there. He also spread news that Yuun was *infected* by this wicked spirit, put her under many strict taboos. He cautioned anyone to eat from her cooking pot. And, if Yuun ate a bit of walrus meat, any woman who ate from the same walrus would never bear another child. The shaman also warned that visiting the couple would cause body weakness or the spoiling of limbs. Soon after, no group would have Cupun to hunt, and other members of his clan no longer traveled to see them. Yuun and her husband were banned from all the communal ceremonies, no matter how important. Even his own father and brothers slowly broke away to seek new hunting grounds and wives of their own.

Despite this misfortune, and his brothers' pleading with him to abandon or kill her, Cupun provided Yuun with kinship. Never did he raise his hands to her or make hasty words against her. They may not have loved, truly, but worked always as a strong team. Sometimes, when a hunt had gone particularly well and they were not too tired, and the air not too frizzled with ice, they would sit at their fire and make fun of each other. He would speak of her feet, larger than bear paws, or match the shape of the mottles across her wide face to lights in the sky. She would imitate the whistle that occasionally sounded from between his crooked teeth or the way in which he sucked roe. They lived in peace. They lived.

YUUN UNWRAPPED THE slice of skin from her summer tent and placed a handful of Cupun's bloodied hair in the shaman's hand. She watched him leave the shelter to rinse it in a small pool, and then enter again to dry it over the fire. Nikalik then skillfully pressed the clump of hair bet-ween two halves of a rattle. One side of the shaker was carved with the face of a man, and the other, that of a bear showing many pointed teeth. The shaman then covered Yuun's head briefly with the same tear of tent, for it would be an offense to look upon the body of an elder as he dropped his clothes to put on the skin waist apron needed for the ritual.

Crouching near her, he spat into the flames twenty times and then lifted a driftwood mask, edged in rows of speckled brown feathers from a hanging place above both their heads. He put it on. It was only now, as her eyes were becoming accustomed to the dark, that Yuun really began to see the inside of his home. Though bare of all other furniture, except for fur skins, some in bundles and some laid in the far corner for bedding, masks and rattles of every kind hung around them, in tight cluster. So many that they completely obscured the posts and sod walls behind, much the way carefully laid snow bricks might block all but slivers of the sun. Large. Small. Feather, bone, wood, stretched skin. Frightening beasts and comforting spirits. Yuun wondered if this shadowy clan was meant to perhaps bear witness, a community in secret from the prying eyes of those outside, to give his ritual power.

Nikalik slowly rose to his feet. Fully in trance, he began to circle the room rhythmically, spirit rattle in one hand, and ivory-handled knife in the other. Shaking the rattle, he sang out so loudly, it nearly made Yuun drop her cup. Before, at the door, brandishing his stick, she thought he had seemed so old and weak, but now he was a frightening visage to behold, and seemed to have the energy of a man half his years.

When the first spirit was present among them, the shaman cried out as if struck by a spear and communed with it in a frenzied dance. When a different spirit entered him, he cried out again, but now staggered, sometimes falling, and began to growl like a beast. This repeated many times over. Each time his cries were more passionate, his snarls became more terrifying, and the falls, much more violent. He left skin and blood on the ground as the two spirits within him battled. At times it was so piercing, Yuun fully expected others to break through the door of the home to see if someone was being murdered within.

When it was finally over, the shaman lay crumpled in the center of the floor. His breathing was labored and his body was glistening with sweat. Now he seemed as before. She offered him a sip of her tea, but he waved it away, and instead, pulled himself up to his knees, slowly dragging his spent body ever nearer the stool. He coughed, and violently spit something into his hand. She thought it might be blood and wondered where she might seek help for him if it was so. Stretching out his arm to Yuun, he turned over his fist. He held out his open palm to reveal a rounded piece of walrus tusk upon which was carved the image of a smiling, swimming seal with five pairs of eyes.

UPON ARRIVING HOME, Yuun lit a fire and fed the dogs first. It had been a longer wait than usual for them, so for a few moments there was the typical baring of fangs and snapping rushes only meant for display. Though there were chores to begin, the day's burdens had driven her body to its very limits. She was too tired to even make tea. Reaching into a deep pocket of her parka, she pulled out the amulet. He had strung it for her on a piece of blackened, braided sinew, and she looked at it in the light. Nikalik had promised that it would bring the protection of her husband's helping spirit. Unable to keep her eyes open, she dropped it into the dry cooking pot. After that, she lay under fur and slept.

YUUN AWOKE TO a puzzling sound, that of her pot banging against stones. Without fully dressing, she left the tent to chase away whatever animal had gotten to it, confused that the dogs had not frightened away any creature which might approach the camp. But it was Cupun! Seated at a fire, crush-rolling dried berries with his hands into melting snow. At first, she could not believe her eyes, and felt as if she might still be asleep, as the hunter who dreams of a silver sea overflowing with char. But no, it was him. His face and body as before the attack. Coarse hair, equally black and grey, woven into the long braids. Fat cheeks. The heavy broad jaw, tucked inside the furry hood of his only parka. No outer glow. No red demon eyes. Just her husband, crouched over a pot, making tea. He told her to ready quickly, so they might not lose time for their hunt. He also said his hunger was great. Cupun did not make mention of his death, and she did not question him.

THE HUNT DID not go well. Instead of remaining at the one crossing place for caribou, Cupun became impatient and moved several times, all the while telling of painful rumbles in his belly. So great it seemed was his frenzied appetite that the mere appearance of game caused his entire body to shake with want, and his spear to miss. And, he blamed her for it and told her she could not hunt with him again.

After one sleep, he had eaten all of the fresh fish drying on the rack. After three sleeps, he had devoured the remaining dried ones. And, though he would leave to hunt or fish each day, he would almost always return with an empty kayak. What little he managed to catch, he stuffed into his mouth at the place where his prize fell dead. Cupun brought very little home for her. If she trapped the game herself, he would take it. Starved though she was, the real terror for her was that this maddening desire for food drove him to dishonorable kills. He did not clean his tools, or sing the songs, or return the innards to the water.

And when there was no more meat or fish left to eat, and recklessness had claimed all of his arrows (save the ones she hid from him), Yuun gave him seaweed with seal fat to stave off his shouting. And when there was no more of that, she gave him hot tea by the potful to keep him from crying. And when there were no herbs or dried berries left to cloud the tea, she gave him the soul of her shoe to chew upon so he would not bite her. But, when she found him, under an orange sky, legs tangled among the traces and loops of the dogsled, feasting on one of the team, she could stand no more. The dog was not yet even dead. He had not killed it first. He had tied it and was using the *ulu* to slice the raw pieces to his liking.

Without thinking, Yuun ran at him, pulling the *ulu* from his hands. But the loss of the tool did not slow Cupun. This time, he brought his face down into the animal's open stomach and bit off a large chunk of the meat. Cupun's mouth and cheeks were covered red, and he was breathing heavily through his nose so he did not have to stop chewing. He looked up and smiled at her as a child might. It was a site more terrifying than any one of the shaman's fearsome masks. Yuun plunged the *ulu* into the side of his neck, and pressed it there, until he was stone cold dead. She fell to her knees and screamed up to the heavens in pain. The dogs joined her with their own howls. By dark, Yuun had burned and buried her husband for the second time, glad that she did not own a mirror to see how she might look this night. Before lighting the pyre, she had removed the amulet to weaken his spirit and any chance of more mischief.

THIS TIME, YUUN awoke to sharp pain. Cupun was poking her in the ribs with the dull end of his harpoon. He demanded she wake up and come hunting with him though it was not yet that time. Again, he looked as her husband. The same man. But a much angrier one, so it seemed this morning. And all at once she remembered! She had hung the amulet over the sharp end of the harpoon this time. A hungry husband brought by pot, a hostile one brought by a weapon. She had learned the secret of Nikalik's amulet! She would need time to think greatly on how to use it best before the journey to winter grounds. But in the days that followed, there was no time for her to think or plan or sleep or tend to herself in any way. Cupun was upon her at every moment, with stick and sometimes with knife. Either driving her to impossible tasks for which she did not have strength or roaring about having married so useless and ugly a creature as herself. His hunts were successful now, but wasteful. Greedy. Too many animals were laid at her feet to scrape and boil and preserve. More than once he beat her for discovering rot among the game. And there was more. The strange sounds of his ferocious outbursts disturbed the dogs terribly, and often set them to attack one other. This time, Yuun used a large rock on the back of his head while he was steadying his aim on a fish. Only enough of a hit to make him sleep. She tied him tightly into a bundle and dragged him to the place where the bear had killed him. She used the knife to break through the skin of the wrapping and cut a chunk of flesh from his arm. The bloody trail she left behind made it easy for the wolves or bears to find him. She hoped he would be awake when they did. That night, Yuun hung the amulet between her breasts.

ONE LAST MILE

—————◆—————

Erica Ruppert

DES CLIMBS THE slight rise to the riverside path and reaches up high, stretching her legs and her back. Her muscles slowly loosen. She walks a tight circle, shaking them out. The morning is warm and misty, the air still heavy with the river's low fog before the sun burns it clear. Her eyes are gritty and her head still a bit clouded. The wet air doesn't help.

She got out later than she wanted this morning, out of sync with the day. When the alarm began its grating complaint at six Des had struggled to surface. She did not expect to find her husband still beside her. He had rumbled angrily as she slapped the clock into silence and rolled free of the damp, sticky sheets. Once up it took her too long to feed the cats, too long to clean the kitchen from the night before, too long to lace on her running shoes. Even asleep upstairs her husband inhabited the entire house, crowding her with his potential presence. He stole her morning solitude, and standing in the dim morning light she feels every lost moment.

She looks at the path before her. It is empty as far as she can see, unfurling past the edge of town. She is here too late for the rush hour of dog walkers and joggers, and there is no one else moving on the path to inspire her. She resents her husband having filled the house like the taint of smoke, clinging to her. She needs the lack of him. His reality is too demanding. She shakes her head, unsatisfied. Sounds from the town filter through to her. The day has begun.

For a long while Des stands with her hands on her hips, deciding if she will run at all. If the house were empty she would go back home and dawdle. She sighs and reaches up to smooth her frizzy dark hair back down into its ponytail. An unseen animal crashes through the brush down near the water, more immediate than the human noises. The space behind her eyes hurts. At last she pushes off, hoping to find enthusiasm as she moves.

The path is an abandoned railway bed, reclaimed, that traces the line of the river for seventy miles. The rails were torn up and sold for scrap, but the decayed wooden ties lie buried under fine gray gravel to make a trail. It was only made a few years ago but already saplings have made inroads at the edges, and grass grows up in the middle over the long swaths beyond town. But this section of path is better traveled and still tame, a tree-lined cloister stretching through and away from tidy civilization, curving gently to the horizon. She runs it, only half-aware of the scenery, unsettled. The gravel crunches and slurs under her feet, each footfall a disturbance in the dull humid morning. Nothing feels right. Des's mind drifts, worrying small domestic angers, winning arguments she never had the energy to have. She hates when he stays home. She can smell the river beside her, flat with the squatting heat and with none of the fresh sweetness she remembers from spring. Already a slick of sweat coats her back between her shoulder blades, and beads form on her upper lip. The day will be wretchedly hot, again. A song hook repeats itself in her head on an endless loop to the cadence of her steps. She hates the song. She wishes she had gotten out earlier. She wishes her husband had gone to work today. She takes a pull from the water bottle she carries, knowing already that it does not hold enough to see her through.

The sun looms indistinct in the heavy air, its yellow light hazy. Latticed branches isolate her from the rest of the world. A county road parallels the path in an echo of the river, but behind the scrim of trees she is invisible to the passing cars she hears. It is a strange sensation, the busy solitude, like being behind glass. Her own breathing fills her head, ragged and thick. The feeling of separation eases as she reaches a clearing, and she stretches her arms over her head as she crosses the open field. She can see the busy road, she can see the river, she can see the houses built on stilts on the far bank. But a few yards ahead the trees loom over again, thick here where they have been left to grow as they will.

Des speeds up as she runs into the tunnel. Just under the shadow of the branches, the remains of a demolished house crouch between the path and the road. A steep, broken stone wall opposite the ruin shores up the eroded bank where the river has cut in. This is an abandoned place, lonely no matter who is on the path. She never trusts it here. She imagines things hiding here, waiting for their chance.

The light dims beneath the branches but the ground is spangled brightly where the sun scatters through the leaves. Flashes of sunlight pull at her attention, suggestive of movements in the brush. She does not turn her head. She is not sure how far she is willing to go today. She wishes there were other people on the path. Even her husband would be welcome company here, but he will not run with her. He blames her for running without him, and for his refusal. He blames her for his drinking, too. He says she took the joy from him. He says she doesn't want him to be happy, that her running is a slap in the face to him, that if she cared about him she would stop. Sometimes she believes him. She feels watched. She pushes herself to run faster.

It wasn't supposed to be like this.

Another clearing becomes visible not too far ahead. The thought of the open sky eases her mood. Des slows to a walk, takes a long pull from her water bottle, wipes at her blurry eyes. The purr and rattle of late summer insects fills the air around her. Humidity presses on her skin like a wet pelt. Sweat covers her, runs down her ribs. She flaps her

T-shirt to make a breeze, then gives in and takes the shirt off. Her bra is soaked through, but the air on her bare skin is a thin relief. She can see the next mile marker in the middle distance, a dark vertical line against the golden light. For a moment Des stops moving entirely, letting her shoulders slump. Behind her, hidden by the path's curve, she hears someone running toward her with long strides, sneakers scuffing the gravel. She can't judge the distance between them. So she waits, bent over with her hands on her knees, for the companionship.

It does not come. The crush of footfalls is lost in a locust buzz as it reaches her, outswelled and invisible and then suddenly past. The sound emerges distinctly again ahead of her down the path, out of sight behind the next curving stand of trees, moving away.

Des stands stiffly upright, suddenly cold, fine hairs prickling on her neck and arms. There is silence on the road she cannot see. She strains for the sound of a car, of anything normal. All she hears is the noise of the insects and the slowly receding footsteps. Tension hums along her bones. She turns on the ball of her foot and runs hard back down the path toward home.

Her heartbeat hammers in her ears. She cannot hear anything above her own thick noises. Light flickers between leaves at the periphery of her sight, disturbing her balance. A stitch burns deep into her side and she presses her knuckles against it. She fights not to slow her pace against the pain. Ahead of her, between her and the town, a figure runs on the path at her speed. It is at the far range of visual clarity in the heavy air, suggestive and undefined. She cannot tell if it is moving toward her or away. She hopes it is away. She hopes it isn't there at all.

She can't keep up her pace. Des drops into a walk, pressing her hand hard against her side. But the figure ahead of her also slows to a walk. Des stops. It stops, too. Goosebumps rise on her arms. She dreads the idea of catching up to it. She looks behind her down the empty path. Haze hangs in the air, shadows and light. There is no answer there.

She forces herself to jog forward, her gait uneven until the stitch works itself out. Gradually the pain lessens and her stride grows smoother.

She can no longer see the figure ahead of her. She allows herself to hope it is gone. She needs it to be gone. She wants to get home. Her face is slick and her mouth sticky, but she does not pause to drink the warm dregs in her water bottle.

As she jogs she peers back over her shoulder, afraid of what she can't see. Branches and sunlight tangle into a standing form beside the path.

She bites down on a scream, stumbles hard, regains her balance. She tells herself that it is a trick of the moving light, a curl of her hair seen wrong at the corner of her eye. She has to get home. The sounds of her footsteps and her own breathing drown any sound of the river or the road, but she still hears something heavy moving fast through the brush beside her. She forces her field of vision into a narrow slit. She does not want to see what travels with her.

The path is too long, as if it had melted and stretched in the heat. She should have been home by now. She does not recognize what should be familiar. Even the ruined house would be a marker, but all she can see are thin, glistening trees. The sun overhead is a pale blur eaten away by the misty sky. Des looks straight ahead, running hard. From behind, she hears an echo of footsteps. They may be her own. She cannot tell.

She looks back over her shoulder again. There is nothing to see, but her imagination nearly overwhelms her. She pulls herself back. She knows she is somehow to blame for this, for her fear, her exposure. Her husband has said it enough times. She wishes he were here now, the devil she knows. Blood thrums in her ears. She runs. It is all she can do. The heat-haze grows thickly into fog, crushing her view of the world into a soft cocoon to be torn through but not escaped. Against it, closer than she expects, a figure materializes and fades away.

Her chest hurts, the air too thick. There is only one way open to her. Des pushes harder, needing now to reach that other runner. It will dog her until she falls if she does not catch up. Her lips twitch into a thin smile as she thinks, it can't be worse than being alone. Finally, the distance narrows. She wipes the sweat away from her stinging eyes. She sees the figure clearly now, the dark hair pulled back, the scar on its calf from a long-ago bike accident. The figure finally pauses, turns. The face is a blank, only shadows making the suggestion of features in the empty space. This is the company she sought. It lifts its hand to her, and she meets it.

The clockwork stops, wound down to nothing.

She is alone, after all.

ABOUT THE CONTRIBUTORS

TIM JEFFREYS lives in Bristol, and works in a tiny office in a Dental Hospital. The screams he sometimes hears from the clinics occasionally make it into the strange stories he writes when no one's looking. His short fiction has appeared in *Weirdbook*, *Not One of Us*, and *Nightscript*, among other publications, and his latest collection *The Real Rachel Winterbourne and Other Stories* is available now, as is his co-written sci-fi novella *Voids*. Tim is certain that one day he'll be approached by his wealthy, jaded doppelgänger. The doppelgänger, looking to experience a bit of grit and toil, will propose swapping lives for a while. Inevitably, things will get messy when one of them decides they want their life back. Follow Tim's progress at www.timjeffreys.blogspot.co.uk.

CLINT SMITH is the author of the collection, *Ghouljaw and Other Stories*, as well as the novella, *When It's Time For Dead Things To Die*, initially published in 2015 through Dunham's Manor Press, but now slated for an updated re-release by *Unnerving* in March, 2019. Of late, other stories have appeared in *Weird Fiction Review #9* (Centipede Press) and *Weirdbook #40*. His sophomore collection, *The Skeleton Melodies*, is scheduled for mid-2019 publication with Hippocampus Press. Clint lives in the Midwest, not far from Deacon's Creek.

PATRICIA LILLIE grew up in a haunted house in a small town in Northeast Ohio. Since then, she has published six picture books (not scary), a few short stories (scary), dozens of fonts, and two novels. As Patricia Lillie, she is the author of *The Ceiling Man*, a novel of quiet horror. As Kay Charles, her much nicer alter ego, she is the author of *Ghosts in Glass Houses*, a cozy-ish mystery novel. Find her her on the web at www.patricialillie.com.

CHRIS SHEARER's fiction has appeared in places like *LampLight*, *Jamais Vu*, *Xnoybis*, and most recently, *Terror Politico*. He is a graduate of Seton Hill University's Writing Popular Fiction program, where he was mentored by Tim Waggoner and Lawrence C. Connolly, and lives in Central Pennsylvania with his family.

A fan of all things fantastical and frightening, **SHANNON LAWRENCE** writes primarily horror and fantasy. Her stories can be found in several anthologies and magazines, including *Space and Time Magazine* and *Fright Into Flight*, and her short story collection *Blue Sludge Blues & Other Abominations* is now available. When she's not writing, she's hiking through the wilds of Colorado and photographing her magnificent surroundings, where, coincidentally, there's always a place to hide a body or birth a monster. Find her at www.thewarriormuse.com.

CHARLES WILKINSON's publications include *The Pain Tree and Other Stories* (London Magazine Editions, 2000) and his anthology of strange tales and weird fiction, *A Twist in the Eye* (Egaeus Press, 2016). His second collection from the same publisher, *Splendid in Ash*, is now out. His stories have appeared in *Shadows & Tall Trees*, *Nightscript*, *Supernatural Tales*, *Bourbon Penn* and other publications. A full-length collection of his poetry is forthcoming from Eyewear. He lives in Powys, Wales.

CRAIG WALLWORK is the twice nominated Pushcart Prize writer of the novels, *The Sound of Loneliness*, *To Die Upon a Kiss*, and the story collections, *Quintessence of Dust*, and *Gory Hole*. His short stories have appeared in many anthologies such as *The New Black*, *Tales From the Lake Vol. 5*, and the one you now hold in your hand. He lives in England with his wife and two children.

DAVID PEAK is the author of the black metal horror novel *Corpsepaint* (Word Horde, 2018). His other books include *Eyes in the Dust* (Dunhams Manor, 2016), *The Spectacle of the Void* (Schism, 2014), and *The River Through the Trees* (Blood Bound Books, 2013). Recent writing has been published or is forthcoming in *Year's Best Weird Fiction Volume 5* (Undertow Publications), *Thinking Horror*, and *Vastarien*. He lives in Chicago.

JASON A. WYCKOFF is the author of two short story collections published by Tartarus Press, *Black Horse and other Strange Stories* (2012) and *The Hidden Back Room* (2016). His work has appeared in anthologies from Plutonian Press and Siren's Call Publications, as well as the journals *Nightscript*, *Weirdbook*, and *Turn to Ash*. He lives in Columbus, Ohio, USA.

ESTHER ROSE is a full time science fiction nerd living in Minneapolis, where she teaches IT classes, writes mobile apps and sings in the shower. She is often surrounded by art supplies, sewing projects, and cartons of ice cream. The only thing she has more of than unfinished stories are shades of lipstick. She is also a proud member of the local writing community "SMUT University." You can find more of her work and see what she is up to at estherroseauthor.com.

STEVE RASNIC TEM is a past winner of the Bram Stoker, World Fantasy, and British Fantasy Awards. His most recent collections are *The Harvest Child And Other Fantasies* (Crossroads) and *Everything Is Fine Now* (Omnium Gatherum). His last novel *Ubo* (Solaris, February 2017) is a dark science fictional tale about violence and its origins, featuring such historical viewpoint characters as Jack the Ripper, Stalin, and Heinrich Himmler. *Yours To Tell: Dialogues on the Art & Practice of Writing*, written with his late wife Melanie, appeared from Apex Books in 2017. Last year Valancourt Books published *Figures Unseen*, a volume of his Selected Stories. *The Mask Shop of Doctor Blaack*, a middle grade novel about Halloween, also appeared from Hex Publishers.

JACK LOTHIAN works as a screenwriter for film and television and is currently showrunner on the HBO/Cinemax series *Strike Back*. His short fiction has appeared in a number of publications, including *Weirdbook, Hinnom Magazine, Triangulation: Appetites, Helios Quarterly Magazine, Down With The Fallen, Out of Frame, First Came Fear*, and *If This Goes On*. His graphic novel *Tomorrow* (alongside the artist Garry Mac) was nominated for a 2018 British Fantasy Award.

GORDON B. WHITE has lived in North Carolina, New York, and the Pacific Northwest. He is a 2017 graduate of the Clarion West Writing Workshop, and his fiction has appeared in venues such as *Daily Science Fiction, Tales to Terrify*, and the Bram Stoker Award® winning anthology *Borderlands 6*. Gordon also contributes reviews and interviews to various outlets including *Nightmare, Lightspeed*, and *Hellnotes*. You can find him online at www.gordonbwhite.com or on Twitter at @GordonBWhite.

NINA SHEPARDSON is a scientist who lives in New England with her husband. She's an affiliate member of the HWA, and her short fiction appears in numerous publications, including *The Colored Lens, Mirror Dance*, and *Devilfish Review*. She also writes book reviews at ninashepardson.wordpress.com.

TIMOTHY B. DODD is from Mink Shoals, WV. His stories have appeared in *Yemassee, Coe Review, The William & Mary Review, Glassworks Magazine, Anthology of Appalachian Writers*, and elsewhere. He is currently looking for a publisher for his first collection of stories entitled *The Disappearance of Mr. Van Devender... & Others*. He also is a visual artist, his expressionistic paintings on exhibition in the art galleries of Manila, Philippines...and a bit on his not-so-burgeoning Instagram page (timothybdodd) as well.

FARAH ROSE SMITH is a writer, musician, and photographer whose work often focuses on the Gothic, Decadent, and Surreal. She authored *Anonyma*, *The Almanac of Dust*, *Eviscerator*, and numerous short stories in horror and speculative anthologies. She is the founder and editor of *Mantid*, an anthology series promoting women and diverse writers in Weird Fiction, as well as the Community Outreach Director for Necronomicon Providence. She lives in Queens, NY with her partner.

TOM JOHNSTONE lives and works in Brighton, England. His first novella *The Monsters are Due in Madison Square Garden* came out this January. His short stories have appeared in (or await publication in) various publications, including *Black Static*, *Supernatural Tales*, *A Ghosts and Scholars Book of Folk Horror* (Sarob Press), *Making Monsters* (TheFutureFire.net Publishing), *Best Horror of the Year #8* (Night Shade Books) and *A Book of the Sea* (Egaeus Press). More information at tomjohnstone.wordpress.com.

From the day she was born, **JESS LANDRY** has always been attracted to the darker things in life. Her fondest childhood memories include getting nightmares from the *Goosebumps* books, watching *The Hilarious House of Frightenstein*, and reiterating to her parents that there was absolutely nothing wrong with her mental state. Since then, Jess's fiction has appeared in anthologies such as *Monsters of Any Kind*, *Where Nightmares Come From*, *Fantastic Tales of Terror*, and *Lost Highways: Dark Fictions from the Road*, among others. You can visit her on the interwebs at jesslandry.com, though your best bet at finding her is on Facebook (facebook.com/jesslandry28), where she often posts cat gifs and references *Jurassic Park* way too much.

London native **CC Adams** is the horror/dark fiction author whose work includes urban horror novella *But Worse Will Come*. His short fiction appears in publications such as *Turn To Ash* and *Weirdbook* Magazine. A member of the Horror Writers Association, he still lives in the capital—and looks for the perfect quote to set off the next dark delicacy. Visit him at www.ccadams.com

TIM MAJOR's books include time-travel horror *You Don't Belong Here* and YA thriller *Machineries of Mercy*, as well as a non-fiction book about the 1915 French silent crime serial, *Les Vampires*. In summer 2019 his novel, *Snakeskins*, will be published by Titan Books and his first short story collection, *And the House Lights Dim*, will be published by Luna Press. His short stories have appeared in *Interzone*, *Not One of Us*, *Shoreline of Infinity* and numerous anthologies, including *Best of British Science Fiction* and *The Best Horror of the Year*, edited by Ellen Datlow. Tim is also co-editor of the British Fantasy Society's fiction journal, BFS Horizons. Find out more at www.cosycatastrophes.com

J.C. RAYE is Professor of Communication at a small NJ college, teaching the most feared course on the planet: *Public Speaking*. Witnessing grown people cry, beg, freak out and pass out is just another delightful day on the job for her, so she knows a little something about real terror. She has won numerous artistic & academic awards for her projects in the field of Communication & Media, and seats in her disturbing classes sell quicker than tickets to a Rolling Stones concert. Her twisted fiction can be found in anthologies with Scary Dairy Press, Franklin/Kerr, Books & Boos Press, Jolly Horror Press (2019) and Hell-Bound Books. She also loves goats of any kind, especially the ones that faint.

ERICA RUPPERT writes weird fiction and poetry from her home in northern New Jersey. Her work has appeared in numerous magazines including *Unnerving*, *Weirdbook*, and *PodCastle*, and in multiple anthologies. She is, very slowly, working on a second novel that is not what she expected at all.

C.M. MULLER lives in St. Paul, Minnesota with his wife and two sons—and, of course, all those quaint and curious volumes of forgotten lore. He is related to the Norwegian writer Jonas Lie and draws much inspiration from that scrivener of old. His tales have appeared in *Shadows & Tall Trees*, *Supernatural Tales, Weirdbook,* and a host of other venues. In addition to writing, he also edits and publishes the award-winning anthology series *Nightscript*. His debut story collection, *Hidden Folk*, was released in December 2018.

For more information about **CHTHONIC MATTER**, please visit:
https://chthonicmatter.wordpress.com

Printed in Poland
by Amazon Fulfillment
Poland Sp. z o.o., Wrocław
02 October 2022

cefd4053-ba45-4982-aa76-c690559f4440R01